WHERE THEY LIE

CLAIRE COUGHLAN

WHERE THEY LIE

**SIMON &
SCHUSTER**

London · New York · Sydney · Toronto · New Delhi

First published in Great Britain by Simon & Schuster UK Ltd, 2024

Copyright © Claire Coughlan, 2024

The right of Claire Coughlan to be identified as author
of this work has been asserted in accordance with the
Copyright, Designs and Patents Act, 1988.

1 3 5 7 9 10 8 6 4 2

Simon & Schuster UK Ltd
1st Floor
222 Gray's Inn Road
London WC1X 8HB

Simon & Schuster: Celebrating 100 Years of Publishing in 2024

Simon & Schuster Australia, Sydney
Simon & Schuster India, New Delhi

www.simonandschuster.co.uk
www.simonandschuster.com.au
www.simonandschuster.co.in

A CIP catalogue record for this book
is available from the British Library

Hardback ISBN: 978-1-3985-2170-4
Trade Paperback ISBN: 978-1-3985-2171-1
eBook ISBN: 978-1-3985-2172-8
Audio ISBN: 978-1-3985-2183-4

Typeset in Sabon by M Rules

Printed and Bound in the UK using 100% Renewable
Electricity at CPI Group (UK) Ltd

MIX
Paper | Supporting
responsible forestry
FSC
www.fsc.org
FSC® C171272

To Chris Cremin, with love

Chapter One

Monday, 23rd December 1968

Some stories demand to be told. They keep coming back, echoing down through the decades, until they find a teller.

There must have been a time before; when silence prevailed, and Nicoletta's days and nights weren't filled with the hum of voices, guttural shouts of '*Copy!*' at the copy boys' pattering stampede across the grubby lino to grab the black page from the waiting reporter and take it to the case room. But she likes to think her life began here; was forged at this wall of noise. The *clack, clack* of typewriters is a sound she'll never tire of, if she lives to be eighty. The *Irish Sentinel* holds her in the present. It makes sense in a way nothing else does. She observes this peculiar space properly now the newsroom is almost empty. The strip lighting and wide, curtainless windows, fogged with condensation, laying bare the souls within, puts her in mind of a stage.

She misses the sound of the typewriters now they

have fallen still. One of the two copy boys on duty is asleep under his coat, his snores oozing along the floor like spilled coffee. The printing presses have yet to start rolling in the basement, signalling the end of the shift as surely as church bells, but there is already talk of giving up the ghost and going to a nearby pub for some welcome festive cheer. Nicoletta sits resolute, her back ramrod straight. She hasn't been invited on the premature flit to the pub as she's been tasked with working the NightTown shift. She feeds each hour with regular phone calls to Dublin's Garda stations. Pearse Street, Harcourt Street, Store Street, Dún Laoghaire, Howth. Each time someone answers, she hesitates before saying a variation on the same thing. It's like a rehearsed party piece, glib and sing-song. It never comes out quite the way it did in her head. And each time, she gets the same reply. Nothing doing. It's Christmas, after all.

'Good evening, Nicoletta Sarto calling from the *Sentinel* . . . anything to report? OK, thank you . . . Happy Christmas! Bye . . . bye.' She's ashamed of the blush that spreads across her cheeks as she replaces the receiver in its cradle, the toll of easing out the words contrasting with Barney, Price and Dermot's brash nonchalance. The men speak each other's language. They have long-established relationships with the Guards, connections that zigzag across colliding ley lines. Presumably, their hearts don't hammer in their chests every time they pick up the phone.

'What's the story? Grand, buzz you back in a while. Cheers.' Barney, the assistant news editor, sits at his desk, shuffling papers from his in-tray, sighing. She watches him stand up and begin to circle the largely empty room like a nervous hawk, crossing from the news desk to make the occasional call. She longs for him to come over and take one of Dermot's cigarettes, half leaning against her desk to talk. But he doesn't. Dermot, a fellow reporter, is nowhere to be seen, and Barney doesn't lift his head in her direction. A question hangs in the air between them, heavy as stale smoke.

She gets up to look out on the dark blanket of sky. Even the stars are hiding. She leans against the windowsill and waits for something, anything. She is good at waiting, at picking her moment. She accepts that sometimes there are no stories. That's when it's time to sit back and listen. She'll wonder in the ensuing days and years which twist of fate led them to Gloria Fitzpatrick in that late-night lull, as though by design.

It starts with a throwaway remark from Duffy, the editor. He joins Nicoletta at the window, resting most of his compact, meaty frame against a squat metal filing cabinet, lighting one of Dermot's cigarettes, and following her gaze along the murky sludge of the river below to the empty quay, shadowy and silent at this hour. He taps ash into a mostly empty coffee cup. He's not a tall man, though wider than the filing cabinet.

'Is it always this quiet?' When she asks the question, with a nervous laugh, Duffy straightens up.

'It's always half dead on this shift.' He's contemplative for a moment. 'The only major Christmas story I can think of was Gloria Fitzpatrick. Sentenced to hang in '56.'

Nicoletta shivers as an icy draught seeps in through a

crack in the pane. She inclines her head to Duffy, and he catches her gaze in the glass. His round face is shiny, but kind. Still, despite his cuddly appearance, Duffy is feared by some. His bite is much worse than his bark; more Rottweiler than terrier.

Nicoletta forces a tentative smile. 'What was that like?'

There's a tread of footsteps from behind and Price, the deputy editor, joins them, towering above them both. He's quickly joined by Barney, who's already wearing his coat, a full-length camel hair he's inordinately proud of, his sandy hair styled into a rigid peak.

'What's going on?'

'I was telling Nicoletta about the last major Christmas story,' Duffy says thoughtfully. 'Gloria Fitzpatrick. The very last woman in the history of the state to get the death penalty, though of course it was later commuted to life imprisonment on the grounds of insanity.' He blows a stream of smoke straight ahead, which fogs the window. Nicoletta coughs as discreetly as she can.

'A long while ago,' Barney says, shrugging. 'Time now to go to the pub for a pint or two.'

'We'll go when I say we go.' Duffy's voice is soft, but Barney gets the message and shuts up.

Nicoletta taps her foot, unwilling to let the name sink out of sight, the way a seagull will dive after its quarry, right into the murky depths of the river.

'Fitzpatrick . . . I haven't heard that name in a long time.'

Duffy nods. 'The infamous Fitzpatrick. They got her in the end, for Elizabeth Rourke, but she never would give the Guards the whereabouts of the missing actress.'

'You don't mean ... Julia Bridges? Was Gloria Fitzpatrick responsible for her death?' she asks, almost holding her breath.

Duffy rubs a circle in the condensation, round as a ship's porthole, and drops the cigarette stub into the cup, where it sizzles in half an inch of tepid coffee.

'The very same. The Guards were almost sure Fitzpatrick was behind her disappearance but there was never enough evidence to make the charge stick. She just vanished partway through a run at the Athena. The Athena Theatre was prestigious in its day. Bit of a kip now.'

'When was that again?' Nicoletta grips the windowsill and keeps looking straight ahead. She won't give Barney the satisfaction of looking back his way.

'Over twenty years ago. During the war, I guess.'

Price taps the top of the filing cabinet. He's the only one of them who's tall enough to comfortably hunch over it. 'Didn't your interview with Julia Bridges' husband years later bring some eyewitness out of the woodwork?'

Duffy grins. 'It did. The Bridges' landlord, in fact. Brendan Owens was his name. Reading between the lines, he was quite taken with Julia. He'd been to see her at the theatre every night for weeks. Then Julia got sick, and an understudy took over. This fellow eventually told me he saw Julia going into St Bridget's, where Gloria Fitzpatrick worked. This corroborated what the Guards had long suspected; that Gloria Fitzpatrick was behind Julia Bridges' disappearance. Fitzpatrick styled herself a patron of the arts back in the day, when she was flush, but she wouldn't have had anything like that kind of money in the years leading up to Bridges' disappearance.'

'How did she get her money?' Nicoletta finds herself asking.

'I can't honestly tell you that, Nicoletta.' Duffy turns to face her. 'Everyone has a different theory on how she set herself up in business. She was certainly wealthier than any midwife I've ever come across,' he says with a laugh.

Nicoletta bites her lip. 'Did anything come out of the final eyewitness statement?'

Duffy sniffs and shakes his head. 'It gave the Guards something solid to re-interview Fitzpatrick about, but Owens' information came too late. Fitzpatrick popped her clogs in the asylum that very night and they never found Julia Bridges' body.'

'What about the Owens fellow? Was he investigated, whenever this was?'

'Late '50s. Around the time Fitzpatrick died. Nothing came of it.'

Price bangs the filing cabinet this time and Nicoletta jumps. 'Still, what about Christmas Eve, '56? We all assumed Gloria would be let off for Elizabeth Rourke. I'll never forget the shock.'

Nicoletta wraps her arms around herself. She's wearing the tweed and fox-fur suit she'd bought with her first wages as a junior reporter. The skirt is miniscule and the sleeves are three-quarter length. There's a matching turban which sits snugly over her newly shorn hair. It's not suitable for the December weather, but she'd wanted to wear it, on this, her first NightTown shift.

'Neither will I,' she says, turning around.

Duffy looks up from his spyhole. 'How would you remember? You'd only have been a kid.'

But she can recall it just as clearly, if not more so, than the predictable signposts of her own life. She'd been weighing apples in her parents' shop when the verdict came in about Gloria Fitzpatrick. Christmas Eve, 1956. Nicoletta was fourteen, doomed to work at Sarto's newsagents in the school holidays and at Christmas. 'Gloria Fitzpatrick has been sentenced to hang,' the radio announcer's clipped voice said. She'd stopped to listen as he went on to report that the disgraced former midwife had caused the death of mother of six Elizabeth Rourke as the result of an induced miscarriage and had then disposed of Mrs Rourke's body. The apples had rolled onto the floor, red and shiny as giant marbles. Nicoletta knelt on her hands and knees to collect them; one had wedged itself under the cabinet where all the hardboiled sweets were kept in glass jars like scientific specimens. By the time she'd resurfaced, the announcer had moved on to the next item – football results, or a weather forecast, as though there was nothing unusual about midwives and murder being mixed up together. Nicoletta waited until the *Press* and *Herald* vans arrived, delivering the evening papers, then she grabbed a copy of each and sat on a high stool behind the counter, reading all about the culmination of the trial she'd been following for weeks. Her mother had found her poring over them when she was supposed to be arranging boxes of Christmas biscuits, bottles of whiskey, things people would pick up as last-minute gifts. She'd snatched the papers away, as though they were contaminated, inexplicably tossing them in the bin.

'It would fit you better to study your schoolbooks with the same fascination, instead of this rubbish.'

Nicoletta was banned from the front of the shop for the rest of the evening, sent to dust the storeroom shelves. A boxroom tucked in the back of their living quarters, it was later also used as a bedroom, when Enzo was alive, with a cot added to the chaos. A room of odds and ends which no one quite knew what to do with. She'd always hated going in there, being among the old packets of firelighters and greeting cards faded from years of being exposed to sunlight. Those cards couldn't be resold, but nor could Daniela Sarto bear to throw them out, for reasons best known to herself, instead choosing to keep the damaged stock year in, year out. They repeated their bland messages in perpetuity: 'Happy 21st Birthday' and 'Congratulations on your Wedding Day'. Milestones Enzo would never reach.

One grainy photo showed Gloria Fitzpatrick in handcuffs, being led into the back of a prison van, her fair hair lifted by the breeze under her mink cap. Nicoletta shivers as she remembers how she'd felt something like a prickle of recognition at the defiant profile. Fitzpatrick was trapped, a caged animal, but she didn't look like you were supposed to. Nicoletta had wondered if she could detect evil in that defiant tilt by tracing its curve with her thumbnail. A second, sharper photo, had been taken earlier, as Fitzpatrick arrived at court, unsure of her fate, of whether she'd be leaving that day alone in her solicitor's car, to enjoy Christmas with her freedom, or escorted by a phalanx of guards to Mountjoy Prison. A fair, handsome woman, jewels gleaming at fingers and throat, her face inscrutable. Perhaps she'd made her expression deliberately blank, not giving herself away in the glare of the flashbulbs. It was all so public.

Duffy and Price are reminiscing now in earnest. They've lost interest in how or why Nicoletta's fascination with the infamous Gloria Fitzpatrick began. Everyone had followed the story, after all. Everyone knows who she was, what she did, and to whom.

Price stuffs his hands into his pockets. 'Gloria always made good copy.'

'Announcing to anyone who'd listen, "This is not my country!" outside the court before the verdict. Didn't do herself any favours. She made sure she wore all her finery, what was left of it.' Duffy shakes his head and scratches his jaw, scrupulously clean shaven as ever, and turns back to Price. 'Do you remember when Lilian Higgins was convicted of forging the birth register?'

Price nods.

'What was that?' Curiosity gets the better of Nicoletta.

'A couple of years ago,' Duffy says, turning to meet her eye. 'Mrs Higgins was Gloria's employer in her last years of respectability. She died quite recently. Rumours were rife that she'd been carrying out a baby-selling racket for years from St Bridget's Maternal Nursing Home. She only got a fine in the district court for forging the birth register, whereas Gloria got banged up for life.'

Price claps his hands. 'Well, on that note, I think it's

time to go to the pub.' He looks to Duffy and Barney. 'Dermot and Anne are already there.' Duffy holds up his hands in acquiescence, returning to his office. Nicoletta hangs back. Price pats the filing cabinet one last time.

'You should get back to your desk.' He starts walking and when he reaches the plate glass doors to the stairwell, he wrenches them open, and they slam against the walls with a sickening clatter. Barney moves forward alongside Nicoletta and drums his fingers against the window, his nails tapping insistently against the glass. The noise is starting to crowd Nicoletta's nerve endings. She pushes a chair out of her way, almost toppling it in a bid to get back to her desk.

'What's up with you?' Barney asks, as she's halfway across the room.

She takes a few steps back. The longing to touch his cheek, smell the familiar tang of Old Spice, is overwhelming. She stands half facing him, close enough that she can see his breath pluming in an opaque cloud.

'I've been trying to ring you,' he says in a low voice.

'I know Marie's back,' she says, aware Duffy can probably hear every word.

'She's just back to see Liam.' There's a pleading note to his voice, and it sets her teeth on edge. He's already slipped away, along with this new life she's worked so hard to acquire. Maybe she'd only been trying it on for size, like an expensive pair of shoes, or a fur coat; she should've realised that.

She tries to inject a false jollity into her voice. 'It'll be nice for Liam to have his mam around for Christmas, won't it?'

'I'm sorry, Nic.'

She nods. 'Have to get back to my desk.'

'Nic, wait . . .'

She resumes her position beside the phone. She can hear Barney's footsteps receding to his own desk, near Duffy's office. A couple of minutes later Duffy himself bustles out the door with a backwards wave, followed quickly by Barney, who doesn't look back at her once. Quiet prevails, until the doors crash against the walls again and Dermot and Anne sidle into the room, giggling. Nicoletta smiles.

'Where've you been?'

'We went for a drink. Anne forgot her keys. I forgot my smokes.'

Anne's long dark hair looks almost blue under the fluorescent lights. She scrabbles for a bunch of keys wedged in a pen holder on her desk.

'Coming?' she says to Dermot, ignoring Nicoletta.

'Fancy a drink?' Dermot shakes his half-empty cigarette packet and puts it into his trouser pocket. Nicoletta shakes her head.

'I have to ring the Guards. I'm working NightTown.'

'Ah, come for one! There isn't a whisper of scandal. The city's half asleep. Let's go back to the pub and raise some festive cheer.' Dermot gestures towards Anne, who looks at the door pointedly.

Nicoletta shakes her head. 'I'd better stay here. I don't want to go now in case Price comes back and wonders where I am.'

'Suit yourself. But he won't. Price is gone to the pub. And Duffy's gone home.' Dermot mimes someone snoring.

'He's quicker on his feet than he'd have us believe. Probably already half sloshed, asleep on the sofa, a cat snoozing on his stomach.'

Nicoletta laughs, feeling slightly wistful at the imagined cosy scene. She doesn't want to go to the pub in case Anne or Dermot probe her with questions she'd rather not answer. Though perhaps Dermot won't. She watches him stride away until he's swallowed whole by the chilly stairwell. People with their own secrets are less likely to pry into the lives of others, and Nicoletta feels safe with Dermot.

Freezing air gusts into the newsroom before the door slams shut. She looks back at Barney's empty desk. Maybe she'd be better off joining the others in the pub after all, letting a drink or three slip down in delicious succession. She shakes her head. If anyone could persuade her to pour her heart out, it's Dermot. He's her only real friend. She's still inwardly debating whether or not to go after him and Anne when the phone peals. For a moment she lets it ring, working up the nerve to answer it. She thinks it's about to stop, but she picks up the receiver anyway and jams it against her ear.

'Hello, newsroom?'

'Hello. Could I speak to Barney King, please?'

The whole floor is chronically silent. 'He's just left. Can I help you at all?'

'Who am I speaking to?'

'This is Nicoletta Sarto. I'm a reporter.' She can hear the pride in her voice. A creak of breath from the other end of the line and then the suck of a cigarette.

12

'Ah yes, we spoke earlier. This is Inspector David Morris from Pearse Street Garda Station.'

'Good evening, Inspector. What can I do for you?'

She scribbles down what's being said. A motley collection of phrases. When read aloud, outside any context, they mightn't hold very much power. They're just words. But taken together, they amount to something bigger than themselves. *Skeleton ... man digging ... garden ... Seaview House, Sandycove ... early hours of this morning ... wedding ring ... Julia Bridges*. When Inspector Morris rings off, she can feel her world flip on its axis. A flicker of static snakes up from the pit of her stomach to sit tight at the crown of her skull. This story is hers for the telling.

Chapter Two

Tuesday, 24th December 1968
Christmas Eve

Nicoletta appears in the newsroom the next morning, wearing the same clothes as the night before. She's had very little sleep and she can feel the thrum quickening her pulse. The adrenaline has warmed her up, despite the cold. She starts tidying her desk, firing scrunched-up wads of paper into the bin.

'Nic?' Barney's voice echoes behind her. 'You're not rostered to work over Christmas week.'

'I came in to tie up some loose ends.' She smooths her turban over her tousled, feathered pixie cut, before grabbing that morning's city edition from a nearby stack. Her story about Julia Bridges from the night before is on the front page.

'Nice splash.' Barney cracks his knuckles, something he always does when he's thinking. 'Whoever thought Julia Bridges would be found?'

Nicoletta shrugs. 'I was in the right place at the right time.' She picks up her bag.

'Nic, wait.'

She stops. 'Yes?'

'It was a good story. How'd you like to stay on it? I'm about to pay a visit to the morgue, if you fancy it?'

Nicoletta can't help but laugh. 'I bet you say that to all the girls.'

Together they descend the icy stairwell. The wind from the Liffey flays their faces as soon as they step out onto Burgh Quay. They make their way down the river wall, past a swaying drunk in a flapping overcoat, humming loudly to himself. It sounds like 'O Holy Night', his reedy voice carrying over the water. Nicoletta can feel the damp air through her clothes.

Barney rests a hand in the small of her back as they cross the bridge, and she pulls away. They walk in silence until Beresford Place. Barney leans against the coal-black railings of the Georgian terrace and puffs out his cheeks as Nicoletta is almost blown off her feet by a violent gust.

'Nic . . . I didn't know Marie was just going to turn up out of the blue. Please believe me.'

Nicoletta unconsciously grabs the railing, not looking at him. Then she lets go and forces herself to meet his eye. 'What's Inspector Morris like?'

'Bit of a self-important bollix,' Barney says, as they clear the short distance to the city morgue on Store Street. 'But all right.'

Nicoletta's feet are already numb by the time they reach

the morgue. It's smaller and older than the surrounding buildings, its whimsical red brick façade giving it the look of anything other than what it is. Barney leans against the wall.

'What now?' Nicoletta speaks above the sound of a train trundling out of Amiens Street Station.

'Now, we wait,' Barney says with a grim smile. Within minutes, a blue-uniformed garda exits through the front door, alongside a tall, straight-backed man dressed in a brown suit with a beige gaberdine over it. The man in the suit pumps Barney's hand. 'Look, I can't let you in.' He indicates the heavy front door. 'Not today.'

Barney shrugs. 'Can you tell us anything here?'

The man sucks his teeth, before eyeing Nicoletta. 'And who's this?'

'Nicoletta Sarto. I'm new at the *Sentinel*.' Nicoletta allows her hand to be shaken with the same firm grasp as the tall plain clothes man introduces himself as Inspector Morris.

'Ah yes, we spoke last night. Rather you than me, working with this fellow. But a pleasure to put a face to the name.'

He winks at Barney. Nicoletta pretends not to notice. The uniformed garda's gaze falls on her and his mouth twitches in recognition.

'This is Garda Peter O'Connor. Nicoletta Sarto.' Morris steps back on his heels. Nicoletta's scalp tightens as she waits for O'Connor to announce how he already knows her.

'Pleased to meet you, Nicoletta,' O'Connor says after a beat, shaking her hand carefully. Nicoletta exhales.

The moment has passed. He takes off his navy peaked cap, smoothing his bristly red hair. The filmy winter light catches it in a fiery halo.

'What's the story, anyhow?' Barney props one heel on the wall behind him.

Morris looks as though he's considering what to divulge. He's older than he appeared at first, Nicoletta thinks. Hair dappled by grey under his hat, deep grooves around his nose and mouth. His military bearing almost gives the illusion of youth.

'Between you, me and the wall, Jack Bridges has just identified his wife's wedding ring.' Morris glances over his shoulder. 'We're heading to The Confession Box. Coming?' He addresses this solely to Barney.

Barney nods. Nicoletta shifts her weight from foot to foot. O'Connor's pale eyes appraise her. She can feel something unspool in the cold air between them. He looks away first.

Morris gives Nicoletta a wink this time. 'You never know, O'Malley may even join us, it being Christmas. Give us a minute and we'll follow you down.'

O'Connor doesn't look Nicoletta's way once as he and Morris head back into the morgue. Nicoletta and Barney are halfway up Talbot Street when Nicoletta finally breaks the silence. 'Is O'Malley the pathologist?'

'Not for much longer. About to retire.' Barney loops a right onto Marlborough Street. The newspaper sellers are out. A boy with a *Sentinel* sandwich board bearing Nicoletta's story about Julia Bridges struts past the Pro-Cathedral.

SKELETON FOUND IN SEASIDE GARDEN
By Nicoletta Sarto
A human skeleton was recovered in the early hours of this morning from a garden in the Dublin suburb of Sandycove. The remains, which have since been brought to the city morgue, are believed to belong to long-missing Dublin actress Julia Bridges, who vanished in July 1943. Gardaí are conducting a full examination of the scene ...

The thrill of seeing her byline on the front page prompts Nicoletta to buy a copy before she hastily follows Barney into The Confession Box, a tiny pub beside the cathedral. He indicates an empty table by the door.

'Morris may be a self-important bollix, but O'Malley's a contrary bollix.'

Nicoletta doesn't ask what O'Connor is like. She doesn't even want to say his name aloud.

She takes off her gloves and places them in front of her as Barney goes up to the bar. The small room is overheated by a roaring fire facing them, but she realises she's trembling as she rummages for her compact and examines her face. She takes deep breaths right up from her diaphragm, the way Dr Jennings had taught her after the ECT. She gouges the outline of a smile with a shimmery lipstick she finds at the bottom of her bag. Garda O'Connor hadn't let on that he knew her, but he might be telling Morris all about their last encounter this very moment. She hasn't even told Barney and she doesn't know if she ever will. He slides a brandy in front of her.

'Looks like you could do with it.' He frowns. 'You OK?'

Nicoletta takes a pretend sip. 'Just cold. And a bit shook thinking about poor Jack Bridges having to identify his wife by her wedding ring. Jesus.'

Barney takes a gulp of his drink, a pint of Guinness. 'It can get too much for some people. Especially if it's your first big story.'

Nicoletta's about to reply when the door creaks open, followed by a blast of cold air. Inspector Morris' large frame takes up most of the doorway. He's followed by Garda O'Connor and an even taller man distinguished by a dark green homburg and chewing a cigar. He's wearing a dun-coloured corduroy suit, the trousers held up by a length of twine.

Morris claps a hand on the man's shoulder, like a big-game hunter posing for a photograph with much-sought-after prey. 'Look who we found trying to slip off home!'

Nicoletta understands this third man to be O'Malley. He doesn't look like a pathologist. He looks like a farmer, someone who's used to surveying, tending and coaxing. Not someone adept with the grim business of death. He takes Nicoletta's hand and holds it delicately between his surprisingly soft fingers. 'Well, well,' he says. 'I couldn't miss out on the opportunity to take stock of this new lady, now, could I?'

Barney takes a long swallow of his drink. Nicoletta tries to withdraw her hand, but O'Malley holds on to it. 'Nicoletta, is it? What sort of a name is that? It's lovely.'

'Italian. My parents are Italians.' She takes a small sip of her drink, before putting the glass back down, feeling the need to explain herself further. 'My mother's family came from a town called Casalattico, near Rome.' She can feel Inspector Morris' eyes on her, listening to everything being said. She keeps her focus on O'Malley.

'Is that so?' O'Malley sips a pint of stout set down reverently for him by Garda O'Connor. 'My wife and I went to Rome on our honeymoon umpteen years ago.'

'How lovely.' Nicoletta laughs. 'I've actually never been.' Barney is looking into his pint, but she knows he's also now listening intently to their exchange. Inspector Morris and Garda O'Connor begin to speak quietly among themselves. Nicoletta can't make out what they're saying. She turns her attention back to O'Malley. 'Does your wife mind you having to work on Christmas Eve?'

He gives a rueful grin. 'Ah, it gets me out of her hair.' He clinks Nicoletta's glass. 'Poor Julia Bridges, all the same. Never thought she'd be found.'

Nicoletta puts down her glass after the toast.

'The wedding ring is the only indication that it's Julia Bridges?'

O'Malley bows his head. Inspector Morris takes a pause from his conversation with O'Connor to join in. Morris is the same towards her as he was earlier; O'Connor obviously hasn't given her away. She feels a rush of gratitude warm her cheeks.

'It's her all right, Nicoletta. I can confirm that. "Jack and Julia, 15th September 1941" is what it says on the wedding ring.' Morris taps the table with a beer mat. 'Jack Bridges has duly signed off on it.'

O'Malley coughs into a greying hanky. He finally

lights his cigar and sits back, wreathing them in smoke. Nicoletta begins to feel a wave of nausea rise in her throat.

'How was Jack Bridges during the identification?' She concentrates on feeling normal.

O'Malley gulps the smoke, stroking the homburg laid out in front of him like a beloved family pet.

'The thing is, everyone reacts differently, Nicoletta. I've seen a mother identifying her son's broken body who didn't say a word. Just stood there mutely, as though it was happening to someone else. Then there are those who weep and wail, and those who're angry as all hell. Jack Bridges was adamant that the skeleton on the gurney wasn't his wife. Until we showed him the wedding ring. He looked at that ring for a long time, before he said, "I suppose that's Julia's, all right."'

'He almost ran out of the place after that,' O'Connor says, sucking down a mouthful of beer. 'Who could blame him? Horrible places, morgues.' He gives O'Malley a mock salute. 'No offence.'

Nicoletta leans toward O'Malley. 'How do you think Mrs Bridges died?'

O'Malley nibbles on the end of the cigar. 'Hard to say. A long time since she disappeared – what was it, '44, '45?'

''43.'

'Right.' O'Malley directs his answer solely to Nicoletta. 'Twenty-five years is a long time. All that was left of her was a skeleton and that wedding ring. Everything else – her coat, her clothes, even her shoes – had decomposed. No handbag with her either.'

'Fitzpatrick didn't leave us much to work with.' Morris

puts down the beermats he's been shuffling like a deck of cards. Nicoletta can feel his eyes on her.

'How can you be so certain Fitzpatrick was behind it?' Nicoletta addresses the question to Morris. 'Isn't it odd, Julia's body being found in this family's garden in Sandycove? Shouldn't you be looking at these Creightons instead?'

It's O'Malley who answers after he stubs out the cigar. 'There are no certainties, my dear, just the evidence in front of us. A woman's skeleton was found. That's it, as far as I'm concerned.'

Two spots of colour appear on Morris' cheeks. 'Fitzpatrick knew Charles Creighton. He was big into the theatre scene, as was she, when she had the money to flash. None of them wanted to know her once it was gone.'

O'Connor gives him a sideways glance and pops open a bag of crisps as he observes the exchange. Nicoletta bites her lip. 'Are these the same Creightons as the jewellery people?'

Morris nods. 'Charles Creighton was always a bit of a ladies' man. He was briefly considered a person of interest, but we ruled him out. Gloria's behind it; it's as plain as the nose on your face.' Morris sucks in his cheeks, giving him a gaunt look. 'We couldn't get her when she was alive, but you can be damn sure we have her now.'

'How do you explain the body being found at the Creightons'? Miss Sarto's right. It doesn't make much sense.' Garda O'Connor's cheeks have turned as red as his hair from the alcohol and the heat.

'The only person who can answer that with any detail

is Gloria Fitzpatrick, and she's six feet under,' Morris declares, his lips a grim line.

'She'll always be the one who got away.' O'Connor nibbles on a crisp.

'What's that?' Morris inclines his head.

'Gloria Fitzpatrick. She's the one nut you couldn't crack.'

Morris knocks over a teetering pile of beermats. 'Oh, I had her cracked, all right. Unfortunately, she kicked the bucket just as I was making headway.'

'How inconvenient, Inspector. But we've still no definitive way of knowing whether she was responsible for Julia Bridges' death.'

Morris takes the crisps off O'Connor, bag and all, and stuffs a fistful into his mouth. 'I was wise to her,' he says, spitting crumbs. 'Still am. She was quite immoral. A *malfeasant*, the prosecution called her at one point in the trial. The truth will always out, isn't that what they say?'

'I admire your tenacity, Inspector.' O'Malley puts on his homburg. Nicoletta notices that it's dented in the middle. 'Most would've given up by now.'

Morris wipes his face with a hanky; the room has filled up without them noticing.

'How did Miss Fitzpatrick die?' Nicoletta asks in a rush, desperate to keep O'Malley talking before he can leave.

'Officially, it was coronary arrest, my dear. Had to do the post-mortem myself because she died at Clyde Hall Criminal Lunatic Asylum, in the custody of the state,' O'Malley says, adjusting the angles of his hat. 'Coronary arrest, a nice vague term, was reported in the papers.

Unofficially, Miss Fitzpatrick's toxicology was sky high, though naturally the powers that be at Clyde Hall didn't want that getting out.'

'What was in her system?' Nicoletta can't help herself asking. She looks sideways at Barney, but he doesn't seem to be listening.

'A small amount of alcohol. And large amounts of chlorpromazine, brand name Thorazine, a drug Gloria was being given. They kept it out of the papers, but there was a big stink at Clyde Hall in the aftermath. I recall an inquiry was held, as to how Gloria would have laid her hands on possibly fatal quantities of this medication. Presuming it was suicide. They were looking for a head for the chopping block and I believe the nurse on duty resigned. Brennan, I think, was her name. But in the end, Fitzpatrick went peacefully in her sleep, I suppose you'd say, the way you'd want your sainted favourite aunt to go. Just went to bed and didn't wake up.'

Nicoletta makes a mental note to go to the bathroom and write everything down as soon as she can. Meanwhile, she takes another pained sip of her brandy, aware that the glass is still mostly full. She doesn't want to be rude but she needs to stay sharp, and she knows she's doing a mangled job of pretending to drink it. 'What a quiet way to go. After the life she had.'

Morris snorts. 'It was well for her. Compared to the horrible way Julia Bridges went, and Elizabeth Rourke after that. Probably countless others, too, that we don't even know about. And poor Bridges didn't even get a proper burial.'

Nicoletta leans forward. 'What happened to Fitzpatrick after she died?'

O'Malley stands up, grabbing the brass handle of the door. He pulls it towards him before he answers. A wall of chilly air hits Nicoletta's face and her exposed wrists are prickled with goosebumps.

'She's interred in a mass grave for inmates of Clyde Hall Asylum at Dean's Grange Cemetery. None of her relatives came to claim her in the end. Lonely way to go.' He raises a hand. 'Good tidings, all.' The door whooshes shut behind him and smoke rushes to fill the vacuum. Nicoletta swallows. She needs air. She puts on her gloves and stands up. Barney is deep in conversation with Morris. He breaks off and pulls her to one side.

'Where're you going?'

She shrugs. 'Home. It's Christmas Eve. Not much point in staying here, is there?' The words find their target. Barney rubs his jaw with his left hand, as though trying to deflect the sting. There's a light-coloured indent on the flesh of his second finger where his wedding band used to sit. She wonders if he'll start wearing it again.

He lowers his voice, though Nicoletta doubts the two men at the table can hear them above the din. A raucous shout of laughter erupts from nearby.

'I probably shouldn't be telling you this, but Duffy has you in mind for this new gig. He's setting up a women's page on the paper and he wants you in charge. Well, it's between you and Anne. You should really get your teeth into this story. Because he's announcing his decision next Thursday, the day after New Year's. Just to give you a heads-up. He'll probably talk to you about it soon.'

Nicoletta swallows. A sudden wave of nausea is making her mouth water.

'Why are you telling me this?'

He frowns. 'Because I'd like you to get the job. I happen to think you've the makings of a damn fine reporter. And I also think you could be useful on this story. Instead of going home, you could try and talk to Jack Bridges.'

Nicoletta starts. 'Wouldn't he be very upset? Especially as it's Christmas Eve.'

Barney nods. 'But he'd probably open up more to you.'

'All right.' Nicoletta shrugs. 'Why's that?'

'Because you're a woman.'

Nicoletta turns to go, and Barney puts out a hand to stop her. 'Don't you want to know where to find him?'

'Don't worry, I'll find him. I already am a damn fine reporter.'

Barney puts out his hand again, then thinks better of it. 'See you in Groome's later?'

'Maybe. Maybe not.' She's out the door and on the pavement when Barney comes after her. She leans against the windowpane, waiting for him to speak. There's a row of small Santa Clauses on the other side, looking out. Their cotton wool beards and felt hats look like they've been glued on by children.

'Nic? Bridges lives at Percy Place, I think it is. Can't recall the number. Come to Groome's when you're finished with him. We'll take a spin out to Sandycove, to the scene of the crime. Seaview House. Owned by Charles and Sally Creighton.'

She shrugs. 'Depends how long I'll be with Bridges.' She turns to walk away, then pauses.

'Just so you know, Barney. I'm only doing this because we're colleagues. Not for any other reason.'

The words register on Barney's face like a slap. 'Are you worried about giving people ideas?'

Nicoletta gives a sharp laugh. 'Probably a bit late for that. It's your ideas I'm worried about.'

Barney's eyes close for a split second. He holds up a hand. 'All right, Nic.'

She stops at the pawn shop opposite the Abbey Theatre and looks back. Barney is gone but the Santa Clauses in The Confession Box window keep on scanning the empty pavement in vain. On impulse, she returns to the pub, opens the door and goes back in. Morris is at the bar and O'Connor is sitting contemplatively on his own, an empty glass in front of him. Nicoletta sits down opposite, keeping her coat and turban on, and her bag on her arm.

'Thank you,' she says, the words coming out in a rush.

'For what?' O'Connor looks mildly surprised by this ambush.

'For not saying we've met before. Or letting on that you recognised me.' Nicoletta exhales. The room is uncomfortably warm and stuffy.

'It's really no bother,' O'Connor says, as Morris comes back with two more pints.

'Ah, Nicoletta,' Morris says, taking a slurp of his drink, giving her a wink. It makes her feel slightly uncomfortable.

'I'd have got you a drink if I'd known you were staying. What'll you have?'

'No, I won't have a drink, thank you so much though, Inspector.' Nicoletta straightens her turban. 'I'm just going to use the ladies'.' She hesitates and leans over the table, taking a deep breath. 'Though there was one thing I wanted to ask you, Inspector. If you don't mind?'

Morris takes another slurp of his pint. 'Of course. Spit it out, pet.'

'I understand Gloria Fitzpatrick was considered a patron of the arts in the 1930s, and she used her money to fund several theatrical productions at the Athena. Where did she get that money from?'

Morris gives a bark of mirth and swills back half the pint before answering. 'Who knows, Nicoletta? Who knows, indeed?'

Nicoletta hovers at the edge of the table. 'You must have some idea.'

Morris turns pink. 'It's not exactly a secret. She was convicted in the district court in the late '30s for providing induced miscarriages for a hefty fee, in that fancy place she had on Mount Pleasant Square. She lost her midwifery licence after that, but it must have made her a packet, back in the day.' He shakes his head and crosses his arms. 'She was quite immoral.' Nicoletta knows when it's time to quit.

'Thank you so much for your time, Inspector.' She stands up. She can feel sweat trickling between her shoulder blades. 'Happy Christmas to you both.' Morris winks again and O'Connor gives her a smile as she makes her way to the back of the pub and opens the door to the ladies'. She lets the cool, disinfectant-tinged air envelop her, before locking herself into a cubicle and digging in her bag for her notebook and pen. She begins transcribing furiously before she can forget.

Chapter Three

Out of habit, Nicoletta walks back in the direction of the newspaper office, hesitating at the corner of Burgh Quay. The singing drunk has gone. Seagulls crowd the low river wall, squalling and nudging each other out of the way. Watery light seeps through the clouds. The day has barely begun, but she wants that women's page editor job so badly she can taste it. The breeze stings her eyes. If her suspicions are correct and she's pregnant, she won't be able to take the job. *But what will you do then?* The little voice in her head is her mother's. She can't go back to her parents' shop with her tail between her legs. Dusting shelves and serving customers. Forcing a smile and repeating the same things, day in, day out. Chit-chat with the regulars. Endless questions. The sight of the morning papers missing her byline. To admit things hadn't worked out would be more than she could bear.

She can see from here that the windows of the *Sentinel* newsroom are dark. The urgent tableaux filled with life and colour have been replaced by two blank spaces. Her colleagues are probably in Groome's by now. She can picture them, floating around, buying drinks, telling jokes, laughing. She can't join them; she's no good at pretending. She squares her shoulders and starts walking. The wind has died down. Pearse Street is practically deserted. The city breathes easily, almost as one being. A lone woman wheeling her shopping gives Nicoletta a curious look. Nicoletta avoids her eyes, self-conscious at the goosebumps hiving her bare wrists and her nyloned legs meeting the tiny skirt. She takes a deep breath and sets out as she means to go on, drumming an insistent tattoo on the pavement.

She's perspiring when she gets to Percy Place, a neat terrace overlooking the canal. She knocks on the first door in the row before she loses her nerve. The black paint is peeling, though a sprig of holly has been sellotaped to the gleaming brass knocker. An old-fashioned bicycle with a wicker basket attached leans against the railing. A cheerful voice of indeterminate gender calls out, 'Who is it now?'

'Nicoletta Sarto.'

A woman comes to the door and sticks her head out. 'You what-o?'

Her long hair drips onto the mat. Nicoletta realises that she's wrapped in nothing but a towel.

'I'm sorry to bother you. I'm looking for Jack Bridges.'

The woman blinks. 'Bridges ... Oh yes. Other end of the terrace. Last house. Now, if you don't mind, it's bloody freezing!'

'Thank you!' Nicoletta calls, as the door slams behind her. The other end of Percy Place is fronted by a blue door with a glossy holly wreath hanging from the knocker. Nicoletta touches the leaves. Plastic. She lifts the knocker and the wreath falls. She quickly picks it up and re-hangs it before pushing the doorbell instead. She's at the bottom of the steps, about to give up, when the door opens.

'Can I help you?' A woman peers at Nicoletta from the top step. Nicoletta doesn't feel inclined to climb back up to her level.

She forces a smile. 'Sorry to bother you like this. I'm looking for Jack Bridges.'

The woman crosses her arms and shivers, a canary-yellow cardigan slung over her shoulders, the empty arms dangling uselessly. Nicoletta wonders why she doesn't just wear it properly.

'Doesn't live here.'

'Oh? I was sure he lived in this house.' Nicoletta falters and steps back onto the path.

The woman goes to close the door. '*I* live in this house. Mr Bridges lives in the basement flat. I'm his landlady. He comes and goes as he pleases. Why don't you knock on his door and bother him?'

Nicoletta clears her throat. 'I'm sorry, I haven't introduced myself. My name is Nicoletta Sarto and I'm a reporter for the *Sentinel*. Perhaps you haven't heard. Mr Bridges' wife Julia was found this morning.'

The woman swears and blesses herself. Nicoletta climbs up onto the second step. 'I know this must be a shock. Did you know Mrs Bridges, Miss . . .?'

'It's Mrs Owens. Of course, I knew Julia. She was my tenant, too. Jack and Julia moved in after they got married. Jack moved on after she went missing, but he came back a few months ago, pretty desperate. He'd lost his house. I couldn't just throw him out on the street, could I?' Nicoletta remembers Duffy and Price's reminiscences in the newsroom, about a Brendan Owens, Julia Bridges' landlord, who went to see her at the Athena Theatre every night. He was also the last known eyewitness who saw Julia entering St Bridget's, where Gloria Fitzpatrick worked.

Nicoletta smiles. 'You and your husband must be very decent sorts. I'm sure it's appreciated.'

Mrs Owens points a colourless finger down in the direction of Nicoletta's face. 'Brendan was the soft touch. But I'm a widow now.'

Nicoletta lowers her eyes. 'I'm sorry.'

She pauses before she strikes again. 'Did you know Mrs Bridges well, Mrs Owens?'

Mrs Owens swallows sourly. 'I don't make a habit of being chummy with people who pay rent. She was asking for trouble.'

'In what way was she asking for trouble?' Nicoletta can sense Mrs Owens is about to inch the door shut.

'That theatre crowd were a bit loose. Probably still are, if you ask me.'

'Oh?' Nicoletta angles her face towards the diminishing gap, but she knows her time is almost up.

Mrs Owens peers around the door and lowers her voice. 'Undesirables, the lot of them. If you know what I mean.'

Nicoletta has a fair idea what she means but she needs more details. A lot more.

'What did your husband think?'

Mrs Owens' mouth pops into a surprised 'O'. Nicoletta fears she may have overplayed her hand.

'My husband was fond of the theatre at one time. For all the good it did him. Good day.' As an afterthought, she crooks another finger in the direction of Nicoletta's face. 'Don't use my name in any of this or I'll sue.'

The door slams shut. Nicoletta doesn't hear footsteps and she senses that Mrs Owens is standing behind the door, waiting for her to leave. She walks down the steps to the basement, where a bevelled glass door marks the entry point to Jack Bridges' dark flat. She knocks loudly and waits. After a few minutes of trying, she concedes defeat. Just then, a taxi stops, and a woman gets out, laden with shopping bags. Nicoletta lunges forward with her hand out to the driver.

'Where to, love?'

She digs around in her purse for money. She can't face another cold walk.

'The Athena Theatre, please. Bachelors Walk.'

The car comes to a jerky stop at the Ha'penny Bridge. The Athena Theatre is a spindly Georgian building, presumably once magnificent, but now falling into confusion. Bits and bobs have been taken away and added on since it was built, giving it an uneven-looking quality. Nicoletta gives a cursory knock before pushing open the door and stepping inside. The foyer is dark and musty. A few tables and chairs crowd a hollowed-out space at the back. A couple of half-filled bottles of spirits sitting on a long, scuffed wooden table mark out the bar area. Once

her eyes have adjusted to the gloom, she notices an angular
man with a thin moustache polishing glasses on a corner
stool. Nicoletta clears her throat.

'Hello! Beg your pardon. Do you know where I can find
Jack Bridges?'

The man stands up and peers down at her, tucking a
cloth over his arm. He chews on his lower lip. 'Who wants
to know?'

'I do,' Nicoletta says, pulling out a chair and seating
herself. 'I'm a reporter for the *Sentinel*.'

'He's in his office. I don't think he'll speak to a reporter.
It's all been a terrible shock.' The man sniffs and sits down
heavily beside Nicoletta.

Nicoletta coughs politely. 'Did you know Julia? Mrs
Bridges, I mean.'

He fixes her with bloodshot eyes. 'Yes,' he says, taking
the cloth off his arm and twisting it between his fingers.
'I knew Julia. We all did.' He gestures around the empty
room.

'What's your name?' Nicoletta takes out her notebook.

'Graham Swift,' he answers, squinting at what she's
writing. 'I'm the manager here. Have been for years.'

Nicoletta nods. 'How did you feel when you heard that
Mrs Bridges had been found?'

'It doesn't feel real,' he says, clawing at his neck. 'I felt
shocked, still do. I never thought this day would come, to
be honest. Don't think anyone did.'

Nicoletta writes the meagre sentences in her notebook
before putting it away. 'Are you happy to be quoted?'

Graham nods. 'I'll take you up.' He gets to his feet

unsteadily. She thanks him, following him through a low doorway and up a narrow stairwell. At the top, they pass an open door with clothes, props and costumes spilling out of it. She steps over the net skirts of a pink tutu and comes to a door that says 'J. Bridges' in stuck-on gilt lettering.

Graham raps on the door. There's no answer, so he pushes it open. Jack Bridges is sitting behind an untidy desk, his head bowed. Graham clears space on a chair opposite and gestures for Nicoletta to sit down. Bridges' eyes settle on her, slightly out of focus.

'You have a visitor, Jack,' Graham says, unnecessarily loudly. 'A lady reporter from the *Sentinel*. She wants to talk to you about Julia.'

He beats a hasty retreat. Nicoletta sits with her handbag in her lap and waits, before she realises that Bridges is waiting for her to speak. She clears her throat.

'Mr Bridges?'

He gives a resigned nod.

Nicoletta shifts in the uncomfortable seat. 'My name is Nicoletta Sarto. I'm a reporter for the *Sentinel*. I'd like to speak to you about Julia. I understand you must be terribly upset, but I'd like to hear things from your point of view. How you must have suffered.'

'My point of view, eh?' His shoulders slump. He sticks his hands in the pockets of his button-down brown cardigan, blinking. 'There's nothing to say, I'm afraid. I just came in here today for something to do. To feel normal. We're closed. Graham should have locked the door.'

Nicoletta talks fast. 'Please, Mr Bridges. I know this must be a dreadful shock, after your wife was missing for twenty-five years. You must have gone through hell. Our readers will want to know all about that. And wouldn't you like to share your memories of Julia? Instead of being known as a headline in a newspaper. She was a real person. A wife, friend, daughter, mother . . .'

She trails off, aware that she may have over-egged it. She fully expects to be shown the door. But Jack Bridges props himself up on one fist. He looks at Nicoletta with interest and gives a sharp laugh. 'Julia wasn't a mother. Or a daughter. Or a friend, really. But she was my wife. And I suppose that counts for something.'

The desk between them is scattered with old Sweepstakes tickets, theatre programmes and bills marked 'Urgent'. She rummages for her notebook.

'Hold on.' He reaches for a newspaper under a pile of detritus. His small hand is grizzled with lots of very dark hair. 'What did you say your name was? I have this morning's city edition here.'

'Nicoletta Sarto. My story about your . . . about Mrs Bridges is on the front page.'

He glances at the paper, before tossing it on the pile and sitting back, arms folded tightly across his narrow chest. 'So now,' he says. 'What do you want to know?'

Nicoletta puts her bag at her feet and balances her notebook on her knees. 'Could you start by telling me what happened this morning, Mr Bridges?' She scribbles his name at the top of the page, followed by the date, then divides the page in two.

Bridges rakes his fingers across his ruddy cheeks and yawns. He's almost over-shaven, Nicoletta thinks.

'I was at home in bed, when that detective, Morris, arrived with some other fellow, banging on the door. It was six o'clock or just after. I'm not an early riser, more of a night owl. It goes with the job. I knew, even before they said anything, they'd found Julia. Morris had never given up hope; he made finding Julia a special mission of his, if you like. For all the good it did her.'

'What happened next?' Nicoletta transcribes everything he says in shorthand loops and dashes.

'They told me to take my time. I gave them some tea and they drank it while I washed and dressed and shaved. If this was Julia, then I wanted things done right. When I was ready, I joined them.

'"It's about Julia, isn't it?" I only felt able to say it then.

'Morris said it was, they were almost sure, and they'd like me to make a formal identification. We got into the car, with the other fellow driving, and they took me down to the morgue. Brought me into a room, cold as the inside of a fridge, and slid a shelf out of the wall, lifting a sort of blanket. They asked me if it was Julia. Well, it wasn't her. A few bones, that's all. But then they showed me the ring they'd found. "Jack and Julia," it said, and our wedding date. I couldn't deny the skeleton on the slab had once been my wife. Morris said something like: "Can you confirm this is the wedding ring of your wife, Julia Bridges?" It was all very formal. I said it was. I signed a form and then walked out as soon as I could. I've been sitting here ever since.' He plucks at the skin around his mouth.

Nicoletta notices the wedding ring finger on Bridges' left hand is bare.

'It must have been awful for you, Mr Bridges.'

He blinks at Nicoletta and looks away.

'How do you feel now?' Nicoletta doesn't know for a moment or two if he's heard her.

'How do I feel?' he echoes finally, resting his chin on his knuckles and considering the question. 'In one way, I always dreamt Julia would be found alive. I know it sounds foolish, when all the evidence was stacked against it, but part of me never stopped hoping.'

Nicoletta nods. 'I understand, I think.'

They sit in silence for a moment, while Nicoletta scratches more notes on the page in her lap. 'How did you and Julia meet?'

The question seems to take Bridges by surprise. He grips his side of the desk with both hands, as though it's about to topple out from under him. 'Why do you want to know that?'

Nicoletta gives what she hopes is a gentle but encouraging smile. 'It'd give more insight into Julia as a person, as your wife. Your memories together. Our readers would be interested.'

He puts his hands up to his face, as though checking the stubble for growth. His fingers begin to tremble. Nicoletta leans forward. 'I'm sorry. It's a lot, I know. Would you like me to fetch you a drink, Mr Bridges?'

He shakes his head. 'I don't drink or smoke anymore. Haven't for ages. It never did me any good. I'm not about to start again now.'

He stands up and reaches over to the other side of the desk, plucking the notebook out of Nicoletta's lap, closing it, and placing it beside his right elbow. She flinches, all too aware of his fingertips grazing the exposed part of her nyloned thigh. 'What did you do that for?' The words come out in a splutter, and she stands up in a bid to take the notebook back, but Bridges motions for her to sit down.

'You seem like a nice girl, Miss Sarto,' he says, his gaze missing hers completely and landing level with the door handle. 'But this is not for publication, you understand.'

'All right,' she says, sitting back down, crossing her arms, and eyeing her notebook balefully across the desk. He looks at her for a moment, before looking away. She smiles. 'So. Tell me.'

'I opened the Athena in 1940. It was always a dream of mine. And I've kept it going since.'

'I see.' Nicoletta feels naked without her notebook. She can't help fidgeting.

'I didn't think I'd ever get married, and then one day, in the middle of the war, Julia walked in. Off the train from God knows where, asking for directions to some boarding house. She asked if there was any work here. I asked her what kind of work she was looking for, and she said, "Anything, really." I asked her if she'd like to read a few lines, for the part of Portia in *Julius Caesar*. "I'm no actress," she said. But she read the lines anyway. Six months later we were married.'

He steeples his fingers against his forehead. Nicoletta can feel perspiration begin to prickle her underarms.

'Did Julia have a lot of friends?'

The corners of Bridges' mouth turn down. 'All the

theatre folk were her friends. Her family, really. I never met her parents.'

'What about women friends?'

'I only met one, someone from the boarding house who was a witness at our wedding. Noeleen O'Shea.'

'Do you know where Noeleen is now?'

'No. I didn't hear anything from her when Julia went missing,' he says, with a snort in the back of his throat.

'What was the name of the boarding house?'

Bridges smears a hand against his forehead. 'Hanahoe's Guesthouse on Gardiner Street.'

Nicoletta discreetly wipes her palms on her skirt. 'How did the production of *Julius Caesar* go?'

'We opened at the beginning of May 1941 and ran for a month.' He stands up and Nicoletta stands, too, eyeing her notebook on the desk between them, still within his grasp. She presumes the interview is over.

'Follow me.' He leads her into the room next door, stuffed with costumes on two long clothes rails running the length of the wall. The rest of the space is filled with props – cigarette holders, telephones, tables and chairs, crockery, a policeman's hat. Bridges seizes a glinting grey object beside the hat and clutches it to his heart, before twirling it in his right hand and tapping it irregularly against the top of the clothes rail, with a sickening metallic *clink*. Nicoletta jumps. When she realises it's a gun, she takes a step backwards into a sea of scratchy fabric.

'We've used this in various productions. In *Julius Caesar*, as a matter of fact.'

'That . . . isn't real, is it?'

'Oh yes,' he says, smiling. 'It's a .22 automatic. Belonged to my father.'

The room is hot and close. At this proximity, she can almost see Bridges' pulse quickening beneath his skin.

'The man drank himself to death.' Bridges cocks the gun at the wall and takes imaginary aim. 'This is a reminder not to turn out like that prick.'

Nicoletta gives a soft cough. She knows she has to keep him talking.

'Tell me about Julia in the play.'

Bridges lowers the gun and puts it back on the table. The planes of his face visibly soften as he relaxes into the telling. 'She was wonderful. But on the last day of May, the Nazis decided to bomb Dublin and the husband of the other actress in the play – she was Calpurnia – was killed. We were meant to run for another month, but we stopped after that as a mark of respect. Everybody loved Julia though. They said she was brilliant. And for the next two years, she was in loads more productions at the Athena, each one better than the last. She blossomed here.' His voice breaks on the last word. 'We were happy.'

'Did Gloria Fitzpatrick fund many productions here?' Nicoletta feels the walls close in on her. She's desperate to get out.

Bridges blinks and grips the gun. 'A good few,' he says finally. 'Until the money ran out.' He lets out a hoarse laugh.

'What was she like?'

'I think she'd have liked to be on the stage herself. Doing what Julia was doing. What Julia loved doing.'

Nicoletta realises she's been forcing a smile so long that her cheeks ache.

'I see,' she says. She gives it one last shot, before she makes her escape. What's the worst that can happen?

'Did you and Julia want to start a family together?' The words are out before she can stop them.

Bridges looks down at the hand holding the gun. 'Yes.' His voice breaks. 'I always wanted a son. But it was never to be.'

A silence follows, and it's a moment before Nicoletta realises that tears are rolling down Jack Bridges' cheeks. He's behind her now, blocking the door. She's wondering if he'd stop her if she were to make a run past him when he beckons for her to follow him back to his office. She's out of the prop room, away from the glint of the gun, before he's taken his first step.

'I'm sorry for intruding,' she says, talking fast, grabbing her notebook off his desk. 'It was kind of you to talk to me. But I won't keep you any longer.'

He doesn't say anything.

Nicoletta bends to get her bag, then pauses. 'What do *you* think happened to your wife, Mr Bridges?'

He wipes his eyes with the back of his hand. 'There was a guy who came to see Julia a lot in the summer revue in May '43. The Guards questioned him, but he had an alibi.'

'What's his name?'

Bridges scratches his cheek and sits back down. 'Brendan Owens. He's dead now, but the wife is still alive. She's my landlady.'

Nicoletta nods. 'Thank you for your time, Mr Bridges.

43

I'll leave you in peace now.' She's almost at the door when she stops again.

'Mr Bridges, do you have a photograph of Julia you wouldn't mind us using in the *Sentinel*? I don't believe we have one on file. One of her on stage.'

Bridges scrubs his eyes with a paper tissue produced from his sleeve. 'Ask Graham.'

She thanks him, making her way back along the narrow corridor, down the stairs. Graham is seated in the bar area, but he's no longer polishing glasses, instead staring into space.

'Graham,' Nicoletta says pleasantly. He looks up with a start. 'Mr Bridges said you might be able to loan me a photo of Julia appearing on stage? To accompany the article.'

He stands up. 'I got rid of most of them in the last few years. I knew Jack didn't want to be reminded.' He walks over to a small photo in a clear glass frame beside a door that says TOILET in peeling black letters. 'This is the only one left.' He lifts it down off the wall, tapping the glass. 'The opening night of *Julius Caesar*. 1st May 1941. Probably time it went anyway.'

Nicoletta takes the picture, sliding it into her bag, frame and all. She thanks Graham and steps onto Bachelors Walk, before taking the photo back out, holding it up to the light. It's a postcard-sized, faded black-and-white print. A group of men in military costumes face the camera, their gazes unwavering, flanked by two women. The woman on the right is pale-skinned and dark-haired, wearing the fashions of the time – a two-piece suit with an extravagantly plumed Robin Hood hat, her hair pinned in a roll at the nape of her neck. Her chin is held up, shoulders straight, a regal bearing. Nicoletta checks the caption at the bottom. Julia Murphy. Her eye runs over to the other woman in the group, on the opposite side. She is wearing similar clothes to Julia, but she's smaller, darker, not as defiantly posed, a fragility about her stance that's as brittle as the glass frame. Nicoletta looks at the caption. 'Daniela Stagg,' it says. She puzzles over it as her heart slows down. The surname is all wrong. Her mother's maiden name was Corso. Though the petite, dark-haired woman in the photograph, hardly daring to look at the camera, is unmistakably her mother.

Chapter Four

The city has woken up. O'Connell Street is darkening with Christmas shoppers, scurrying to and from the various department stores, lines of fevered ants. A tall Christmas tree adorns the window at Clerys, decorated from top to bottom with tasteful red bows. The space where Nelson's Pillar was bombed by the IRA is conspicuous as a jagged tooth.

The sharp point of the framed photograph from the Athena Theatre presses against Nicoletta's hip. She wonders if she'll have the nerve to ask her parents about it the next day, at Christmas lunch. She knows she should join them for this evening's traditional *La Vigilia di Natale* dinner. But Julia Bridges has turned up after twenty-five years. Stories like this don't come along every day. And the women's page editor job is hers for the taking.

Hanahoe's Guesthouse is at the end of a cluster of small, shabby hotels and bed and breakfasts on Gardiner Street, a Georgian building that has seen better days. Someone has left a rusted bicycle on the top step, upended like a dead insect, exposed to potential thieves and the elements.

A gaudy Christmas wreath hangs from the brass knocker on the front door. Nicoletta is about to lift it, when the door opens and a woman with a beaky nose takes her measure through horn-rimmed glasses. Nicoletta stands frozen for a moment, unsure of whether to stay where she is, or back away.

The woman makes a face. 'We're closed until the New Year. No room at the inn.' She looks Nicoletta up and down. *Can she tell?* Nicoletta feels her cheeks burn.

'I'm not here about a room. I'm looking to speak to Mr or Mrs Hanahoe.'

'I am *Miss* Hanahoe.'

Miss Hanahoe blows her nose into a large handkerchief and opens the door a fraction wider, so Nicoletta can see into the dim hallway. 'I was wondering if I could speak to you about a girl called Julia Bridges. Julia Murphy, she would have been then. She stayed here a long time ago, during the war, I believe.' In the background, she can make out a rickety desk with a large, silent wireless on top of it.

The woman exhales, as though she's been meditating for a few seconds. 'I haven't heard that name in a long time. What do you want to know for?'

Nicoletta shifts her weight. She realises that she desperately needs to use the bathroom. 'My name is Nicoletta Sarto. I'm a reporter for the *Sentinel*. I'm writing a story about Julia.'

'A reporter. Writing a story about Julia. As if she's a film star or royalty. I've just about heard it all now. You might as well come in, but, as I've said, it was a long time ago. I don't know how much I'll remember.'

Nicoletta doubts very much that this woman ever forgets. She follows her into the dark little hallway, its plaster walls as effective as cardboard at making extra divisions to create the illusion of space. 'Thank you,' she says. 'You're very kind.' The adjective hits a false note. Miss Hanahoe seems like someone who notices everything and lets nothing go, a seething morass of resentments and slights. She pulls out a chair for Nicoletta on one side of the desk and indicates for her to sit. She settles herself on a high stool, hunched forward, like a small bird of prey on a perch.

'I'm sorry for intruding on your work.' Nicoletta crosses her legs and sits back.

'I'm cleaning before I close for Christmas.'

Nicoletta looks around appreciatively. 'I'd say you run a tight ship.'

Miss Hanahoe sniffs. The compliment may have found its target. 'I have to. It's a respectable place. I mostly take in young, single girls and I'm strict about rules and regulations or they'd run rings around me.' She leans forward. 'Some of them can be very devious.'

Nicoletta starts jiggling her leg up and down, then stops herself. 'Do you remember Julia Murphy?'

Miss Hanahoe nods. 'I do remember Julia, as it happens. She was only here for a few months, in the spring of 1941. A quiet girl, but open to being led astray, if you know what I mean. Still, it's all such a long time ago. Why are you writing about her?'

Nicoletta shifts in her chair, the pressure in her bladder making her imminent escape a matter of urgency. 'Julia's body was found this morning.' She pauses. Miss Hanahoe blinks. Nicoletta continues, 'Julia was last seen in the summer of 1943, entering the premises of Miss Gloria Fitzpatrick – I'm sure you know the name. I thought I'd speak to those who knew Julia.'

Miss Hanahoe blinks again, her eyes fully closing for a couple of beats. 'Fitzpatrick . . . why would that name mean anything to me?'

Nicoletta swallows. 'Gloria Fitzpatrick was convicted of murder in connection with another woman's death several years later. An induced miscarriage gone wrong.'

Miss Hanahoe sniffs again. 'I'm sorry to disappoint, but I'm afraid I don't read the gutter press, so the name doesn't roll off my tongue as readily as it does yours. I can't help you on that front. Julia was a bit of a mouse . . . I didn't know her, not really. And I'd prefer not to have my name in any of this. This is a respectable establishment. Julia didn't decide to disappear when she was staying here, so it's really nothing to do with me.'

Nicoletta stares at her in disbelief. 'Did Julia say where she was from? Or mention home at all?'

Miss Hanahoe leans forward. 'I really can't say. She was from down the country somewhere. I make it a policy of not getting too pally with my guests. Just as long as they pay their bills and behave themselves, then we shouldn't have a problem between us.'

'And did she?' Nicoletta leans forward, mirroring Miss Hanahoe. 'Did she pay her bills and behave?'

'She did, to a point. There was one night when she and her friend Noeleen missed the curfew and banged on my door roaring to be let in. They were inebriated. I won't stand for that sort of thing.'

'I see.' Nicoletta taps her foot impatiently. 'Would you know where I could find Noeleen O'Shea? Though she may have since married and changed her name. She also stayed here and may be the same Noeleen you mentioned. She was a witness at Julia's wedding to Jack Bridges.'

Miss Hanahoe pretends to think for a moment and purses her lips. 'Noeleen married Joe Clancy from around the North Strand. I saw their wedding photo in the *Evening Press*. That's all I care to remember.'

Nicoletta stands up. 'Thanks very much for speaking to me, Miss Hanahoe.' She holds out her hand. Miss Hanahoe doesn't take it. Instead, she stands up, rattling a bunch of keys to let Nicoletta out.

'Don't go mentioning Hanahoe's in your little newspaper article. In fact, don't mention me at all.' She fidgets with a Miraculous Medal, depicting Our Lady of Graces, at her throat, before unlocking the door and seeing Nicoletta out into the pale sunlight. Curiosity compels Nicoletta to speak before she can stop herself.

'Aren't you the tiniest bit sorry to hear that a woman's body – and not just any woman, but someone who was in your care – was found today?' Her voice is hoarse from the brute force of the sentiment.

Miss Hanahoe narrows her eyes through her thick glasses. 'Miss Sarto, I would hardly say Julia was in my care. She is someone who stayed here almost thirty years ago. I do not have a duty to the girls who stay here. They are adults, well able to fend for themselves. Julia wasn't even staying here when she disappeared with that Fitzpatrick woman. It was a couple of years later. She was a silly girl. Easily suggestible. I could have predicted this outcome.'

Nicoletta begins to speak but Miss Hanahoe, eager for the last word, cuts her dead.

'You can tell Noeleen, if you manage to get hold of her, that she owes me a month's board. Good day to you.' And, with that, she shuts the door with a bang.

Nicoletta stands for a moment, inches from the flaking door, feeling a hot burst of anger flood her bloodstream. She starts walking, unsure of her next step. Her uncomfortable bladder is her most immediate concern. Beyond that, she can't think. She won't. Though a thought finds its way through the fog regardless. A bright winter's day like this one. Hauling evening newspapers out of a van, ignoring offers of help. Locking up, lowering herself into a scalding bath. Letting nature take its course, hoping for the best. The thought burrows into her brain like a parasite.

A string of gaily coloured lights illuminating the words *Nollaig Shona Dhuit* guides her to a pub at the end of Gardiner Street. She has to focus on this story; this is what matters. She darts inside to use the ladies', half hoping to see the familiar spots of blood. But still knowing there'll be nothing. Then she buys a packet of crisps and a lemonade at the bar and asks for the telephone directory. Under cover of a skinny, over-decorated Christmas tree, she tears open the crisps and devours them by the handful, almost licking the salt off the packet. She looks around, hoping no one has noticed. The bar is empty. A couple of men in suits sit in a snug beside the fire, sipping pints, open newspapers in front of them, eyeing her curiously. The lemonade is bittersweet, and she gulps it as quickly as the fizz will allow. There are several Clancys in the phone book. One looks promising, Nicoletta decides, a Mrs N. Clancy at Summerhill Parade, not far from the North Strand. Noeleen Clancy, née O'Shea, must be a widow.

Out in the street, an empty wrapper skitters across her path. A small child kicks a football into the road and darts out through the traffic to retrieve it. She can't help but notice that he's in his stockinged feet. A horse and cart clop towards them at a brisk pace, the horse's hooves narrowly missing both the child and football. If Enzo were still alive, would he like football? Nicoletta can't imagine her mother would allow him out of the house without shoes. 'My little man,' Daniela used to call him, cradling his head against her neck, crooning the only Italian lullaby she knew, one Nicoletta had never heard until Enzo arrived. She wills the thought away.

The houses on Mrs Clancy's street are over a century old, and yet there's a divide in the chimney at the number listed where a new bit has been tacked on. Nicoletta's father had said something about the Germans dropping the first bomb accidentally on Summerhill Parade. Her mother had told him to shut up, she remembers now. She thinks of the photograph in her pocket, of the cast of *Julius Caesar*. Daniela Stagg, her mother from another life. A life she realises she knows nothing about. She hears the sound of a faltering piano from the front room, along with a woman's voice giving instructions.

She pauses for a moment, listening to the tinkling of scales. Raffa used to play piano at the Broadway Café tea dances on Sunday afternoons. Her mother took her there as a teenager, in the hope that she'd meet someone 'nice', meaning someone of Italian stock. Nicoletta had expressed an interest in learning music and her mother had approached Raffa and paid for a term of six weekly lessons. Thursday afternoons from mid-October, between three and four, were spent sitting perched on the sofa in his tiny, rented front room, listening to him play what he called 'the Greats' while his wife was shopping. He'd only ever let Nicoletta play scales. 'You have to start at the beginning,' he'd say, the slight roll on his 'r's still detectable despite years in England, and later, Ireland. After the third lesson, he walked her to where her bicycle was propped against the wall at the side of the red brick terrace. She'd waved and prepared to cycle off.

'You're a beautiful woman,' he'd said, almost as an afterthought, before kissing her squarely on the mouth, his hands in his pockets. She was so surprised, she almost fell off her bicycle, her hands wobbling on the handlebars. As she pedalled home, she couldn't be sure if he'd really said it, or if it had been the sound of the wind sweeping through piles of dead leaves at the corner of the street. Things had progressed after that, until one day she turned up at his house to find it empty, the blinds drawn. She'd peered in, through the gap, to see light spaces on the wooden floor where armchairs, tables and chairs had once stood, along with one large light rectangle indicating where the piano had been. Nicoletta holds herself up straighter. That's not who she is anymore. Someone who peeps under closed blinds, hoping for the scraps of somebody else's life. The scales have stopped, and the unseen pianist is now playing a shaky version of 'Yankee Doodle'. She rings the bell and waits.

Chapter Five

The music stops and the door opens an inch or two. A woman stands, half obscured by what looks like a sheaf of sheet music bundled against her chest.

'Yes? Can you come back later? I'm in the middle of a lesson. Last one before the New Year.'

Nicoletta clasps her hands in front of her. 'Mrs Clancy? My name is Nicoletta Sarto. I'm a reporter from the *Sentinel*.'

Mrs Clancy calls something to the occupant of the room behind her, before opening the door a bit wider. 'A reporter? What about?'

'It's about Julia Bridges.' Nicoletta says the name in a low voice, in case any of the neighbours happen to hear. 'I believe you also knew her as Julia Murphy. I'm so sorry to tell you that Mrs Bridges' remains were found this morning.'

Mrs Clancy's shoulders shoot up. She opens the door further. 'Oh God. Jesus Christ. Poor Julia.'

'I hoped you'd have a few minutes to speak to me. About Julia.'

Mrs Clancy looks at her for a second longer than is

necessary. 'You want to talk about Julia.' She makes a brittle sound, halfway between a laugh and a cry. 'I wouldn't even know where to start.'

The piano has stopped. Mrs Clancy lowers her voice. 'Look, I'm all too aware of little ears eavesdropping.' She gestures to the adjacent open door, which leads to a cluttered-looking room. Nicoletta can see a dusty bookshelf crammed full of books, decorated with gold and red tinsel in joyful, gaudy loops. 'There's about fifteen minutes left in this lesson. Wait for me here and I'll speak to you then. I'll tell you, I'm in bits to hear about Julia. I want you to tell me what happened.'

Nicoletta takes a seat on a low-backed chair in the hall-way while Mrs Clancy glides back into the parlour and the sound of scales starts up again. This woman is being so kind, the first person who seems like they want to tell her what they know. Something might finally make sense. She is lulled almost to sleep when Mrs Clancy reappears. She puts a finger to her lips.

'Emer is just packing up her things,' she says brightly. Then in a low, urgent voice close to Nicoletta's ear, she says, 'I need to know now, Miss Sarto. Did that bastard kill her?'

The door opens to reveal a studious-looking girl with thick plaits. Nicoletta is suddenly claustrophobic in the cramped hall. The girl and Mrs Clancy fill the space with murmurings of *Happy Christmas, keep practising now, Emer, send my regards to your parents*. Mrs Clancy eventually returns alone, indicating Nicoletta to join her in the parlour. She stands over Nicoletta, her back to the small, boarded-up mantelpiece.

'I'm not much of a housekeeper,' Mrs Clancy says proudly, taking in Nicoletta's eyes sweeping the room. The dining table is crammed into one corner, piled with books, papers and magazines, its chairs scattered through-out the room. 'I don't see the point of cleaning when I could be doing something else. Something *fun*.'

Nicoletta nods politely and hovers, waiting to be told where to go. When no instructions are forthcoming, she sits gingerly on one of the dilapidated dining chairs, its back pushed against the wall. Mrs Clancy sits on a small settee beside her, a bit closer than Nicoletta would like, but she takes the housekeeping confession as a promising sign.

'Where was she found?' Mrs Clancy is the first to speak. The question takes Nicoletta by surprise.

'Mrs Bridges was found buried in a shallow grave in the grounds of a private house in Sandycove. Her husband was able to identify her remains by her wedding ring.'

If Mrs Clancy is satisfied with this explanation, she doesn't show it. 'Poor Ju,' she says, twisting a hank of dark hair behind her ear. It immediately escapes and falls forward.

'Who were you referring to a few minutes ago as "that bastard"?'

Mrs Clancy shrugs. 'The husband, of course. It's always the husband.'

'Do you know Mr Bridges at all?' Nicoletta slides her notebook out of her bag and opens it in her lap, making a few notes. She is conscious of Mrs Clancy being so close, and she wonders how those shorthand lines and loops must appear to someone who can't read them. At least, she hopes Mrs Clancy can't.

'Jack Bridges? Well, I was a witness at their wedding. I'm sure you already know that if you've come to find me.' Mrs Clancy sits back, and Nicoletta observes her profile. There's no accusation in her matter-of-fact tone. Her soft, white hands are folded in her lap. If Nicoletta were of a mind to draw, Mrs Clancy would make a good subject.

'Were he and Julia happy?'

Mrs Clancy laughs, an unexpected flutter of mirth that ripples out from her lips.

'I mean, really. God, you're young. What does that have to do with anything? Julia would've hated all this. She was such a quiet, private person. She detested being the centre of attention, even though I suppose that was essentially the nature of her profession, being an actress. But she did it because she liked pretending, I think. She was damn good at it.'

'Were you surprised when she went missing?'

Mrs Clancy swivels around to look Nicoletta in the face. 'Of course. I couldn't stop thinking about it. I never did, really. And I never thought the truth would come out.' She wrings her hands. It's all a bit theatrical, Nicoletta can't help thinking.

'Yet you didn't think to contact Jack Bridges after you heard she'd gone missing. Did you really think he'd killed her?'

Mrs Clancy sighs and sits back again. 'Somehow, I kept hoping all this time that Julia had just disappeared, the way people do; that she'd taken the boat to England, or America, with a new name, to seek her fortune, leaving everything behind her. But to hear that she's been found ... well, Jesus wept.' Mrs Clancy pauses to pat her cheeks with a handkerchief. 'Julia wanted to leave him. Oh, yes.'

Nicoletta tries to frame her next question. But there's no delicate way of asking it. 'Why? Was he violent, Mrs Clancy?'

Mrs Clancy sighs. 'I don't know. She wouldn't say a bad word about him. She stayed here for a little while, you know. But then when I heard she'd gone missing, I didn't want to ... I preferred to believe some romantic notion that she'd escaped from her life – do you know what I mean? Otherwise, it was too much to think about how she'd ended up. I can see why Julia loved pretending. It's far more appealing than the alternative.'

'I understand.' Nicoletta scribbles some notes, but Mrs Clancy is lost in her own thoughts, and doesn't seem to notice. 'You must have cared about her a great deal.'

The other woman's mouth lifts at the corners. 'I did, I suppose. She was half daft, was Julia, but that was part of her charm. We had so much fun when we stayed at Miss Hanahoe's. Both of us up from the country and green as grass. We'd do silly things, like go into Clerys and try on all the hats, then leave without buying anything, or take the tram out to Howth and back again, for no other reason than we wanted to. We got into some scrapes with Miss Hanahoe, but it's funny now, looking back.' A tear rolls down her cheek, followed by several more. Nicoletta offers her a clean hanky.

'I met Miss Hanahoe. I can imagine.'

Mrs Clancy raises her eyebrows. 'I hadn't seen Julia much after she got married. Then one day, it must have been a few weeks before she disappeared – I remember it was a hot, sticky day in early July and I went into Bewley's on Grafton Street for a glass of lemonade – I bumped into Ju. We ended up talking for hours and she told me all about how desperate she was feeling. She still couldn't say anything bad about Bridges. But I got the sense she was scared to leave. She came here then for a night or two. And it was like old times, we were the silly girls we'd been when we stayed with that old goat Miss Hanahoe. I was on my own and, to be honest, I was glad of the company.'

'It must be terribly sad for you,' Nicoletta interjects.

Mrs Clancy nods without saying anything and Nicoletta waits until she's ready to speak again.

'Julia did say a married man had been paying her attention, but she didn't give me too much detail. We mostly reminisced about old times. She didn't want to talk any further about Bridges. And I never did find out who the married man was. Julia was secretive. She didn't like to talk about herself, or her people, or where she'd come from. She never once mentioned her parents, for instance.'

Nicoletta frowns. 'Did they ever come forward when she went missing? Any idea how I could get in touch with them?'

Mrs Clancy shakes her head vigorously, the effort dislodging several strands of hair. 'I have no idea. I know their name must be Murphy, but I can't even give you a county. It changed all the time, wherever she decided she was from, depending on her mood. Her accent didn't give much away.'

'I see.' Nicoletta closes her notebook.

Tears are streaming down Mrs Clancy's cheeks, and she doesn't make any move to wipe them away. 'The thing is, even after all that, I don't think I ever really knew Julia at all.'

Nicoletta shifts in her chair. 'How well can we ever really know another person?' She's aware of the unintentionally flippant tone as soon as she's said it. Mrs Clancy doesn't answer.

She looks around, as though noticing the room for the first time: the books, the dust, the half-hearted Christmas decorations. 'I'm sorry, I should have offered you something. Tea, or what have you. I could do with a drink myself.'

Nicoletta hesitates. 'I'm sorry I've taken up so much of your time. I know it's been a shock.'

Mrs Clancy stands up without a word and disappears into the kitchen. She comes back with a bottle of brandy and two smudged glasses, pouring a generous measure into each and handing one to Nicoletta. 'Please join me in a drink. It's Christmas, after all.'

Mrs Clancy cradles her glass against her chest, lolling back against the sofa and kicking off her shoes, her toes at a diagonal, pointing towards Nicoletta. It occurs to Nicoletta that this isn't Mrs Clancy's first drink of the day. She takes a reluctant sip and it hits her insides with a jolt. She puts down the glass, wondering how she'll manage not to drink it. She tries to sit upright, pressing her back into the hard chair.

'Mrs Clancy, you mentioned earlier that when you heard that Julia had disappeared, a part of you hoped she'd somehow "escaped" her life and made a new one for herself overseas. Why would you think her husband might have killed her?'

Mrs Clancy wrinkles her nose, before taking a dainty sip. 'I don't know what you thought of Jack Bridges, and maybe he seemed like he wouldn't hurt a fly, but the truth is he always gave me the creeps.' She looks over the rim of her glass.

Nicoletta jumps as a cuckoo springs out of an old-fashioned clock on the far wall, chiming the hour. Mrs Clancy raises a slim hand and waves in its direction with an indulgent smile. 'Oh, don't mind him. I don't even notice him anymore.'

The thing stops shrieking and retreats into the clock. Nicoletta resists the urge to shudder. 'When you say Mr Bridges gave you the creeps, how do you mean?'

Mrs Clancy blinks. 'I don't know if you know what Julia looked like, but she was a stunner. She could've had anyone. Yet she married the first so-and-so who asked her.'

Nicoletta waits for her to continue. Mrs Clancy contemplates this for a moment, her head slackened to one side. She's finished her drink. 'What does that tell you about Julia?'

Nicoletta smiles. 'That she was ... maybe insecure?'

Mrs Clancy bangs a cushion with her fist, as though Nicoletta has just come up with a solution to a complex algorithm. 'I've known plenty of girls like that. None quite like Julia, but plenty with rotten taste in men. They think they won't find anyone, so they settle for the first Tom, Dick or Harry they happen to meet.'

She refills her own glass and glances at Nicoletta's. 'You've barely touched yours.' She raises the brandy and takes a gulp, smacking her lips. 'Bridges was all flattery at the start. That type always is. I think Julia was dazzled by him, because of that ramshackle theatre, because he told her she was a brilliant actress, because no one had ever told her anything like that before. And she was. She was brilliant. I could've told her that.'

'What was he like once they were married?' Nicoletta takes a small sip of the brandy. The burning sensation in her throat isn't altogether unpleasant.

'Miserable. Wouldn't let her out of his sight. That's why, when I heard she'd disappeared, I sort of hoped she'd done a runner. The alternative was just unthinkable . . . that somehow Bridges had done something to her, and bloody well got away with it after all this time.'

Nicoletta maintains a level gaze with Mrs Clancy, who's well on her way to being merry now, her words sliding all over the place like dropped musical notes.

Mrs Clancy leans forward, her elbow sliding off the armrest. 'Tell me this, Miss Sarto – that private house in Sandycove where Julia was found, who does it belong to?'

Nicoletta hesitates. But what harm can it do? It won't be long before it's public knowledge. 'It's the house of Charles Creighton and his family. They're the jewellery people.'

'And no doubt regular patrons of the theatre as well. That explains everything.'

Nicoletta sits back. 'Does it? I don't think it explains anything, Mrs Clancy.'

'Julia said her married man was involved in the theatre.'

'But if Jack Bridges found out about an affair between his wife and Charles Creighton, and killed her, why has Julia's body been found in Creighton's garden?' Nicoletta makes her voice gentle, but she can tell the question stings as soon as it lands.

Mrs Clancy slumps against the sofa. 'Do you know what she told me one time? Bridges said that if he ever caught her with another man, he'd kill them both. But then she laughed it off, said he was only joking.'

Mrs Clancy meets Nicoletta's eye and Nicoletta puts her notebook down. 'There was a sighting of Julia entering Gloria Fitzpatrick's premises in Ranelagh. This struck the Gardaí as significant, in light of Fitzpatrick's subsequent murder conviction.'

Mrs Clancy's face crumples. 'Poor Ju,' she breathes. 'She must've been desperate. And she was so secretive right until the end.'

Before she can think twice, Nicoletta pulls the photograph of the cast of *Julius Caesar* out of her bag and hands it over to Mrs Clancy, who takes it and reaches for her spectacles. 'The manager of the Athena gave me this. For my article.'

Mrs Clancy peers at the photo, before breaking into a smile. 'Ah yes, I remember it well. Opening night of *Julius Caesar*. God, she was gorgeous.'

She hands the photo back to Nicoletta, taking another gulp of brandy.

Nicoletta puts the picture back in her bag. 'I believe the show ended abruptly when the North Strand area was bombed. The other woman in the play lost her husband. Her name is Daniela Stagg. Do you know her?' She tries to appear casual, taking a sip of brandy to wet her lips. Mrs Clancy doesn't seem to notice.

'That's right. This very house was bombed, and I lost my Joe. You can probably see where my husband's family had to replace half the chimney. Of course, it only took them ten years.' Her voice cracks and she kicks the leg of the table in front of her. 'Anyway, it was dreadful. Caused devastation. Another fellow my Joe knew was killed; Tommy Stagg was his name. Knew the family well. He was married to Daniela, an Italian, I believe. Her parents didn't like her marrying Tommy.'

Nicoletta feels her head prickle with heat. She forces herself to focus on Mrs Clancy. 'What happened then?'

'They had to stop the play. She'd just lost her husband in tragic circumstances; they couldn't go on. Didn't want to in any case, though Bridges was raging his production was stopped. But what else could they do?'

Nicoletta pauses. 'No, I mean what happened to the girl whose husband was killed? Do you know?'

'Oh, yes. I believe she remarried fairly quickly after that. Found a fellow Italian in Fairview. Can't remember the name.' She pronounces it 'Eye-talian'. She gives Nicoletta a curious look. 'Is Sarto an Italian name?'

'It is, yes.' Nicoletta is about to elaborate, the way the transactions of social niceties have taught her she must, when Mrs Clancy asks for the photograph again.

Nicoletta glances at it before she passes it over. Dark-haired, pale-skinned Julia, the way she held herself with cool precision. Was she still in character? She didn't look like someone who might be desperate enough to seek the services of Gloria Fitzpatrick a couple of short years later. And the woman beside her, Daniela Stagg, smaller, slighter. Her mother, before she knew her. It's like looking at a total stranger. Mrs Clancy stares into space for a moment or two, before accepting the photograph again and gazing at it as though she's never seen it before. She wipes her eyes with the back of her hand.

'Poor Julia. She could've had anyone.' She hands the photo back and sits very still, putting her fingers to her temples, her eyes closed. 'I still wonder if that bastard did it.' She throws her head back against the sofa.

'I'm sorry. This must be difficult for you.'

Mrs Clancy goes over to the piano and sits down heavily, lifting the lid. Nicoletta shoves the photo back in her bag and stands up. 'Thank you, Mrs Clancy,' she says, quietly letting herself out. A jumble of staccato piano notes reaches her as she contemplates the cold, clear afternoon.

Chapter Six

By the time she gets to Groome's on Cavendish Row, the lunchtime rush is over, the others have gone, and Barney is sitting alone, nursing the remains of a pint. He stands up when he sees her, automatically pulling out a stool. She hovers for a moment or two, considering what to do, before sinking onto the low seat.

'You're here,' he says, downing what's left in his glass and wiping the foam from his upper lip. 'I'm glad.' He takes a breath, as though he's about to say something else, but Nicoletta rushes ahead before he can speak. 'Barney, I want that women's page editor gig. I mean, I really, *really* want it.'

'OK, I get it, I get it.' His brow creases in confusion. 'So, what do you want from me?'

Nicoletta picks up his empty glass and rolls it between her palms. She takes a deep breath and puts it down.

'Information,' she says, smoothing her turban back into place. 'What's the next port of call with this story?'

Barney signals to the barman and Nicoletta taps him on the elbow. 'I definitely won't have a drink,' she says.

Barney swings back around and looks at her for several seconds too long. She drops her gaze, self-conscious.

'All right,' he says. 'Next stop is the Creighton residence in Sandycove. Seaview House.'

'What sort of house is it?' Nicoletta asks, idly tapping her foot.

'I'm sure it's quite the pile. That jewellery business must be worth a lot. I think the wife, his second, is independently wealthy, too. Nice for some.'

'What are the Creightons like?' Nicoletta draws out her notebook, pen poised.

'Who knows? They'll tell us nothing, of course, but it'd be good to get some colour on the area. Also try to speak to John Dawkins, the guy who found Bridges' body. A son-in-law of the Creightons. Lives in the mews, married the daughter, Delia Creighton.'

Nicoletta looks down at the slender gold watch on her wrist, a gift from her parents on her 21st birthday. She'd wanted an Art Deco ring she'd seen at Charles Creighton and Son on Grafton Street, but they'd insisted on buying her this from a jeweller on the other side of town. She'd been disappointed but she hadn't wanted to make a fuss. She finishes jotting everything down, before closing the notebook and tapping her foot.

Barney looks amused. 'That all right for you?'

She smiles her thanks.

'We might as well go now. I'm glad you're coming with me; a woman's always more likely to be let past the front door.' He looks at her expectantly. 'How was Jack Bridges?'

Nicoletta pauses, scraping back her stool. 'A loose

cannon. He was in shock, though, as to be expected,' she says. 'You're right, that theatre's a kip now. Was Bridges ever questioned over his wife's disappearance?'

Barney lifts his coat from the back of his chair and puts it on, shoving his hands into the pockets. They're out on the street before he answers. 'I'm sure he was interviewed, but just so he could be crossed off the list. Morris always had the bit between his teeth about Gloria Fitzpatrick. One of his hunches.'

'I spoke to somebody else who seems convinced Jack Bridges was behind it.'

'Who?'

They skim past the pawn shop window of earlier, and Nicoletta's attention is caught by a typewriter, a garnet ring and a set of saucepans. The sum of someone's worldly possessions, their lives turned inside out for public viewing. She taps the glass, decorated at the edges with bunches of fluffy cotton wool in lieu of snow. 'I hope whoever pawned their saucepans gets them back before Christmas.'

Barney waves at someone he knows as they zigzag across O'Connell Bridge. 'You're too soft, Nic. Has its place, don't get me wrong. But not in this job.'

'What do you mean?' They duck down an alley to where Barney has parked his wreck of a car, the factory badge long missing.

He unlocks the driver's door and reaches in to open the passenger's side. 'Stay focused. Keep your eye on the ball.'

She crosses her arms as the engine starts with a splutter of protest and the car chugs out onto Inns Quay. He looks sideways at her.

'It's just a friendly bit of advice.'

She clutches the dashboard, her knuckles pale as chalk. 'Maybe you don't get to give me friendly advice anymore. Unless, of course, I ask for it.'

He smiles thinly. 'So, you spoke to someone who thinks Jack Bridges killed his wife? Who?'

Nicoletta reaches into her bag for her compact and lipstick.

'Noeleen Clancy, a friend of Julia's,' she says, blotting with a crumpled tissue. 'Apparently, Julia stayed with her for a couple of nights right before she vanished, and confided in her.'

At the traffic lights she traces circles of condensation on the window with her finger. Barney catches her eye and gives her one of his broad grins, where his eyes crease so much they almost disappear.

'Great work, Nic.'

She looks back out the window.

'Nic, I told you, Marie just turned up. It's about Liam, not about me and her.'

Nicoletta clamps her lips together. The lipstick is cloyingly perfumed. 'Let's just do the job we're supposed to do and stop talking about bloody Marie for once?'

Barney looks suitably chastened. He avoids her eyes, flooring the accelerator, the car narrowly missing the pavement. The way Barney drives matches who he is, she thinks. 'Keep your eyes on the road.'

They're winding along the coast, the Poolbeg Lighthouse a red pillar in the distance, when Nicoletta relents and explains further. 'Noeleen Clancy said Jack

Bridges told Julia if he ever suspected her of having another man, he'd kill them both. Mrs Clancy seemed to think he meant it, and she said Julia told her a married man had been paying her attention.'

She colours and looks at the dashboard. 'Could Jack Bridges be a reasonable suspect? Sounds like he had plenty of motive. Also, there was someone else, mentioned by Jack Bridges so it may not hold much weight. A Mr Owens, now deceased, whose widow is Bridges' landlady. According to Bridges, he was "quite taken" with Julia and went to see her in the revue every night during the summer of '43. The Guards initially treated him as a person of interest.'

'Owens.' Barney shakes his head. 'No. He's the one who came forward reporting that he saw Julia at Fitzpatrick's place of work around that time. The Gardaí ruled him out of enquiries. And you can hardly think Bridges did it? If he did, why would he report his wife missing?'

'Appearances can be deceiving.' The sky has darkened now, to the same poured cement colour as the sea. On the horizon it looks like one angry mass. 'Then there's Charles Creighton and the not insignificant fact that Julia's body was found in his garden.'

Barney gives her a sharp look. 'You're not suggesting that Morris has been wrong about Fitzpatrick? Nic, he eliminated Bridges, Owens and Creighton from his enquiries for some solid reason. Morris knows what he's doing. His hunches are usually correct.'

As they pass the outdoor public baths at Blackrock, Barney steps on his brake to let a young boy in short trousers and a woman in a pink tulip coat cross the road. Nicoletta hugs herself. 'They must be freezing,' she says to Barney, but he's not listening. The boy dashes ahead, a red kite tucked under his arm, the plumed tail twisting behind like a living thing. The woman calls him back, her profile sharply defined against the dark asphalt of the road, her coat and the red of the kite stark against the grey horizon. There's something about the scene: the sea, the kite, the woman. Nicoletta's vision blurs and her chest tightens. She coughs, and Barney turns back to her side-on, concern scored on his forehead. 'You OK? Do you want to go home? I can drop you back into town if you like.'

Nicoletta takes a deep breath and pulls her notebook from her bag. 'Keep your eyes on the road,' she repeats.

Barney floors it and they shoot on until they reach Dún Laoghaire. A ferry honks its way into the harbour, bringing people home from England for Christmas. Nicoletta holds on to the sides of her seat until they roar into a cul-de-sac called Seaview Terrace, and he slams on the brakes. An uneven concrete wall, marked with dense graffiti, separates the end of the street from the coast road. The words 'Brits Out' have been spray-painted in huge red letters over some minutely scrawled initials and obscene doodles.

'Not much of a sea view, is there?' Nicoletta feels glad of the brisk air that enters her lungs as she emerges from the car. They loop through the gap in the concrete wall for pedestrians only, which winds back to the coast road where the entrance to Seaview House sits at the top of Seaview Terrace. Nicoletta can't see the mews Barney mentioned from the road. He takes the lead, looking like he knows where he's going. She used to think she'd follow him anywhere. The first time they'd spoken had been on the phone, two years earlier. It was her first job with the *Sentinel*, as a copytaker. She'd been waiting to wake up from the fugue she'd been in. She'd been waiting for something new, something important to happen to her. She just didn't know what that was. She recognised it when Barney King called her desk one day, to file his story straight from the Four Courts, covering some High Court dispute between two neighbours over a boundary line. He'd said he liked the sound of her voice. He said it was like something you'd hear on the radio.

'Is that part of the story?' she'd said, only half joking.

'Where are you from?' he asked her, as the pips were about to go on the call. 'Richmond Road, Fairview,' she'd said, aware that these bland words, evoking a dull suburb, sounded so inadequate. They didn't sum her up, not even nearly. All her hopes and ambitions seemed squashed right down into their ordinariness.

He laughed, a low chuckle. 'You don't sound like anyone from Fairview I've ever met.'

He came over to her desk the next day to introduce himself, leaning a dripping black-and-white umbrella against the wall. He was eating an apple, crunching it down in huge bites.

'Nice to meet you, Nicoletta,' he'd said, before lobbing the apple core into the wastepaper basket on the other side of the room.

It became a habit for him to come over early every morning to say hello, after the first-post editions of the newspaper had come in. At the beginning, they just talked about what was in the paper that day, and she drank in everything he said about the stories he'd worked on. Then gradually he started mentioning his wife, Marie, who complained about the hours he worked, and was often ill, and their son, Liam, a fretful, anxious child. Marie's parents had bought their house, Nicoletta learned, and they didn't approve of Barney. In turn, she told him about her parents' shop in Fairview, the long hours they worked, and how she'd wanted to get away from it and from them, to do something different with her life. Exactly what, she still didn't know.

Sometimes, after these intense conversations had ended and he'd resumed his place at the news desk, she could feel Anne's eyes on her from where she sat opposite Nicoletta, and she always made sure to bury her face in her bag, pretending to look for something, or shuffle the jumble of her ever-expanding in-tray.

Their stolen conversations had gone on for a year. When two junior reporter positions opened up, Barney encouraged Nicoletta to apply for one of them. She was elated the day she found out, on a bright Friday afternoon in June, that she'd got the job. Anne had got the other one.

'This calls for a celebration,' Barney had said. They'd been walking to the pub when he told her. 'Marie's left me,' he said. 'She's gone.'

Nicoletta hadn't known what to say. She'd been so shocked, she'd stumbled at O'Connell Bridge. Barney had helped her up, taking her hand. The unexpected touch of his skin on hers evoked a rush of excitement, of the unknown.

'When did this happen?'

'Three months ago,' he said.

She felt ready to rebuild herself, and his news changed everything. She didn't want what her parents wanted for her; she wanted fun, and she wanted life. Was that so bad? She felt prepared to follow Barney wherever he was prepared to take her. She hadn't let go of his hand.

Now, she's two steps behind him as he approaches an imposing Victorian villa, 'Seaview House' painted in raised white lettering on a black plaque affixed to the gate. The house is large and turreted, with brick the colour of dried blood. She smooths down her skirt and inwardly rehearses what she'll say, should they get inside. The windows are half shuttered, so that they bear a vague resemblance to sleepy eyes. A pair of fastidiously clipped yew trees flanks the top of the short driveway. She shudders. She thought they were meant to be associated with graveyards. She's never liked old houses.

'Ready?' Barney straightens his narrow tie and opens the gate, stepping through.

'As I'll ever be,' she says, trying to match his stride.

Barney charges towards the door, waiting a beat before he sounds the bell, an antique jangly job. It peals gaily, and they wait in silence until they hear faint footsteps. Several bolts are slid back, a key is turned, and a latch is undone. Finally, the door gives a couple of inches inwards.

'Yes?' A thin girl wearing an old-fashioned frilly maid's cap stands inside the door, her small hands clutching the edge, as though she may need to slam it with all her might at any moment.

Barney takes charge. 'Are Mr or Mrs Creighton in? We'd like to speak to them, if you please. Urgently.' He scuffs his shoe for emphasis against the rough granite step.

The girl gawps at them, her lips making a slight popping sound.

'Mr and Mrs Creighton are not here,' she says, as though repeating something she's been drilled to say.

Barney sucks in a pocket of air and grimaces. Nicoletta knows that look, and she steps forward, smiling. This requires a softly-softly approach.

'You must've had loads of upset here this morning,' she says, lowering her voice and holding out her hand to steady the door, mirroring the girl's stance on the other side. 'It's been a shock, I'm sure.'

The girl nods. 'The Guards were here. Lots of them. Asking questions.' She swallows, looking behind her, then shifts her weight back to the other foot. 'Are yous from the Guards?'

'No, we're not from the Guards. We're just interested in what's happened.' Nicoletta keeps her hand on the door. It's still open, at least. 'Is there anyone else in, besides Mr and Mrs Creighton? We can come in and wait if that's convenient.'

The girl glances behind her again, her voice falling to a whisper. 'Mrs Creighton . . .' she says. 'Mr Creighton's mother. I don't know . . . I'll have to check.' She releases the door and turns to go, before popping her head through the gap. 'Who did you say you are?'

'We're reporters from the *Irish Sentinel*.' Nicoletta knows from the bewildered look on the girl's face that she might as well have said that they're astronauts from Apollo 8.

She leaves the door ajar and Nicoletta walks through into a spacious hallway, tiled in black and white, the walls papered an austere burgundy colour. There are two ornate, heavy-looking chairs facing each other, beside a telephone resting on a table with a small chair attached to it. She wonders if last night's call to Dún Laoghaire Garda Station was made from here. She's tempted to sit down, but decides to stay standing, and so does Barney. The maid disappears through a doorway at the end of the hall, giving Nicoletta a minute to take in their surroundings. A grand-looking staircase winds up to another floor, and a poinsettia on a nearby occasional table angles its petals towards a domed skylight high above.

Nicoletta can hear raised voices. They sound blurred at the edges, as though they're submerged. She closes her eyes and swallows, her recently applied make-up melting like a warm waxwork. Suddenly there's too much saliva in her mouth, which tastes of old pennies. She's afraid her legs might go from under her. She looks around. Barney is examining a row of framed photographs on the wall opposite. Nicoletta sinks into one of the telephone chairs and dips her head between her knees. She's about to risk standing up so they can get out of there, when she hears a soft, breathless voice in her ear.

'Are you all right, Miss?'

Nicoletta raises her head, mortified. It's the maid who

answered the door. She gives a nod, swallowing bile. She knows she hasn't much time.

The girl takes her by the elbow and Nicoletta stands up. 'You're like a ghost. You don't look well,' the girl says. Barney is still at the other end of the hall, now examining a framed copy of the 1916 Proclamation of the Irish Republic.

'Could I perhaps use the bathroom?'

The girl nods, leading Nicoletta by the elbow towards a narrow door off the main hall. She turns the small, brass doorknob to reveal a toilet and tiny porcelain sink within. Nicoletta steps inside.

She weighs up her options. This girl could be extremely useful. 'Could you come in with me?' She swallows. 'I know it's a bit strange but it's just in case I faint. It'd be so embarrassing.'

The girl gives a slight nod, hovering in the open doorway.

'Thank you,' Nicoletta murmurs helplessly, closing the door, trapping her like a fly in a spider's web. There's barely enough room to accommodate one of them in the space.

The girl blinks but stays put. 'Is it your monthly? Our Mary used to get them pretty bad.'

Nicoletta runs the cold tap and turns her back, splashing three handfuls of icy water onto her face. When she looks in the mirror, she can see the girl's large doll-like eyes fixed on her. She takes a tissue from her handbag and wipes away the smudged make-up. The taste of grubby metal is gone, and the colour is back in her cheeks. She smiles.

'I'd best get back,' the girl says uneasily, with a hand on the doorknob.

Nicoletta splays her fingers on the sink as though to steady herself. 'Oh, I'm sure they won't miss you for a bit. Stay here, keep me from keeling over and knocking my head. Besides, it's nice talking to someone besides Barney. What's your name?'

'Una. What's yours again?'

'It's Nicoletta.'

Una frowns, but doesn't query the unusual name, the way someone older might.

'How long have you been working for the Creightons, Una?' Nicoletta digs in her bag to find her make-up. She's going to spend at least a minute fixing her face in a bid to get Una to say something about the Creightons and what happened here in the early hours. She rubs some blush into her cheeks and starts on her eyes. Through the mirror she can see Una's hand still resting nervously on the doorknob.

'A year.' Una bites her lip. 'I took my sister Mary's job.'

Nicoletta rings her eyes in kohl, then smudges it with her little finger.

'Oh, that's nice. Did Mary get a better job somewhere else?'

Una puffs out her cheeks, then takes a couple of shallow breaths through her mouth. She suddenly looks no more than eleven or twelve, though Nicoletta supposes she must be older. 'She died.' Her tone is flat.

'Gosh, I'm so sorry,' Nicoletta says with a genuine gasp. 'What happened?'

Una rubs her bottom front teeth across her top lip, as

though she's deciding something in that split second. 'I really better get back,' she says.

'Una, you can trust me,' Nicoletta promises. She picks up her bag. 'Is there anywhere we could meet shortly to have a chat? Not here. Somewhere you can talk.'

'Sullivan's,' Una says, in the same flat voice. 'A pub in Glasthule. I'll be there as soon as I can, but I won't have too long.'

She opens the door and Nicoletta follows her back into the hall, where Barney is pacing. He raises his eyebrows but doesn't say anything. Una coughs and stands up straighter. A far-off door bangs, followed by footsteps. Nicoletta tenses at the idea of whoever it is seeing her coming from the bathroom with the maid.

A door at the far end of the hall opens and an angular, grey-haired woman approaches them, heels clicking against the chessboard tiles. She has an unshakeable air of class and authority, like the wife of a politician. When she reaches them, Nicoletta clears her throat to speak, but the woman beats her to it.

'I'm Ruth Creighton. What can I do for you?'

Barney holds out his hand, but she doesn't shake it. 'We're reporters from the *Irish Sentinel*. We'd like to ask some questions about the incident that occurred here this morning.'

Nicoletta is surprised to hear a tremor in his voice. She's never heard it before. It must be the effect this woman has.

Ruth Creighton blinks hard. Her full lips are painted the same shade of burgundy as the walls. She sighs.

'Una, you're needed in the kitchen.' She gives the maid

a curt nod. Una almost genuflects into a curtsey before scuttling back the way she'd come. Nicoletta feels a pang of sympathy. The girl is so young, and at this family's mercy. Mrs Creighton ushers them away. 'Your guess is as good as mine,' she says, pointedly, when they've reached the front door. Neither Nicoletta nor Barney make any move to step through it. Mrs Creighton sighs. 'I don't know much about it, and I really wouldn't like to speculate. The Guards are looking into it. Sorry you've had a wasted journey.'

She doesn't sound sorry at all. She steps into the natural glare from the skylight. She's wearing no other make-up apart from the lipstick. The light throws the shadows under her eyes into stark relief, mottled as bruises. Still, Nicoletta finds it hard to put a guess on her age. She's far from a frail old lady. She looks from Nicoletta to Barney, blue eyes bright as bullets, issuing a pointed challenge. She boldly opens the door herself, a clear invitation for them to get the hell out.

Nicoletta walks towards it, though stops short of stepping through. Barney is already back on the step before she decides what she'll say. There seems to be a tacit agreement between them that she'll handle Ruth Creighton from here. She holds out her hand and Mrs Creighton takes it gingerly. Her hands are soft and warm. The blue eyes take in Nicoletta's miniskirt, the crossed fox-fur collar, the feathered haircut curling out of the turban. She's sure she's being found wanting, but she gulps and smiles. 'I'm sure this has been very upsetting for you all. You must want to put it behind you as much as you can.'

Mrs Creighton nods and lets go of Nicoletta's hand, shaking her head as though she still can't quite believe it. 'It's been a strange morning, you might say. Of course, I'm deeply sorry for the poor woman's husband and family, whoever she was.' She bows her head in a simulacrum of piety. Nicoletta snaps to attention.

'Mrs Creighton, do you have any comment to make to the *Irish Sentinel* on speculation that Gloria Fitzpatrick was behind Julia Bridges' death and her burial here?'

Ruth Creighton's eyes are wide with incredulity. She purses her lips, as though she's tasted something sour and isn't quite sure whether to spit it out or swallow it. Finally, she shakes her head. 'I have no comment to make. This is a matter for the police. A private matter, nothing to do with you people.'

Nicoletta takes a step forward. 'Mrs Creighton, a skeleton was found in your garden this morning, belonging to a woman who's been missing for twenty-five years. I would say that's very much in the public interest, wouldn't you?'

Mrs Creighton shakes her head again. Her whole body trembles. She sticks out an unsteady finger, adorned with the biggest ruby Nicoletta has ever seen. It's so ostentatious that it looks false to her untrained eye. Mrs Creighton points towards the doorstep, wordlessly commanding her to leave. Nicoletta stands firm.

'Did you know Gloria Fitzpatrick?'

Mrs Creighton blinks. 'No. And I thank God for that.'

'If Miss Fitzpatrick was responsible for Mrs Bridges' death, why do you think her body was found in your garden?'

Nicoletta knows she's pushed her luck. Just then, she hears slow, deliberate footsteps on the hall tiles and a slim man with very dark, slicked-back hair and a light tan approaches them. She gets the feeling he's been listening to this exchange the whole time.

'Haranguing an elderly woman in her own home,' he says, with a practised smile. 'You should be ashamed of yourselves.'

Nicoletta looks to Barney, but he's already out on the front path. She smiles and sticks out her hand. 'Nicoletta Sarto from the *Sentinel*. I was just asking Mrs Creighton for a comment on the discovery of Julia Bridges' body.'

The man takes Nicoletta's hand and holds it between both of his for a second too long. His nails are pink and manicured. He's freshly shaven, with the kind of piercing blue eyes Nicoletta is sure some women love. He's wearing a pressed, open-necked shirt and fawn slacks. This morning's discovery doesn't appear to have knocked a feather off him. Nicoletta withdraws her hand while he appraises her for a moment or two, like a birdwatcher observing an exotic species in an unprecedented sighting.

'Charles Creighton,' he says. 'Pleased to meet you.' He raises a hand. 'Mother, I'll take it from here. No need to upset yourself further.'

Mrs Creighton huffs her way back down the hall, heaving tiny puffs of air with each step. Nicoletta can see that she has a limp and the effort of walking with such ramrod posture is causing her immense discomfort. She wonders what it must be like living with this son of hers and his wife, wherever *she* is, and whether or not they pay her any heed, or if they're simply waiting for her to die. She feels her dislike of earlier dissolve.

Once his mother's footsteps recede, Creighton takes Nicoletta by the elbow. 'Why don't you come into the drawing room, and we can talk there? I apologise for my mother. With the best intentions in the world, she can often make things worse.'

He begins walking towards a door on their right, pausing to ensure Nicoletta and Barney are following him. Barney gives Nicoletta a thumbs-up behind Charles Creighton's back as they proceed deeper into the house.

Chapter Seven

Charles Creighton huddles by the fireplace, where a low fire burns in the grate. Nicoletta can see the outline of large, muddy footprints on the pale green carpet. She scans the room. Every bit of it is crammed with what she supposes are antiques, each one jostling for attention. Ornate urns, bronze statuettes of frolicking nymphs and furniture of all periods and styles, including a peculiar-looking musical instrument Nicoletta has never seen before, like a mix between a tiny piano and a church organ. She eyes it curiously. Creighton eventually indicates a plump armchair for her beside the fire and she sinks down into it. A tall Christmas tree stands in the window, decorated with an assortment of old-fashioned porcelain ornaments and small red bows. It looks like the kind of tree cut down specially from a grove of firs in the Dublin mountains, a different league entirely from the shrivelled things her parents sometimes sell. Barney hovers awkwardly behind Nicoletta's armchair until Creighton pulls out a low, hard-backed dining chair for him, and he sits down, his knees sticking up at right angles.

Barney flicks her an approving glance. He's letting her run this.

'What a lovely room,' she says to Creighton, who's still hovering beside the fire, warming his hands.

'Thank you,' he says, turning to face her.

'I hope you don't mind if I ask what kind of instrument that is?' She indicates where the strange-looking piano rests against an oak-panelled door.

Creighton looks relieved. He probably thought she was going in for the kill. 'Oh, you mean the harpsichord? Sally's the one who plays. On her good days. I don't know what my wife would do without her harpsichord and her peacocks.'

'Have you lived here long?' Nicoletta keeps her face open.

'As a matter of fact, all my life. I was born here, and Mother gave me the house when I got married. To my first wife. I've never lived anywhere else.'

Nicoletta nods, hoping she looks impressed. 'Where's Mrs Creighton now? Sally, did you say?'

Creighton warms his hands at the fire. 'She's in bed. She's had one of her nervous turns. Sally has what you might call a weak constitution.'

Nicoletta doesn't ask what a weak constitution entails. She gets the gist.

'It must have been a terrible shock.'

'Do you know, it was.' Creighton steeples his hands in front of his mouth in an attempt at being casual. 'A terrible shock, as you say.'

Nicoletta opens her notebook with quick, deliberate movements.

'Can you confirm who found the deceased woman's remains?'

Creighton clears his throat. 'My son-in-law, John Dawkins, was digging in the garden very early this morning.'

'Does he live here?'

Creighton smiles. 'He lives in the mews at the end of the garden with my daughter, Delia, and my granddaughter, Hayley. Their pet dog died last night, and Dawkins was burying the animal in a plot where my mother used to bury dead pets when I was a child. I suppose Dawkins was doing it so that Hayley wouldn't be upset to see it when she woke up this morning.'

Nicoletta's hand aches with the effort of transcribing everything, but she keeps going. 'What happened then, Mr Creighton?'

Creighton wends his way towards a glass-panelled drinks cabinet at the far end of the room. 'I never offered you anything. You'll have a drop of something.'

It's more of a statement than a question, but Nicoletta manages to shake away the offer. Barney settles for a Jameson, and Creighton joins him, lighting a cigar as he does so. He offers Barney one from a mother-of-pearl box and Barney accepts a match. Creighton doesn't offer Nicoletta the cigar box. She can't help bristling as he turns his attention back to her. She wonders if he's noticed.

'The area of the garden where Dawkins was digging was used as a pet cemetery when I was a child, as I've said. Dawkins found some bones, which he rightly thought too large to belong to a long-lost family pet. He rang the doorbell here, a gibbering wreck. My wife called the Guards straight away. The rest is a matter for them, as I don't have to tell you.'

'Did you know the deceased woman, Julia Bridges?'

Creighton takes a sip of his drink and looks Nicoletta in the eye. 'I did not, no.'

'And did you know Gloria Fitzpatrick?'

Creighton narrows his eyes and sets his drink down on the mantelpiece. 'No. Why do you ask?'

'Because she is thought to be responsible for Mrs Bridges' death.'

Creighton nods. 'I knew of Miss Fitzpatrick many years ago, of course. Everybody did.' He picks up his drink, downing it in one.

Nicoletta finishes taking down what he's said. 'Why were Julia Bridges' remains buried on this property, Mr Creighton?'

Charles Creighton blinks as though he can't quite believe her forthrightness. 'Miss Sarto, between ourselves, I believe the Guards are working on a theory.'

'Which is?' Nicoletta leans forward. Barney is puffing away on his cigar, and he looks ready to drop off from the effects of the whiskey and the warm room.

Creighton turns inwards towards the fire, looking into a huge gilt-edged mirror above the mantelpiece. His reflection is softened by the firelight.

'I'm afraid I can't share that with you.' He turns back around.

'I see, Mr Creighton. Is there anything you can share?'

Another smile plays around his lips before he speaks.

'Naturally, my condolences go to the husband and family of Mrs Bridges.' He closes his eyes for a moment, as though he hopes that when he reopens them, he will be alone.

'Naturally.'

'I'm sure you understand, this is a private matter for all concerned.' He drums his fingers on the mantelpiece. Nicoletta thinks of Una possibly waiting for her in the pub right this minute and she doesn't bother to argue. She closes her notebook. Barney doesn't seem to register any disappointment at Charles Creighton's trailing off.

'We'll leave you in peace now, Mr Creighton. Thank you, you've been most helpful.'

Creighton walks them to the door and opens it courteously. When they leave, Nicoletta can hear the myriad locks and latches being reinstated as on impulse she takes a narrow footpath and leads Barney around the side of the house. Una can wait for a few minutes.

'Where're you going?' Barney takes her by the elbow.

A low white building is visible at the end of the garden. 'Now we're in, let's try and find the son-in-law, John Dawkins.'

Barney nods. 'All right. According to Morris, he's an artist of some sort. The neighbours have made dozens of complaints to the Guards about loud parties, and he's said to be smuggling dope on the ferry.'

They fall into step as they walk along a winding path, through stark rose beds, pruned shrubs and ornamental trees. They pass a sturdy-looking glasshouse through which Nicoletta can see the trails of withered vines, creeping like tentacles. She shivers. The mews is tucked away just behind the glasshouse, in its own cosy nook. The sea wall is a few metres away, and a flank of several newish-looking poplar trees has grown up to roof level and given the area an air of seclusion. Nestled among the poplars is a slatted wooden outhouse. A pair of large birds emerge from between the trees, pecking around the gravel, squawking at the sight of Nicoletta and Barney. Their strange, prehistoric-looking beaks are poised to jab Nicoletta's bare wrists, seeking flesh.

'They must be Sally's peacocks.' Nicoletta points to the wooden outhouse. 'And that must be where they live. Come on now, that's the girl. Calm down, old thing.' The female, smaller than her mate, with dull brown feathers, responds to her voice, looping around in greedy circles. The male flaps and struts, sliding out the sly fan of his feathers, until they reach the door of the mews.

Chapter Eight

Where the main house is all sombre brick and curlicues, the mews is its modern antithesis. Its flat roof is painted the same blinding shade of white as its walls, and its boxy windows are neatly shuttered by Venetian blinds, gazing into the weak winter sun. Neither building compares to what Nicoletta is used to. The peacocks are hovering dangerously close, pecking relentlessly at the hard ground.

An atonal *bing-bong* reverberates through the small house. Footsteps clatter in the hallway, the sound of sandals slapping against tiles, and someone opens the door.

A young woman in a short pink kaftan hanging loose over smooth, brown legs stands in the doorway, a little girl asleep in her arms. The child looks too old to be carried around. The woman has masses of dark hair piled on top of her head in a beehive style with a pink and yellow patterned headscarf tied around it. Her expression doesn't change when she sees them. Nicoletta glances at Barney out of the corner of her eye. His hands are clasped in front of him. He gives Nicoletta a barely perceptible nod. She wonders if the woman thinks they are gardaí, come to ask more questions, and perhaps that's the only reason she opened the door in the first place.

'Hello, are you Mrs Dawkins?'

The woman frowns and shifts the child to her other hip. She waves half-heartedly at the peacocks. 'Antony, Cleopatra, shoo. Go on. I'm sorry, they're my mother's peacocks. I don't think they've been fed this morning. I'll have to go out and give them something.' She looks back to them, impatient. 'And you are?'

Nicoletta takes a deep breath. 'I'm Nicoletta Sarto and this is Barney King. We're reporters from the *Irish Sentinel*. We'd like to speak to your husband about finding Julia Bridges' remains this morning.' Antony darts forward, squawking his disapproval at the interlopers.

Mrs Dawkins frowns slightly, an ugly line marring her lovely forehead. 'Who? Oh, so they've identified who it is. Or was, I suppose I should say. How awful. But we've told the police everything we know.'

She takes a step back to close the door, and Nicoletta swears inwardly. The little girl rouses. She angles her silken head at Nicoletta and yawns, showing off a row of pearly milk teeth. 'I want my daddy,' she says haughtily, before closing her eyes again and promptly settling back into the crook of her mother's arm. Mrs Dawkins shifts under her weight and grimaces. 'Daddy isn't here, Hayley,' she says, glancing at Nicoletta and Barney.

'He is,' Hayley says sleepily. 'He's right behind you.'

A man with fairish hair curling into the collar of an Afghan coat steps forward, looking sheepish.

'What's going on?' He looks from Mrs Dawkins to Nicoletta and Barney.

'Daddy!' Hayley puts out her arms to her father.

Nicoletta smiles. 'You must be John Dawkins?'

The man gives her an easy grin.

'We've already told the Gardaí everything they needed to know. Good day.' Mrs Dawkins nudges the door shut with her hip, but it doesn't close all the way. Nicoletta can hear mumbled voices on the other side. She and Barney stand there dumbly.

At last, the door opens again. John Dawkins gestures for them to come in. 'From the *Sentinel*, you said? I was actually on my way out, but seeing you've come all this way, you might as well come in.'

He leads them through a hallway, painted white and lined with dozens of modern paintings, several just blobs of colour, with the initials 'JD' clear in each corner. Nicoletta stops in front of one. 'Did you paint this?' She peers at the canvas. It's two orange circles contained within a larger blue circle.

'Sure did.' Dawkins bows his head.

'It's very good,' Nicoletta says, for want of anything else to say. She hears the front door close, and a white cat follows Mrs Dawkins and Hayley as they bring up the rear.

'Pity they don't make him any money,' Mrs Dawkins says, with a short laugh. 'As painting is all John wants to spend his time doing.'

John pretends not to hear. He leads them into a small kitchen with terracotta tiles and an orange L-shaped couch taking up one corner. He indicates for Nicoletta and Barney to be seated. Nicoletta instantly feels at home. She can imagine living in a house like this, bright and modern to the nth degree, cooking meals for Barney at the electric stove, a child or two at her feet. She shakes off the image and perches on a small three-legged stool, the only old-fashioned item in the room.

'Can you tell us what happened this morning, Mr Dawkins?'

Mrs Dawkins joins them at the end of the sofa. Hayley is now asleep in her lap, curled around her mother like a pet monkey. 'Please,' she says, putting up an elegant hand. 'It's Delia and John.'

John bustles around making coffee and hands it out before joining them.

'I was digging around in the garden. Apparently, Delia's father used to have some sort of cemetery for pet dogs and cats there years ago. Of course, no one told me that. No one tells me anything.' He grimaces. 'I found some bones, looked too big to belong to a dog or cat or anything else with four legs.' He pauses, scrutinising Hayley, but her breathing is slow and peaceful. 'I didn't want to make a fuss but then Sally, my mother-in-law, rang the Guards before anyone could stop her. Right before she had one of her turns.'

Nicoletta takes a scalding sip of her coffee and puts down the cup. She looks around. The fluffy white cat winds itself around Dawkins' legs before jumping into his lap. 'Seriously, come on. Off the record, why were you digging in the middle of the night? You don't have to pretend. We're not the Guards.'

John Dawkins reddens, but he brazens it out. 'I lost something. And I was looking for it.'

'What did you lose?'

'Just some stuff.'

'Right.' Nicoletta draws out the word. 'I bet there never was any dog, was there?'

Delia half closes her eyes, embarrassed. 'No,' she says. 'Just Victor.' She gestures to the white fluffy creature sprawled across her husband. 'Vicious little fecker. He'd kill any dog.'

'I see.' Nicoletta laughs suddenly. It's too ridiculous for words. Barney guffaws, and Delia lets out an unexpected shriek of mirth, before covering her mouth with her hand. She coughs, trying to compose herself.

'It's not really a laughing matter,' she says finally, giving her husband a stern look. 'You mentioned this person has been identified?'

Nicoletta nods. 'It was Julia Bridges. An actress who went missing twenty-five years ago. During the war.'

'Bridges?' John stands up and tosses off his coat. 'The wife of the same fellow who owns the Athena in town? I did an illustration for one of his theatre programmes last year. Never got paid.'

Nicoletta clicks her tongue. Coming to speak to these two has been another waste of time. Though it's clear the rumours are probably true: John Dawkins is a dope peddler on the side. She stands up. 'Thank you,' she says, shaking John's and Delia's hands in turn. Barney drains his coffee and puts on his hat.

John hovers by Nicoletta. 'I don't suppose you've any illustration work going at the paper?'

The reason Dawkins invited them in is now becoming apparent. 'I don't think so, no,' Nicoletta replies. 'But if we do, I'll let you know.'

John gives her another easy grin. 'No worries. No harm in asking, is there?'

Nicoletta smiles back. 'Could I please use your bathroom?'

Dawkins directs her to a tiny room containing just a toilet off the kitchen. She can hear the little girl, Hayley, talking to her mother, and Barney's gruff leave-taking as he steps outside and closes the front door with a click. Nicoletta hovers at the entry to the small WC. She's about to step in when an open door next to it catches her eye. It's a utility room, with a twin tub in one corner, and an empty wicker laundry basket resting on top. But apart from that, the room is stuffed full of colour-filled canvases piled together in order of size. Two chairs with moulded plastic bucket seats have been pushed into the corner, along with a tub filled with tubes of paint and brushes. A bottle of clear liquid and a couple of streaked rags have been left on one of the chairs. She looks around. A wash of light falls through a long window, and a swathe of the murky Irish Sea is partly visible through the line of poplar trees. This must be John Dawkins' studio. Nicoletta considers it. A pleasant place to spend time, she supposes. She turns her attention to a collection of large canvases, stacked neatly against the back wall, reaching almost up to window height. The first one is a frenzy of blues and greens. But there is order in the chaos, and you can see the sea and sky take form. Nicoletta puts it aside and catches her breath at the sight of the one underneath. It's a female nude, the flesh all shades of rose and blush. The woman, a girl really, is small, with thin, wiry arms, and jutting, pointy breasts. She is washing in a basin, her profile visible to the artist, fine dark hair rippling down her shoulder. The initials 'JD' are visible in the bottom right-hand corner. The intimacy of the painting makes Nicoletta feel slightly uncomfortable, but she can tell immediately that it's very good. She feels eyes on her.

'See anything you like?'

She turns, and John Dawkins is standing behind her, arms folded, an amused twist to his lips.

'Very nice,' Nicoletta says, putting the painting down. 'You're talented.'

He flexes his arms over his head and yawns. 'Want to buy anything?'

Nicoletta can't help the laugh bubbling up to her lips. 'I'm afraid not. Maybe another time.'

'Hey, we're having a New Year's Eve party here next week,' he says, stretching long fingers towards the ceiling. 'You're welcome to come. And bring your boyfriend if you like.'

Nicoletta's hand flies to her throat. 'Oh, you mean Barney? He's not my boyfriend. Thank you, bye now,' she says in a rush, pushing past him, desperate to get out of there. In the hallway, Delia and Hayley are nowhere to be seen. She opens the door, not waiting for John Dawkins to follow her. Barney is standing in front of an armless Greek nymph, at the centre of a hexagon of flower beds, scuffing the gravel with the toe of his shoe. He beckons her towards a side gate, impatient to get going.

Antony the peacock gives a desultory screech after them, but his focus is redirected when the front window opens. Nicoletta looks back to see Delia Dawkins throwing out food of some kind. Her bright scarf-covered head disappears, and the food, whatever it is, glistens on the cold, fissured earth. Nicoletta breaks into a trot to keep up with Barney. He tries the gate. It's locked. They walk back around to the main entrance and emerge onto Seaview Terrace.

He turns to face her.

'Where to now?'

She points towards the car. 'Wait for me there. I've arranged to meet Una, the maid, at Sullivan's, a pub down the road.'

Barney grins. 'You're a fast mover, Miss Sarto. I'll be in the car. Take your time.' He walks off whistling. She momentarily basks in his praise, and things between them feel like they used to.

Halfway down Seaview Terrace, her eyes and nose streaming from the cold, she has a spring in her step. She's on a mission. Barney is waiting for her. Her pride catches at the back of her throat when she imagines him dropping her off at the flat on Eccles Street, before he inevitably goes home to Marie and Liam. The sun dips in the sky, past its afternoon zenith; dusk surely isn't too far away. Lights twinkle in windows up and down the street, curtains are drawn, fires have been lit. She stops to take in her surroundings. Seaview Terrace has given way to a hamlet of some sort, with three pubs, a shop and two churches, one Catholic and one Protestant.

Sullivan's is the nearest of the pubs, a tiny place with thick windows of coloured glass, opaque like a bottle of stout. She yanks open the door and is immediately hit by a wall of warm, smoky air. Several pairs of eyes look up from around the bar, where a cluster of men sit hunched over pints. Nicoletta is acutely aware of being the only woman in the place. The men's wives, if there are any, are most likely in the lounge at the back. She straightens her shoulders and walks up to the bar, ordering a lemonade. The middle-aged barman, in shirt sleeves and braces, takes a good look at her, then extracts a bottle of pop from a dusty row above his head and knocks the cap off, sloshing the contents into a Slim Jim. She takes the last seat at the end, horribly conscious of each pair of eyes feasting on every bit of her. The barman is talking to one of the men, agreeing with something he says; their brief conversation over, he folds his arms and lapses back into silent contemplation of the dusty glasses and the fuzzy radio. Nicoletta checks the lounge but it's completely empty. She goes back to the bar. After a minute or two, she clears her throat. The barman doesn't look up.

'Excuse me,' she says, without raising her voice. Eventually he sidles over. She smiles. His expression doesn't change. 'Has a girl come in, anytime in the last hour or so? I'm meeting her here.'

'Is that so?' He wipes the counter.

Nicoletta tries again. 'Do you know the Creightons?' she asks, brightening her voice.

The barman shrugs. 'They live down the road. Why don't you try there?'

Nicoletta smiles again and lays her palms out on the table. 'I'm trying you. What are they like?'

The barman leans forward. 'Do they owe you money?'

'No, no. Nothing like that.'

'What did you say your name was?'

'Nicoletta Sarto.'

The barman frowns. 'What sort of a name is that?'

'The perfectly good kind,' Nicoletta returns.

The barman looks her up and down again, and the corners of his mouth arch upwards in a reluctant smile. He leans over.

'They never come in here, so I wouldn't know,' he says, then pauses. 'But if it was someone like you ... I'd remember.' Nicoletta picks up her drink, retreating to the lounge. It's empty, save for a lopsided Christmas tree in the corner she didn't notice earlier. She takes a slug of her lemonade and makes a face.

There's pop music playing in here, completely separate from the toneless wireless of the bar. Nicoletta recognises the song: 'I Think It's Gonna Rain Today', by Dusty Springfield.

She's about to drain her drink and go when the door from the bar crashes open and a slight figure erupts into the room and plonks herself down on a stool opposite Nicoletta.

'Una! Would you like something?'

Una takes off her frilly maid's hat, shaking out a tight bun. The female nude in the Dawkins' kitchen pops into Nicoletta's head, the dark hair cascading around the shoulders, and she wonders if Una might've been the sitter.

Una pulls the stool right in so her bony knees are uncomfortably rammed against Nicoletta's and shakes her head. 'I've to get back soon. Someone will notice I'm gone.'

'Here, have my lemonade.' Nicoletta slides her drink across the table and Una accepts it, her mouth finding the lip of the glass like a baby latching on to a teat. She gulps the lemonade in three swallows until it's all gone.

'Wow, impressive.' Nicoletta can't help a smile. 'I'd hate to see you with a real drink.' She pauses. 'Hang on, what age are you?'

'Fifteen,' Una says finally, looking around the featureless room. 'I've never been in a pub before.'

'A bad habit you don't want to start.'

Una shakes her head and gives Nicoletta a rueful grin. 'I'm only messing. I've been in loads of pubs. Getting my da. He's never out of them since Mary died.'

'Fair enough.' Nicoletta can feel Una's bony knees getting restless under the table. 'Where does your da live, Una?'

'Seaview Terrace. Number eight.'

'Who else lives there?'

'Just me, my mam and dad. And my little brother Michael.'

'I see.' Nicoletta surreptitiously checks her watch. The walk from the house takes ten minutes, and Una would almost certainly be missed by now. 'Why don't you tell me about Mary, Una?' She gives the girl's hand a gentle pat. The small knuckles are blanched into fists.

Una inhales sharply through her mouth. Then she begins to sob, and Nicoletta moves and puts an arm around her.

When Una's sobs subside, she scrunches a beermat and gives Nicoletta a fierce look.

'It's like no one cared what happened to Mary. I just replaced her, and things went on as normal. It's not right.'

Nicoletta hesitates before taking her notebook and pen out of her bag and placing them on the table.

'Una, I'm going to ask you some questions and I'm going to write down the answers. Is that OK? But I won't say you told me if you'd prefer for me not to use your name.'

Una gives her assent with a vigorous nod.

Nicoletta briskly writes the date and time at the top of the page.

'Una, what's your surname?'

'Little.' She gives Nicoletta a tiny smile. 'Me and Mary used to laugh about it because we're not a tall family. We really are the Littles.'

Nicoletta continues to scribble notes as she talks.

'How old was Mary?'

'Two years older than me, just. She'd have had her seventeenth birthday last month.'

Nicoletta scores a line under the age. 'You said you replaced her. Do you mean at the Creightons'?'

Una nods.

'How long did Mary work there?'

'About a year and a half.'

'Was she happy?'

Una shakes her head, then thinks better of it. 'At first, maybe. She was a hard worker, they paid her OK, if that's what you're asking.' She twists her fingers around her bony wrist. 'She was all right. Well able.'

'What happened then?'

Una sighs. 'It's no use telling you. It's not going to bring Mary back. I'd best be going.' She stands and Nicoletta grabs her by the elbow.

'Una, listen to me. There's every point in telling me. I might be able to help you. Mary deserves that, doesn't she?'

Una thinks about it and nods. Nicoletta looks her in the eye.

'Una, can you tell me exactly what happened to Mary?' she asks.

Una clamps her lips together, before releasing a pent-up gasp. 'One evening last summer, she went out for a walk. She . . . hadn't been feeling well, so I thought it was strange that she'd want to go out.'

Una stops, opening and closing her fist.

'And?' Nicoletta prompts gently.

'I followed her. But Mam started talking to me and I got delayed leaving. In the end, I was too late.'

'Too late for what?'

'To save her. She walked into the sea and just kept going until she drowned.'

Nicoletta feels a shiver at the base of her skull, sharp as an electric current.

Una begins to cry quietly, and Nicoletta squeezes her hand. 'Where was this?'

'Sandycove Beach.' Una wipes her eyes and nibbles the edge of the empty glass. Nicoletta wants to get her another drink, but she's afraid in the time it would take to go to the bar and back, Una might bolt. She pats the girl's shoulder.

Una scrubs her eyes with her fist. 'I have to go. They'll be looking for me.' She picks up her things and heads off, before stopping halfway to the street entrance. 'Did I do the right thing, telling you?'

Nicoletta walks with her to the door. 'Yes, you absolutely did the right thing, Una. Poor Mary. Do you've any idea at all why she might've done what she did?'

Una opens the door and a blast of freezing wind slams it into the wall, chilling the room. She retreats a couple of steps. 'Mary had a baby. Two weeks before.'

Nicoletta can barely formulate the questions bubbling below the surface. But she's only hanging on to Una by a thread now. The words sound more forceful than she means.

'What happened to the baby, Una?'

The barman chooses this moment to stick his head around the inner door leading from the bar. 'All right in here?' He winks at Nicoletta.

'Fine, thanks,' she assures him, but he continues to stand there.

The door crashes shut with a whoosh of cold air and Una is gone, hair flying, her frilly maid's cap in her hand. Nicoletta rushes to follow her onto the quiet street. The cold hits her like a bucket of icy water. She can hear a dog or a fox barking, the far-off sound of the sea lapping the harbour, a distant engine revving, then silence. Una is nowhere to be seen. She goes back to the lounge to get her things. The barman is sitting at her table.

'I've definitely seen that girl in here before.' He indicates the door through which Una just made her dramatic exit.

'Oh yeah?' Nicoletta grabs her bag, still standing. 'Who with?'

The barman grins. 'Some guy in an Afghan coat. Far too old for her.'

The top two buttons of his shirt are undone, and she can see faint tufts of fair hair across his chest. 'Thought I might join you for a drink?' His tone is hopeful. She thinks of Barney, cursing his rust heap of a car at Seaview Terrace, shivering in his coat.

'It's late. I was just going,' she says, picking up her turban and gloves.

Outside, dusk is falling, shrouding the air within minutes. She passes a derelict house, the weeds taller than she is. Her heels tip-tap past its low concrete wall, the wild garden as cavernous as a small jungle in this light. Big enough to hide a body, she thinks. Poor Mary Little, walking into the sea until it was too late. She can feel her guts roiling at the injustice. The nausea is building now, and she doesn't know how she can go on hiding it. She's reached the bottom of Seaview Terrace before she has to double back, vomiting bile over the perimeter of the abandoned garden. She straightens up and wipes her mouth with a tissue, hiding her burning cheeks in the rising dark.

Chapter Nine

Wednesday, 25th December 1968
Christmas Day

Nicoletta listens for the thrum of human noise on Christmas morning, but her flat on Eccles Street is cold and still. She huddles under the vast continental quilt on her single bed and savours the quiet. For once, Jean, her flatmate, isn't here, and being alone is exactly what she has craved. It feels both welcome and illicit. Nicoletta tucks her hand under the pillow and shuts her eyes, though she knows she won't go back to sleep. The nausea seems to be settling. She luxuriates in feeling normal for the first time in ages. She's always liked her own company, though she couldn't afford to live alone. She's been here with Jean for just over two years now, ever since she saw the ad in the *Evening Press* for a flatshare. 'Single girl, quiet, non-smoker, no pets,' the notice had specified. She'd gone to meet Jean at the flat. It was grotty, a unit of nine at the top of a ramshackle Georgian house divided up with crooked plasterboard walls. Jean was loud, talkative, a primary school teacher from Tipperary. She'd shown Nicoletta the room, and Nicoletta had loved it on sight. When she looked out the window she felt like a bird safe in its nest.

'What do you do?' Jean had looked at her sensible blouse and unfashionable mid-length skirt with un-ashamed curiosity.

'I'm a copytaker at the *Irish Sentinel*,' Nicoletta had said, unable to hide the pride in her voice. 'Since last month.'

Jean had pursed her mouth, as though considering this occupation, its merit and whether it would fit into her life. 'What do you do for fun?'

Nicoletta had thought for a moment. 'I listen to music. And I read.'

She hadn't been able to read Jean's face as she'd turned and led her out of the bedroom, chattering about the fraying carpet, the lack of wardrobe space, the lingering smells from the other flats. Nicoletta knew then she hadn't a hope.

'I'll take it,' she'd said, interrupting Jean mid-flow.

Jean looked doubtful. 'I've three more left to see.'

'I can give you two months' rent in advance,' Nicoletta said boldly. She knew her mother would rage about it, but she was ready to fly. In the end, her father gave her the money for the deposit on the quiet. She'll always be grateful to him for that.

She gets out of bed and stands at the window. A small boy of four or five pedals past on a shiny red bicycle, ring-ing the bell energetically as he goes. She wonders what sort of child Enzo would have been; if he'd have enjoyed bikes, climbing trees and playing with other children, the usual things that small boys do. Or if he'd have been like her, preferring his own company. The icy sun has started to creep out from behind a lair of cloud to crowd the glass. She stands for a moment, in no hurry to begin the shortish walk to her parents' house. The small boy has reached the end of the street and now turns back in a noisy relay. Nicoletta smiles down at him, though he wouldn't be able to see, her heart closing like a fist.

The three or four years after Enzo died are a blur. It had been her father who'd seen the ad for a secretarial course in town, in a last-ditch bid to 'get you out of yourself'. He'd cut it out of the paper and thrust it across the table at dinner.

'You'd learn typing, shorthand, that kind of thing,' he'd said, avoiding his wife's eye and focusing on persuading Nicoletta. 'In case you decide you don't want to work in the shop for the rest of your life with your old pair.' He'd gestured between himself and her mother. 'It'd give you options. You're a bright girl.'

Her mother had put down her knife and fork with a clash. 'God forbid she should help her parents in the family business,' she'd said under her breath, but she hadn't objected when Nicoletta had gone to the secretarial school on O'Connell Street two evenings a week for the next six months and come out top of her class. It was Nicoletta who'd seen the ad for a copytaker at the *Sentinel*, and she'd applied for the post without telling either of her parents. She couldn't face more questions, more recriminations, more disappointment. Ettore had been so delighted for her when she told him she'd got it that he'd closed the shop early for the only time Nicoletta can ever remember, and opened a dusty bottle of sherry from the top shelf that had been there for years without being sold.

She eventually heats water in the kettle for bathing; she knows she won't find a sixpence for the metre. The bath is strewn with dried stockings, girdles and knickers belonging to Jean. She wraps up warmly, still chilled from the sea wind the day before, teaming flared jeans and a cable-knit sweater with one of her flatmate's old overcoats. She feels like she wants to hide.

She stalls as long as she can, in the futile hope that Barney might ring, but the phone stays as still and silent as an unexploded bomb. When she steps onto Eccles Street, there isn't a soul around. It's still early. She'd been uncommunicative in the car on the drive back into town with Barney the previous evening. When they'd passed the twinkling Christmas tree at the Central Bank, she'd averted her eyes. It reminded her of that last Christmas when Raffa had left. After she'd found his house shut up, deserted, she'd walked back into town from Portobello, her thoughts keeping her warm, trying to make sense of it all. It was the first Friday in December, and Grafton Street was thronged with families having a first look at the Christmas lights in the late afternoon dusk.

She'd peered into one of Switzer's windows, her reflection flanked by dozens more either side of her, children's faces lit up with the magic of it all. Her own gazing back from the glass showed her eyes huge in her head. She'd felt foolish, and she'd walked home, dragging her feet. When she passed the Nativity scene at the Central Bank, she knew something had shifted within her, as though her heart had moulded over itself a layer of plastic as hard as the star sitting atop the towering fir tree. This was the last time she'd be taken for a fool.

Now she feels a lightness inside as she starts walking. The wind picks up and blows through her, as though it might allow her to levitate above the ground. Nicoletta can feel the colour coming back into her cheeks. A walk is just what she needs, she thinks, as she rights herself after a forceful gust with a giddy skip forward. At Fairview Park, she speeds up into a brisk trot. She's glad of the exercise, positive that by the time she reaches her parents' two-up, two-down on Richmond Road her period will have started. That she's been worrying for nothing, dreading the worst, as she always does.

Sarto's Newsagents occupies what was once the front room of their part of the narrow, pale-bricked terrace. It's closed today, the only day of the year apart from Good Friday when it is ever shut to customers. It looks all wrong, shuttered up. She thinks about all the times she's walked through this door, the steep descent into the hall embedded in her movement as muscle memory. It often took visitors by surprise, this step down, instead of up. Not that they ever had many visitors, especially after Enzo. The thought that she might be carrying a new life over the threshold makes her suck in her stomach. A car exhaust wheezes from the next road, a far-away radio blares. She exhales. Her mother probably won't be able to tell just by looking at her.

Chapter Ten

She rings the bell, despite having a key. Her mother answers, her forehead a mass of squiggly lines which have only deepened as the years have progressed. Nicoletta suspects that she's been the cause of quite a few of them.

'You're here,' her mother says, by way of greeting. 'We didn't know if you were coming.'

'Yes, I'm here,' Nicoletta replies. It seems like a wholly inadequate response.

The door widens to allow Nicoletta to enter the cramped hallway. She stands in front of her mother for a moment or two, neither of them reacting.

'You've got fat,' her mother pronounces. 'I've always managed to keep my figure. Are you eating a lot of white bread?' Nicoletta opens her mouth to reply, but then thinks better of it. Daniela Sarto is tiny, her frame no bigger than a songbird's. Nicoletta is easily five or six inches taller.

'*Buon Natale, Mamma*,' Nicoletta says finally. She goes to kiss Daniela's cheek, but instead gets a mouthful of hair. She can feel her mother stiffen. When Nicoletta was a child, Daniela worked long hours in the shop until it closed. 'Let me put my feet up,' she would say, when Nicoletta wanted to show her a drawing, or a report from school. It established a pattern between them. Nicoletta feels hurt pricking her eyes. She doesn't know why she bothers.

'*Anche te*,' Daniela says, responding to the greeting, though she hasn't spoken Italian since she herself was a child and her own parents were alive. Nicoletta had always wanted to learn. She hopes it's a sign that her mother is in relatively good form. She follows her towards the immaculate kitchen at the back of the house. There are two bedrooms and a bathroom upstairs. The Sartos have sacrificed their sitting room for the shop. Nicoletta often thinks her mother has sacrificed her whole life along with it. Selling newspapers, packs of cigarettes and loaves of bread has sucked up every ounce of joy she ever seemed to possess. Nicoletta is hit by a familiar pang of guilt. Her mother provided for her and gave up a lot to do so. But in the end, Nicoletta was not the kind of daughter Daniela might've hoped for.

The dim, narrow hallway has scant decoration. Nicoletta catches her breath as she lingers at its only photograph, a framed black-and-white print of Enzo at his christening. The photo had been taken at a professional studio in town, and Nicoletta can see now that the child has a slight scowl on his tiny face, as if sensing the indignity of wearing a long white gown. She scans the picture for some resemblance to her. They have the same fair eyebrows, the same slight upturn in their nose. She wonders if Enzo might have been tall, like her. She doesn't want to think about the swell of people who'd pressed her hand, telling her how sorry they were about her little brother. She'd had to quell the roar inside to an acceptable level somewhere underneath the surface and say, *thank you, we appreciate you coming, yes, poor Mam.*

She wonders how much her mother's feelings towards her are complicated by the fact that she survived. The urge to talk about Enzo rises, though she knows it will probably upset Daniela, who is already fussing around the kitchen, making tea. Now is not the time for reminiscences. There never is a right time.

'I brought you a present,' Nicoletta says brightly, taking an envelope out of her bag and leaving it on the kitchen table. A long oak plinth too big for the room, it is zealously over-scrubbed by her mother. Nicoletta remembers it came from a neighbour who was going to give it to a skip or the St Vincent de Paul if the Sartos hadn't taken it. 'I know you don't like surprises. They're theatre tickets. For you and Dad. *The Importance of Being Earnest* at the Imperial. I thought you might like to go before the New Year.'

Daniela scalds a teapot with hot water, before tossing in a handful of tea leaves. 'Thank you, but you shouldn't have bothered. We won't have time. Who would look after the shop?'

Nicoletta bites her lip. 'I could do it. It'd give you a chance to have a nice evening out.'

Daniela looks up, the lines on her forehead deepening. 'On your own? I don't think so. But thank you anyway.'

Nicoletta sits down at the kitchen table and accepts a cup of tea. It is unremittingly strong. She adds a couple of spoons of sugar and folds her arms across her chest. 'Where's Dad?'

Daniela sits down opposite her. 'Your father has gone for a walk. We didn't know exactly when to expect you.'

Nicoletta takes a sip of the scalding tea. She makes a face and puts it down.

'How is everything?' Her own voice sounds artificial to her ears. There's a note of desperation beginning to creep in.

Daniela shrugs. 'The same as it always is. If we saw you more often, you'd know.'

'I was working yesterday. That's why I couldn't make it.' Nicoletta dumps milk into her tea and stirs it furiously.

'Ah yes, your precious job. How is that?'

Silence descends, the only sound the water gurgling through the pipes set in the walls. The house is not yet a hundred years old, and those pipes will survive long after them all, according to Daniela.

'Great, actually.' Nicoletta rolls up the sleeves of her sweater. The kitchen is warm and perspiration prickles at her neck. 'A big story came in yesterday. I was sent out to cover it. It went well, I think.'

Her mother raises her brows, smoothing her forehead back to how it had been when Nicoletta was a child, a million worry lines ago. Nicoletta takes her silence as an invitation to go on.

'Julia Bridges was found. An actress who went missing

114

during the war ...' She falters for a moment, before resuming her thread. 'Gloria Fitzpatrick was thought to be responsible, but the Gardaí could never prove anything. Remember Fitzpatrick, the midwife who was convicted of murder?'

Daniela stands up and begins clearing away their tea things, though Nicoletta hasn't finished hers. She bangs around the kitchen, washing and drying the cups and saucers. Nicoletta knows there's no point offering to help when her mother is like this. When she's finally restored everything to its rightful place in the crowded dresser by the back door, she wipes her hands on her old green apron. Nicoletta doesn't ever remember seeing her without it. When she's at home she wears the apron, and when she's in the shop she wears the blue shop coat with 'Sarto's' embroidered on the breast. She is only ever in either of those two places, as defined by what she wears. Clothes are for utilitarian purposes, never to be looked at for their own sake.

'I hardly think that's the right sort of job for a young lady.' Daniela stands over her daughter, her warm breath ruffling the top of Nicoletta's hairline.

Nicoletta clenches her jaw. She tries to turn around, but her mother blocks her, moving from foot to foot, like a boxer.

'What do you mean?' She speaks slowly, as though the longest possible time that passes between each word means less chance of losing her temper.

Her mother comes back over to the opposite side of the table but doesn't sit down. Instead, she wrings her hands.

'Your father will agree with me. Getting mixed up with murders and undesirable types ... it's just, it upsets me. My nerves certainly can't take it.'

Nicoletta glances down at her hands. Her mother's reaction is strange, even for her. She looks around the small, overheated kitchen and sighs. There is not a thing out of place here. You could probably eat your dinner off the floor if you were so inclined. She knows she won't be able to explain herself to this woman. But maybe she should try. This is as good an opportunity as any.

'I'm getting really good experience as a reporter. I'm even in line for a promotion. And it's not just that. I enjoy it. When I'm writing for the paper, things make sense, somehow. I feel useful.'

Daniela laughs, a harsh, brittle sound, and sinks back into her chair. 'That's a load of nonsense. Things might make more sense if you helped your parents out with their business. Then you'd be useful. Or found someone decent to marry. You've missed a lot of opportunities now.'

Nicoletta digs her nails into her palms, then gathers the sleeves of her sweater over her hands. She knows this old lament of her mother's. She hadn't met anyone 'nice' at the tea dances at the Broadway Café on Parnell Street after all. Now she never would. Nicoletta knuckles her fist into her chin. 'I'm sorry I've disappointed you.'

Daniela shrugs and bites her lip.

Nicoletta looks at her mother as though for the first time. Disappointment has eaten into her youth and dis-coloured her like a jaundice, and Nicoletta can't help but feel that she has become its focus.

She blinks back tears. 'I was just looking at Enzo's christening photo. When did you put that up?'

Daniela bites her lip again. 'Let's leave that poor little angel out of all this.'

The tears start to spill, and Nicoletta is helpless to stop them. 'I can't.' She wipes her face with the back of her hand. 'I'm sorry.'

Daniela shrugs and stands up, moving back over to the kettle, filling it with more water for tea. 'You're just indulging yourself now,' she says, without looking at Nicoletta. 'Pull yourself together.'

Nicoletta doesn't hear her father come in until the kitchen door opens and lets in some welcome cold air. Ettore Sarto's dark hair is gleaming, his jacket pressed, his shoes polished. When he sees Nicoletta, his face splits into a smile.

'There she is,' he says, kissing her soundly on both cheeks.

'Hi, Dad,' she says, standing up and meeting his hug. She is glad of the embrace.

Ettore stands back. 'Hey, hey. What's with the tears? It's Christmas.'

Nicoletta lets out a shuddery sigh. 'I got upset. We were talking about Enzo.'

Ettore's face clouds over. 'I see.' He squeezes Nicoletta's shoulder.

'You were speaking about him.' Daniela can't even bring herself to say Enzo's name. 'I wasn't.'

Ettore takes off his jacket and hangs it on the back of a chair. 'Phew, it's warm.' He rubs his hands together. 'What's to eat?'

'We're having leftovers from last night. I might put a chicken on later. There doesn't seem much point for just the three of us.' Daniela leans against the counter and closes her eyes, as though it pains her to have to speak at this moment.

Ettore smiles at Nicoletta. 'It's wonderful to see you. Tell me everything.'

'Her precious job means she doesn't have time for her family.' Daniela sits back down and crosses her arms. She's so petite, she looks like a child seated at the table.

Ettore doesn't acknowledge what she's said, instead looking from one woman to the other, his face unreadable. 'I'll make more tea, OK?'

'Don't bother,' Daniela says shortly. But Ettore ignores her, placing the kettle back on the hob, setting a match so that a blue flame encircles it like the atmosphere of a distant planet.

Nicoletta looks down at the table, where the grain of the wood swirls outwards in concentric lines. She wonders if it's true what they say, if you can tell the age of the tree when it was cut down by counting the lines. She thinks of poor little Enzo, forever frozen in time in her mother's hallway, never to age much more than he was in the picture, never to disappoint or say a cross word.

'I'm sorry you're stuck with me,' she says to Daniela's profile. The words are out of her mouth before she can stop them. There's a sharp intake of breath from Ettore and he places the filled teapot on the table. He is no stranger to playing the role of referee between his wife and daughter.

'That's quite enough now,' he says firmly.

It had been Ettore who'd encouraged Nicoletta at school. He'd taught her to read, supervised her homework and brought her to join the library. And he'd told her he'd pay for her to go to UCD to study English and History, that she might become a teacher, or anything else that she wanted. But then Enzo had arrived, in her last year of school, and she'd had to help her mother, followed by all the grief in the years following his death. UCD had never happened. Nicoletta puts her head in her hands and takes a deep breath. 'I'm sorry,' she says finally. 'Let's not allow Christmas to be ruined.'

Ettore gives her a wink. Daniela doesn't stir.

Nicoletta thinks back to the photo that Graham Swift, the manager at the Athena Theatre, had given her. Julia Bridges, née Murphy, had been only one of two female cast members of *Julius Caesar*, along with someone called Daniela Stagg, whose resemblance to her mother when she was young is seeming less likely, now that the real article is seated in front of her. All the woman in the photograph shares with her mother are dark eyes pooled in a round face. In the end, curiosity wins out.

'Mam, did you ever act in a play at the Athena, along-side Julia Bridges?'

Her mother looks up, startled, her forehead wrinkled. 'Whatever put that into your head?'

Nicoletta finds herself faltering as she struggles to get the words out. 'I spoke to Jack Bridges, the widower of Julia, the actress who died. For the story I'm covering. And he let me have a photo of the cast of *Julius Caesar*, the first play Julia appeared in. The only other female cast member was called Daniela Stagg. She looked an awful lot like you. I thought I'd ask you about it.'

Ettore continues drinking his tea. Daniela turns to face Nicoletta, her bottom lip trembling furiously. 'We don't see you for ages, and now you're back causing trouble. Upsetting everyone.'

'So, it's not true?'

'The notion of me playacting is ridiculous,' Daniela hisses with finality, standing up and inexplicably taking the teapot away, though it's still mostly full.

'Why?' Nicoletta idly lifts the tiny spoon in the sugar bowl and pours a cascade of white granules. 'What's wrong with doing something like that?'

Her mother snatches the sugar bowl away. 'Your father and I work all day, every day, making the best of things. That's called living in the real world. A place you don't seem to occupy.'

Nicoletta scrapes back her chair and stands up. 'I just called in to say Happy Christmas to you and Dad. I didn't want a row. I think I'll go.'

Daniela pinches the bridge of her nose, the way people do to staunch nosebleeds.

'As you wish. Walk away. That seems to be your solution to everything.'

Nicoletta shrugs on her coat. As an afterthought, she grabs the envelope containing the theatre tickets. She hovers at the door to the hallway, but Daniela has busied herself with yet more furious washing-up, her shoulders rigid. She is angry, Nicoletta knows that, but she's not quite sure what about. Or if there needs to be a specific reason anymore.

She steps out into the dim hall, markedly cooler than the kitchen.

'Bye, Dad,' she calls back into the room, but there's no reply.

She pauses in front of the photograph of Enzo, tiny and perfect, immortalised in black and white. Her eyes swim with a too-familiar grief, and frustration. Her mother will never want to try and understand her new life. She's about to go back in and offer a tentative olive branch, but Daniela slams the adjoining door, physically closing the gap between them once and for all. Nicoletta is out the front door before she can change her mind.

Chapter Eleven

Rage propels her home at speed. She doesn't even feel the cold as she replays the conversation with her mother again and again. She's surprised to see Dermot Mahon standing outside her flat, his finger pressed to the bell.

'What're you doing here?' She drags her key out of her pocket.

'We never got to have that drink yesterday.' He pulls two bottles of Blue Nun out from under his coat and brandishes them at her sheepishly.

'You'll drive the neighbours mad with all that bell ringing.' She leans up on her tiptoes and hugs him. 'It's good to see you,' she says hoarsely.

She puts her key in the lock and beckons for him to follow her. When they reach the door to her flat, she turns her head. 'How'd you know I'd be here?'

'Lucky guess.'

Inside he takes off his gloves and coat, collapsing on the sagging sofa, which has sprung a couple of leaks in its belly, revealing errant springs and stuffing that no one can be bothered to repair or replace. He regards the stained carpet, ringed where drinks have been left and forgotten, without comment. Nicoletta fumbles for her purse. Dermot takes sixpence from his pocket and slots it into the gas metre. A blue flame pops into the funnel and the whole thing shoots to life.

'Thanks. It'll warm up soon.' She discards Jean's overcoat on the back of a chair and fetches some glass tumblers from the kitchenette. 'We don't have wine glasses,' she says apologetically.

He pours them a full glass each. They clink. Nicoletta takes a sip, intending not to drink any of it, but then she finds herself taking another, and another. She sits back, basking in the afternoon sun seeping through the gap in the curtain.

'How's your Christmas been?' She holds the tumbler of wine with both hands. It's supposed to be chilled, but by dint of being in Dermot's pocket, it's warmer than the room.

He stretches his large frame towards the meagre heat coming from the gas heater. 'The same as any other day. My parents live down the country and I didn't go home . . .' He leaves the sentence hanging between them and Nicoletta doesn't probe further.

'Lucky you,' Nicoletta says cheerily, knocking back a glug of wine, feeling the warmth from the alcohol spread. She takes another sip and laughs. 'I just had a bizarre row with my mother – over what, I'm still not quite sure.'

Dermot smiles and raises his glass. 'Happy Christmas.'

They both drink, before Dermot tops up each of their glasses.

'So, what's the latest with the world's greatest love story?' He sits back, his hands behind his head.

'You mean Barney and me? I wouldn't exactly call it that.'

'What would you call it, then?'

Nicoletta puts her glass down. 'Well, it is a love story, but it's not as straightforward as all that. Barney's still technically married, after all.'

Dermot turns his head without moving his body. 'He's not married. His wife deserted him. There's a difference.'

Nicoletta takes a sip of wine. 'Yes, but it's not as though he can just get a divorce. If we wanted to get married, we'd have to go to England.'

Dermot sits up straight. 'Seriously? You'd marry him?'

Nicoletta curls herself into the arm of her chair. 'Of course. What's the point otherwise?'

'Sounds pretty straightforward to me.' Dermot drains the rest of the bottle into each of their glasses.

'Hardly. Marie came back for Christmas, to see Liam. I hope that's all she wants. And . . .' It's on the tip of her tongue to confide in Dermot about her own fears, that she's pregnant and she doesn't know what to do, but he's on his feet before she can say anything.

'Are you hungry? I haven't eaten today. I'm starving.'

'I don't think we have anything in the house,' Nicoletta says. 'We could go out.'

'Are you mad? There'll be nowhere open on Christmas Day.' Dermot starts walking towards the kitchen and Nicoletta trots behind him.

She manages to unearth some eggs, rashers and

sausages belonging to Jean, and half a loaf of bread, a couple of days old, but which should be fine toasted, Dermot assures her. He cooks on their scalded frying pan over the two-ring stove, while Nicoletta does the toast under the grill and makes them some tea.

They eat by the light of the gas fire. Nicoletta puts the Rolling Stones' *Beggars Banquet* on her record player. When they've eaten every last morsel on their plates, Dermot pours them more wine.

'Where'd you disappear to yesterday?' He settles back on the sofa. The room has heated up beautifully. Nicoletta stretches her stockinged feet out in front of her.

'I was working on that story. About Julia Bridges being found.'

'And? Did you find out anything interesting?'

'Lots of things. Some interesting. But none of it seems to make sense.'

'What do you mean?'

'Nothing adds up. No one seems to know anything. Take the Creightons. How could they not have known there was a body buried in their garden?'

Dermot shrugs, his head lolling. He's completely relaxed where he is, right in his own skin, Nicoletta notices. She could do with taking a leaf out of his book, she decides, and stop caring so much what others think.

'Some people are just like that. They choose to turn a blind eye.' His own eyes are half closed now.

'Someone must have known something.'

'Isn't Gloria Fitzpatrick the one we should be blaming? Inspector Morris still seems convinced she was rotten to the core, according to Barney.' Dermot doesn't open his eyes.

The record has come to an end and Nicoletta gets up to set it back to play from the beginning. 'So everyone says. But nothing stands up. Jack Bridges and some other fellow were initially questioned, apparently, though they were later ruled out of enquiries. Dermot, if you saw Jack Bridges, you'd know what I mean. He can't be all there. And don't get me started on the Creightons. Their maid told me that her sister, who worked there before her, killed herself just after she'd had a baby. What if that's somehow connected to the body that was found?'

Now Dermot opens his eyes. 'You seem to really care about this.'

Nicoletta takes a sip of wine, then another. 'I suppose so.'

He pours a generous amount from the second bottle into both glasses. 'But why? Nicoletta, it's Christmas. You're allowed to take a day off.' He gives a lazy chuckle.

Nicoletta uncrosses her legs and leans forward, their knees touching. 'I don't know, I just can't stop thinking about poor Mary Little, walking into the sea, until the water dragged her under.' She stops, aware how strange she probably sounds, and looks down at her hands. 'It's getting to me, I suppose.'

Dermot takes her hand and holds her fingers lightly in his large square palm. 'You're doing great,' he says sleepily. 'Things get to me all the time. It just shows you're not made of stone. You're all right.'

She doesn't know what it is, the hand-holding, the wine,

the rising heat of the room, or just her need to hear the words spoken out loud.

'I'm pregnant,' she says, shaking her head, taking a gulp of her wine before the tears can start again. 'Or, at least, I think I might be.' The record whirs to a stop, and the room is filled with static: the rush of gas at the fireplace, the whoosh of faraway traffic, Nicoletta's stuttered heartbeat.

'Have you told him?' Dermot's voice is kind, without accusation.

She shakes her head. 'I haven't told Barney, no. I haven't a clue what to do.'

'You should tell him.' Dermot takes her hand again and crushes it with all his might. Nicoletta winces from the force.

'Should I?' She looks into his face, shiny now with perspiration. The room has got too warm. 'What if he goes back to Marie?'

'He won't,' he says quietly, and she doesn't say anything else for another minute.

'Do you think everyone knows?'

'About you and Barney?' He shrugs. 'Dublin's a small place. No one's allowed any secrets.' He catches her eye. 'Do you think everyone knows about me?'

'About you? You mean ... that you're ...?'

'Queer,' he says, with the ghost of a smile. 'Come on, I'm sure it's been mentioned.'

'So what if it has?' She kisses him on the cheek. 'We're all entitled to our secrets.'

They hug at an awkward angle, still holding hands,

until she disentangles her fingers from his and gets up to go to the bathroom. There's still no sign of blood – though she knew it would be highly unlikely, the hope is still there. She sits down on the edge of the bath and picks out a tub of lavender-scented cold cream she'd bought for her mother but forgotten to wrap, much less actually give as a gift. It's too late now. Nicoletta twists off the round blue plastic lid and breathes in the familiar scent. Her mother used to smother her face with this at night when Nicoletta was a child, though it hadn't stopped the worry lines from deepening as the years went on. Perhaps the worries simply outnumbered Daniela. Nicoletta pokes her finger into the pot and smears a blob of cream over the back of her hand. It sits on her skin, refusing to be spread or absorbed. She presses the back of her hand against her cheek. A memory pops the bubble of her thoughts, sharp as a pinprick – her 'night terrors', as her mother called them. She could never remember the particulars once she'd woken up, but the feeling they left would last all day. If she had to describe it now, distil it into a logical sentiment, it was that something bad was her fault. On one occasion when she was maybe five or six, Daniela must've seen how distraught she was and taken Nicoletta into her bed. Ettore had already risen to meet early deliveries to the shop. Nicoletta had been near hysterical, shaking with a grief she didn't know how to express.

'What is it, *cara*, what is it?' Daniela had been patient, locking her arms around her daughter, resting her chin on top of Nicoletta's head, until she calmed down, until the sobs lessened to mild shudders, and she was anchored to her mother's embrace.

'How would I know if I'm bad?' Nicoletta had said into her mother's neck, feeling slightly silly now, already somehow aware that it wasn't a question her mother would be able to answer. But Daniela had surprised her.

'You could never be bad. You are a good girl. And I never want to hear you say those words again.'

The sound of gentle snoring greets her when she arrives back to the sitting room. Dermot is fast asleep, his mouth half open. She covers him with the quilt from her bedroom, before sinking back into her chair, her thoughts whirring as she sets the record to play again.

Chapter Twelve

Thursday, 26th December 1968
St Stephen's Day

The newsroom hums when Nicoletta returns in the mid-afternoon. She's not rostered to work over Christmas but she can't wait to get back to this story. The buzz from the fluorescent strip lighting and whatever is happening in Duffy's office are music to her ears.

Barney has left some old news clippings he'd obtained from the library on her desk. She recognises his illegible scrawl on the attached note. She reads them standing up.

Irish Sentinel, **17th March 1959**
A HUSBAND'S ANGUISH
By Tim Duffy

'Someone must know something. People don't just vanish into thin air.' It is now almost sixteen years since Dublin actress Julia Bridges was last seen by her husband Jack, the owner of the renowned Athena Theatre at Bachelors Walk. Mr Bridges is today appealing to *Sentinel* readers to come forward if there's anything they may remember which could assist the ongoing investigation. Today is particularly significant as it would be Julia's thirty-sixth birthday, a day she shares with our patron saint, Patrick.

'If she were here, she'd be going to the parade, making a day of it. She loved to see everyone enjoying themselves,' Mr Bridges tells me from his home in Ringsend, where he moved from the flat he shared with his wife at Percy Place. He holds a framed photo of Mrs Bridges in her last role as a mermaid at the Athena's summer revue. 'She was a natural. That's what everyone said,' he tells me, before emotion gets the better of him. The part was taken over after a month's run by Carole Swift, Mrs Bridges' understudy, after Mrs Bridges fell ill.

Mr Bridges last saw Julia in July 1943. He says it was 'out of character' for Mrs Bridges to have gone off somewhere without telling her husband. 'She was very considerate and always more concerned with how everyone else was than with herself. It was just her nature. None of it makes sense.'

Mr Bridges thinks that someone, or more than one person, might know something, no matter how seemingly inconsequential, which could prove instrumental in finding out what happened to his wife.

'If you know something, no matter how big or small, it could make the world of difference to the investigation.'

Anyone with relevant information should contact Detective Inspector David Morris at Pearse Street Garda Station in strictest confidence.

Irish Sentinel, **23rd April 1959**
MISS FITZPATRICK DIES IN ASYLUM
By Tim Duffy

Miss Gloria Fitzpatrick died on Tuesday morning at Clyde Hall Criminal Lunatic Asylum in Dublin. She was transferred to the asylum in January of this year, after serving two years of a life sentence at Mountjoy Prison.

It is believed that Miss Fitzpatrick suffered a cardiac arrest in her sleep and was found shortly before 8am by a ward nurse.

The former midwife was sentenced to death for the murder of Elizabeth Rourke, a married mother of six, after performing an illegal operation on the deceased person. Mrs Rourke's body was found on the pavement outside Miss Fitzpatrick's flat in Ely Place in April 1956 by the driver of a bread van, who immediately alerted the Gardaí.

After a lengthy and often shocking trial, the sentence of death by hanging was commuted to life imprisonment on the grounds of insanity.

Miss Fitzpatrick was outspoken in the course of the legal proceedings, making it clear that she did not recognise the Irish state. It is expected that Miss Fitzpatrick will be buried at Dean's Grange Cemetery, where inmates of Clyde Hall Asylum are usually interred. This is subject to her remains being claimed by relatives in the meantime. She is said to be from the townland of Knockgan, in County Laois.

An official spokesman for the asylum said that they couldn't comment on Miss Fitzpatrick's death.

Mrs Bernadette Brennan, the nurse at Clyde Hall Asylum who found Miss Fitzpatrick on the morning she died, has said that she and many of the residents and staff are 'in shock' in the wake of Miss Fitzpatrick's demise.

Nicoletta has only just taken off her coat when the door to the inner sanctum opens. Robert Price and Barney exit sharply, followed at a leisurely remove by Duffy. They appear to be making a beeline for her desk. Nicoletta sits and smooths down her skirt.

'Ah, Nicoletta,' Duffy says by way of greeting, rubbing his small hands together. 'You're not meant to be here, but how and ever. Just the lady. I see you already got the clippings Barney ordered.' He perches his fleshy behind on the corner of her desk, his checked sports coat straining at the weft, his hand balancing on her shoulder. 'Nice Christmas?'

'Very nice, thank you,' she says, glancing from Barney to Price, who flank him on either side, arms folded across their chests. 'How about you, sir?'

'Ah, you know yourself. Came back in here for a bit of peace.'

Nicoletta smiles politely, waiting for whatever's coming.

'The thing is, Nicoletta, we're setting up a new women's page in the new year. And we're looking for the right lady to edit it. Are you interested?'

Nicoletta nods without missing a beat. She's about to speak when Duffy takes a laboured breath.

'It's between you and Anne. Haven't quite decided.' He looks around pointedly at Anne's empty desk, before leaning forward, speaking almost directly into her ear. She feels too uncomfortable to move away. 'I'll be announcing my decision next Thursday. 2nd January.'

Nicoletta falters, unsure of what to do. Price glares at her. He's about to say something but Duffy speaks first.

'Barney tells me you made great progress on Christmas Eve with the Julia Bridges story. Fancy staying on that?'

'Yes,' she says. 'I do. I feel like there's a lot more I could get.'

'Great.' He claps her on the shoulder. 'We want you to do a longer-read piece about the background surrounding Bridges and what happened to her. Anyone who'll speak to you.'

Nicoletta glances at Barney but he's in silent conference with Price, mouthing furiously. Duffy clambers to his feet and Nicoletta's desk heaves an audible sigh of relief. 'Right,' he says, striking the surface with a perfectly aimed fist. 'Go out there. Speak to as many people as you can about how Julia disappeared, leaving Jack Bridges a broken man. Lots of colour. A real tear-jerker.'

Nicoletta looks up. Duffy is already red in the face from all the excitement, but she won't let her blood pressure be raised to his level just yet. 'So, this might lead to the women's page editor job?'

Duffy leans forward and almost shouts in her ear. 'I hope so, Nicoletta.' He straightens up.

Nicoletta stands and picks up her handbag. 'Well, I suppose I'd best be off.'

'Attagirl.' Duffy throws an arm around her waist and squeezes. She flinches, but he doesn't seem to notice. 'Off you go, now. Don't let me down.'

She disentangles herself, buzzing with purpose, and strides to the stack of telephone directories beside the bank of phones on the news desk. She flicks the frayed edges of the flimsy paper and comes to 'B'. She can see Barney's head bobbing in agreement to something Duffy is saying and looks away. There are hundreds of Brennans listed. She finds three that sound vaguely promising, including a B. Brennan, and a Miss Bernadette Brennan, but she knows that can't be right, as the Nurse Brennan who'd found Gloria was Mrs. Then she finds a listing with a Mr Cyril and Mrs Bernadette Brennan, Windy Arbour. She makes a note of the address and phone number. It's not far from Dundrum, where Clyde Hall Criminal Lunatic Asylum is still located. Without looking back, she marches out the door. Barney follows her into the chilly stairwell, where they eye each other in the gloom for a moment before speaking.

'So. You OK to keep doing this?' Barney says eventually.

'More than happy to.' Nicoletta puts on her gloves, the soft kid leather connecting with her hands finger by finger. Anything to avoid eye contact. 'It's a great opportunity. Thanks for the clippings you left on my desk. See you later, so.'

She turns to go. Dermot sticks his head around the door. 'Nicoletta? Thought I might just catch you. Phone!'

She adjusts her bag on her wrist. 'Who is it?'

Dermot looks down at a scrap of paper in his hand. 'Garda O'Connor. He says it's urgent.'

Nicoletta feels the cold hand of fear press its icy fingers into her throat. 'And he asked to speak to me?'

Dermot nods, biting the inside of his cheek. Barney frowns. Nicoletta reverses up the concrete steps and back through the plate glass newsroom door. She picks up the phone.

'Nicoletta Sarto speaking,' she says, her tone brisk.

'Miss Sarto, it's Garda O'Connor.' The voice is soft, earnest.

'Good morning, Garda,' she says, the fear spreading into the pit of her stomach and settling there like lead. 'What can I do for you?'

She takes a glance around. Barney has drifted off to speak to Duffy. Dermot is shouting something to a copy boy. She lowers her voice and clears her throat. 'Is this call business or personal?'

'Oh, it's business, no, it's a story, actually.' Garda O'Connor sounds alarmed. 'You're probably wondering why I asked for you.'

Nicoletta relaxes slightly and laughs. 'A bit, yeah.'

O'Connor sounds like he's tapping a pen against his teeth. 'This particular story might need a woman's touch. Can you meet me in Sandycove in an hour? At Seaview Terrace?'

Nicoletta tugs at a clump of her hair, which has escaped from the turban. Barney has disappeared. She sighs. 'Sure. What's happened?'

She can hear what sounds like the repeated clicking of a pen lid. 'We've found more human remains. At Seaview House.'

'The Creightons' place again?'

'In their grounds anyway.'

She's about to say something else when O'Connor cuts across her. 'I'm on my way now. I'll see you there, Nicoletta.'

'Thank you,' she says, but the line is dead.

Chapter Thirteen

She picks up her bag and stands up, squaring her shoulders. But she doesn't meet a soul as she passes the row of vacant typewriters. Dermot is still shouting to the copy boy. Duffy's office door is closed. She rushes headlong down the concrete staircase until she's out the door and onto Burgh Quay. The wind is muted to a soft whisper. There are no trams running today. She gives an inward shrug and hails a taxi on Westmoreland Street.

When her taxi pulls up, she sees O'Connor leaning against the staggered concrete partition between Seaview Terrace and the main coast road leading to Seaview House. He whistles and she blushes.

'Arriving in style,' he says, indicating the retreating saloon.

She shakes her head. 'No trams today. And I can't drive.'

'You couldn't get a lift from Barney, no?' He tilts his head and beckons her to follow him through the concrete divide. The suck of sea air pulls her into its embrace as soon as they're facing the harbour and she's glad. Out of the corner of her eye she can see several Garda cars, with uniformed gardaí sitting in the drivers' seats, watching, waiting.

She falls into step beside O'Connor. 'I didn't want to ask him, actually,' she says. 'Wanted to see what you had to say first. Besides, this is my story now.' She looks at him side on. 'You asked for me specifically when you called. I presume you had a reason for that?'

O'Connor turns around to face her. He stops the wind blowing his hat clean off his head with a swat of his hand.

He coughs. 'Morris mentioned you're in line for the new women's page editor position.'

Nicoletta's eyes begin to stream from the wind. She turns the other way. 'How did he know about that?'

'Barney told him.' O'Connor's gaze is frank. 'It seems like a great opportunity.'

Nicoletta doesn't say anything for a minute. 'Why are you helping me?' He doesn't immediately answer, and for a moment she wonders if her voice has been carried off by the wind.

'You could do with a break.' O'Connor presses his palms together and they start walking in the direction of the James Joyce Tower.

Nicoletta stops suddenly. 'I don't need charity,' she says quietly. 'I'm not a special case. I don't need your help again.'

O'Connor raises his hands in surrender. 'Jesus, relax. The word is you're a good reporter. Would it help if I said that Morris wanted me to ring you as he knew it might piss Barney off something rotten?'

Nicoletta breaks into a smile. 'It might.'

The Martello tower where James Joyce once lived sits hunched over the harbour, squat as a toadstool. The sea below them is riveted with trails of pale foam, as each wave piles on top of the last and breaks on the shore, a minute replica of the one before it. She's always loved the sea. Its changing moods. She's about to say as much but thinks better of it. It would sound foolish considering how she and O'Connor previously met. He lifts his hat and wipes his forehead with the back of his hand, readjusting the peak so it sits perfectly straight. His hands are pale and speckled as eggs, the palms wide and strong. She remembers those hands grasping her under the arms, tackling her in a rough embrace, pulling her back up, forcing her to meet the surface, a reluctant rebirth. She hadn't fought him in the end. Relief had enveloped her, and she'd let her body float on the water, thick as freezing oil, the kicking and thrashing stilled. She'd known she'd made a mistake as soon as the current sucked her under. She hadn't wanted to die; she'd just wanted it all to stop, she'd wanted to join Enzo wherever he was. O'Connor was a strong swimmer, she remembers. Maybe you have to be; a requirement for the job. She'd never asked him. Or if she had, she doesn't remember. She can't even remember how he got to be there. Whether someone telephoned the Guards, or he just happened to be nearby. Parts of that night are shadowy and dark. She just knows that one minute she walked into the water, hoping for oblivion, and the next she was gliding along the surface, him pulling her on his back, the sheer strength of him, his legs paddling furiously out of sight. The heave of his breath as he set her down like a wounded bird on the wet sand. The relief as the water left her lungs, as life fought to reclaim her. He'd sat with her in the ambulance all the way into town, asking her questions about where she lived, what she did, who she was, what she liked. So many questions, though the one he never asked was why. She'd liked him for that. Then her parents were clinging to her bedside, dry-eyed and tight-lipped. It was for them to ask, but they could not.

She takes a sidelong glance at him. They keep walking, the silence of tacit understanding between them. They pass the tower, the path winding on around the coastline.

She coughs. 'Aren't you going to tell me what happened?'

'We found more human remains, as I said.' He braces himself to continue. 'A baby this time.'

Nicoletta's throat tightens. She feels a heave in her gut. 'Who found it?'

O'Connor doesn't look at her but keeps walking. 'I did. Poor little mite.'

They walk in silence for a minute, scanning the horizon. 'Who is it?'

'We don't know yet,' O'Connor says. 'We've known for a while what John Dawkins is up to, with his dope racket.' He gestures towards Seaview House and its expanse of grounds. 'Up until recently Dawkins worked as some sort of educational supplies salesman and he was going back and forth to the UK a bit for his work. We searched the garden and discovered a cache of his stuff buried in the rose beds – purple hearts and reefer with a street value estimated at several thousand pounds.'

Nicoletta lets out a breath through her teeth, an unintentional whistle. 'Will you arrest him?'

'In due course. That's the least of our worries at the moment. A couple of feet away from Dawkins' stuff is where I found the baby.'

He wipes his forehead with a paper tissue, which he shoves back in his pocket. 'We don't have much more than what I've just told you, and we won't know anything further until after O'Malley's examination.'

Nicoletta takes a deep breath. 'Is that off the record, Garda?'

O'Connor nods. 'Between ourselves, Morris is working under the assumption that this child was Julia Bridges'.'

Nicoletta bites the inside of her cheek. 'Doesn't that seem highly unlikely, Garda? If Julia was pregnant, it was only in the early stages. No one who knew her was aware of a pregnancy. How could she have given birth to a baby without anyone knowing?'

They pass the tower, and he stops. 'It happens, Miss Sarto. It was a long time ago and people's memories aren't exactly reliable. I'm just telling you what Morris thinks. I trust his judgement.'

Nicoletta lowers her voice. 'Una Little, a maid at Creighton's, had a sister, Mary, who worked there until she died last year. According to Una, Mary drowned herself.' She takes a deep breath. 'She'd just had a baby. I thought you should know.'

O'Connor's brow furrows. 'Jesus.' He nods. 'I'll look into it. Now I'd better get back inside. Thanks for coming all this way. Let me know if you've any other questions.'

'I might go and talk to some of the Gardaí at Seaview House. Would that be all right?'

O'Connor nods. 'OK, but don't say I sent you.'

Nicoletta sits down heavily on the low sea wall. 'I won't. I'm going to stay put for a minute and take some notes. Thank you, Garda.'

He nods and walks back the way they came. She swings her legs around to face the sea, drawn to look at the water. The pale winter sun has turned it a sparkling blue tourmaline. She closes her eyes, thinking about the poor little baby. The morning she'd found Enzo, she'd cradled him against her chest, crooning to him, the Italian lullaby she'd heard her mother singing when she thought she was alone. Pleading with him to wake up. Her mother had heard her and called the doctor. But Nicoletta already knew it was too late. Her stomach heaves like it's being dragged by an unseen current. When she opens her eyes, the sea has changed colour again, back to a chilly grey.

She's shivering by the time she advances along the path to Seaview Terrace. The wind is relentless, riffling a diagonal pattern through the flat-topped yew trees at the front of Seaview House. Compared to their immaculate appearance a few days earlier, the grounds are now a sea of mud, tape cordoning the land into zones. They've done a thorough job of searching it. She can hear a distant squawk as Antony or Cleopatra, or both – Sally Creighton's peacocks – give the cops a hard time. Nicoletta counts six uniformed gardaí milling around the garden, and another two sitting in parked cars. She tries the side gate, but it's secured by a tiny padlock. Nicoletta stands for a moment, before vaulting the wall. Her knee grazes the blood-coloured brick as she gains a foothold and swings a leg over it, jumping into a muddy flowerbed on the other side. She's greeted by a volley of outraged squawks, as Antony and Cleopatra peck at the ground in front of her. She advances slowly, her shoes sliding in the mud, crooning the lullaby at the peacocks, fresh from her head. Antony cocks his head to one side and fans his tail, quietening down. Cleopatra takes a step back as it starts to spit rain. Nicoletta takes the opportunity to make an awkward dash for a parked Garda car beside the armless Grecian nymph in front of Delia and John Dawkins' house. The hexagon of flower beds surrounding it has now dissolved into a blank sea of mud. There's one uniformed, though hatless, garda sitting stock-still inside. He's motionless, not smoking, or reading or making notes, just sitting and observing the scene from the driver's seat. Nicoletta taps on the window. He's very young, with very white skin and a smattering of raised red acne around his mouth. He rolls the window down and gives her a doubtful look. Nicoletta bends towards him and smiles, though the rain spilling down her face has taken all her make-up with it, and her shorn hair is hidden under her now soggy turban.

'Mrs Dawkins,' the garda says, with a jump of recognition, an air of deference in the way he places his hat on his head and opens the door, stepping out into the rain. 'What can I do for you?'

'I'm not . . .' Nicoletta hesitates. She knows she has a split second to decide what to do. If she says she's a reporter, she'll be thrown out on her ear. This guard obviously thinks she's Delia Dawkins, for some bizarre reason, so maybe she should just go with it.

'Could we perhaps have a chat?' She smiles again, hoping she won't be found out.

'Of course,' the garda says, nodding at the mews. 'Inside?'

'Oh no,' Nicoletta says, panic beginning to rise. 'Maybe we could stay here? Could I get into your car?'

'Of course,' he says, coming around and opening the passenger door for her. She hops in, dripping water in a puddle at her feet. When he's seated beside her, they both look straight ahead at the blur of rain flooding the windscreen. The garda starts the ignition and switches a knob. Warm, dusty air blows towards Nicoletta's face. She coughs.

'Well now,' he says, with a nervous flick of his head in her direction. 'What can I do for you?'

Nicoletta takes a tissue out of her bag and wipes her face. 'I'm so sorry for bothering you like this,' she says hesitantly. 'It's just, this has all been most distressing. And nobody's told me anything.' She touches his elbow. 'I'm completely in the dark. Could you tell me what's happening?'

The young garda bites his lip, as though considering. 'What do you want to know?'

Nicoletta leans forward. The warm air has stopped. She shivers. 'How did these bones get into my garden, Garda?' She gives a plaintive upwards inflection on the last syllable for dramatic effect.

He shakes his head. 'We don't know yet, Mrs Dawkins. We're investigating.'

Nicoletta's teeth have started to chatter, and she can't stop them. 'Where was the baby's skeleton found?'

The garda blinks before he answers. 'Julia Bridges was a skeleton. But her baby wasn't quite a skeleton.'

Nicoletta gulps. 'You mean, the baby's body hadn't decomposed fully? In that case, it probably wasn't Julia's baby.'

He shakes his head again. 'Inspector Morris thinks that this area of the grounds, which was apparently used as a pet cemetery many years ago, had a special kind of soil that meant decomposition was delayed.'

'If that were the case, why wasn't Julia Bridges' body more substantial than a skeleton?'

The garda looks at her sharply. 'I'm just telling you what Inspector Morris thinks.' There's a note of suspicion in his voice as his eyes bore into Nicoletta's profile. She keeps looking straight ahead, reaching for the handle on the passenger door.

'Thank you, Garda. It's good to finally know what's going on.' She's out of the car and back sliding around in the mud before he can answer. She eyes the wall ruefully. She doesn't know if she has it in her to climb it a second time. The front gate has been opened to allow a Garda car entry. Nicoletta is down there as fast as she can. A flash of red hair gleams from the driver's side as O'Connor manoeuvres the car into a tidy angle beside a yew tree. He gets out of the car and chuckles.

'You look like you've been mud wrestling,' he says, not unkindly.

Nicoletta thinks of how she just impersonated Delia Dawkins and a flush of shame warms her cheeks. 'I'm going to speak to the Littles,' she says in a rush. 'At number eight Seaview Terrace. The home of the Creightons' maid who died.'

O'Connor nods before going up the steps and ringing the Creightons' bell. Nicoletta is out the front gate before someone can lock her in.

Chapter Fourteen

Seaview Terrace is deserted, save for a small boy of six or seven polishing a black bicycle outside number eight. Nicoletta stops at the gate. Rust is flaking through the paint. The unvarnished door is bare, save for a squiggly numeral someone has dashed on with grey paint.

'Are you Michael Little?' She looks down the street. There isn't another soul around.

The boy looks startled. He nods. 'Who're you?'

Nicoletta smiles. 'I'm a friend of your sister's. Are your parents in?'

Michael indicates the door. 'Resting.' He mouths the word in a whisper.

'Ah, I see.' Nicoletta stands up straight. An upstairs curtain twitches. 'Maybe I can come back some other time. Did you have a nice Christmas?'

Michael pokes his tongue between his teeth. 'I got a bike.' He pats the saddle. The rubber binding is coming away at the edges, Nicoletta notices, and it looks much too big for this small boy.

'It's very nice,' she murmurs. 'Did Santa Claus bring it?'

Michael looks incredulous. 'Santy is only for kids. That's what Da says. This is a real bike, for a real man.' He kicks the front tyre doubtfully. 'Only I know it's really Mary's old bike he took out of the shed.' He grasps the handlebar with his small fingers. 'It's still mine.'

'It's very nice,' Nicoletta says again, with a smile.

Michael looks over his shoulder. 'Una's getting me a brand-new racer soon. She has the cash, so why not?'

The curtains twitch open, and Nicoletta lowers her voice. 'How come Una has the cash?'

The upstairs window lifts up and a woman's torso is framed in the gap, her face slightly obscured. 'What do you want?' The voice is pointed, used to meeting confrontation before it meets her.

'She's a friend of Una's, that's what she said,' Michael calls, taking a run at the bicycle and swinging his leg over the saddle, mounting it like a cowboy. He pedals off down the empty street.

'Una isn't here,' the voice calls. 'What did you say your name was?'

'It's Nicoletta Sarto.' Nicoletta shifts from foot to foot. She's loath to have this conversation out on the street but there doesn't seem to be any alternative. 'I'm a reporter for the *Irish Sentinel*. I'd like to talk to you.'

'A reporter?' The voice sounds muffled. 'What do you need to talk about Una for?'

Nicoletta clamps her bag tightly to her side. 'I'd like to speak to you about Mary.'

The window slams shut. Nicoletta waits anyway. After

a few minutes, the front door opens a cautious couple of inches.

The voice from upstairs belongs to a tall, thin woman with dark hair tightly coiled at the nape of her neck. She's wearing a blue padded-satin housecoat, and her feet are bare.

'What do you want?' Her voice is hoarse now, though still needle sharp.

Nicoletta casts a quick glance over her shoulder. There's no one around.

'It's about what happened to Mary, Mrs Little. I want to help.'

Mrs Little scrunches her toes against the lino behind the threshold. She yanks the door towards her chest like a shield. 'You want to help us, do you? Well, go on, so. Knock yourself out.' She folds her arms tightly.

Nicoletta senses they are being watched. Out of the corner of her eye she sees Michael doubling back in circuits on his bicycle. He's within earshot. Mrs Little's eyes are dark blue, almost purple, ringed with smudged circles. 'Mrs Little, I know that Mary died, I'm so sorry. It was when she was working for the Creightons, I believe. The Guards found a baby's body buried in their garden today. Did Mary have a baby?'

Mrs Little takes a sharp breath. Michael is still circling the street in tight loops. He doesn't give any indication whether he's heard.

A man steps forward into the hallway, edging Mrs Little out of the way. Nicoletta didn't hear footsteps and assumes he was there the whole time. He's at least a head shorter than his wife. Nicoletta remembers Una saying that she and Mary suited the name Little. They must've taken after their father in this regard. He reaches an arm up the doorframe in an attempt to take up as much space as possible. His arms are grizzled with fine dark hairs. Nicoletta doesn't budge.

'Mr Little, I'd like to ask you about Mary.'

He takes a moment to consider this, looking Nicoletta up and down and turning away quickly.

He raises his voice. 'Michael, get in here.' He takes a step towards Nicoletta. His breath is sour, like stale milk. 'Get the fuck away from my house.'

Nicoletta can feel the fear rise in her chest. She's about to step back when she feels a hand on her breastbone, pushing her. She stumbles back, losing her balance, and turns awkwardly on her ankle. When she staggers to her feet, Mrs Little has brought Michael inside and it's just Mr Little leaning against the doorframe in that same languid way, the way a much taller man might.

'You've no right to lay a hand on me. I should call the Guards,' Nicoletta says, biting her lip and turning to go.

A vein throbs in Mr Little's temple. 'A good ride would be just the thing to sort you out.'

Nicoletta is trying to think of something to say when he kicks the door shut. She can hear raised voices beyond and she's helpless to do anything. She limps to the gate and back onto Seaview Terrace, every window on the other side of the street squinting at her. Tears smart her eyes. She swipes at her face, self-conscious. She gets to the top of the road and stops just inside the concrete wall, where she'd

151

originally met O'Connor. She's shaking. Whether it's with shock or rage, she's not sure. She sits down on the pavement, suddenly not caring who sees her. She dips her head between her knees. She hasn't felt like this since before the ECT. She closes her eyes. Her memory of that time is hazy, but she can see herself as she was, barely sentient, scant flashes of light across her vision, people's voices drifting in and out with the hum of a crackling radio. She takes deep breaths and counts, the way Dr Jennings had shown her, waiting for the seconds to pass. She'd thought these turns had gone away. She knows she'll never be the same person she was before: before Enzo died, before the ECT. It feels like a foreign country to her now, and she's travelled too far to go back.

'Need a hand up?' The sound of an engine running nearby, and a kind voice, comes into focus.

She opens her eyes. It's O'Connor. She smiles weakly. He pulls her to her feet, concern on his face.

'Jesus, you're shaking. Get in.'

She nods as the tears scald her cheeks. He opens the passenger door for her and she slides in, grateful to be out of public view.

'Need a lift home?'

Nicoletta sinks into the seat and the engine growls to life. O'Connor reverses onto the terrace, coming back around to the coast road.

After a few minutes, she says, 'Actually, could you stop here? Just for a minute? I want to talk to you.'

O'Connor gives her a quizzical sideways glance but stops the car at the outdoor public baths at Blackrock. They sit for a moment in silence, taking in the lone figure in the water – a young man, head bowed in concentration – resolutely swimming lengths. Nicoletta feels cold just looking at him. She's counted length number nine before she speaks.

'You've got to look into what happened with Mary Little's baby. Her parents won't talk about it at all.'

O'Connor looks straight ahead at the lone swimmer. 'I'll certainly relay what you've told me to the station and hopefully I can get Una Little to make a statement. But between you and me, Morris has pretty much decided the baby was Julia Bridges'. And once he gets something into his head . . .' He sighs.

Nicoletta digs into her bag. 'Couldn't be. There's no way Julia Bridges had a baby without anyone knowing. She was an actress; people would've noticed her being at an advanced stage of pregnancy. And that baby wasn't a skeleton. Which means he or she died more recently than Julia Bridges.' She pauses. 'A lot more recently.'

'How'd you know that?' O'Connor starts and turns to look at her.

She shrugs, tearing a page from her notebook, scribbling down the Littles' names and address at Seaview Terrace.

O'Connor extracts his own notebook from his pocket and folds the page carefully inside. 'I'll look into it.'

The light is changing, the sky darkening quickly. They sit in silence for a minute.

She swallows a pocket of air. 'I've never acknowledged what you did for me. But you saved my life. Thank you.'

He continues looking straight ahead. 'I did what anyone would do in that situation.'

'And you never asked me any questions I didn't want to answer. I appreciate that.'

He swallows. 'It's none of my business.'

A knot of pressure in her stomach bursts like a balloon. She gives a strangulated laugh. O'Connor passes her a clean hanky. She scrubs at her eyes, then takes a compact from her bag and checks her face. Her real eyebrows without the heavy pencil are curved and blonde, the way Enzo's had been. An image flashes into her head: Enzo's perfectly smooth features, peacefully sleeping for eternity. A wisp of the Italian lullaby her mother had sung to him surfaces in her mind.

Fai la ninna,
fai la nanna,
ninna oh, ninna oh,
Lo darmemo alla Befana . . .

Her mother's voice, singing him to sleep, long ago. The tears return, and she redoes her face. They watch night settle, the lone swimmer gone.

'OK now?' Garda O'Connor asks with a gentle cough, breaking the silence.

'Fine.' Nicoletta tilts her chin and gives him a forced smile. The evening chill is falling around them, finding its way through every available gap. O'Connor lets the engine run, switching on the windscreen wipers. 'I'll drop you home,' he says, reversing and turning, the car nosing its way back onto the road. 'Where to?'

Nicoletta hesitates, thinking what would happen if she went home, let the threads of this story hang. What harm? The women's page editor job would go to Anne. Nicoletta would have to return to Fairview and tell her mother the job at the paper hadn't worked out after all. Oh, and by the way, she's pregnant. *No*. The word echoes in her mind, a smothered scream.

She collects her thoughts and smooths her damp turban back into place.

'Actually, Garda, would you mind dropping me to Store Street?'

O'Connor raises an eyebrow but doesn't say anything. When they reach the funny-looking morgue on Store Street, she raises a hand.

'Thank you,' she says, opening the door.

'Look after yourself, Nicoletta,' he says, drumming his fingers on the steering wheel. He waits for her to cross the road, his headlamps shooting arcs of light into the gloom. When she reaches the door, he's gone.

Chapter Fifteen

She tries the door. It's open. Stepping inside, she asks a stern-looking woman at the front desk if she can speak to Dr O'Malley.

'*Professor* O'Malley is busy.' The woman picks up a phone but appears to have no one to speak to. Nicoletta resists the urge to tap her foot. She wanders over to a plastic bucket chair, sits down and waits. After a few minutes she's half thinking of giving up and going home, but a connecting door opens, sending the temperature shooting down. O'Malley stands with his foot wedged in the doorway, a sandwich in one hand, his mouth full. He's wearing exactly the same clothes as on Christmas Eve. Nicoletta notices a patch of dried mud on the hem of one trouser leg.

'Miss Sarto!' A shower of crumbs flies out of his mouth. 'To what do I owe this pleasant surprise?'

Nicoletta hovers, unsure of what to say and positive she doesn't want to state the real reason for her visit in front of this woman, until O'Malley indicates for her to join him on the other side of the door. She gives the woman a smile as she passes the front desk.

O'Malley directs her into a small, untidy office, papers and files covering every available surface. The radio is on low, playing classical piano. It sounds like one of the pieces Raffa used to play. Nicoletta takes a deep breath and counts to five, steeling herself to stay in the present. She smiles as O'Malley swallows the last of his sandwich and eases himself into the chair behind his messy desk.

'I'm trying to put a shape on things before I retire in the new year.' He shrugs. 'I always say a tidy desk is the sign of a disordered mind.'

'You're probably right,' she says with a laugh. 'What's that music, if you don't mind me asking? It's ... nice.'

O'Malley looks pleased. 'It's Chopin's *Nocturnes*. It helps me concentrate.'

Nicoletta swallows a mouthful of air. 'You're probably wondering why I'm here. It's about Julia Bridges.'

'Ah yes.' O'Malley takes a plate holding a slice of apple tart and a dollop of cream out from behind a pile of medical textbooks and whips a spoon out of his breast pocket. 'Would you like some?'

Nicoletta declines, though her stomach rumbles in protest. She waits for him to finish eating. 'Professor O'Malley, can you tell me about the child's bones found in the Creightons' garden? Off the record, if you wish.'

'Ah, the latest discovery.' O'Malley wipes his mouth with the back of his hand. 'The bones belonged to a baby boy, born full-term, though the poor little chap didn't survive beyond a few hours outside the womb, by my estimation. It's a cruel world, my dear.'

'Thank you.' Nicoletta takes out her notebook. 'Is that on or off the record?'

'On, if you like.'

'How did this baby boy die?'

O'Malley chews for a minute, before swallowing. 'Hard to be exact, in this instance. Quite probably natural causes.'

'No signs of foul play?'

'None I could ascertain,' he says, sitting back.

Nicoletta writes everything down, moving across the page in deliberate, methodical lines.

'Does it follow that this baby was Julia Bridges' child?'

O'Malley steeples his fingers and puts his feet up on the desk. 'My examination of Mrs Bridges' skeleton indicates she had never given birth to a full-term baby. So, no, in answer to your question.'

Nicoletta leans forward. 'Was Mrs Bridges pregnant?'

O'Malley takes his feet back down. 'It's really hard to say, after twenty-five years. Mrs Bridges was a skeleton by the time she was found, and any foetus would have fully decomposed as well. Some additional tiny bones were found at the site, which tally with the age of Mrs Bridges' skeleton. But it's difficult to get the full picture because of animal activity. However, as for the latest discovery, those are newer bones with some additional hair and tissue. Those belonged to the baby boy I examined.'

He stops and looks at Nicoletta expectantly. 'Is that what you want to know? The full-term baby the Guards found did not belong to Julia Bridges. I'd stake my reputation on it. Hell, I'd stake my house on it.'

Nicoletta stares back at him contemplatively for a

few moments. The music has stopped, and the radio announcer is speaking in a soothing, quiet voice, almost a whisper. She closes the notebook, putting it back in her bag. 'A maid at Seaview House said her sister, Mary, gave birth to a full-term baby the summer before last. Mary later drowned herself. No one seemed to know she was pregnant or is prepared to talk about it.'

O'Malley lights a cigar and puts his feet on the table, exhaling a cloud of thick smoke. Nicoletta almost gags at the smell. 'That's very unfortunate,' he says, frowning. 'The poor girl.'

Nicoletta flattens her hands on the desk. She's ashamed to see her fingers trembling. 'I think Inspector Morris would like to square off this baby as Julia Bridges'.'

O'Malley stubs out the cigar and, to Nicoletta's relief, opens a window. 'I heard. Unfortunately, it's out of my control now, my dear. I'm gone in two weeks. My job was to look at the evidence before me. That's what I did. I can't help how it got interpreted.'

Nicoletta picks up her handbag. O'Malley rubs his nose with a long, thick finger. 'Actually, that's all off the record. Please don't quote me on any of it, Miss Sarto. It's a tricky one for all concerned.'

Nicoletta inhales the cold air coming through the window. O'Malley reaches over and gives her hand a gentle pat, the way a farmer might a wayward calf. She smiles at him. She likes O'Malley, she decides.

She laughs, despite herself. 'Sometimes my job feels like I'm banging my head against one brick wall after another.'

O'Malley gives her an indulgent smile. 'You're good at

banging it though. Keep doing it. The walls come down eventually.'

'I'm just so sick of lies.' Nicoletta clasps her hands in her lap.

O'Malley smiles conspiratorially. 'The truth always comes out,' he says. 'Sometimes it just takes a bit of time.' He drums his fingers on the desk. 'You can quote me as saying that last bit if you like. Just so you haven't had a wasted journey.' He gives her a wink.

'Thank you for speaking to me so frankly,' Nicoletta says, plucking her notebook out of her bag and scribbling down the quote. She beams at O'Malley. 'I appreciate it.' She picks up her bag again.

'I've enjoyed it immensely.' O'Malley pats his homburg onto the crown of his head. 'I'll see you out. I'm going for a walk.'

He stops at the front door and surveys the dark street like it's a field of beets. 'I hope you'll come in to see me again before I retire.'

'If I can.' Nicoletta can feel the stern woman taking in every word being exchanged.

'And keep doing what you're doing,' O'Malley says, with a tip of his hat. 'Because the dead can't speak. More's the pity.'

Chapter Sixteen

Friday, 27th December 1968

Nicoletta gets to the newspaper office mid-morning. She's determined to keep herself busy over Christmas with this story and take her mind off her own predicament. She'd been horribly wide awake since the pre-dawn, only to fall into a deep sleep after her alarm went off. The newsroom is mostly empty when she arrives. A glow emanates from the copy room. The overhead fluorescent lights sting her eyes, but she continues to busy herself with the Dublin telephone directory, as though nothing is wrong, as though she's carrying out a perfectly mundane task.

She remembers Diane, one of the copytakers whose stint at the *Sentinel* had briefly overlapped with Nicoletta's, mentioning a Mr Morton on Merrion Square. Diane had pointed out one of his ads in the back of the paper – starkly worded, couched in coy generalities, promising cures for 'psychosexual problems'. Diane had made a joke, some euphemism Nicoletta hadn't quite grasped at the time, about him 'having it out as quick as your tonsils. He's pricey, but.' Diane had left shortly afterwards; there had been some sort of scandal, Nicoletta can't quite remember the details. But that throwaway comment stuck with her. She doesn't know exactly what was meant by 'pricey', but she's getting desperate. Her period is five weeks late, and it's always on time. She knows for sure that she can't let anyone see what she's doing.

She flicks through the directory to 'M', finds the address for H. Morton and writes it down. 12A Merrion Square. She doesn't want to phone in advance. Someone might hear her. The sound of a guffaw drifts from the copy room, the clink of a spoon in a cup, someone enjoying his elevenses. She'll go tomorrow, she decides. Not today, not yet.

She replaces the directory back with the others and sits down at her desk, contemplating the day ahead. O'Malley had been adamant that the baby boy wasn't Julia Bridges' child. He'd also told Nicoletta about Gloria Fitzpatrick's suspected suicide at Clyde Hall Asylum. Both sets of information weren't exactly common knowledge. She shuffles through her in-tray and finds the cuttings Barney had obtained for her from the newspaper library. She checks the back of one of the sheets where she'd written the address of Bernadette Brennan, the nurse at the asylum who'd been quoted in Duffy's ten-year-old article about Gloria Fitzpatrick's death. She resolves to try and find her. Maybe today. She thinks about getting up, making a cup of tea and flicking on the radio, then thinks better of it. She looks up with a jolt. Dermot Mahon is towering over her desk, a mug of tea in hand. He slops it down in front of her.

'You're white as a ghost. Were you out last night?' He walks over to the window ledge and switches on the radio. The weather forecast blares out in a meaningless jumble. Nicoletta takes a grateful gulp of the sweet tea.

'Nope.' She takes the scalding mug between both hands and crosses over to stand beside him, looking out over the low smudge of buildings. The river slithers a trail alongside them. 'Nice shirt. How are you not freezing?'

He's wearing a light, teal-coloured shirt today, tucked into brown suit trousers.

'I never stop moving,' he says, taking a brown jacket from the back of his chair and buttoning it. 'Much like yourself. You've been busy.'

Nicoletta nods. 'I have. Been speaking to lots of people.'

'Did you forget about the Bridges' funeral?'

Nicoletta feels a surge of panic rise in the pit of her stomach. 'I didn't think it was for another couple of days. Shit, when is it?'

Dermot turns his attention away from the radio. 'Price was meant to let you know. The funeral's in about ten minutes. He obviously didn't tell you.'

'No.' Nicoletta picks up her handbag. 'He didn't.'

Dermot knocks back his tea as though it's last orders at the pub, setting his mug down too fast beside the radio. He makes a face. 'It's a double burial, as I understand.'

She can feel her cheeks prickle with heat. 'That's ridiculous. There's no way that poor little baby belongs to Julia Bridges.'

Dermot shrugs. 'Ask Duffy.' He's about to walk off when he lowers his voice. 'Listen . . . about what you told me on Christmas Day . . . Maybe you should go home? I'll tell Duffy you have the flu.'

Nicoletta picks up the empty mugs. 'I'm fine,' she says, in a too-bright voice, on her way to the kitchenette off the copy room.

Dermot looks sceptical but turns his attention elsewhere. Time is running out, she thinks, as she strides the couple of feet to Duffy's office. The frosted glass door is closed, so she raps on it lightly, until she hears a gruff voice saying, 'Come in.'

'Nicoletta,' he says, feet on the desk, without looking up. 'What are you doing here?'

'I'm on my way to Julia Bridges' funeral,' she says brightly, loath to draw attention to Price's failure to call her. 'I wanted to confirm it's a double interment?'

'It is, indeed, my love. Do you know where you're going?' Duffy drops his feet to the floor with a neat *clunk*.

Nicoletta takes a step back, her face flushing. 'No, actually.'

'Ah, it's just around the corner.' Duffy puts his arms over his head in a noisy stretch. 'St Kevin's Chapel, around the side of the Pro-Cathedral.'

Nicoletta bites her lip. She'd gone to the Italian Mass at St Kevin's every week for as long as she could remember with her parents, only stopping when Enzo died. 'Right-o,' she says, with a backwards wave. 'See you later.'

'Try and go on to the burial at Glasnevin. And don't get yourself thrown out,' Duffy barks, as she closes the door softly behind her.

Out on the street, it has started to drizzle. On Thomas Lane, Nicoletta holds her bag over her head in a vain attempt at shielding herself from the slanting rain. A large black hearse takes up the whole narrow road, and a Telecom van coming from the opposite direction has to stop and immediately reverse with an indignant squeal of brakes. St Kevin's is a newish-build rectangular chapel to the north of the main cathedral, accessible by what was once a service laneway to the grand Georgian townhouses of Marlborough Street and O'Connell Street.

Nicoletta can see from the hallway that the congregation is comprised of mostly empty pews. As a matter of habit, she sticks a gloved finger in the holy water font and presses it to her forehead. She slips in and takes a seat at the back, shivering. The seven semi-circular windows at ceiling level are dense with condensation. Nicoletta knows there are seven because she'd counted them many times as a child while she'd been bored at Mass. Two closed coffins lie in front of the altar: a modest pine adult-sized casket, beside a tiny white box. The sight greets her like a punch to the solar plexus. She looks away and focuses on steadying her breathing, training her sight on a small knot of people around a slight man, seemingly rubbered with grief, in the top pew, beside the coffins, bookended by a man and woman. The woman is wearing a large black hat, under which is stuffed a lot of gilt-coloured hair. Nicoletta wonders who they are. She presumes the grief-stricken man is Jack Bridges. She hugs herself for warmth. She wonders if she should go, get far away from the white coffin, the cold grief, this bizarre intrusion into these strangers' intimacies.

She could tell Duffy she got thrown out. But she just can't lie. Not anymore. And what would happen to the women's page editor job? It would slip out of Nicoletta's grasp and swim straight into Anne's.

She blesses herself when she sees what everyone else is doing, and stands up. The priest, a large man with a shock of white hair whom Nicoletta doesn't recognise, is wrapping things up, leading the way as Jack Bridges shoulders the little white coffin on his own and carries it quickly, almost sprinting down the short aisle, followed by Graham Swift, the manager from the Athena, who'd been the man sitting beside Jack. Swift takes charge of Julia's casket, carrying it along with three altar boys. Swift meets Nicoletta's eye as he reaches the back of the chapel, and she holds his bloodshot gaze for as long as she can bear before dropping it and reaching for her bag.

Outside, the small knot of people from the church stand miserably in the downpour, waiting as the two coffins are placed side by side in the hearse with grim precision. Swift claps Bridges briefly on the back, before a tall woman in a dark wool coat, whom Nicoletta remembers as Mrs Owens, steps forward and says something to Bridges, leading him away. Swift notices Nicoletta.

'What are you doing here?' His tone isn't friendly, but it seems more resigned than anything else.

'I came to pay my respects.' Nicoletta wipes her face with the back of her hand. She is now fully soaked from the rain.

Swift puffs out his cheeks. 'I saw you slipping in near the end.' His thin moustache quivers with the accusation.

He comes over to stand beside her and takes her by the elbow, awkwardly manoeuvring her towards the wall. He's at least a head taller than she is, and he has a slight stoop, Nicoletta realises now.

'I don't mean any harm.' She disentangles herself from his grasp.

'Do us a favour, will you? Leave Jack alone. He's not in a good way,' he says, leaning down towards her, so that she gets a tang of sour breath.

Nicoletta takes an involuntary step back into the rough granite. 'All right,' she says. 'Poor Jack.'

'Who's this, Graham?' The woman with the big black hat takes his arm in a proprietary way as Nicoletta tries to inch away. Her gilt hair curls out from under the hat, which is topped by black flowers made from the same fabric.

'Just some lady reporter,' Swift tells her. 'Don't worry about it.'

The woman holds out her hand to Nicoletta. She looks vaguely familiar. 'Carole Swift. What are you reporting on this for?' She smiles, revealing a spot of lipstick on her teeth.

Nicoletta is momentarily disarmed. She smiles back, her teeth chattering.

'I'd like to speak to those who knew Julia. Especially those of her friends from the theatre. I believe they were like her family.'

The woman nods. 'I was Julia's understudy,' she says. 'In the summer revue of '43, right before she went missing.' She gives Nicoletta another smile, leaning into earshot somewhat conspiratorially. 'I could tell you a few things.'

Graham's sallow face looks even more pinched as he holds a big black umbrella over their heads. 'It's very sad,' he says. 'But we've nothing more to tell you.'

'I'm not here to intrude,' Nicoletta says. 'I just wanted to speak to Julia's friends, those who knew her best.'

Carole looks at Nicoletta with a slight curve to her lips and winks at her husband. Nicoletta feels as though there's a joke she's not quite in on. Carole nudges Graham. 'Come on, what harm can it do? Look, the girl's freezing.'

Graham frowns resignedly at his wife. Everything about him is thin, Nicoletta thinks. His mouth is a down-turned line, in contrast to his wife's gaiety.

Carole takes Nicoletta's arm in her own. 'We're parked around the corner. You could come with us to the cemetery? We can talk in the car, sure.' She licks her teeth and guides Nicoletta down the narrow lane, as the hearse reverses and makes its slow, final journey towards Glasnevin.

Carole deposits Nicoletta at the passenger side of a red Cortina, indicating for her husband to hop in the back. Nicoletta climbs in, twisting her head, but Graham avoids her eye. The rain has stopped now, just as suddenly as it began. Nicoletta can feel a chill start at the base of her skull. Carole wends her way through a warren of lane-ways until they're in familiar territory, out on O'Connell Street. She's a slow, cautious driver, and they're creeping past the Gresham Hotel when Nicoletta decides it's time to break the strained silence. She doesn't know how long this journey will take, but she probably doesn't have much time.

'So, how long did you know Julia?'

Carole lets out a short breath. The gaiety of earlier has evaporated and Nicoletta senses that she's perhaps regretting letting a reporter into her car. 'A couple of years, that's all. But we were like family, that's for sure. Me and Graham, her and Jack. That right, Graham?' Graham lets out an unintelligible grunt from the back.

'You socialised together, that kind of thing?'

'Yes. In each other's pockets the whole time. Too much, you might say.'

'Oh?' Nicoletta waits for Carole to elaborate on that comment, but she doesn't. The roads are awash with the recent heavy rainfall and water sloshes the car's tyres on either side. The hearse has made more business-like progress through the traffic, and they are part of a very small cortege, so they have now lost sight of it. Carole swears under her breath as the car cuts out. When they're back moving again, she gestures to Nicoletta. 'Pass me a cloth, could you? In the glove box? I can't see a bloody thing.'

Nicoletta extracts a grubby yellow cloth and obliges by rubbing the condensation from the windscreen. 'You knew Julia well, would you say?'

Carole clicks her tongue. 'No, I wouldn't say that,' she says, catching Nicoletta's eyes before looking back at the glimmering expanse of road that stretches ahead. 'I don't think I knew Julia at all. She didn't want people knowing her.'

Nicoletta makes a mental note of the phrase, registering

its peculiarity. She doesn't want to spook this odd pair by making physical notes in front of them. Graham has so far been silent from the back. There's a strange dynamic at play here, she decides.

'Was Julia hiding something?'

Carole clicks her tongue again, but it's Graham who speaks next. 'Ignore my wife,' he says, with an exhale. 'She's upset. We all are.'

'I see,' Nicoletta says. But she doesn't see at all. She turns back to Carole. 'You were Julia's understudy?'

'Yes. From about mid-July of '43. Ju got some kind of flu, we don't know. That's what we were told. But the revue only went on for another couple of weeks after that.' She looks up again, an unexpected little glance at Nicoletta. 'We'd a packed house for those two weeks.' She looks back at her husband. 'Isn't that right, Gray?' There's an edge to her voice as she looks back to Nicoletta. 'Everyone said I just looked the part.'

Nicoletta makes an indeterminate noise in the back of her throat. Carole continues, 'Julia had to wear a blonde wig, you see. I didn't. She didn't have my figure either. Or my voice.' The engine sputters. Carole swears, before coaxing it to continue with a gentle rev.

'Julia was a very fine actress.' Graham speaks gruffly into the back of Nicoletta's head. 'She was taken long before her time. You can quote me on that.'

As they approach the cemetery gates, Nicoletta can see the hearse inching into place beside a huge, marble statue of the archangel Michael slaying a dragon.

'Thank you,' she says, turning to catch sight of Graham

170

eyeing his wife's profile. 'What do you think happened to her?'

Graham sighs, his hand on the door handle. 'That fellow, Owens, went to see Julia every night for a month in the revue. He says he saw Julia entering the house of that Fitzpatrick woman. So . . .' He tails off.

'Did Julia mention a pregnancy?'

'Not to me,' Carole says, looking straight ahead to where a watery sun peeks through the sodden sky.

'Did she mention being afraid of anyone?' Nicoletta asks the question in a rush before Graham can open the door.

'No,' he says shortly. 'Although,' he adds, releasing the door handle, 'Gloria Fitzpatrick went to the summer revue quite a bit that year, now I come to think of it. She was down at heel by then, of course, all the finery gone.'

'Her finery?' Nicoletta echoes lightly, trying to keep him talking.

'Oh, yes. She had money hidden all over the place back in the '30s when she had that swish home for having babies, didn't she, Car? What was it called, The Downings?'

Carole doesn't answer.

Graham gets into his stride now. 'We used to say, if you lifted up the floorboards in that place, you'd find a rake of stockings stuffed with cash. She fancied herself as a patron of the arts at one time. But once she lost her midwifery licence, that was it.' He sits back, pleased with himself.

'Where did she get the money to set herself up at The Downings?'

Graham shrugs. 'Probably from Charles Creighton.

Who knows? If you ask me, probably illegally. Julia used to say anything was possible with that woman.' He frowns, as though not quite believing he's bandied Julia's name around so casually.

'Could Julia have been afraid of Miss Fitzpatrick?' Nicoletta tries to keep her voice level.

'Possibly,' Graham says, taking a cigarette out of his pocket and lighting it without offering the box around. 'She was mad. She used to come and sit in the audience and stare at Charles Creighton. He came to the revue quite a lot that summer, too.' He lets the sentence hang between them.

Nicoletta pounces. 'Was Charles Creighton keen on Julia?'

Carole breaks the trailing conversational thread by clearing her throat. 'Look, I'm sorry we haven't been very helpful,' she says with a rueful slant to her lips. She pats Nicoletta's arm and takes the key out of the ignition, getting out of the car. Graham follows and they walk on ahead, slightly apart, towards the sea of headstones, crosses and religious icons. Nicoletta ducks into a small portico to transcribe their conversation in frantic loops and dashes. It's started to drizzle again by the time she reaches the heaped pile of earth and stones marking the freshly dug grave for Julia Bridges and the baby. Carole and Graham Swift, Jack Bridges and Mrs Owens line the muddied plot, the Swifts flanking Jack, with Graham mostly holding him upright. The priest cuts a solemn figure as he swings incense over the two coffins, lowered into the single grave, fitting neatly together like Russian dolls. As Jack Bridges casts the first clod of earth, a stone hits the tiny white coffin on top, with a hollow thump. Nicoletta wills herself to keep on looking, until she just can't bear it any longer.

Chapter Seventeen

The bus from Glasnevin village is oppressively hot, damp and slow, with not a window open, and by the time it deposits Nicoletta back on O'Connell Street, she's dying for some fresh air. Her chest is so tight it feels close to bursting, her coat clammy and uncomfortable. The short walk to Burgh Quay returns her breath to normal. The newsroom is deserted in the early afternoon lull, and she sits down stiffly at one of the typewriters against the wall, quickly shedding her coat on the back of her chair, wanting now to get this story over with. She pulls her notebook out of her bag and tries to make sense of what just happened. She sits for a minute, staring at the reams of blank copy paper in front of her, waiting to be filled. She starts typing. She doesn't know what she'll do with the strange exchange with Graham and Carole Swift from the car, but she decides to write this as a short colour piece on just the funeral itself. That's all Duffy asked for, after all. When she gets to the end, she tears off the flimsy sheet of paper and looks around for a copy boy. She can see Price shuffling around the back bench, fiddling with the radio aerial, but she doesn't want to talk to him. She wants to see someone she can trust, a friendly face. She thinks about ringing Barney, but what if Marie picks up? She peeks around the copy room door and hands her story over, before scooting back over to the phones. On impulse, she dials the operator.

'Pearse Street Garda Station, please,' she says. When the call goes through, she asks for Garda Peter O'Connor and gives her name. Nicoletta is thinking about hanging up by the time he comes to the phone.

'Hello, Garda,' she says, mustering some cheer into her voice from the depths. 'How are you?'

'Miss Sarto,' O'Connor's voice sounds gruff and faraway, though not surprised. 'To what do I owe this honour?'

Nicoletta flushes despite herself.

'Ah, I was wondering if you're free in the next little while? For a drink maybe.'

A pause crackles through the line and Nicoletta is mortified. He's going to say no.

'All right,' he says. 'See you in Chaplins in a few.'

He rings off before she can either agree or disagree.

She's the first to arrive at Chaplins, a popular pub beside the Imperial Theatre and not too far from the station. She sits down beside a lively fire and waits, taking off her coat, gloves and hat, luxuriating in the warmth.

'What can I get you?' a familiar voice says in her ear.

O'Connor is there, in uniform. He takes off his hat and puts it on the chair beside him. 'A brandy, please,' Nicoletta says. 'It's . . . been a rough day.'

He comes back with a brandy and a cup of tea for

himself, and they sit in silence for a moment. Nicoletta watches the fire dance into the chimney beside them and she can feel herself relaxing for the first time all day.

'So,' O'Connor begins. 'What did you want to talk to me about?'

Nicoletta downs half the brandy before she speaks. 'I wanted to ask you, why is Inspector Morris so adamant it was Gloria Fitzpatrick behind Julia Bridges' disappearance?'

O'Connor rubs the palm of his hand against the top of his head. He's very recently had a tight haircut, and the hair left behind is fine and bristly.

'It's funny you should ask that.' He looks contemplative.

Nicoletta picks up her glass, then puts it down again. 'He was dead wrong about that baby belonging to Julia. So, why should he be right about Gloria's involvement? It doesn't make sense.'

'I was thinking the same thing myself.' O'Connor's face is turning pink from the heat of the fire. 'So, I did a little digging.'

'Oh? What did you find?' Nicoletta crosses and uncrosses her legs. The room is now uncomfortably warm, and she can feel her eyelids growing heavy, but she doesn't want to suggest moving away from the fire.

'I've been working my way through all the witness statements relating to the Bridges file. It was all long before my time. Just trying to get some sort of picture.' He mops his face with a hanky. His eyes on Nicoletta's are the colour of the sea on a clear day. He widens them and shakes his head, putting his hanky back in his pocket. There's something so genuine about him, so honest. Nicoletta takes another sip of her drink. She drums her fingers on the table, idly stretching them into one of the scales Raffa had taught her. She folds her hands back in her lap, snapping back to attention. 'Garda, there's no way that baby should have been buried with Julia Bridges.'

O'Connor looks into her eyes. 'That's as may be,' he says. 'But I'm just telling you what I came across when I went through all the evidence on this file.'

'I see, Garda,' Nicoletta replies, folding her arms.

'In July 1943, three days after Mrs Bridges was reported missing, Inspector Morris – Garda Morris, as he was then – interviewed all the residents of St Bridget's, where Gloria Fitzpatrick lived and worked at the time. As well as all the theatre folk.'

'I see. Can you show me those statements?'

'No.' O'Connor lays his palms flat on the table. 'I'm afraid not. But I can tell you more or less what I'm telling you now.'

'Thank you, Garda.' Nicoletta waits for him to continue.

'Between ourselves, it does seem as though Inspector Morris had the bit between his teeth about Gloria Fitzpatrick. He was the arresting garda when she had that fancy nursing home on Mount Pleasant Square in the '30s, and he made sure she lost her midwifery licence.'

'So I gather.' Nicoletta can feel the sweat trickling down her back. She doesn't want to interrupt O'Connor's flow, but she can't help herself. 'But what made Inspector Morris go after Fitzpatrick again when Julia Bridges was reported missing? She didn't have a midwifery licence anymore. She just worked for Lilian Higgins at St Bridget's. Surely he didn't have any evidence to support her involvement.'

O'Connor sighs. 'Initially, he had what he calls one of his hunches. Once Jack Bridges reported Julia missing, Morris seems to have been utterly convinced Fitzpatrick was behind it all. He raided St Bridget's and took statements from all there.'

'Anything interesting, or a total waste of time, do you think?'

He mops his face again before answering. 'The Guards found an appointment book belonging to Miss Fitzpatrick. A lot of the pages were ripped out, but Morris says that the words "Black Coat" were written on a date in July 1943, and a time, 7pm. A maid who worked there changed her original statement to say she'd let Julia Bridges into the house to see Gloria Fitzpatrick in the early evening, but they didn't consider her particularly reliable – thought she might have had some kind of grievance. It wasn't enough to implicate Fitzpatrick at the time, but Brendan Owens, Jack and Julia Bridges' landlord, later claimed that Julia was wearing a black coat on that date, when he saw her entering St Bridget's at approximately 7pm.'

Nicoletta nods. 'Jack Bridges gave an interview to my editor at the *Sentinel*, appealing for witnesses with any relevant information to come forward. Do you think Brendan Owens was credible?'

'I don't know.' O'Connor rubs his chin and puts his hat back on. 'He was a person of particular interest for a while. Until Morris decided it couldn't have possibly been him.'

Nicoletta sits up. 'Why did Morris decide that?'

O'Connor drains the last drops from his cup. 'He was interviewed on and off, from the summer of 1943 when Julia disappeared, up until spring 1959, when your colleague Mr Duffy ran Jack Bridges' appeal in the *Sentinel*. In all his previous interviews Owens had been unable to account for his whereabouts satisfactorily, but after that piece ran, he trotted into the station, saying that he hadn't wanted anyone to know that he'd followed Julia from her home, as he was too afraid of being thought of as her killer. He was adamant that he saw her entering St Bridget's on that date at that time, wearing a black coat, which corroborated the maid's account. The solid connection to Fitzpatrick was enough for Morris to drop any other suspects.'

'What happened then?' Nicoletta is desperate to keep O'Connor talking for as long as possible, though she can tell he wants to go.

'Morris went to interview Fitzpatrick at the asylum the very next day. However, she died in her sleep that night, and no satisfactory outcome was attained.'

'O'Malley says it was suicide.'

'Yes, I know.' O'Connor looks at his watch. 'My own thinking is that Morris' last interview with Fitzpatrick sent her over the edge, perhaps provoked her into taking her own life. He can be a little . . . dogged in his approach.'

Nicoletta looks down at her hands. 'O'Malley mentioned there were large quantities of medication in her system. How would she have got hold of it unless she had saved her own medication without taking it for weeks in advance? That shows she might've been planning it. And why? Was she protecting someone?'

'Who knows?' O'Connor stands up. 'There's probably no real way of finding out now. No one we can ask.'

Nicoletta holds out her hand and smiles. 'You're wrong there. There's always someone we can ask.'

He takes her hand and shakes it. Something passes between them in the hot, smoky pub. 'You've got tenacity, Miss Sarto. That'll get you far.'

'Thank you, Garda.' Nicoletta takes out her notebook. 'I appreciate you speaking so frankly.'

He quietly leaves her to her own thoughts. After a moment, she puts on her hat and gloves and stands up. She remembers the name and address of the nurse from Clyde Hall, Bernadette Brennan, who'd been quoted in Duffy's long-ago report on Gloria Fitzpatrick's death. Now's the time to go and speak to her. Nicoletta hails a taxi from the quay to Windy Arbour.

It's a quiet, suburban enclave, a stone's throw from the high wall and secure gates of Clyde Hall Criminal Lunatic Asylum in nearby Dundrum. Bernadette Brennan lives in a neat, pebble-dashed house off a small cul-de-sac, where a group of young girls play hopscotch in the road, despite the cold and creeping dusk. Nicoletta wonders if what O'Malley said is true – that this Nurse Brennan was forced to resign from her job after Gloria died – as she considers the hanging baskets covering the bottle-green doorframe. A home-made Christmas wreath adorns the knocker; Nicoletta can see the twisted wire coat hanger beneath its threaded sprigs of holly. A child-sized bicycle lies on its side on the square of lawn and a huge black cat sits washing itself on a windowsill. It eyes her up as she rings the bell, before running over and winding itself around her legs. She likes animals, and they always seem to like her. If only humans were as straightforward. As the door opens a crack, she can hear music, and the din of people talking, the clink of cutlery upon plates. The cat runs through the open door and into the hallway.

'Who have we here?' It's a man's voice, the words sodden with drink. The door opens wider to reveal a short, well-built man of forty-odd, with a full reddish beard. Nicoletta presumes it's Cyril Brennan, the man listed in the phone book, Bernadette's husband. 'You're a bit late for the party.'

'I'm sorry to intrude.' Nicoletta nods towards the noise. 'I'm looking for Mrs Bernadette Brennan.'

'Well, the missus is a bit busy at the moment. We've had twelve here for lunch. We should be rid of them by next Friday.' He laughs, showing a lot of teeth.

Nicoletta politely echoes his laugh and shifts from one leg to the other. She's still perspiring, despite the cold. 'Perhaps I could come back later.'

The man shrugs. 'How did you say you know Bernie?'

'I don't. I'm a reporter from the *Irish Sentinel*. I'd like to ask Mrs Brennan about Gloria Fitzpatrick.'

A child appears, a girl of nine or ten, holding the cat. It struggles in her arms, outraged by the indignity of being picked up. The man looks down, momentarily irritated by this intrusion.

'Mam said to put him out,' the girl says, by way of explanation, dumping the cat on the doorstep and retreating back into the hall. The cat lunges back through the gap, and there's a shriek as the girl goes off in hot pursuit. Nicoletta waits for the man to speak, examining the house's number, painted in royal blue on a ceramic plate. It's almost obscured by ivy.

'Hey, I knew Gloria Fitzpatrick from Clyde Hall too. I'm still an orderly there. Why are you writing about her?'

Nicoletta grips her bag in both hands. 'I believe Miss Fitzpatrick was questioned about Julia Bridges' disappearance up to her last day alive. There've been some recent developments.'

'Ah yes. I heard about that. Read about it in the paper.' The man rubs his beard with his palm.

Nicoletta nods.

He opens the door wider, beckoning her through. 'Listen, we were just about to have dessert.'

'Thank you, Mr Brennan.'

'Call me Cyril,' he says, leading her past a Christmas tree in the hall and into the kitchen, a light-filled room that looks onto another patch of neat lawn scattered with children's toys. He indicates for her to take a seat. She pulls out a chair from a small circular wooden table and sits, taking off her gloves and stuffing them into her bag.

Cyril Brennan busies himself at the sink, rinsing something, drying it, before deciding to dump whatever it is back into the basin. He comes back and sits beside Nicoletta, almost toppling his chair sideways. He's drunker than she'd realised. This could go one of two ways, she thinks, chancing it and taking out her notebook.

'I'm in charge of dessert,' he says. 'Meant to be, anyway. That lot are so pissed by now, I'm sure they won't notice.'

'What did you make?' Nicoletta crosses her arms. The kitchen is chilly and she's glad she's kept her coat on.

Cyril takes a cigarette out of his pocket and lights it, letting it trail between his fingers for a while before taking an absent-minded drag. 'Oh, didn't make a thing. Bought a Tea Time Express coffee cake. But the bloody cat got at it. So now it's in the bin.'

'I see.' Nicoletta can hear her tummy rumbling. She'd murder a slice of cake. A chorus of laughter breaks out from a nearby room, and she figures she doesn't have much time before someone is dispatched to find Cyril and the cake. She decides to dive straight in.

'How long have you worked at Clyde Hall, Mr Brennan?'

He considers the question with a lazy roll of his chin. 'About fifteen years. My wife worked there for a while, but she left just before our daughter was born. Ten years ago, or thereabouts.'

'So, you were working there in the spring of 1959, when Gloria Fitzpatrick was a patient?'

Cyril narrows his eyes, which are slightly bloodshot at the corners.

'Yeah, I knew Gloria then. Inasmuch as anyone did. Bernie knew her better though. Gloria was sort of her pet.'

'Her pet? What do you mean by that?'

Cyril stubs out his cigarette and reaches for a new one from the packet in his pocket. 'Want one?'

Nicoletta shakes her head. She can hear what sounds like someone collecting the dirty dishes in the other room. They'll be on their way in here soon. 'What would you say your wife's relationship with Miss Fitzpatrick was like?'

'Oh, the best of chums.' Cyril waves his hand, letting it fall on the table between them. 'Gloria followed Bernie everywhere, wouldn't let the other patients get a look-in. My wife, bless her cotton socks, has a heart of gold, but she could do with a lower tolerance for fools. She felt sorry for Gloria, used to give her bottles of stout in the evenings. That got her into trouble with Fleming, the matron, to say the least.'

Nicoletta's pen flies over the page, and she turns it over, almost ripping the notebook at the spine. She can hear chairs being pushed back as the child exclaims that the cat has been sick. A spate of high-pitched wailing ensues, followed by the sound of a woman's voice making soothing, cajoling noises.

'Do you think Gloria was dangerous?'

Cyril laughs and smoke comes out of his nose. He coughs and runs his hand through his longish, untidy hair. 'No. She was a bit of a wagon, if you ask me – prone to the odd outburst. Bernie always used to say she was harmless though. Personally, I never felt afraid of her.'

His hand, which had been resting on the table between them, idly picks up Nicoletta's notebook and scans the page. He frowns and drops it into her lap, standing up.

'Where was this Julia Bridges woman found? It just said

in a Dublin garden in the paper. Didn't give specifics. I've been wondering. And do the cops still think Gloria did it?'

Nicoletta hesitates. 'Two skeletons were found in recent days, in a garden. The remains are believed to belong to Julia Bridges and a baby. Gloria Fitzpatrick was widely believed to have been responsible for Mrs Bridges' disappearance, but the Guards are still investigating every available lead.'

Cyril wrinkles his forehead. 'Open and shut if you ask me. No need for any investigation. Gloria was already a convicted murderer, for Christ's sake.'

'Is that right?' Nicoletta murmurs. She's starting to get jittery. 'I should get going. Could you tell your wife I called?'

Cyril glances over her shoulder and laughs. 'My wife will kill me if she finds out I've been talking to you. She hates me talking to anyone better-looking than her.'

Nicoletta shoves her notebook into her bag and stands up, her cheeks burning. Cyril holds up his hands. The index and middle finger on his right hand are tarred yellow. 'Look, it seems to me you've been sent out on a bit of a fool's errand. I think it's rotten luck that they've sent you out over Christmas to boot. But you seem like a nice girl ...'

He seems to hover, unable to leave the room. Nicoletta holds her breath. The child's wailing has slowed down to intermittent whimpers.

'It is a bit rotten, I suppose,' Nicoletta says with a forced laugh. 'No harm in trying, all the same, though I knew there'd be nothing new to find out. As you said, it's open and shut, and, besides, it was all such a long time ago. No one could possibly remember anything by now.'

Cyril hesitates. 'Bernie's the best person to ask, memory of an elephant. Maybe come back another time?'

'All right.' Nicoletta closes her notebook and smiles. 'Sad the way none of Gloria's relatives came to claim her body, isn't it?'

Cyril snorts. 'Good enough for her.'

'What happened to all her personal effects?' Nicoletta can't stop herself asking.

'Oh, she didn't have anything of value by then, if that's what you're asking,' he says. 'It was divided up among the patients, every last bottle of shampoo and kirby grip. There was some cheap jewellery. Her knitting.' He laughs and gives her a sly sideways glance. 'And an envelope.'

'What was in the envelope?' Nicoletta's scalp prickles with static but she tries to remain nonchalant.

Cyril gives a hoarse laugh. 'Don't know. The solicitor, that White fellow, took it away. It was addressed to him.'

'What's his full name?'

'A woman's name. But he's not a woman ... Leslie, that's it. Anyway, Bernie swore me to secrecy. But seeing as you've had this wild goose chase for no reason, it's not going to do any harm.'

He beckons Nicoletta to lean forward. 'You know, Gloria once told Bernie she'd had a child. But then, she told a lot of tall tales – she was an awful liar, really.'

Nicoletta clutches her handbag tightly. 'Why are you telling me this?'

Cyril laughs. 'I've always thought it'd be a good angle if someone found Gloria's child. What would he or she think, having a killer for a mother? Especially now that whatsername, the actress, has been found. There's your story,' he says, pleased with himself.

'If this child exists,' Nicoletta says sharply.

Cyril shrugs as a blonde, delicate-featured woman comes through the door, leading the little girl by the hand.

'Cyril!' She sits the child down in one of the kitchen chairs and fetches her a glass of milk. 'What's going on? I came to get the cake.' She looks to Nicoletta, who opens her mouth to speak, but Cyril cuts her off.

'This lady knocked on the door. She was lost. I gave her directions, is all.'

Nicoletta turns, hand outstretched. 'Nicoletta Sarto, Mrs Brennan. I'm a reporter for the *Irish Sentinel*. I'm writing a story about Gloria Fitzpatrick.'

Mrs Brennan's face drains of colour. She opens her mouth to speak, but the little girl asks about the cake. Cyril explains that the cat ate it, setting the child off crying again.

Nicoletta nods and mouths her goodbyes as Cyril turns to face his wife. By the time she reaches the front door, she can tell they are already in the throes of a humdinger of a row.

Chapter Eighteen

Nicoletta walks for a while, in the opposite direction from which she'd come, as the afternoon dissolves into a mist of drizzle, until she comes to the asylum's high stone wall, topped by barbed wire. It goes on for half a mile. The gate, black and forbidding-looking, is manned by a security guard, seated in a small hut, leafing through a newspaper. He doesn't stop to notice her or wonder why she's there.

She hails a passing bus heading for Baggot Street Bridge. The rain has stopped by the time she ducks into a pub to gather her thoughts and use their phone book. Leslie White doesn't live too far away, in Ballsbridge. She decides to walk, the streets becoming wider and leafier at Pembroke Road. Leslie White's house is a sprawling, modern red-brick, set back from the road. Though the name on the gate says Magpie Cottage, it's as far away as it could be from Nicoletta's idea of a traditional cottage. Dozens of magpies and rooks circle the chimney stacks on the large steepled roof, calling to each other with glee. There's no doorbell she can see, so she gives a brisk knock. Several seconds pass, a door bangs and a woman's voice calls something to an invisible presence within. The door is opened by a tall man, stooped at the shoulders, dressed to go out in a three-piece suit, an overcoat and a hat. They're all far too large for him and the effect is that of a boy playing dress-up. The man carries a large umbrella with an insurance company logo on it. When he puts it down, Nicoletta is surprised to see sunken cheeks and papery skin. He looks almost as surprised to see Nicoletta.

'You're not our taxi, by any chance, are you?'

'I'm afraid not. Are you Mr White?'

The man laughs, which turns into a cough. 'I am. Please don't be offended. I had to ask. Can't assume these days that a woman can't or won't drive a taxi.' He looks at her quizzically from under the brim of his hat. 'Who's looking for Mr White, anyhow?'

Nicoletta talks fast. 'Nicoletta Sarto. I'm a reporter for the *Sentinel*. I'd like to speak to you about Gloria Fitzpatrick.'

White leans into the doorframe as though the effort of standing upright is making him tired. 'I haven't heard that name in a long time. I'd ask what she's done now, but she's dead. God love her, and all that.'

White shuts the door gently behind him and joins Nicoletta on the front step. 'A bit late in the day to be writing about poor old Gloria, I would've thought. Nothing left to say.'

Nicoletta catches his eye. They're about level in height, his eyes muddily bloodshot in the greyish midwinter light. They seem to take everything in, yet give little away.

'The body of Julia Bridges was recovered on Christmas Eve, along with the remains of a baby, as I'm sure you've heard by now. I believe Miss Fitzpatrick was questioned about Mrs Bridges' disappearance up to the last day of her own life. Can you tell me about that? Off the record if you'd prefer.'

White coughs into a handkerchief. 'I wasn't present for that last interview. Miss Fitzpatrick and I had parted company by then. After the trial, she said she never wanted to see me again.' He looks her up and down. 'Off the record, of course.'

Nicoletta pauses. 'I wondered if you'd have any comment to make on the record about Julia Bridges' remains being found on Christmas Eve in a suburban garden?'

White shakes his head. 'Look, as you might've guessed, this isn't an ideal time, Miss Sarto. My office is closed. My wife and I are on our way now to catch the last few races at Leopardstown.'

A car backs into the short driveway and the driver gives one long beep of the horn, followed by two short beeps. White waves at him.

Nicoletta acts fast.

'What was in the envelope Gloria left for you?'

White looks her up and down again. Nicoletta realises she may as well play the possible ace in her hand.

'I know Gloria committed suicide in the asylum. And I know about her child.' The second bluff seems as loud as a shout. Just then, a woman opens the door and shuts it firmly behind her. She's all dressed up in a pink two-piece suit, a matching hat pinned to the back of her head, cream gloves and handbag clasped in one hand. Nicoletta guesses that Mrs White is an admirer of Jacqueline Kennedy.

'Leslie!' She looks from White to Nicoletta, with something bordering on distaste. 'We don't have time for this. Our lift's here.'

Whatever she means by 'this' is obviously a fairly commonplace occurrence in the White household. Nicoletta keeps her shoulders straight, as Mrs White gives her one last impatient look, before stepping neatly into the back of the taxi. She calls back to her husband. 'If you're not in this car in three minutes, I'm leaving without you. We're late enough as it is.'

White leans on his umbrella. 'I have no idea what you're talking about, Miss Sarto.'

Nicoletta rocks back on her heels. 'Miss Fitzpatrick left a letter among her personal effects. And you took it. Where is it, Mr White?'

White takes a long look at Nicoletta before turning his face into the wind. 'I'm sorry, Miss Sarto. My illness makes me boiling hot.' He wipes his face with a hanky. 'Gerard didn't want it.' He starts walking towards the car.

'Who's Gerard?' Nicoletta calls after him.

He pauses, wetting his thin upper lip. 'Look, I've said too much. Gerard was, or is, Miss Fitzpatrick's elder brother. Miss Sarto, off the record, if indeed any of this is true, and if indeed Gloria had a child, why stir up grief for that child now, after all that's happened?'

Nicoletta trots after him. 'Mr White, wait! Can I come and speak to you in the new year when you're back in your office?' After a moment, he comes back over to her, hands clasped in front of him.

'Miss Sarto, I'm dying. I may not live to see the new

year. Blasted stomach cancer. The only thing I can do is hope for the best. As for this article you're writing, all I can say is that Miss Fitzpatrick always denied liability for Mrs Bridges' death, though I was not present on the last day of Gloria's life when the Gardaí re-interviewed her.'

'Didn't the Guards dig up the garden at St Bridget's after that interview?'

White looks as though he's just swallowed something rotten. 'I believe so, Miss Sarto. And found dozens of babies' skulls, if erroneous reports in your newspaper were to be believed.' The car horn beeps again and White closes his eyes, as though the sound causes him acute discomfort. 'Glory paid to ashes comes too late. The Latin escapes me, but the words may be worth keeping in mind, Miss Sarto.'

Chapter Nineteen

Saturday, 28th December 1968

Nicoletta examines the flesh around her midriff, pressing her hands into the skin, sure she can sense the first signs of life, that she's passed the point of no return. She's memorised Henry Morton's address. Is today the day?

She rushes to the hall and perches at the edge of the tiny table on which the telephone sits, its silence cavernous. She snatches up the receiver and dials Barney's number. She taps her foot while the call connects. She needs to hear his voice. A woman answers, her voice unfamiliar, and yet Nicoletta knows at once it must be Marie. 'Hello?' she says. 'Who's there?' The words are sibilant with sleep.

'Who was that?' Nicoletta can hear Barney's voice nearby, a creak as he stands up. Are they in bed together? Her hand starts shaking as she grips the receiver to her ear. Finally, she drops it back into its cradle. She sits for a moment, her heart ticking like a clock. So that's how it is. She walks into the sitting room, remembering the last time Barney had been here, in early November. Jean had been away somewhere for the weekend and Barney had been meant to stay for two whole nights. Nicoletta had made lasagne, the only Italian dish she knew, soaking the pasta sheets overnight in preparation, simmering the ragu for hours, filling the tiny flat with smells of home. When Barney arrived after finishing a late shift at the newspaper, they'd eaten by candlelight at the tiny table at the edge of the kitchenette. The next morning, they made love in Nicoletta's bed, high up under the eaves, the rain drumming on the roof close to their heads. Afterwards, they'd been in no hurry to disentangle themselves from each other. Barney propped himself up on his elbow and smiled, the smile taking over his whole face, the way it did when he was about to suggest something unexpected: 'Let's go to the beach; let's go to the pictures; let's take Liam to fly a kite!'

Nicoletta hadn't known what he was about to say. 'I'm sick of this,' he'd said eventually, gesturing at the unmade bed. She hadn't known what to think.

'No, no,' he'd said, lacing his fingers with hers in reassurance. 'I mean, I'm sick of all the cloak and dagger stuff. Marie's gone. Let's make it official.'

Nicoletta had drawn her knees up to her chest and covered them with the quilt. 'Why? Everyone knows. Dublin's a small place. Let's just leave it.'

Barney's face had fallen. Nicoletta bit her lip. Not only would everyone at work know her business, they'd feel free to make their own unadulterated judgements to her and about her. The thought made her feel sick. This was the new life that she'd fought so hard for.

'No,' she'd said, shaking her head with a vigour that dislodged the quilt. 'I like things the way they are for now. I need more time. Please.'

Barney had wordlessly slid his trousers on, buckling the belt with icy precision. 'If that's what you want,' he'd said, walking out of the flat.

He'd avoided her at work after that, stung by the perceived rejection, and she hadn't gone after him. Those days were over, she'd reasoned with herself. She wasn't about to chase after anyone. At the end of November, she'd started to suspect she was pregnant. She'd spent the first two weeks of December waiting for her period to start, and she'd been about to tell Barney when Marie had shown up. She's afraid now she's left it too late, and Barney is back with Marie. When all she'd wanted was a bit more time.

She dresses quickly, putting on the skirt suit with the crossed fox-fur trim, matching it with her block-heeled suede shoes. She paints on her eyebrows and gouges heavy circles of kohl around her eyes, brushing stripes of blush onto her cheekbones to liven up the ashen face underneath. When she's finished, she stands in front of the small bathroom mirror, regarding herself with grim satisfaction. They don't call it war paint for nothing. She fastens a single piece of jewellery, the gold watch that her parents had given her for her twenty-first birthday, wondering what its absence will feel like. Will she even notice it?

Frost clouds the windshields of the cars parked in higgledy-piggledy rows as far as the eye can see around the Mater Hospital. It's bright with signs of activity. People don't stop getting sick just because it's Christmas. There are people inside, lying prone on neatly made beds, much worse off than she is. She should stop feeling sorry for herself, she knows that. She keeps walking, her bag clamped to her shoulder. She doesn't know how much to expect of Henry Morton's fee; Diane the former copytaker had simply said he was 'pricey'.

The pawn shop on Marlborough Street is open, as she suspected. Christmas is a busy time for these places. Emotions run high; debts are incurred. And debts must be paid. Everyone knows that.

The bell chimes when she walks in. She's pleased to see that she's the only customer. A man in shirt sleeves and braces, standing over a newspaper and a steaming tin mug, looks up from behind the counter and smiles, as though he's not surprised to see her at all. He's seen all types, the smile assures her, all classes and creeds. Everyone is desperate at one time or another.

'Good morning,' he says, taking a hearty gulp from his mug, closing the newspaper. 'What can I do for you?'

Nicoletta stiffens. But it's too late to change her mind. She wrenches the watch off her wrist and presents it on the counter, like a piece of meat ready to be weighed. Trays of watches, bangles and rings are visible under the glass.

'How much?' It comes out in a whisper. The man whips the watch into his hands and turns it over, murmuring. He puts on what looks like a tiny set of glasses while he inspects it without saying a word. Finally, he picks up his mug of tea.

'I'll give you £35.'

Nicoletta pretends to consider this for a moment, before giving a tiny nod. The man runs her up a ticket.

'Oh, your money,' he says, thumbing a series of notes from the till and writing the transaction down in a leather-bound ledger. He holds out the money in his palm and Nicoletta snatches it, shoving it into her bag, along with the ticket. She's vaguely aware of the man taking an obscenely loud gulp from his mug as she flees the shop and continues to her destination.

She walks the perimeter of Merrion Square twice before she notices the laneway she's looking for. There's barely any traffic on a day like today, sandwiched in the no-man's-land between Christmas and New Year. A few of the grand houses on the square have remained complete private residences, and through these ground floor windows, Nicoletta glimpses perfectly symmetrical Christmas trees, plump with pine needles. She's reminded of the casual picture-book festivity of the tree in the drawing room at Seaview House, when she and Barney had spoken to Charles Creighton.

A small brass plaque announces the rooms of H. Morton. She rings a bell and waits. After an interminable minute, a woman opens the door. She is very tall and thin, her hair framed in a blunt bob. Nicoletta can't decide whether or not her clothes – black trousers and a fitted black tunic – are some kind of uniform. Glancing at the woman's feet and her red embroidered Chinese slippers, instead of regulation white nursing shoes, she doubts it. Perhaps sensing her uncertainty, the woman smiles, and Nicoletta can't help but smile back.

'Welcome,' the woman says. 'Do you have an appointment?'

'No, I don't ... should I come back another time?'

The woman opens the door wide and indicates for Nicoletta to follow her into what appears to be a small waiting area, crowded with a leather couch scattered with tassled red cushions. The air is ripe with the scent of something musky, and Nicoletta realises that a freshly lit joss stick is burning away on the low coffee table in front of her. There's a gramophone on top of a high wooden counter running the length of the room; when Nicoletta looks closer, she sees that it's actually a wood-panelled shelving unit, with hundreds of books, their spines facing out. *Memories, Dreams, Reflections*, by Carl Jung, says one, in raised, blocky type. She runs her finger lightly over it and gazes at the rest. She wonders if H. Morton has read all of these. This is a place of learning, of skill. She was right to come here. The music from the gramophone is Indian-sounding, lyricless and repetitive, with a sitar or some other instrument. She can feel herself relax slightly. She turns back to the woman, who has been watching her. She gives Nicoletta a neat smile, before leaving through another door and coming back holding a clipboard with several sheets of paper secured to it.

'I am Mrs Morton,' she says, resting her lithe frame on the couch and crossing one slippered foot over the other. 'But you can call me Silke.' Nicoletta nods. Now that Mrs Morton has said her first name, she can detect a trace of a non-Irish accent in the hard way she pronounces her consonants.

'I need to take some information from you, and then we can see whether or not my husband can help you today.'

Nicoletta sits diagonally opposite Silke, the smell of the joss stick and the warmth of the room starting to send her to sleep. Silke turns over the page and puts down the clipboard. She clasps her hands in her lap. 'My husband deals mainly with psychological, nervous or sexual troubles,' she explains, giving Nicoletta a long look. 'But he takes a holistic approach, as I'm sure you're aware.'

Nicoletta nods, not sure she understands. 'What kind of approach do you take, Silke?' She sounds bolder than she feels.

If Silke is surprised by the question, she doesn't show it. 'What's your name, dear?'

Nicoletta hesitates. She clears her throat. 'Mary Clarke,' she says, finally.

Silke takes up the clipboard again and duly writes down the name Nicoletta has given with a newly sharpened pencil.

'Age?'

'Twenty-six.'

'And tell me, dear, are you married?'

Nicoletta shakes her head. 'No,' she says, making a meal over such a simple word, one she's said thousands of times before.

'And what appears to be troubling you, Mary?'

Nicoletta licks her top lip, but it immediately feels dry as paper. 'I'm going through some ... family stuff,' she says carefully.

'I see.' Silke puts the pencil and clipboard down and sits back. 'What kind of family stuff?'

Nicoletta can feel her scalp prickle from the overwhelming heat, the cloying smell of the joss stick, the unfamiliar music and the scrutiny of this woman. She just wants to breathe.

'I think I might be pregnant.' She exhales through the pit of her stomach. 'And I'm not sure what to do.'

'I see.' Silke swipes at an imaginary speck of dust on her trouser leg. 'What would you like to do?'

'I don't know.'

'You haven't told your boyfriend?' Silke scribbles something down on the second sheet and quickly covers it over with the first.

Nicoletta doesn't say anything. A tear finds its way down her cheek and lands on the shiny surface of the couch. Silke blinks. Eventually, Nicoletta shakes her head. 'I haven't told him, no.'

Silke stands up, clasping the clipboard under her arm. 'Right,' she says, restoring the cheery manner of earlier. 'I'll fetch you a glass of water. Then I'm going to consult with my husband, and we'll be with you shortly.'

After about ten minutes, Nicoletta rouses herself and considers walking out. She doesn't owe these people anything. They don't even have her real name. Yet something – maybe it's simple exhaustion – compels her to stay rooted in her seat, until the door opens and Silke comes out accompanied by a slight, dark-haired man with a brush moustache, flecked with grey. He nods at his wife, who melts into the background.

'Miss Clarke,' he says. 'I am Henry Morton. You're very welcome.'

He indicates for her to follow him back into the room and she shuts the door behind her while he takes a seat at a small rolltop desk. This consulting room is like the waiting area in that one wall is panelled floor-to-ceiling with books, but there's no colourful furniture, no musky scent of burning joss sticks. Instead, a stainless-steel examination table complete with medical equipment resembling medieval torture devices flanks the other wall, beside a huge X-ray machine on wheels. She shivers. The ECT machine she'd been connected to had looked similar, with a bewildering number of wires zigzagging in and out of it. She'd always been healthy, with not much need for doctors, until she'd been admitted to St Teresa of Ávila's Hospital on a beautiful day in May, the ruler-straight driveway scattered with a confetti of pink cherry blossom. Daniela and Ettore had plundered their savings so that Nicoletta had her own room. She didn't plan on staying long. Her parents were hopeful that this new hospital with its small wards, acres of gleaming tiles and manicured lawns would be just the place to promote what Dr Jennings called a 'good rest'. The day she got the ECT marked a dividing line in her adult life. As though everything had been building up to that point. Some of the procedure itself is a blur, of mismatched memories and half-formed perceptions, until the side effects wore off. But when Dr Jennings put the protective mouthguard in place and the first jolt was administered, Nicoletta had a moment of blinding clarity, like a forked flash of lightning illuminating her brain. This was the moment that would change her path. Enzo's existence had not been in vain. She'd made a mental note to tell

Dr Jennings about her epiphany. Now Nicoletta wonders what Dr Jennings would say if he knew that lightning really does strike twice.

An armchair is set up opposite Mr Morton's desk. He points at it without looking up from his notes.

'Please,' he says. 'Let's get started. There's nothing to fear in this room, I can assure you.'

'Oh, I'm not afraid.' She sits on the edge of the armchair and waits for him to finish reading whatever it is he has in front of him. Eventually, he looks up, seeming to see her for the first time. There are dark smudges under his eyes.

'Have you really read all these books?' Nicoletta sits with her handbag on her lap, aware of the vast sum of money inside.

He laughs, an unexpected sound in this hushed little room. It has the high Georgian ceilings synonymous with the rest of the square, but it looks as though it's part of a subdivision, Nicoletta notices. This diminishes its initial grandeur. The sudden mirth animates his thin face. 'I'd say so, Miss Clarke, wouldn't you? They are the tools of my trade.'

She nods, eager to cut to the chase. 'And what is it, exactly, your trade?'

He laughs again, though not as raucously as the first time. 'I'm a psychoanalyst, Miss Clarke. I specialise in the mind. Troubles of the psyche. Tell me, what's troubling you?'

Nicoletta touches her wrist. She'd never much cared for the watch her parents had given her, but she feels its absence as acutely as the loss of a front tooth.

'What about the body?' She indicates the examination

table and the X-ray machine. 'Surely you can't X-ray minds as well?'

He cups his mouth, sighing.

'We take a holistic approach. The body affects the mind, and vice versa. One can't exist without the other.'

'How much?' Nicoletta says, gripping her handbag. 'What will it cost for you to cut the bullshit?'

Morton pales visibly and gives her a faint smile. 'No need for language, Miss Clarke. We'll proceed in due course.'

He taps his pen against the sheets already filled in by Silke in the waiting room.

'I believe you're here to allay some concerns over relationship trouble.'

Nicoletta sighs but relaxes her grip on her bag slightly. 'Yes, I suppose so.'

'Date of last menstrual period?'

'I think it was around the end of October. Halloween.'

He writes something down. There's a knock on the door and Silke reappears.

'My wife is now going to take your measurements in weight and height.'

Silke locates a scale under the examination table and gestures for Nicoletta to get up onto it. She's about to take her handbag with her, until the other woman gently wrenches it out of her hands and sets it on the floor beside her. She allows Nicoletta to keep her shoes on, slipping a tape measure out of her pocket and mouthing the results to Morton, who writes everything down.

'Now, Miss Clarke,' he says, getting up from his chair.

'We're going to X-ray your abdomen, to see if there's anything out of the ordinary which we should be aware of. It's standard practice for all our clients at the initial consultation.'

Nicoletta pauses for a moment. She sees her future with Barney, their sleek modern house on one of the new estates, a child at their feet, vanish before her eyes. She steps in front of the machine. This Mr Morton knows what he's doing. She waits while Silke draws down the blinds and flicks off the light switches. She closes her eyes in anticipation, but there's no light that she can see. Morton wheels the machine back against the wall.

'Excellent,' he says, motioning for his wife to pull the blinds back the way they were. 'I'm off downstairs to develop these plates now. I'll be back shortly.'

Silke accompanies him out of the room and Nicoletta is directed back to the too-comfortable armchair, from where she tries to read the spine of each book within her line of sight, until her eyes start to swim.

Silke comes back after a couple of minutes with a cup of tea and some biscuits on a saucer. 'He won't be much longer,' she says, waving at her husband's empty seat. Nicoletta knows the words are meant to reassure, but they manage to do the opposite. Once again, she feels like getting up and walking out. However, Morton is back before she can muster the will to stand up. If he notices the untouched tea, he doesn't comment.

'All right, Miss Clarke,' he says, making a note of something in front of him. She couldn't summon up the energy to check his notes while he was gone.

'You're approximately seven weeks pregnant,' he says, cupping his chin and looking her straight in the eye. 'I can offer our services for you right here. We can also give you a week's board in one of our apartments on-site, to recuperate after the operation. My wife will look after you in recovery.'

Nicoletta starts. This is what she's been waiting to hear, all this time, after all this interminable mumbo-jumbo, but what he's said still shatters her eardrums like a scream.

'How much?' She grips the handles of her bag, not trusting herself to stand up at this moment.

'The operation, plus accommodation and all increments, etc., would be an even £120.' He splays his hands over the notes he's taken, as though it's just occurred to him that she might have read them while he was away developing the plates. His hands are smooth, with long fingers. Would she trust those hands to open the most intimate parts of her?

She exhales very slowly through her mouth, getting to her feet. Her legs hold, though she grips the edge of his desk with her fingertips for balance. 'I'm afraid I didn't bring that amount with me,' she says. Her voice sounds measured, but bright, the same voice she uses at work. Not the one that's screaming inside her head. 'I'll have a think about it.'

He sighs. 'I'll tell you what.' He takes a package from his drawer and hands it to her. 'Take these. Both of them together, at the same time. Preferably on an empty stomach. And if they don't work, come back to us. With £120.'

She feels the small package, snug in the palm of her

hand, and slides it into her bag. She holds the bag over her wrist, hesitating. She can feel Henry Morton's eyes clocking her every move.

'Why do you do what you do?' Her voice is high and piercing, like the jolt of lightning from the ECT, and the light she'd been expecting from the X-ray.

'I beg your pardon?' Morton puts down the page he's been peering at.

'What's in it for you? Being an abortionist.'

Morton winces. 'I would be very careful about using that word, if I were you, Miss Clarke,' he says, his voice gliding over her like the repetitive sitar music from the waiting room.

'Which word would you use?' Nicoletta looks him boldly in the eye. He stares down at the page in front of him.

'I provide a service and I help people.'

'But you charge them a vast sum of money to do so.'

He gives her a sharp look. 'I have bills to meet, same as anyone else. Now, if you'll excuse me, I have work to get on with. Good day, Miss Clarke.'

She hesitates again. 'How much for today?' She feels for her purse, where the crisp money from her watch is folded tight.

'Free of charge,' he says. 'All initial consultations are gratis, until we know how we can help you.'

She sighs. 'How much for the pills?'

'I'll take £30,' he says, with a wave of his hand. 'They're just a menstrual regulator.' She hands over the money. He doesn't quite meet her eye.

He stands up and shows her out, past the garish waiting

room, before wordlessly shaking her hand and closing the door to the street behind her. It's only when she's walking past a children's playground further on, the empty rubber swings slick with rain, that another thought occurs to her. Hadn't Dr Jennings displayed all his medical qualifications on his walls in polished wooden frames? She hadn't noticed any in Henry Morton's office, but nor had she thought to ask. It doesn't matter anyway. If she's desperate enough, she'll go back.

Chapter Twenty

Nicoletta is glad of the milky sun on her face as she marches to the newspaper office. She isn't rostered to work today, but she can't wait to get to a typewriter to type up her notes. She thinks back to her conversation with Leslie White the day before. He hadn't seemed in any way surprised when she'd mentioned Gloria's suicide, which lent O'Malley's theory further weight. *Disgraced former midwife may have planned suicide in asylum ...* She can already see the front page in her mind's eye. The sky hangs sullenly over the water when she reaches Burgh Quay. She thinks back to that first photo of Gloria she'd stolen a look at in Sarto's Newsagents when she was fourteen. The way she'd traced it with her thumb, looking for evil in the aquiline nose, in the high curve of the mouth.

There are only two other members of staff on the newsroom floor. Robert Price is shovelling a sandwich into his mouth and poring over that morning's *Irish Times*. He looks up when she walks by.

'Good morning, Robert,' she says.

He furrows his too-wide brow and shakes his paper.

She checks her in-tray, which is empty, then sits down at a vacant typewriter and pulls out her notebook. Dermot walks by, whistling.

'Wasn't there a message for Nicoletta?' He pokes Price in the shoulder. Price visibly recoils.

'Inspector Morris called,' Price mumbles at Nicoletta.

Dermot shakes his head. 'And?'

Price glares at Dermot. 'And nothing. Ring him back.' Price goes back to his paper.

'Prick,' Dermot mutters under his breath, plonking himself down at his desk.

'What was that?' Price calls from the back bench. Dermot jumps a mile in the air.

'Why are you such a prick to Nicoletta?' he calls back, brazening it out.

Nicoletta shrinks back into her seat. 'Dermot, there's no need ...'

Price is by Dermot's desk in a second. 'Do you really want to know?'

'Yep.' Dermot is still sitting, his hands behind his head in a put-on laconic pose, though Nicoletta can see his hands shaking.

'Look at me when I'm talking to you.' A spray of saliva flies from Price's lips.

Dermot holds Price's gaze, unflinching. 'I'm looking,' he deadpans.

'She's nothing but Barney's bit of skirt.' Price backs away, wiping the excess saliva from the back of his mouth, as though demonstrating his contempt for both of them, before striding into Duffy's office and slamming the door.

Nicoletta takes a deep breath and looks down at her notes. In the ensuing hush, she can hear Dermot fiddling with something at his desk. Duffy's door remains closed. Barney is nowhere to be seen.

She's wondering whether or not to leave, the heat rising in her cheeks, the atmosphere feeling more and more oppressive, when Anne walks in, her black hair pulled tightly off her face. She catches Nicoletta's eye and gives her an unexpected wink.

'All right? Any joy on the Julia Bridges story?'

Nicoletta shrugs, trying to seem casual, all too aware of the scene that has just played out, and that Anne is also in competition for the women's page editor job.

'Hard to say.'

Anne gives one of her looks, her nose wrinkling. She's clutching the *Irish Times* crossword and she squints down at it in her hands. 'See if you can get this. Secrecy or confidentiality, two words.' Anne turns half away, as if to head to her desk. 'You and Barney know all about that,' she adds, under her breath, though Nicoletta knows she is meant to hear.

Nicoletta feels her face flame, but she rises as calmly as she can and takes a few steps closer, to look over Anne's shoulder at the shape the letters would make.

'*Sub rosa*,' she says, and her voice sounds gratifyingly calm and matter of fact. Anne scribbles furiously but doesn't answer.

Nicoletta goes back to her typewriter as Dermot approaches. 'Did you ring Morris back? He specifically asked for you. Sounds juicy.'

'Thanks, yeah,' Nicoletta says with a weak smile. 'I'll do that.'

She takes a deep breath and crosses to her desk, scraping back the chair. Inspector Morris takes a long time to come to the phone. When he eventually answers, he sounds irritated at the disturbance, though once he hears Nicoletta's voice his tone changes.

'Miss Sarto.' He clears his throat. 'We have a delicate matter at hand. It might be within your interests to pop down to the station at your convenience. Actually, no, on second thoughts, meet me in Chaplins.'

Nicoletta rings off none the wiser. She puts her coat back on, giving Dermot and Anne a wave on the way out.

'Off again?' Anne calls, as Nicoletta dives headlong into the stairwell's chill air, leaving the smoky newsroom behind.

When she pushes open the door of Chaplins, Inspector Morris stands up, indicating a chair he's pulled out in front of him.

'Nice to see you,' he says, waiting until she sits down before he resumes his own seat.

They speak in pleasantries for a bit, until he offers Nicoletta a drink. 'I'll have a lemonade,' she says, in a low voice. 'I've had a bit of stomach flu this week.'

'It's the week to have it,' Morris agrees, signalling effortlessly to the barman.

A glass of lemonade arrives at the table. Nicoletta takes a sip and smiles. 'You were very mysterious on the phone,' she says. 'I sense a story.'

'Your senses are correct, Miss Sarto.' Morris claps his

hands and gives her a grim smile. He has a glass of water in front of him. Nicoletta notices bubbles forming on the surface. It looks like it's been there for a while. He dips his head and adopts a confidential tone.

'We arrested John Dawkins this morning, at his mews in Sandycove. We came with a search warrant and found enough purple hearts and reefer to keep the whole city laughing for weeks. We haven't charged him yet, but it'll be interesting to see how the family reacts to this one.'

'You mean his in-laws, the Creightons?' Nicoletta whispers, even though the nearest occupants of the bar are two old men sitting companionably back-to-back reading newspapers, each minding his own respective business.

'Yes. I'm sick to the back teeth of the lot of them.'

'How did you get Dawkins?'

Morris grins, showing off a row of grey-looking teeth. 'Good police work combined with an old-fashioned bit of luck. When Julia Bridges' and that poor child's remains were found, John Dawkins gave us a cock and bull story about digging a grave for a family pet. A dog, I believe. He never even had a dog. He was digging up his stash from the garden. He was working as some kind of sales representative for a supplier of educational materials. Must have made a pittance doing that, but he was over and back to England on the ferry a lot. We have reason to believe he's been bringing in drugs. We found this lot buried close to where he found Mrs Bridges and Garda O'Connor later found her baby.'

Nicoletta shifts on her stool. She can feel Morris' eyes evaluating her, so she doesn't want to seem too excited.

'Do you think you've enough to charge him?'

Morris waggles his fingers. 'I might just.'

Nicoletta takes another sip of the lemonade. It's simultaneously too sweet and too bitter.

'Do you still think Gloria Fitzpatrick was behind Mrs Bridges' disappearance? And isn't it possible the baby belonged to someone else, not Julia Bridges?'

Morris sighs. 'You're full of questions. But I don't have an iota of a doubt about either, Miss Sarto. Do you?'

Nicoletta's blood pounds in her ears. She's aware her face and neck have gone red, but she's so angry she doesn't care.

'I think it's one hundred per cent impossible that poor baby is any relation to Julia Bridges. O'Malley even said so.'

'O'Malley's got one foot in the grave himself. I wouldn't put any store in what he's said. He can never be one hundred per cent sure about anything.' Morris' tone is flippant but he's watching Nicoletta closely. He frowns.

She keeps going. 'I gave Garda O'Connor the address of a family, the Littles, on Seaview Terrace. Their daughter Mary worked as a maid for the Creightons and may have given birth in secret in the past year before killing herself. I think that seems more likely than connecting this poor baby to Julia Bridges. Don't you, Inspector?'

Morris pats her hand. The emboldened gesture takes her by surprise. 'Garda O'Connor told me about your little hunch, and we've since eliminated Mary Little's baby from our enquiries. There simply isn't enough evidence.'

Nicoletta clears her throat. 'What about Una Little?'

Morris pats her hand again, resting his beside hers on the table. 'She declined to make a statement. I can finally sign off on Julia Bridges as a solve.'

'But that's a complete fabrication, and you know it!' Nicoletta smacks her hand lightly against the tabletop, then snatches it back and nurses it in her lap. Morris glances at the space her hand occupied with distaste. Her outburst may be more than he'd bargained for that evening.

'No offence, pet, but you've been a reporter, what, a wet week? I've been in the force for over thirty years. I think I can be trusted to read this better than you.'

Nicoletta clears her throat. She's wondering how long politeness dictates she stays. 'What about Gloria Fitzpatrick's employer at St Bridget's, Lilian Higgins?'

'What about her?'

Nicoletta eyes him. 'One of my colleagues mentioned that just before she died, Lilian Higgins was fined in the district court for falsifying the birth register. Maybe she'd had more to do with Gloria's side of the business than anyone realised.'

Morris waggles his fingers again. 'Don't mind your colleagues.' He sits back, taking a pack of Rothmans from his pocket. He offers her one. She declines. 'Barney, was it? He's always on the lookout for a conspiracy theory angle if you ask me. He's an amateur.'

'Is that so?' Nicoletta picks up her lemonade glass. The smell reminds her of curdling milk and she's afraid she'll get sick. She puts the glass down. 'It was Tim Duffy, actually, who said that. My editor. Did you know Mrs Higgins?'

'I did.' The act of smoking soothes Morris' nerves. The flutter of his hands quietens, and he looks at Nicoletta contemplatively. 'She was a fine woman. A friend of my mother-in-law. I don't know what she was thinking taking on Fitzpatrick, but it was to be her undoing. Sometimes it just takes one rotten apple.'

'You thought well of Mrs Higgins then.' Nicoletta tries to look agreeable. She has a suspicion she may not be succeeding.

Morris stabs his cigarette into the ashtray. 'Everybody did,' he says, the irritation in his voice palpable. 'She was very respected. At one stage St Bridget's was the place to go if you wanted to book into a state-of-the-art place to have your baby. Not only that, but she was compassionate. She knew there were many unfortunate girls around, who found themselves in trouble, and who wouldn't be able to afford the kind of fees she charged. I don't like to speak out of turn, but she often took them in, gave them food and board, and looked after them until they had their babies. Most of them couldn't go back to wherever it was they came from. When it came to forging the birth register, what harm did it do, really?'

'Interesting.' Nicoletta drums her fingers on the table. Her bitten nails don't create much of a tap against the wood. She stops when Morris clenches his jaw. 'Thank you, Inspector. It's so helpful to get the inside track from someone with your knowledge and experience.' She doesn't know if she's laying it on too thick, but Morris inclines his head, looking slightly mollified.

'Speaking of which,' he says, blowing out his cheeks.

'A little birdie tells me there's a bit of a promotion riding on the Bridges story.' He takes a large manila envelope out of his inside pocket and holds it up. 'I thought you might be interested. I made copies of all the statements we took from key people after Julia Bridges went missing. Residents of St Bridget's and a few others. Just to give you a flavour of the case for your piece. Off the record, of course.'

'Thank you, that's very kind, Inspector.' Nicoletta reaches for the envelope. 'I appreciate it. If I can ever do anything for you in return . . .'

Morris holds the envelope against his chest. 'You can have dinner with me! I'm celebrating, as it happens. The solve on Julia Bridges has brought me promise of a little promotion of my own.' His tone is jovial, but he looks down into his drink as though about to take a long swallow, but not quite able to bring himself to do it.

Nicoletta picks up her bag. 'I might go back out to Sandycove and speak to some of John Dawkins' neighbours, now he's been arrested. Maybe even his wife, Delia. She must be in shock at what her husband was up to behind their backs, in such a respectable neighbourhood.'

Morris snorts. 'You'd be surprised. The wife always knows.'

Nicoletta laughs. It sounds bright and false to her own ears. 'Well, if you say it, then it must be true. I wouldn't say there's much gets past you, Inspector.'

Morris gulps and pats the back of her hand again. 'I've to go now and throw the book at this chancer. Tell you what, though, wait here for me. I'll only be an hour or so, and we'll go for a meal then. I'll go over these statements with you. My treat. I can tell you all about it, and Lilian Higgins, and anything else you'd like to know about. Consider me an open book.'

Nicoletta half closes her eyes, shaking her head. 'Thank you, Inspector, but I think I'll keep going with this story. Then it's time I went home and got some rest, as dull as that might sound. I haven't been feeling right all week with this flu.'

'Ah yes,' he says, sliding the envelope back into his inside pocket. 'Your stomach flu. How could I forget?' He gives her a wink.

She can't quite make out his expression as the room is half in shadow and he turns his face away. She stands up, but he doesn't this time. She's about to walk out the door when he calls her back. 'You're a woman of the world, Miss Sarto. Tell me, what does Barney have that I don't?'

By the time she's thought of a suitable answer, she's already out the brass-trimmed door. She walks as briskly as she can towards the nearest bus stop.

Chapter Twenty-One

The bus stops with a gasp every five minutes, and by the time Nicoletta gets off at Dún Laoghaire and walks the final stretch along the sea front to Sandycove, dusk is creeping in. There's barely anyone around. The wind is cold, but somehow flat, and the sea looks dulled by it.

When she reaches the Creightons', she pauses. The giant yew trees at the front are stiff and unyielding in the breeze, the curtains of all the front windows pulled tightly closed. She tries the main gate, but it's padlocked shut. The garden is a sea of mud. Nicoletta keeps walking, passing through the graffitied snicket in the wall dividing Seaview Terrace from the coast road. Before she can stop herself, she knocks at the first house on the street, a red-brick Edwardian, two-up, two-down, with a peeling green door and black railings. Immediately, she hears the sound of bolts sliding back, as though someone was hovering in front of the door the whole time.

'Who is it?' a husky voice calls, through a gap where the latch has been left on. Nicoletta can make out the outline of a tall elderly woman with rheumy blue eyes. A pair of

218

pink-slippered feet nudge a large black dog away from the door. 'You don't look like the police, but if you are, you've taken your sweet time.'

'I'm not the police.' Nicoletta can see the gap in the door visibly shrink, so she starts talking faster. 'My name's Nicoletta Sarto. I'm a reporter. I wonder if you'd have a few moments to speak to me? It's about John Dawkins.'

The latch slides back, and the shrewd blue eyes look Nicoletta up and down.

'A lady reporter,' the woman says, bending down to yank the dog by its collar. 'Well, I never. Sarto, did you say?'

Nicoletta nods. 'Yes.'

The woman ushers her inside. 'You'd best come in before Nero bolts.'

The woman leads her to a very warm, cluttered kitchen at the back, and motions for her to sit down. Nicoletta can't decide on her age. She looks anywhere between fifty and eighty. A pair of black eyebrows has been carefully drawn on her pale, powdered face, along with a slash of red lipstick. Her hair is the colour of dull brass, with an inch of grey showing at the roots. She's wearing a two-piece khaki suit with an unfashionable midi-length skirt, and a cigarette in a long black holder smoulders in a nearby ashtray. The woman yanks the dog's collar, pulling him back before he noses forward to sniff Nicoletta's feet. He yelps with resignation.

'I hope you're not afraid of mutts. Some people are, never could understand it. I'd be more afraid of some people than I would of this fellow.'

'No, I'm not afraid.' Nicoletta smiles and sits down in the seat opposite the woman. 'I'm fond of dogs.'

'I'm glad. Can't abide people who don't like animals.'

Nicoletta smiles again. The woman picks up the smouldering cigarette by the holder and takes in a brisk lungful of smoke. 'You know, since I called the cops, I was half expecting a reporter to come sniffing around.' Her eyes rest on Nicoletta's face. 'I wasn't expecting a lady though. Especially one who looks like death warmed up.'

'I've had stomach flu all week.' Nicoletta pats her stomach, then feels foolish for doing so.

'I'll bet,' the woman cackles, standing up and flicking on a kettle. 'Not much of a job for a woman, is it?'

'It's the best job,' Nicoletta blurts out.

The room is like a Turkish sauna, with most of the heat emanating from a wood-burning stove in the corner. The large black dog plods over to a basket beside it and settles himself in a resigned fashion, head hanging out over the top, tongue lolling to one side, eyes never leaving Nicoletta.

'I feel the cold,' the woman says, as though sensing Nicoletta's thoughts. She plonks an overflowing teapot and some chipped, gilt-edged cups on the table.

'Yes,' says Nicoletta. 'Some people do.' She takes a hasty sip of tea, scalding her tongue. 'I'm sorry, I'm afraid I didn't catch your name.'

'Didn't give it. It's Helen Leonard,' the woman says. 'Miss. But I don't want my name in any of this. I don't mind telling you what I know, as it's the God's honest truth, and it's nothing I wouldn't say to their faces anyhow. But the thought of having my name in the paper is a bit . . .'

Nicoletta waits for her to finish. 'A bit . . .?'

'Nasty,' Miss Leonard says with relish. 'No offence.'

'Absolutely none taken,' Nicoletta replies with a laugh. 'Have you lived here long?'

Miss Leonard thinks about it. Her old cigarette appears to have extinguished itself and a fresh one is duly lit, before being cast into the ashtray and forgotten about. 'I was born in this house,' she says. 'Everyone was born at home then. There were no fancy places to go and have babies. Women didn't make a fuss. Weren't supposed to.'

'They're still not supposed to, if you ask me,' Nicoletta says, with a rueful smile.

Miss Leonard gives an appreciative cackle.

'So, you've lived here all your life?' Nicoletta takes another sip of tea. Nero is lapping water from a bowl by his basket, and she looks at it longingly. Another sliver of perspiration slides down her back.

'Yes, in fact. Apart from my time in London with the Wrens during the war. Best time of my life. Everything just seemed so dull after.'

Nicoletta takes her notebook and pen out of her bag. 'Can you tell me why you called the Guards, Miss Leonard?'

Miss Leonard takes a suck of her cigarette, from which curls a long tail of ash. She doesn't appear to notice, and it falls to the floor. 'I've known the Creightons all my life. Charles was actually sweet on me once. A long time ago, before he met Maureen, the first wife.' She laughs girlishly, a talon brushing against her throat. 'Then Maureen died, and he met Sally during the war. An English girl, an evacuee from London, an orphan. He married her within six months. It only took another six months for her to take to her bed. Those Creightons think they can do whatever they like.'

Nicoletta shifts in her seat. 'What exactly do you mean, Miss Leonard?'

Miss Leonard snorts and slams her cup back into its saucer. 'Every dog on the street knows that Dawkins was peddling drugs. I'm not afraid of the likes of him. A long-haired pansy in an Afghan coat.'

Nicoletta suppresses a smile. 'Did you call the Guards to complain about him?'

Miss Leonard stops to light another cigarette off the butt of the old one. Nicoletta can't help but notice that her hands are trembling, and it takes her several attempts to light up.

'At first I threatened to, and he laughed,' she says, looking Nicoletta straight in the eye. 'Didn't seem to knock a feather out of him. My Nero was always chasing Sally's peacocks. Charles came down here, threatening to poison Nero. I said I'd call the cops and tell them about Dawkins. So, I did. They said they were about to arrest him anyway. When you knocked on the door, I thought they'd come back to check on me.'

'That's terrible.'

'It is.' Miss Leonard sniffs in agreement. 'I think the general feeling is that Delia threw herself away on that hippy she married. I don't know, maybe she did it out of spite. I think Charles wanted to evict them from the mews quite recently though.'

'How do you know that?'

Miss Leonard goes to say something, then stops as though she thinks better of it. Nicoletta leans forward in her chair.

'I'm not going to write about any of this, Miss Leonard,' she says. 'It's purely for background information. You're being so helpful, but I understand if you'd like to stop.' The loud tick of the kitchen clock intrudes into the momentary silence and Nero grunts softly in his sleep, blissfully unaware of the threat against his life.

'No,' Miss Leonard says, finally, clearing her throat. 'That's what they'd like me to do. Keep my mouth shut. Charles Creighton and I have known each other since we were in nappies. He's always done whatever his mother said. She's the only woman he'll really listen to.' She pauses, flicking a glance at Nicoletta. 'I wasn't eavesdropping, but I couldn't help but overhear them arguing a couple of weeks ago.'

'Who was arguing?'

'Charles and his mother. Ruth.'

'What were they arguing about?'

'About John Dawkins, of course. And what a bad influence on Delia he is, and how Ruth wants him out of the mews. But this time Charles talked her round. Told her to leave them be, that he'd have a word with Dawkins.'

Miss Leonard raises her overplucked eyebrows so high they almost shoot off her forehead. 'Ruth would do anything for that son of hers. That'll be her undoing if you ask me.'

Nicoletta smooths back a stray tuft of hair. 'What do you mean by that, Miss Leonard?'

Miss Leonard doesn't answer. Instead, she opens and closes her mouth in a couple of goldfish-like gulps. She begins massaging her temple with the tips of her clawed fingers.

Nicoletta persists. 'Miss Leonard, some context would be so helpful. Do you think Mrs Creighton would err on the wrong side of the law to protect her son? Or her grand-daughter and grandson-in-law, for that matter?'

Miss Leonard gives her head an almost imperceptible shake.

Nicoletta leans across the table, stretching out her hands toward Miss Leonard. She doesn't want to scare her. 'You mentioned earlier that you didn't want the Creightons to "get away with it" anymore. What have they got away with in the past? You can trust me, Miss Leonard. I hope you know that.'

Miss Leonard gives a derisive snort, before closing her eyes. When she finally answers, it's only a tone or two above a whisper. 'I have to feed Nero. It's getting late.'

Nicoletta gathers her things and stands, knowing she can't push the woman any further. Nero raises his silky head and plods after her on her way to the door. She strokes his ears. After a moment, she goes back. Miss Leonard is still at the kitchen table with her eyes half closed.

'Miss Leonard, do you know the Littles at number eight?'

Miss Leonard's eyes fly open. 'He's a horrible creature. She's like a ghost. Why?'

'Their daughter Una works at Seaview House as a maid.'

'I know. I see her over and back to the mews quite a bit.' Miss Leonard purses her mouth.

'Her sister Mary worked for the Creightons, too, but she died recently,' Nicoletta presses.

Miss Leonard massages her temples with the points of her fingernails.

Nicoletta hovers, before sitting back down at the table. 'Did you know Mary had a baby?'

'No,' the older woman says stiffly. She rises from the table and walks with Nicoletta into the dim hallway. Nero tries to slip out too and Miss Leonard drags him back by his collar.

Nicoletta thanks her, with a reminder of her phone number in case Miss Leonard wants to talk about anything else. She closes the door carefully, drinking in the icy sea breeze. As she passes onto a deserted Seaview Terrace, she can hear Nero whining and scratching to be let out.

She passes through the snicket and heads to the top of the street, stopping in front of Seaview House. A light gleams behind the drawn curtains and she wonders if whoever is behind them can see her. She walks on self-consciously, around to the side of the house. On impulse, she pushes the side gate. It's unlocked and she steps quickly towards the mews, wading ankle-deep through the mud. There's no sign of the peacocks. They must be roosting, Nicoletta imagines, in this weather. Her finger punches the bell before she can change her mind. After a minute or two, the door opens and Una Little appears, her eyes red and puffy.

'Una! What are you doing here?'

Delia Dawkins steps into the gap before Una can answer. She looks nothing like the last time, her back-combed beehive loose and lank around a pale, unmade-up face. She's wearing an unbecoming paisley housecoat with hanging threads around the hem. Una freezes for a moment, until Delia pats her on the shoulder.

'Go on back now, Una. We'll talk later.'

Una hurries away without a word, giving Nicoletta a sulky look.

'Hello, Mrs Dawkins,' Nicoletta begins. 'How are you?'

Delia scrunches up her face. Her eyebrows are plucked to almost non-existence. She sniffs. 'It's been the week from hell.'

'I'm sure it's been extremely difficult. What's happening to John now?'

Delia steps out and closes the door, taking some breadcrumbs from her pocket and scattering them on the flagstones around the mews. Antony lurches towards her, as though out of nowhere, fanning his tail for Nicoletta's benefit, before pecking as fast as Delia can throw. Cleopatra bobs behind at a more ladylike pace.

'He just phoned from the Garda station.' Delia throws another handful of crumbs at Antony, waiting for Cleopatra to join him before she continues. She lowers her voice. 'He's on his way home. They've had to let him go on a technicality. The search warrant was out of date.' She throws one last handful of crumbs before clapping her hands. The dark has crept into every corner. She turns back towards the door, wiping her feet on a mat.

'Mrs Dawkins, you must be delighted about John coming home. Do you have any comment to make to the *Sentinel* on your husband's arrest?'

Delia opens her door as the peacocks tussle over a single remaining crumb. 'We're still throwing our New Year's Eve party,' she calls, with a crooked grin. 'You should still come.'

'Did your father threaten a neighbour with poisoning their dog?' Nicoletta says, half to herself, but Delia, whether or not she has heard, closes the door with a soft *thud*.

Nicoletta stands for a moment, contemplating the smoothly painted wood in front of her. The whisper of the sea rushes back into the silence. For the first time in days, she feels normal. It must be the sea air. After the heat of Miss Leonard's, it has cooled her off. As she walks back to the bus stop, she casts a look back to Seaview House. Someone has pulled back the drawing room curtains, but kept the blinds partly drawn, so that the window resembles a huge glassy eye.

Chapter Twenty-Two

The walk from the bus stop feels charged. Nicoletta is seething at the way Inspector Morris has put the baby found by Garda O'Connor down as Julia Bridges' child to copper-fasten a solve on the case. She thinks of poor Mary Little, desperate and alone, her baby presumably taken from her, walking and walking into the sea until it swallowed her up. She passes the window of a small toy shop on Hawkins Street, where a large, flaxen-haired doll is on display. 'Cries real tears,' says the label. Its wide, plastic eyes follow her as she tries to walk away. She turns sharply on her heel. What if she were to keep this baby? She could manage, she knows she could. She crosses the street and stops, rummaging in her bag for the envelope of menstrual regulators given to her by Henry Morton. She tosses them into a litter bin and almost gallops back to Burgh Quay.

There's a bit of chat in the newsroom, as Anne and Dermot sit side by side at adjoining typewriters, bashing out their respective stories. Anne whispers something when she walks in, and Nicoletta pretends not to notice. Dermot gives her a friendly wave and stands up. There's no sign of

Duffy or Barney. She tries to slide unobtrusively into her seat, dumping her handbag under her chair, but Dermot is standing over her before she can take off her jacket.

'Evening, sunshine,' Dermot says, with a sly grin.

'What are you so cheerful about?'

'Wouldn't you like to know?' He drags over a chair and matches it to hers.

He blows smoke towards the yellowed ceiling. 'Hope the long face isn't catching, dear.'

She smiles, despite herself. 'Anything strange or startling?'

'Now, that's more like it.' He takes a large manila envelope out of his breast pocket with her name scrawled on it. It looks like the one Inspector Morris hadn't quite given her. 'Garda O'Connor left this for you. You seem to have built quite a rapport with him.'

'I wouldn't say that.' Nicoletta's cheeks colour as she reaches for the envelope.

Anne walks by, brandishing a black at one of the copy boys. She glances her way and Nicoletta senses that she's dying to sidle over to get the latest read on Barney and Marie. Without thinking any further, she rips open the envelope. There's a neatly written note from O'Connor on top: 'Think this is meant for you.' Ten typed pages. She reads them from the top. They're copies of the promised witness statements that Morris had wanted to give her, on the proviso she have dinner with him. Mostly from mothers 'lying in' at St Bridget's in late July 1943, when Julia Bridges was allegedly seen entering the premises. None of them had heard or seen a thing out of the ordinary. She's glad now she didn't agree to dinner with Inspector Morris.

Nicoletta skims until she reaches something of interest.

Statement from Miss Marian Swan, date of birth, 24/11/1915:

I have worked for Mrs Higgins at St Bridget's since 1941. In that time, I have delivered many babies. Most of the mothers come back for all their confinements; Mrs Higgins is well-liked. On the night in question, I spent the afternoon and evening up to midnight with Mrs Haskins, delivering her baby, Patrick. It was a long, drawn-out labour and I was tired after. I went and sat in the kitchen and had something to eat with Eilish, a domestic. We turned on the wireless and listened to a wonderful play on the BBC World Service. At around 12:30 I heard a car on the gravel. I was surprised as I hadn't known we were expecting anyone.

I got up and looked out. I saw Miss Fitzpatrick's sports car in the drive. She must have sat in the driver's seat for a while, just looking straight ahead. She didn't come in for about ten minutes. I heard the back door open and shut but I didn't go out to speak to her as I was tired after the day's work and wanted to be alone. Miss Fitzpatrick suffers from terrible insomnia and often goes for night-time drives. I have known Miss Fitzpatrick for quite a long time, since I started working as a midwife at St Bridget's in the early '40s. I do not consider her to be a close personal friend.

Marian Swan, 2nd August 1943

Statement from Miss Eilish Smith, date of birth, 28/11/1928:

It was a long night delivering Mrs Haskins' baby. Miss Swan had me running between the bedroom, kitchen and the bathroom fetching water and emptying buckets. My arms were hanging off me by the time baby Patrick made his appearance. His face looked like a squashed turnip, but I didn't say that to Mrs Haskins. I wanted to get away from Miss Swan, but she insisted I keep her company. She put on the wireless and I had to sit through an hour of one of her plays. At one point, she went to the window and saw Miss Fitzpatrick's car outside. When she sat back down, she said: 'Gloria must be having another sleepless night.' We sat there until 1am. By the time I got to my bed, everything was quiet. I didn't see Miss Fitzpatrick until the next morning.

Eilish Smith, 2nd August 1943

Statement given in the presence of Garda Sergeant David Morris at Pearse Street Garda Station, by Eilish Smith, of St Bridget's, Ranelagh, Dublin:

I wanted to come in to talk to you because something terrible has happened. I can't sleep and I feel like I'll explode if I don't tell someone. I'm not good at keeping secrets. I don't see why I should. I was afraid I'd lose my job. It was Miss Fitzpatrick who got me the position at St Bridget's. I also worked for Miss Fitzpatrick at her previous residence, The Downings,

when I was younger, age twelve or so. She is a difficult, peculiar woman.

On the evening of 23rd July, while Mrs Haskins
was screaming and shouting and having her baby,
I left the room where Mrs Haskins was and let a
woman into St Bridget's. I now realise it must have
been Julia Bridges, the actress. She was very drunk
and slurring her words. I had to give her a fireman's
lift to get her to Miss Fitzpatrick's room. Everyone
else was busy with Mrs Haskins and her baby, so no
one else saw but me. I don't know what happened
after that.

Eilish Smith, 2nd August 1943

**Statement from Gloria Anne Fitzpatrick, of
St Bridget's, Ranelagh, Dublin, date of birth,
25/12/1900, taken at Pearse Street Garda Station,
2nd August 1943:**

I know the name Julia Bridges. She's an actress. I
have seen her in several productions and revues at
the Athena Theatre. A pretty girl.

I have recently been diagnosed with rheumatoid
arthritis and it has affected my sleeping habits. As
a result, I suffer from fairly extreme insomnia. My
poor sleep is well known at St Bridget's. I tend to go
out driving when I am afflicted as I find it meditative
and calming. On the night in question, yes, I did go
for a drive, I suppose. I must have driven up and
down the coast road a few times. I got back just after
midnight. A few people must have seen me, but no

one commented on it the next day. I didn't speak to anyone when I came in. I arrived through the back door as I didn't wish to disturb anyone. I did wonder what had happened to Mrs Bridges and it's an awful pity to hear that she never turned up. Unless, of course, she planned the whole thing that way.

Gloria Anne Fitzpatrick, signed in the presence of Garda Sergeant David Morris

Statement from Mr Jack Bridges, date of birth, 01/02/1902:

The last time I saw Julia it must have been mid-July 1943. It was on stage, at the Athena's summer revue. I've seen her give better performances. After the curtain went up I had to see to a problem with the lighting – a trip wire had blown. Julia went off without saying goodbye. I got the feeling she was in a huff with me; about what, I really don't know. She didn't come home at all that night and then phoned me the next day to say she was staying with a friend. I didn't hear from her again. I reported her disappearance to the Guards in the early afternoon of 30th July. I didn't want to make a fuss in case she turned up, but deep down I knew something was very wrong. Julia may be headstrong, but she is my wife and I love her, always have. We were meant to be together forever.

Jack Bridges, 2nd August 1943

Statement from Mr Graham Swift, manager at the Athena Theatre, date of birth, 10/03/1905:

Julia came to my flat at Herbert Place on the evening of 23rd July. She wanted to talk to me. She loved me, she said, and she wanted us to go to England together. My wife, Carole, was out. I told Julia I wouldn't leave Carole. She seemed upset but she accepted it. We went for a drink in the Sackville Arms off O'Connell Street and later we said goodbye at Nelson's Pillar at around 6:30pm on 23rd July. She didn't say where she was going. That's the last time I saw her.

Graham Swift, 2nd August 1943

Statement from Mr Brendan Owens, Jack and Julia Bridges' landlord, date of birth, 19/11/1895:

Julia and Jack Bridges were my tenants. I am coming forward because of a recent newspaper appeal for information on Julia's whereabouts. On the evening of 23rd July 1943, I saw Julia arrive back at her flat. I knew Jack Bridges had been looking for her, so I couldn't help but notice her arrival out of interest. Mr Bridges wasn't home. Julia emerged wearing a short dark coat a few minutes later and departed on foot. I remember thinking it was odd to wear such a warm coat on a hot day. I followed closely behind her to make sure she was all right. She stopped just over the canal in Ranelagh and went into a house, which I knew to be St Bridget's nursing home, where Gloria Fitzpatrick lived and worked, a fact which now strikes me as significant. Mrs Bridges went in and was only there for a minute before she came out again and went into a pub nearby. She came out a long while later, inebriated, and then went back into St Bridget's. I waited for about half an hour, but she didn't re-emerge.

Brendan Owens, 15th April 1959

As soon as she stops reading, Nicoletta grabs her coat. She needs air. On the street, the wind bites her cheeks. She turns up her collar. She longs to speak to Barney, but she won't ring him again. Marie's soft, breathy voice answering the phone is seared into her brain. Her head is swimming with so many fragments.

Cassidy's is half full, as always, no matter the time of year. She orders an orange and sits at the bar with the old men, despite the disapproving looks and outright hostility. She puts her back to them and picks up the perspiring glass, the ice tinkling as she takes a gulp. That first time, when Barney had taken her hand on the bridge and finally told her that Marie had left, they'd come here. It had been early summer, and the city had been teeming with life. Lovers were everywhere, it seemed, gliding around in pairs like swans. She'd dropped his hand as soon as they'd stepped over the pub's threshold in case they bumped into anyone they knew from work.

The snugs had all been full, so they'd had to take a table by the door, in full view of the whole place. He'd come back with drinks for them both, a pint for himself and a gin and orange for her, because that's what she'd asked for.

She didn't usually drink, not really, and her stomach had
fizzed with nerves. She'd taken a couple of grateful gulps
from the cold glass. None of the windows had been open,
so a girl in a short, fringed dress and teetering espadrilles
wedged the door wide open using a mound of beer coast-
ers, until it was pinned back as far as its hinges. Gasps of
air from outside had drifted in from the exhausts of the
cars and buses of Westmoreland Street.

'Is Marie coming back?' She'd surprised herself by the
boldness of the question, as direct as an arrow in flight,
fortifying herself with another gulp of orangey gin.

'No.' Barney banged his fist on the table, as though the
word by itself wasn't enough. He succeeded in upending
her glass and spilling most of the rest of her drink, so
that it slopped onto the ancient green carpet. 'That's it.
She's gone.'

She didn't know how he could be sure. Nicoletta didn't
know anyone who had gone to England for a divorce.
The word sounded so brutal. Barney and Marie had been
together since they were kids. They had a whole shared
history with a child, a home. It was impossible to split it
all down the middle.

'What about Liam?' She'd half hoped he'd say Marie was
taking him, yet felt instant, horrible guilt for the thought.

'The boy's staying with me.' Barney had leaned forward, his cheeks flushed. 'She decided to walk away. The
law will take my side, I know it.'

'Will it?' she'd asked, as a wave of laughter erupted from
the table where the girl in the fringed dress sat on the floor
with her bare legs crossed at the ankles.

Barney had looked deep into his diminishing pint. 'Yes. If a mother deserts her children, the law is on the father's side. But that's beside the point. That boy is the most important person in my life. He has to come first.'

She'd swallowed a gush of jealousy and nodded. 'I understand,' she'd said, feeling her new gold hoop earrings brush against her jaw. She'd had her ears pierced the week before, as part of this new life. Fortunately, her mother was yet to see them, as her disapproval was almost certainly guaranteed.

He'd smiled then, taking her hand again and squeezing it. She winced, but his grip stayed strong. 'Someone might see.' She indicated the open door behind her.

'Don't care,' he'd said. 'Couldn't give a damn, Nicoletta. Five minutes with you is worth a hell of a lot more than twelve years with her.' He'd leaned forward then and kissed her without preamble, his lips surprisingly warm and soft. She'd kissed him back, despite herself, despite them all: the girl on the floor only a few feet away, the colleagues who could walk in at any moment, the hordes of thirsty revellers traipsing in and out of the pub. Her spilled drink dripped steadily, already forgotten.

When they'd broken apart, he'd stood, wallet in hand. 'Sorry about your drink.'

'Where are you off to?' She hid her uncertainty with coyness.

'To get you another. Same again?'

She shook her head. 'No, I don't think so. That's enough for me.'

Barney's face fell from a height. He looked like a boy whose hopes had just been stamped on.

'I meant, let's get out of here instead,' she'd said, righting the sticky glass and picking up her bag. This was new to her. If her mother found out, she'd have something else to be disapproving about, along with the newly pierced ears, questionable job and flat in town. What was one more thing to add to the list?

Now Nicoletta feels the barman's eyes in her peripheral vision. She takes a sip of the orange in front of her. It's gone flat.

'Same again?'

'Yeah,' she calls, rooting around in her bag for change. 'Why the hell not?'

He sloshes orange into a glass and slides it towards her. 'On the house,' he says with a wry wave. 'You look like you could do with some cheering up.' He's gone to pour a pint for one of the old men before she can open her mouth to either thank him or protest.

They'd walked back to her flat on Eccles Street from here. Though she's walked that same route many times since, there was something about that long summer evening that doesn't feel fully real now, cast in her memory in an artificial light.

She'd turned the key in the lock, knowing Jean was out and praying that she hadn't come home early. She'd never mentioned Barney to Jean, who was going out with a fellow teacher from the primary school where she worked. Jean often spoke about Stephen and their plans for the future. She'd tried to engage Nicoletta with questions about anyone at work she might have designs on, but Nicoletta had told her she didn't have time for dates. Jean told Nicoletta once that she found her secretive, and Nicoletta tried to laugh it off by saying she was too boring to have secrets, but she knew from that moment she'd never trust Jean.

Barney had taken off his jacket and hung it on the back of the door. He'd sat on the sofa in the tiny sitting room, without passing comment on the cluttered table, the mismatched wobbly chairs, the grimy windows.

She'd sat too, unsure of what should happen next, her jiggling leg almost overturning the chair. He'd stood and walked over to her then, kneeling before her on the old, stained carpet, steadying her and the chair.

'What if people find out? They'll talk about us. About me.'

Barney considered that for a moment. 'So what? We're not doing anything wrong.'

When he kissed her again, it felt as natural as breathing in a lungful of air. They made love on the sofa in short, greedy bursts, with most of their clothes still on, though Nicoletta was afraid Jean might surprise them by coming home early and she couldn't relax properly.

Afterwards, he held her, cupping her hip. 'I always wondered,' he said, while their breathing returned to normal.

She'd shrugged off his embrace, sitting up and straightening her clothes, before heading for the bathroom, terrified she'd hear Jean's key in the lock. When she got back, Barney was fully dressed and sitting in the same place on the sofa. 'You have to go,' she said. 'My flatmate will be back any minute.' He wordlessly walked out of the room. She heard him opening the door and she followed him onto the landing.

'Well, bye,' she'd said, miserable that he'd obviously got what he wanted and now that was it. He'd turned and come back into the flat, closing the door behind him, catching her around the waist.

'Can this happen again?'

The expression on his face had been fragile as glass. She'd never seen this Barney before; outside of the newsroom he was a different person, one she knew she could never hurt. She'd kissed him, not the way people did in films, or the way she'd kissed Raffa, but as though she'd been programmed to do it. 'Yes,' she'd said, when they finally broke apart.

Later, she'd been surprised to find that only a handful of hours had passed since they'd left the pub together, yet her world was transformed beyond recognition. This was her new life. Since Enzo had died, time had been riveted into two distinct compartments, each with its own lock and key: there was Before and there was After. But sometimes things spilled messily from one into the other, bleeding into each other's corners like half-remembered dreams. Now, thinking of those first few months with Barney felt like looking through an old photo album. Had any of it been real?

The buoyant mood of earlier has seeped away and she's mortified to find that tears are rolling down her cheeks now, in the middle of this stuffy pub. The barman begins walking over to her, but she stands quickly, grabbing her things and escaping to the ladies', in a bid to pull herself together. After redoing her face and blowing her nose, she emerges into a cold, drizzly evening, with people drifting in and out of pubs in dribs and drabs. Most are at home with their families at this time of year. Who else would be in a pub the week after Christmas, but someone who has to be? She feels restless, like staying out. She needs a purpose. She heads back to the *Sentinel*, feeling its magnetic pull. Dermot is one of only a few people in the newsroom. He's reading the *National Geographic*, slowly flipping through its glossy pages.

'Hey,' he says, without lifting his head. 'Where'd you get to?'

She sits at her desk and drums her fingers on the table-top. Her notebook is full of names, yet she still can't prove anything about that poor baby and his mother, and she's no closer to knowing anything about Gloria's child, if that child exists. One name catches her eye, from the conversation she'd had with Leslie White. Gerard Fitzpatrick, Gloria's only known next of kin. The man who had declined to claim her body when she died.

Nicoletta flips the notebook closed. 'Dermot, do you have a car?'

Dermot looks up. 'You know I do. Need a lift somewhere?'

Nicoletta perches at the corner of his desk. 'How'd you feel like driving me to Knockgan in County Laois tomorrow?'

Dermot splutters. 'Laois? On a Sunday? It's my day off. Don't ask for much, do you?'

Nicoletta sits down beside him. 'I'd owe you big time,' she says, in a wheedling voice. 'Anything you want.'

'All right,' Dermot says doubtfully. 'I'm not doing anything anyway. I might just call in the favour though. Be prepared.' He gives a short laugh.

Nicoletta throws her arms around him. 'Thank you,' she says.

She picks up that day's racing edition of the paper, flicking through the pages, skimming an ad for a run of *The Importance of Being Earnest* at the Imperial Theatre. Starring Carole Swift, the ad says. The name rings a bell. Carole Swift. She remembers the woman from Julia Bridges' funeral. Her understudy in the 1943 summer revue. Graham Swift's wife, who didn't know she was being cuckolded by Julia Bridges. Or did she? Nicoletta checks her bag for the tickets for *The Importance of Being Earnest* that she'd got her parents for Christmas and which they hadn't taken up, before clipping over to the phone and dialling Pearse Street Garda Station. She asks for Garda Peter O'Connor, and he comes to the phone right away.

'It's Nicoletta Sarto,' she says. 'Hello, Garda.'

They exchange pleasantries before Nicoletta dives in. 'Thank you for earlier,' she says in a low voice, though there's no one besides Dermot to hear. But you never know. 'The statements.'

'No problem, so,' he says, sounding like he's about to ring off.

'I have two tickets to *The Importance of Being Earnest* at the Imperial. For tonight. Would you like to go?'

O'Connor is waiting for her in Chaplins half an hour later. He stands up when he sees her. She insists on getting the drinks and returns a few minutes later with a glass of orange for her and a pint for him. They sit in silence for a moment or two, their knees jammed together on uncomfortable stools, listening to the increasingly raucous sounds of nightlife in the bar around them.

'So,' O'Connor says, taking a sip of his pint. 'What's all this about?'

His gaze is direct and honest. It makes her feel safe.

'I . . . wanted to thank you for the statements.' Nicoletta feels the words sticking in her throat. 'And I had the tickets anyway. Carole Swift is in this play. She was Julia Bridges' understudy in the 1943 summer revue. Her husband is the manager of the Athena Theatre and, according to his statement, he was having an affair with Julia. I'd like to try and speak to Carole now.'

'You never stop,' O'Connor says with a chuckle.

Nicoletta smiles. 'I like being busy.' She gives a shaky laugh. 'No rest for the wicked.'

'Come on now.' O'Connor matches her smile. 'You're hard on yourself. You're doing great work.'

Nicoletta looks down at her glass, feeling his eyes on her. When she looks up, he doesn't look away. 'Thank you for all your help,' she says. 'You're a really nice guy.' She looks back down at her glass, the sudden silence awkward. 'We should drink these. It's curtain-up in ten minutes.'

The play seems to go on forever. Nicoletta can feel O'Connor shifting in his seat several times, and when the curtain goes down for the interval, he thinks it's the end. His face falls when Nicoletta tells him there's forty-five minutes left. Carole Swift plays Lady Bracknell with high camp, swaggering around the stage with a large black feathery fan and matching hat. When the curtain finally goes up, there's wild applause and a standing ovation. Nicoletta nudges O'Connor. 'I'm going to try and speak to Carole Swift now,' she says in his ear.

'Right so,' he says, looking relieved. 'I'll leave you be.'

Nicoletta slips through backstage in the after-show rush, and no one stops her. She knocks on a door with Carole's name on it, and doesn't wait to be told to come in. She finds Carole touching up her make-up in front of a brightly lit mirror in a room crammed with costumes. It's similar to the set-up at the Athena when she'd visited Jack Bridges, but here everything is clean, and the costumes are neatly ordered on metal rails.

Carole's reflection in the mirror raises her heavily kohled eyebrows when she sees Nicoletta. 'What're you doing here?'

Nicoletta stands, half in, half out the door. 'I came to see the show,' she says, talking fast. 'I thought you were great, by the way!'

'Oh, thanks.' Carole blots her lips on a tissue, which she throws in a wastepaper basket at her feet. 'Why're you really here?'

Nicoletta puts her weight on one foot. There's no easy way of saying this. 'I wanted to speak to you about Julia Bridges again,' she says. 'A friend of Julia's said Julia told her that a married man had been paying her attention. It was your Graham, wasn't it?'

Carole takes a gold cigarette case out of a drawer and lights a thin brown cigarette, inhaling greedily.

'You've got some nerve. I don't see how that's any of your business,' she says finally.

Nicoletta hops onto her other foot. She's about thirty seconds away from being thrown out, she knows. 'Julia's body was found on Christmas Eve after twenty-five years,' she says mildly. 'It's in the public interest.'

Carole raises a sardonic smile at that. 'Smart little cookie, aren't you?' She continues powdering her face. 'Look, I'm heading out with the cast, don't have long. But yeah, Graham would get up on a cracked plate, that much is true. It's harmless. He and Julia, it was just what you'd call an infatuation.'

Nicoletta clears her throat. 'Did he ever give any indication that he and Julia were planning to head to England together, anything like that?'

Carole's eyes narrow in the mirror. 'All talk,' she scoffs. 'That's all it ever was. And it was so long ago now, what does it even matter? You can't prove anything about Julia and Graham. Besides, it's not relevant.' She closes her compact and blows her reflection a kiss, before standing up and turning to Nicoletta. 'I'll walk you out.' She puts her hand on Nicoletta's shoulder and gives her a little push towards the door. Nicoletta shakes her off.

'All right,' she says. 'But what if Graham was one of the last people to see Julia alive? That would make it very relevant.'

Carole flicks off the light switch and slams the door behind her, gesturing for Nicoletta to follow her down the corridor, towards a fluorescent 'Exit' sign. 'What exactly are you saying, my dear? Watch your step.'

Nicoletta trots after her in a bid to keep up as she comes to a set of double doors leading into the lobby. 'Mrs Swift, why did you ask me to join you in your car on the day of Julia's funeral? If you knew about your husband's, ah, flirtation with Julia.'

Carole gives her a hundred-watt smile, before pushing open the doors. 'Just to make him sweat, my dear.' She gives a tight, bitter laugh. 'He still doesn't know that I know.'

Chapter Twenty-Three

Sunday, 29th December 1968

It's early afternoon by the time they set off the next day. From Dermot's car window, Nicoletta watches roadside fields unfold in patchworks of greens and browns, herds of cattle standing resolute against the wind. Somewhere in Kildare, Dermot stops to take out a map from his glove compartment, along with a thermos of something which steams up the glass. He offers it to Nicoletta, and she declines. Once he's checked his map that they're on the right road for Knockgan, he restarts the engine, but doesn't move off.

Nicoletta takes out her compact. 'Why did you agree to drive me?'

Dermot shrugs, waiting for a lone tractor to pass before pulling out onto the road, which is beginning to crisp. 'I hope you get the job, Nicoletta.'

'Thanks,' Nicoletta murmurs, as they pass hedgerows already dappled in shadow, dusk settling thickly over the land.

Dermot gives a throaty chuckle that seems to warm up the whole car. 'Barney told me you really want it.'

He brakes suddenly as a lone figure steps out from a footpath and narrowly misses their fender. Nicoletta grips the handles of her bag, unmoored at the mere mention of Barney's name. She tries to picture his face, to hear his laugh, but Henry Morton's grey-flecked brush moustache keeps intruding. She won't even entertain the idea of telling Dermot about her visit there. If she files it away in a distant compartment of her brain and tells no one, then it'll be as if it never even happened.

They enter a small, neat village, with a sign welcoming them to Ballybeg. 'This is it,' Dermot says. 'Knockgan is the next townland over. Have your questions ready, I guess. You probably won't have long before doors are slammed in your face.'

Nicoletta looks doubtfully out the window as they pass a post office, several poky-looking bars and a dingy terrace. There's no one on the main street as they drive slowly by. This whole village is already giving her the heebie-jeebies. She doesn't blame Gloria for leaving.

'Could you pull in here, Dermot?' She indicates the side of the street where the terrace ends, and the countryside begins again.

'What're you thinking?'

She checks her face one more time before answering. 'We could do with a drink anyway. Let's try the pub.'

Nicoletta slips her arm through Dermot's. There's a faint light coming from a downstairs window of a pub she hadn't noticed when they'd driven by. Dermot trips over the step as they enter and swears as he stumbles into the tiny bar, disturbing a group of men playing cards on the countertop. The men look astonished as Nicoletta flashes a smile and settles herself beside them. Dermot joins her, red-faced. A woman puts down her newspaper and gets off a stool before stepping forward, nodding. She's not exactly unfriendly, Nicoletta decides.

'Good evening,' she says, trying to sound cheery. 'Could we have a brandy and a lemonade?' She doesn't bother asking Dermot what exactly he wants to drink. This is her show. The woman wordlessly turns to fetch two glasses and measure out the brandy.

Nicoletta hands over the money efficiently, freeing the landlady to go back to her newspaper.

'Cold enough out,' she says mildly. 'We've travelled down from Dublin and the roads are starting to ice up already.'

'Indeed.' The woman nods, disinterestedly. 'It's not a day for travelling.' The latter remark sounds as though it's intended as a rebuke. Nicoletta already regrets mentioning the word Dublin, as she's sure this woman's back is already up and she's on her guard. She sits down heavily on the stool and peers over the deaths page in the *Irish Independent*.

Nicoletta clears her throat. Dermot takes a sip of his drink and smacks his lips.

'I don't suppose you'd know the Fitzpatricks in Knockgan?'

There's a sharp intake of breath as the men stop talking and gawp at Nicoletta as though she's said something obscene. The landlady gets up off her stool and comes back over to them.

'Why do you wish to know?'

Nicoletta can feel the blood pumping around her face. 'I'm a reporter for the *Irish Sentinel*. I'd like to ask what you remember about Gloria Fitzpatrick.'

The woman's expression looks as though she's been turned to stone. When she answers, she speaks carefully. 'That was all such a long time ago.'

Nicoletta leans forward and lowers her voice in a futile attempt at preventing the card players from overhearing. 'A woman's body was found with the remains of a baby a few days ago and Miss Fitzpatrick is believed to have been responsible for their deaths.'

The woman closes her eyes. When she opens them, she returns to her stool and picks up her newspaper. 'I don't know the Fitzpatricks at all,' she says with finality. 'I must've been confusing them with someone else.'

One of the card players says something and all the others erupt with laughter. The game itself seems to have stopped and one or two of them keep looking over, before saying something to the group. Did she hear the word 'poof'? The atmosphere has now taken a slightly dangerous turn.

'Let's go,' she whispers to Dermot.

Dermot extracts a five-pound note from his wallet. 'Same again,' he says to the pub's landlady, but she continues reading her newspaper, studiously ignoring them. On his third attempt, Nicoletta stands up and grabs her bag. Dermot reluctantly follows.

'Where are you dragging me now?'

'We're going to try another pub.'

'After that reception? We'll be beaten up.'

Nicoletta sighs, admitting defeat. 'Let's go back to the car. Maybe we can try and speak to a neighbour of the Fitzpatricks.'

Dermot mutters something under his breath which Nicoletta doesn't quite catch. He's silent as he restarts the engine. It splutters and coughs. He lets it run for a minute or two. The seats are cold beneath them, their breath gathering in thick plumes. The headlights slice through the dark before Nicoletta speaks.

'Do you think the neighbours will speak to us?'

'You.' Dermot doesn't take his eyes off the road. 'Speak to you. This is nothing to do with me. Doubt it though. Judging by that crowd, we'd be as well to head back to Dublin right now.'

Nicoletta hugs herself in a futile bid to warm up. 'I'm not ready to throw in the towel just yet. We might find out *something* about Gloria. And I really, really want that job, Dermot. It's not as if I have anywhere better to be.' She forces a laugh.

Dermot gives her a sideways smile. 'That's the spirit. You might just get the job after all.'

He drives around for a while, turning off the main road onto a narrow laneway with barely room to admit one vehicle. Nicoletta hopes they don't meet any oncoming traffic at this hour.

'This is Knockgan, I guess,' he says doubtfully, slowing down as their headlights illuminate a nondescript modern

251

bungalow. All its windows are blank and uninviting. They appear to be curtainless.

Nicoletta swallows. She can feel a tight knot forming in her throat. 'Are there any other houses down here?'

Dermot does a sudden U-turn, and his headlights sweep over a cottage at the end of the lane. Nicoletta grips on to the door handle. Dermot slows and stops, turning off the engine. 'Sorry about that,' he says. 'I can see you're a nervous passenger. How you'd ever get into a car with Barney is beyond me.'

It might be the mention of Barney's name again, but this time she's galvanised into action. She picks up her bag.

'We'll try there first.' She gets out of the car and Dermot hastily follows suit, turning off the engine. The headlights fade and die. 'You're coming, too?' Nicoletta pauses at the grass verge, ghostly still in the dark.

'Can't let you go on your own.' Dermot heaves open the trunk and retrieves a torch. He switches it on and aims it at Nicoletta's feet.

'Here,' he says, tracing the shape of a large pothole with the sharp beam. 'The ground looks pretty lethal. You'll kill yourself in those shoes.'

They approach the front gate. A rusted sign says 'Blackberry Cottage'. Nicoletta can see where the house got its name as the modest patch of ground at the front is almost completely covered with wild brambles. They're already coated with a layer of frost.

She hesitates at the gate, turning back to Dermot, who has stopped to fiddle with the torch. 'This place doesn't look occupied. What do you think?'

Dermot rocks back on his heels before answering. He always sounds authoritative, Nicoletta thinks. That goes a long way. People tend to listen more closely if you sound like you know what you're talking about.

'You've come this far. Might as well see if there's anyone home. At the very least, they might feel like talking. If not, well, no harm done.'

The gate squeals long and loudly on its hinges. It feels as though it might disintegrate with one well-aimed push. Dermot lags behind her. Something scurries across the overgrown path, dashing under cover of darkness from one mass of brambles to the other. She shudders and gives the door a loud rap with her knuckles. Silence. She raps again and is just about to signal to Dermot to retrace his steps when the handle turns, and the door opens a crack. It wasn't locked at all to begin with. Nicoletta wonders if that's the way with all the houses around here, or if it's just particular to this one.

'Who's there?' a voice booms.

Nicoletta takes a deep breath. She can feel the adrenaline begin to course through her body, down to the tips of her toes. She doesn't feel the cold anymore.

'I'm a reporter for the *Irish Sentinel* newspaper. I'd . . . I'd like to talk to you about Gloria Fitzpatrick, if I may.'

Silence. Nicoletta knows the person is still there because she can hear them breathing through the crack in the door.

'I . . . why?'

Nicoletta stands up a little straighter. She looks back to Dermot. He nods encouragingly, the torch trained on the crack at the bottom of the door. 'New information has come to light in connection to Miss Fitzpatrick.'

'What is it?' The voice has descended to an urgent whisper.

'The body of Julia Bridges . . .'

'Another body.' The door opens and Nicoletta is face to face with a stooped man of indeterminate age, wearing blue cotton pyjamas under a terry cloth dressing gown despite the fact that it's only early evening. A sour smell hangs over him, a mixture of unwashed flesh and stale booze.

'Yes.' Nicoletta's eyes adjust to the gloom of the narrow hallway. It's bare – devoid of pictures, photographs, furniture or ornaments. After a minute she notices that there's no carpet either.

Nicoletta looks around helplessly to where Dermot is now leaning against the bonnet of his car. He has the headlights dimmed but she's glad he's there. 'I'm sorry, may I come in? If you'd like to speak to me, of course, Mr . . .?'

'You might as well,' he says. 'And Fitzpatrick is my name. Gerard Fitzpatrick.'

Chapter Twenty-Four

Nicoletta wonders later what might have happened if they'd kept going and ignored this particular house. The door closes and she can't see anything. She clears her throat.

'Where's the light switch?'

She feels something brush against her shoulder, and jerks her head, the solidity of a cold wall at her back.

Gerard pauses for the flare of a match, which suspends his face ghostly pale in front of her. 'Didn't mean to frighten you. The electricity has been cut off, I'm afraid.'

She's tempted to rush past him to the door and flee into the sanctity of Dermot's car. But there's something reassuring about his voice, kindly and apologetic. *This is Gloria Fitzpatrick's brother*, she reminds herself.

'Why has your power been cut off?' she can't help asking.

He sighs, almost snuffing out the guttering candle which he's placed on a low shelf at his elbow. He sits down on a small wooden crate, and she takes a stool opposite without being asked. 'There was a storm just before Christmas and the power hasn't come back yet.'

'Do you live here alone?'

Gerard hugs his knees to his chest, as though deflecting the question, and nods. Nicoletta observes him in the flickering light. The pose is a child-like one, but Gerard is stooped, and his hair is streaked with silver. He's a slight man.

'Have you always lived here?' She stops herself. 'I'm sorry. I'm already asking far too many questions. I'd like to speak to you about your late sister, Gloria, if I may.'

He angles his face towards her. 'Nobody's asked me about Gloria in a long time.'

'Is that so?' Nicoletta shifts her weight, and the stool almost topples over. 'As I mentioned, a body was found on Christmas Eve. The remains of Julia Bridges, an actress, along with a baby. Your sister is believed to have been responsible for their deaths many years ago. Do you have any comment to make on that?'

'Is that what the Guards think? It was Gloria?' Gerard briefly looks up as something small and determined scuttles past his feet. It takes all her willpower for Nicoletta to stay seated and quiet.

'Yes,' she says finally. 'It seems to be what they think.'

Gerard stands up, grabbing the candle and making his way to a room at the back. 'Can I get you something to drink?'

She considers asking if Dermot can join them. But Gerard Fitzpatrick may be about to talk to her. He's the closest she's been so far to Gloria. She doesn't want to spook him.

'Yes, please,' she says, her eyes following the candle as its light bounces drunkenly around the opposite wall.

A moment later he comes back with a glass of something tepid. She takes a pretend sip. It might be lemonade, but she can't be sure. To ask would be to insult him. She'll try and pour it away somewhere when he's not looking. He puts the candle back down. This really is a miserable room. A large armchair crowds one wall. There are several empty bottles and packets on the floor. The fireplace is piled with ash. She tries to draw her focus away from the squalor of it and onto his face, but it's difficult in the dim light. She wonders if he's even noticed her taking it all in.

'When was the last time you saw Gloria, Mr Fitzpatrick?'

He gives a hollow laugh, swallowing a mouthful of something, which goes down the wrong way. He makes a big show of coughing for ages.

'All the questions.'

Nicoletta smiles, unsure of how to proceed. 'Asking questions is my job. Why did you let me into your home, Mr Fitzpatrick?'

He hangs his head. 'I don't get many visitors,' he says miserably. 'Anyone who mattered is dead.'

'I see. I'm so sorry.' Nicoletta slides her notebook out of her bag.

Gerard stands and Nicoletta starts. 'You're not drinking what I gave you. I'll get you something else.' He indicates the gleam in the glass. Nicoletta picks it up and takes a pretend sip.

'No, it's fine. Please don't trouble yourself.'

Gerard grunts and shuffles back over to his position against the wall, looking out on the brambles in the back garden, which are cast in a hallucinogenic glow. Nicoletta marvels at their sheer scale. The spikes twist and turn inwards, forming a series of cavernous tombs.

'How did Gloria get the money to set herself up in business as a midwife, Mr Fitzpatrick?'

Fitzpatrick sighs. 'It broke Daddy's heart. As soon as she qualified in midwifery, Daddy made over a parcel of land in her name. Hoping she'd stick around here, have a family or what have you. But she sold the land and bought that fancy place above in Dublin.'

'Did Gloria ever have a child, Mr Fitzpatrick?' Nicoletta tries, as Gerard goes to the kitchen. He doesn't seem to have heard.

As he walks back, the room is flooded with light, bringing each shabby corner into chaotic relief. Nicoletta blinks. 'The power's come back.'

Gerard flicks off the light switch in the kitchen and shuffles around, plugging in a lamp. He sits back down on the floor beside her.

'It was my idea for her to give the baby up,' he says, as though they're picking up the threads of an ongoing conversation. He takes a glug from a bottle of clear liquid he's brought from the kitchen. She drops her pen, but he doesn't notice. His words are starting to slur, and she thinks about whether or not she can trust him and the veracity of what he's saying. *Why not?* she thinks, scouring his name onto her page. He's sure to be no more or less of a liar than anyone else.

'When was this, Mr Fitzpatrick?'

He takes another mouthful from the bottle. If he passes

out from drink, she'll have to get Dermot in to help. She wants to handle this one on her own, she decides.

'A long time ago.' Gerard wipes his mouth with the sleeve of his pyjama top. 'Daddy was still alive then. Gloria had already been in Dublin for nearly twenty years.'

'Was this when she owned The Downings nursing home?' Nicoletta writes quickly in the sharpened light.

'Yes. She'd just received a fine in the district court for supplying miscarriages. That nearly finished Daddy off. She was deep in debt. She used to splash her money on every theatre type who asked for it. Then, after the first court case finished, she came to me, in the winter of 1941, saying she was having a baby and asking could she stay with May and I for a while.' He snorts. 'May wouldn't have it. What would people say? Gloria had already done enough. Now, forty years of age, unmarried and in the family way. It was embarrassing.' He sounds almost pleading.

'What did she do?'

'I asked her if the chap would marry her. She laughed at that. He was already married. I thought about it. And of course, I didn't breathe a word to Daddy.'

'So, what then? What did you do?'

Gerard stretches his legs out and gazes at his feet, like a baby newly fascinated with these bodily appendages. 'May knew Lilian Higgins of St Bridget's from way back. They'd been at school together with the nuns. She wrote to Mrs Higgins, asking her to look after Gloria until the baby was born, suggesting that Gloria work for Mrs Higgins if she'd take her on. Gloria had lost her midwifery licence, so she went to Mrs Higgins as a live-in manager, if you like.' He makes a noise in the back of his throat. 'She was even allowed to keep that awful flashy car of hers. Mrs Higgins was very understanding, or so I thought.'

Nicoletta can feel her temperature rise, despite the dankness of the room. For once, someone is actually telling her information worth hearing. The fact that he doesn't exactly seem reliable is beside the point.

He lifts his sleeve to wipe a spool of drool from one corner of his mouth, as if to illustrate her point. 'Maggie and Sean are in England. They got away as fast as they could.'

'Who are they?'

'When our stepmother died, Gloria was like a mother to those two. But in the end, she couldn't wait to get away, too.'

Nicoletta murmurs sympathetically. 'How did your stepmother die?'

Gerard looks up. 'Gretta died giving birth to Eamon. Another half-brother. Gloria worshipped Gretta. She said afterwards that she'd never seen so much blood. I sometimes wonder ...'

'If it drove her to do what she did?' Nicoletta's breath plumes in front of her. She thinks of Dermot in the cold car, but she doesn't want to move and stop Gerard from talking.

'My wife never got on with Gloria. It was May who suggested Lilian Higgins. Said it was the kindest thing to do.' He gives a brittle laugh. 'But Gloria never forgave me. She said that baby was her last chance.'

'Last chance at what?' Nicoletta's chest feels tight.

Gerard doesn't look at her. 'Who knows? Happiness, I suppose. I should have asked her at the time.'

'Do you know what happened to Gloria's baby?'

Gerard settles his hands in his lap and turns to peer at Nicoletta. 'May used to always say that I couldn't be in my own company. When she died, I realised she was right. A few months ago, I saw this advertisement in the news-paper.' He rummages among the debris on the floor and comes up with a scrap of paper. He wordlessly hands it to Nicoletta, and she examines it in the silvery light.

'Leopold Slift,' the ad reads. 'Complete discretion, results guaranteed. Reuniting friends and loved ones since 1919.' Nicoletta hands it back to him and he stuffs it in his pocket.

'Of course, I'd already tried to find Lilian Higgins. Told her I wanted to contact Gloria's child. She said that was impossible as Gloria had suffered a stillbirth. I said, no, *that* was impossible. "Why?" Mrs Higgins said. Well, because Gloria blamed me for encouraging her to give her baby up. It was one of the reasons why she refused to see me when she was in prison. All that time to think, and I suppose she took it out on me. Had to take it out on someone. But she would have mentioned if the baby died, wouldn't she?'

Nicoletta lets out a tense breath. 'Did you try looking for her child?'

Gerard sighs. 'That's when I saw the ad. And Mr Slift did some poking around for me.'

'What did he find?' Nicoletta no longer feels as though

she's coaxing the answers out of Gerard. He answers readily, as though he's been dying for some time to talk to someone – anyone – about all this.

'That's the funny thing, Natalie.'

She doesn't say anything to correct him, just waits for him to tell her the funny thing.

'As I've said, Mr Slift did some poking around and ringing doorbells. He got talking to someone, a Miss Marian Swan, who'd been a midwife at St Bridget's in the early '40s. Miss Swan said there were some practices going on there, not quite above board . . .'

He trails off and Nicoletta sits forward. 'Practices? Such as . . . ?'

Fitzpatrick gives her a wary look, his voice barely above a whisper. He seems to have sobered up, or at the very least, drunk himself sober. 'Such as the fact that another woman at St Bridget's registered a live baby and Gloria registered a stillbirth when Miss Swan knew for a fact it was the other way around. And Gloria had a healthy baby girl and the other woman's baby boy was stillborn. Slift asked this Miss Swan if she'd ever questioned it. She had, she said. She raised her concerns with Mrs Higgins, eventually, after Julia Bridges went missing. Mrs Higgins gave Miss Swan her notice the next day. She was out on her ear, dismissed.'

'And what about the baby?'

'I decided to let the whole thing lie. That child, grown up by now, is better off not knowing.'

Nicoletta exhales, realising she's been holding her breath. She licks her lips, but her tongue feels dry and cracked. She takes a swig out of the forgotten glass and the clear liquid within nearly blows her head off. She coughs and splutters.

'Are you all right, Natalie?' Gerard turns in her direction. 'Grief can send you spare, you know.' He bats at the air, before his hand flops back down to his side. 'You wouldn't understand. You're too young.' His voice booms across the gloom like a foghorn. She digs her nails into the skin around her wrist before she speaks.

'I do understand, actually. When my son died, I couldn't tell anyone, and it nearly killed me.' The words come out in a rush, and she isn't sure if he's heard her.

'You were on your own?' His voice reaches across to her, soft.

'Yes,' she says, hardly daring to say it aloud. 'My boyfriend didn't want to know. I never saw him again. And my mother pretended the baby was hers. But Enzo was *mine*. And I couldn't even say.' Tears roll down her cheeks. The whole situation is surreal. She stands up to leave.

'Are you getting all of what I said, Natalie?' Gerard is beside her in an instant. 'I want you to report this. I want Mrs Higgins to have the book thrown at her.'

Nicoletta plucks at the air in front of her. She swallows. 'It's Nicoletta. And it's too late, Mr Fitzpatrick. Mrs Higgins is dead a few years. And she was already fined in the district court for forging the national birth register.'

Gerard's shoulders sag in defeat. Nicoletta walks into the hallway. He doesn't follow her. 'Thank you, Mr Fitzpatrick,' she says over her shoulder.

She stops on the doorstep. He appears in the hall-way now, a frail, sad shadow of a man in stained blue pyjamas.

'Mr Fitzpatrick, did Mr Slift manage to find out the name of the other woman? The one who registered Gloria's baby as her own?'

Gerard goes to lean against the doorframe, but he stag-gers against the flimsy pine, and narrowly misses a steep fall, his eyes half closed. When he opens them, he squints, as though trying to bring her back into focus.

'Sarto. It was Sarto. Daniela, or Danielle. Unusual. I knew I wouldn't forget it.' He pinches his nose at the bridge and closes his eyes. 'I'm sorry,' he says. 'Nosebleed. I often get them.'

Blood rushes to Nicoletta's scalp. Gerard's face swims out of focus, the night spiralling around them. She braces herself on the corner where the door meets the outside wall.

'Are you sure?' she asks.

But he's already closed the door softly, leaving her to navigate the brambly path on her own. Dermot is asleep in the driver's seat when she gets into the car beside him. He wakes up with a start and grunts.

'How'd you get on?'

'Not great,' she says, her voice flat and low.

'Are you all right?' Dermot leans forward, concern etch-ing his face. 'You look like you've seen a ghost.'

'It was fine.' Her teeth start to chatter. 'A drunken mono-logue of not very much coherent information.'

Dermot whistles. 'Were you on the sauce, too?'

Nicoletta nods tightly. 'I couldn't say no. I feel sick.' She stares mutely at her reflection in the windscreen as Dermot sparks the engine.

'Have you told Barney about your condition? Please tell me you've told him.' Dermot squeezes her arm.

Nicoletta shakes her head. 'Look, Dermot, can you keep this to yourself? I'll tell him in my own time.'

Dermot gives a wordless nod at her sharp tone.

'Thanks, Dermot. I owe you for this,' she says in a scratched whisper.

He waves away her thanks as the car shoots back onto the main road, before clicking on the radio, turning up the volume. Nicoletta clenches her fists, curling into herself, gratefully burying her head in her notebook. Gerard Fitzpatrick doesn't know her name. She's sure it didn't go in properly and on the law of averages he won't remember this exchange in the morning. Her eyes mindlessly scan her notes again and again, until the words run together on the page and rain spatters the windscreen.

Chapter Twenty-Five

Two rectangles of light gleam from the top of Burgh Quay, tantalising as a port. Dermot turns around when they reach the wooden shuttered doors to the *Sentinel*.

'You haven't said a word since we left that shithole in the sticks.' He rests a hand gently on her shoulder, as though she's made of porcelain. 'Jesus, Nicoletta, you're shivering. Maybe you should go home. You OK?'

She nods and steps forwards, thrusting the door open, not trusting herself to speak, trotting up the stairs ahead of him before he can ask her questions she doesn't want to answer.

There are a few copy boys milling around the newsroom. Price is seated at the back bench, an ear cocked to the radio, his chair back, feet on the desk. He looks away when he sees Nicoletta. She sits down at her desk in her coat, her shoulders rising and falling with the violence of holding her composure. She rifles through her notebook and scans through her notes from the conversation with Gerard. If what he said is true, then she is the natural child of Gloria Fitzpatrick. Her fingers clench back into savage fists. She thinks of Daniela, the woman she's thought of as her mother all these years, with her worry lines, and the navy shop coat and the lavender-scented cold cream. With a start, Nicoletta remembers wailing at Daniela as a young child, her wet face pressed into her mother's neck. *How would I know if I were bad?* The words resonate through the years with a slap. Did she know then? Could she sense it?

Her breath catches in her throat, and she shakily stands up, pacing to the window, placing her hands on the cold glass. She tries to think. Gerard Fitzpatrick is not a credible source. He gave her a lot of information, but it could all be completely untrue. Surely she can't put all her trust, the foundations of her very identity, on the ramblings of a lonely old drunk? She takes a deep breath, the river's path below silvery as a snail trail. One name jumps into her mind like a lighthouse beam. Leopold Slift. The private investigator who'd allegedly squirrelled out this information for Gerard. There is only one Leopold Slift in the phone book, with an address in Portobello. She needs to speak to him right now. She rushes back out without saying goodbye to Dermot, almost falling headlong down the steep stairwell. She has no time to lose. She hails a taxi on Westmoreland Street and cradles her bag on her lap, staring intently out the window to avoid conversation, as the departing street shapes lengthen into oblong blobs in the window opposite.

Leopold Slift lives in the end house of a row of eight Victorian red-bricks. His front room curtains are open, and Nicoletta sees the silhouette of someone reading by the light of a freestanding lamp, the bars from a fire glowing beside him. She knocks on the door, a couple more raps than is necessary. The man in the window takes several minutes to disengage himself from his book and armchair to come to the door.

'Leopold Slift? Since 1919?' Nicoletta rasps the words breathlessly, as though she's been running.

The man appraises her. 'That would be my father. I took over the business a few years ago. And you are?' He is wearing steel-rimmed spectacles and worn carpet slippers. His face is kindly, but instead of this putting her at her ease, it makes her more agitated. How can any right-thinking person help her untangle the mess of her life?

'Nicoletta Sarto,' she says. 'I have to talk to you. It's about Gloria Fitzpatrick. You, or your father, obtained some information for her brother Gerard some time ago.' She stops, trying to read his face. He hasn't registered surprise. He's simply waiting for her to say her piece. 'And that information' – she almost chokes on the word – 'relates directly to me.'

'I can't betray a client's confidentiality,' Slift says, pushing at his glasses.

Nicoletta leans dizzily on one foot. 'I've just found out I might be the daughter of a convicted murderer. And you're the only one I can think of who can confirm or deny that.' She staggers as though drunk. Slift raises an eyebrow.

'You'd better come in, Miss Sarto.' He stands to one side to allow her entry. She stumbles on the top step, and he reaches for her hand to steady her. His hand is large, with broad fingers. He gestures towards the front room he's just come from. A couple more lamps glow in the corner and there's a jazz record on the gramophone. A faint scent of mint lingers in the air.

'Have you already taken down your Christmas tree?' Nicoletta blurts out, before she can stop herself.

'We don't celebrate Christmas. My wife and I are Jewish.' He stays standing, warming his hands on a three-bar heater in the fireplace, waiting for Nicoletta to speak. When she doesn't, he leans towards her.

'Are you all right, Miss Sarto? You look like you've had a shock.'

It's only when she goes to formulate words that she realises her teeth are chattering.

'I'll be back in a moment.' Mr Slift edges forward, as though reluctant to leave her alone. At the door, he turns. 'Please make yourself at home.'

Nicoletta sits, hunched over her knees, her breath still rising and falling despite what's happened. Her mind is a blank. It feels fitting to be in this stranger's sitting room, far away from the people who think they know her. She can hear the faint hum of voices, a kettle hissing, some cupboards being opened and closed. Mr Slift comes back bearing a tray piled with tea things and biscuits. He pours her a bright yellow mug of tea and offers her the plate before sitting down gingerly in the chair he'd vacated to answer the door.

'Why are you here, Miss Sarto?' he says finally, his fingers laced around his drink.

Nicoletta looks at him, as though seeing him for the first time. She shakes her head. 'You won't be able to help me.'

Slift puts down his mug and stands back at the fire so he's facing her. 'I might be able to.'

Nicoletta puts down her mug as well. She hasn't touched its contents. 'No. You won't be able to help me. It's too late for that. I just want to hear the truth.'

'I see.' Slift looks thoughtful. 'In my experience, people think they want the truth, but the truth can be far more hurtful than not knowing.'

Nicoletta swallows. A rush of rage warms her blood. 'That's for me to decide.' She regrets the forceful tone, but it's anger alone that's propelling her now. 'I'm a journalist,' she says, the saying of it fortifying her. 'I was investigating a story about Gloria Fitzpatrick ...' She stumbles slightly on the name. 'The midwife who was convicted of murder.'

Slift makes a noise in the back of his throat. Nicoletta tries to read his expression in the soft light but it's not giving anything away.

'I spoke to her brother, Gerard Fitzpatrick. He said he'd asked you to look into the circumstances surrounding Gloria's pregnancy and the birth of her child at St Bridget's Maternal Nursing Home. Gerard seemed convinced that Gloria had given birth to a healthy baby girl, despite what the records show. A woman called Sarto was said to have had a stillbirth at the same time, spring of 1942. The babies were switched.'

Nicoletta looks up. Mr Slift's eyes haven't left her face. 'My mother's name is Daniela Sarto, and I was born at St Bridget's on 14th February 1942.'

Mr Slift gives Nicoletta a slight nod. Can she detect pity in the slight tilt of his mouth? Rage floods her nervous system and she stands up, though her legs threaten to give.

'Don't feel sorry for me, Mr Slift. I simply want you to confirm or deny this. Either it happened, or it didn't.'

Slift rubs his jaw. 'I spoke to the midwife who delivered you. Marian Swan. She spoke at length about how unhappy she was with the practices at St Bridget's, and voiced her concern. She witnessed Miss Fitzpatrick's living baby girl being switched with Mrs Sarto's baby boy, who had died, and when she complained to Mrs Higgins, the proprietor of St Bridget's, she was dismissed. I have no reason to suspect Miss Swan was lying about what she saw. So, yes, I can confirm it.'

'Gloria Fitzpatrick was my mother.' Although she whispers it, her voice sounds too loud for the stillness of the room. She stumbles to the inner door and wrenches it open. A young woman with pale hair pulled back with an Alice band and a concerned look on her face is on the other side. Has she been listening to them the entire time? Mr Slift is right behind her.

'Miss Sarto, wait. You've had a shock, a dreadful shock. I think you should sit with us for a while. Is there anyone we can call to come take you home?'

Nicoletta shakes her head mutely, passing through the hall, her hand pressing on the front door latch. 'I'm fine,' she says, not meeting their eyes. 'Thank you. I have to go now.'

She's down the dark path before they can come after her, and onto the street. The pavement has started to ice over and she skids, then rights herself. She looks around helplessly, wondering how she'll get out of here. There isn't a car in sight. She steps blindly into the road, just as a man on a bicycle slams into her side. The force knocks the wind out of her chest, and she sits heavily on the cold black road for a moment or two, the pain spreading with excruciating speed around her ribcage. She holds her belly, and a sound breaks through the gloom, like the cry of a wretched nocturnal creature. It's a moment before she realises it's her own sob. The man on the bicycle mumbles an apology over his shoulder and cycles on. He's gone by the time Mr Slift dashes onto the road and grabs Nicoletta under the armpits.

'My dear, are you all right? You could've been killed.'

Nicoletta allows herself to be guided back into the house, where she is placed on the sofa with a blanket over her and more tea and biscuits are administered.

'I'll ring an ambulance. She's in shock. But she might be concussed,' Mr Slift says to the woman with the Alice band, who Nicoletta presumes is his wife. Their two heads float over her own, bobbing around like kindly balloons. She wills herself to get up, gritting her teeth as she staggers to her feet.

'Please. Thank you for being so kind. But I'd just like to go home.'

Mr Slift bundles her into the back of his shiny green Ford and drops her back to Eccles Street, his wife in the passenger seat. They insist on waiting until they see her to the door of the cold, dark flat. Jean isn't home and Nicoletta is beyond grateful. She raises a whisper of a smile before closing the door with a reassuring click. She guzzles two aspirin with a small glass of brandy and gets into bed in her clothes, falling into a short, fitful sleep despite herself. When she wakes in the night with a painfully full bladder, she notices bright red streaks of blood in the toilet bowl.

Chapter Twenty-Six

Monday, 30th December 1968

The next morning, Nicoletta feels completely different. The lower half of her abdomen is tender, and she cradles it uselessly for a moment, as though doing so will stop the inevitable, until dull cramps spike into painful spasms. She doesn't want to be by herself, so she takes more aspirin and stuffs her underwear with two sanitary pads, before getting dressed. She eventually finds a taxi at Rutland Street and arrives at the newspaper office almost an hour after she set out. Her fingers shake as she picks a pen out of her bag, wincing at the pain in her ribs. She keeps her head bent over her in-tray as she hears the familiar thunder of footsteps and, within moments, Barney is at her desk.

'We need to talk,' he says, by way of greeting. His eyes are bloodshot, and he's now got several days' worth of stubble.

'Fine,' she says, concentrating all her energy on stacking a pile of notebooks with the spiral binding facing out.

She keeps the notebook relating to this story in her bag. 'Let's talk.'

Her voice sounds flat to her ears.

His eyebrows knit together, in the way they always do. She used to think Barney's age and experience elevated him into a stratosphere beyond her own, but now she notices the threads of grey in his hair, the worn look under his eyes, and he's only thirty. The way he's got thin, all of a sudden. She wonders if that's Marie's renewed influence.

'You look terrible,' he says, the words biting into her thoughts. 'Maybe you should go home, get some sleep. You're not even meant to be here.'

'Thanks very much,' she says tartly. 'You don't look so well yourself. And I'm fine where I am.'

In her peripheral vision, she can see Anne nudging Dermot and nodding at Barney, who's about to say something else, when the double doors from the stairwell clang. Nicoletta jumps, and so does Barney. A tall woman dressed in a full-length black fur coat with a black turban hat and a large black handbag comes striding towards them, dragging a small boy by the hand. Noel, the doorman, appears at the door, too late.

'I told her she couldn't come up,' he says to Barney.

'Marie,' Barney says. 'What are you doing here?'

'Which one of you is Nicoletta?'

The voice is familiar from the phone call a few days ago: soft, the hint of breath. But in person there's a steeliness which Nicoletta hadn't got on the phone. She is finally face to face with the monster from her head, and she doesn't know what to think. She can feel the colour drain from her face and wishes she'd had the inclination to put on make-up. Anne, Price and Dermot are sitting back to enjoy the spectacle, eyes on stalks.

'I am.' She pushes back her chair and stands up, holding out a trembling hand. 'You must be Marie. I've heard so much about you.'

Marie raises an eyebrow. She doesn't take her hand. 'Is that so? I hadn't heard a thing about you until this morning.'

'Hi, Nicoletta,' Liam calls with a wave.

Nicoletta can feel Marie's eyes travel from her toes to her face and back again. Marie is not what she'd been expecting from Barney's wife at all. She'd somehow imagined her to be paler, sicklier. Not this juggernaut of energy. Marie immediately turns her attention back to Barney. 'A word?'

Barney doesn't move. Despite his ragged look of earlier, Nicoletta can imagine now what he looked like as a child, wide-eyed, helpless, a fawn trapped in the headlights. He turns to her, a mixture of pleading and resignation on his face. She looks back down at her teetering pile of note-books, as if to say, *You're on your own here*. He touches her shoulder and mouths something, but she can't make out what it is and he's too self-conscious to say it aloud with everyone listening. Nicoletta watches with almost morbid fascination as Barney lifts up Liam and clutches him under his arm like a football. They follow Marie back out the door. Nicoletta can hear the echo of voices in the stairwell, fading as they descend.

The newsroom releases a collective exhale. Gritting her teeth, Nicoletta takes out her notebook and goes over to the vacant bank of typewriters. She sits down at the nearest one, intending to begin transcribing her conversation with Gerard Fitzpatrick. She rips out a page and scrunches it up. All eyes are on her. A burst of saliva reaches her mouth, and she holds on to the high, metal-topped table for support. She doesn't know if she'll make it in time.

The ladies' is empty, the two toilet cubicles ajar. She slams herself into the furthest one, before doubling over the bowl and being sick until she retches bile. She flushes the toilet and wipes her mouth with a tissue. She feels awful, but the worst must be over, surely. She squats over the seat. And that's when she notices the large, oozing stain spreading from her knickers through to her tights. Her knees go from under her as she passes something large and clotted into the bowl. She doesn't look down. Shaking with hot tears, she flushes the handle as much as it will allow before she hears the suck of the empty cistern. She waits until she hears a trickle as it refills itself with water. She throws the saturated sanitary pads into the bottom of the bin and stuffs toilet tissue down her knickers, staggering to her feet. Then she flees through the newsroom without a word to anyone.

At the bottom of the stairwell, she sits down heavily on the last step. Her tights stick clammily to her thighs, and she can feel something warm and wet rushing out of her. She closes her eyes. She feels light-headed. This is what it feels like to have a terrible accident, she thinks. A part of her wants to lie back and wait for it all to pass, but her higher self takes command. Standing up, her legs wobbly, she approaches the doorman.

'Noel,' she says, in what she hopes is a calm voice. 'Could you get me a taxi? I'm not feeling very well.' She sways, and Noel grabs her under the arm, concern etched on his face. He sits her down on the chair behind his desk and she puts her head between her knees, willing the dizzy spell to pass. Marie and Barney float through her mind. She imagines them having a heart to heart as a family unit about their future and her chest constricts with pain. Liam is taller than she'd remembered from before. She'd only met him once, months earlier, when she and Barney had taken him to fly a kite at the South Wall. Barney had said that he'd wanted her to meet Liam. Marie was still incommunicado, he'd said; she wasn't coming back. And because she was out of sight, Nicoletta had never thought about Marie too much. She was a distant threat, like nuclear war, or communism, far removed from Nicoletta's daily life. Liam hadn't been too fussed by her presence, nor had he asked who she was or how she knew his daddy. He'd been too focused on the large kite she'd brought him, with a bright, plumed tail. She'd watched as Barney raised the kite so that it almost tasted the wind, as it nudged its way into the air, twisting and turning, pulsing in the sky like a living thing. Nicoletta remembers Liam's flushed, laughing face, and Barney's whoops as the kite soared. They'd gone for tea at a hotel in town after, the crusts cut off the sandwiches, the scones piping hot and served with clotted cream. Liam, his face raised skywards, the kite racing away from him, or was it a different kite? Different but similar. Red and green, maybe, with a yellow tail. A slightly different shoreline, with houses in the distance, and a large boat honking its way out to sea. Her mother in a good mood, her hand on Nicoletta's shoulder, as she faced the charcoal-grey heavens, the kite dancing in her hands. Running along the sands, trying to catch up with it, until it plummeted to earth, and she pounced, ready to start again. Expecting her mother to call for her, but her mother had her head thrown back, her forehead smooth, her hair loose and spread out, streaming like a dark flag. There was someone else with them, a woman, much taller than her mother, linking her mother's arm, muttering in her ear, making her mother laugh. It was this someone who'd given her the kite. When Nicoletta launched the kite back into the sky, the stranger had turned to the side, her sharp profile in contrast with her coat billowing out against the grey seascape like a scarlet hot air balloon. She couldn't take her eyes off this woman, with her quick way of turning, the way she stopped to laugh, her whole body shaking, a magnificent silhouette against the dull sand.

'Come on now, Gloria,' Daniela had said. 'We need to get back.'

Gloria, her mother. And Gloria had composed herself and clasped Nicoletta's small bare hand in her gloved one. 'You'll get cold. We can't have that, can we?'

They'd gone to drink sweet, scalding tea, the taste of happiness. A painful spasm causes her head to bob further between her knees and she groans. She doesn't have the energy to look up to see if Noel has heard. She scrunches her eyes, but the memory is overlaid with others. That first time with Raffa, on the sofa in his front room, her eyes shut, his touch taut, rising like music. Spending the two subsequent times chasing the first like a half-remembered melody. Looking through his shuttered window, the glow from a streetlamp slicing the winter dusk to reveal the empty space where his piano once stood. The long, hot summer when Enzo was born. Marooned in her house with her mother, in those final weeks of confinement, sniping at each other, playing games of whist and rummy, waiting until they could start the ultimate game of pretence, a game that would slowly send her mad. Holding Enzo for the first time, looking into his squished little face with wonderment. Holding Enzo for the last time, his face slack with sleep, never to wake up. Barney's face, his expression of pure joy so easily worn. He was always amazed at her reserve. 'I thought Italians were supposed to be emotional,' he'd said once when they'd been lying in bed together, stretching out the minutes until they had to get up. 'That's just an idea people have,' she'd said, lightly. Barney had laughed, but his face is now blurring with Garda O'Connor's, water dripping from his lashes, nose and chin as he'd heaved her out of the sea and laid her on the shore. Nicoletta can feel another sharp cramp building. She shakes her head, the thoughts scurrying through it like blind mice.

An engine purrs and Noel is back with a clean-shaven man, a car with open back doors behind him. She blinks, her eyes not quite focusing. She doesn't look at the man's face.

'Can you take me home? I'm not feeling well.'

She's at her flat on Eccles Street when she realises that she doesn't have any money in her purse. She even turns it inside out. The driver waves her away. 'It's covered, love. Mind yourself.'

Inside her flat, feeling her way to the bathroom, she notices the blood has soaked through her tights, staining her skirt, marking her. Shame floods her body, acrid as bile. She sinks to her knees, tearing through her handbag, looking for more aspirin, tossing aside used tissues and several lipstick stubs. She finds the scrap of paper with Henry Morton's address on it, languishing at the bottom of her bag. She flings it into the toilet and flushes violently until the cistern gives a feeble groan of protest and she fears she's broken it. She lies on her bed listening to it gurgle and refill for what seems like hours, but sleep refuses to come.

Chapter Twenty-Seven

Tuesday, 31st December 1968
New Year's Eve

Nicoletta is still in bed when she hears the sound of thuds and sighs as several bags and boxes are lugged up the stairs and deposited in the tiny hallway of her flat. She groans and crams the pillow over her head. She is still weak and tender, but hopeful that the worst has passed. By the sound of things, Jean is back after her Christmas break. She'll probably be dying to ring in the New Year with gusto later on. That means endless chatter about what she's going to wear and who she's going to see. Nicoletta will have to say she's ill. She rolls over. Dirty light streams through the window. She has the day off, but she feels restless, despite everything.

She takes an exploratory step out of bed and stands for a moment, resting her weight gingerly on first one foot, then the other, bathed in the greyish light. Questions course through her, quicker than blood. Leopold Slift said there'd been an eyewitness to her illegal adoption: Marian Swan, the midwife who'd delivered her at St Bridget's. Nicoletta needs to hear it from the horse's mouth.

She urgently dresses in the only clean things she has, which are a short black babydoll dress with sharp white cuffs over slim black trousers. Speed is of the essence before Jean starts knocking on her door. Jean will demand her time and attention, seeking a conversation that will cement their relationship as flatmates, because that's the kind of person she is. The only people Nicoletta wants to talk to right now are those who can give her answers. She drags the telephone directory out from under her bed, the pages folded and furred. There are three Swans listed. One is a Miss M. Swan, with an address in Rathmines. The worst that could happen is that she has the wrong Miss M. Swan or that it's the right one and Marian Swan refuses to speak to her. But what's worse than not trying?

As she dashes into the bathroom, she can hear Jean singing to herself from the kitchen as she begins to fry sausages. Nicoletta scrubs her face, trying to get some colour back into it. She's brushing her teeth when she hears someone hammering at the door.

She spits out the toothpaste and dries her mouth, before sticking her head into the kitchen. Jean immediately starts chattering about her week. It's a few moments before Nicoletta can ask her if she's expecting someone to call.

'No, why?'

'There's someone battering our door.'

Jean wipes her hands on a tea towel and marches into the hallway, flinging the door open. Nicoletta picks up her bag, keys and an umbrella, before following her.

'It's for you,' Jean says smartly. 'It seems urgent.' She turns back into the kitchen as Barney steps forward, his presence already somehow too big for their tiny flat. 'Oh, and the toilet's broken.' She gives Nicoletta a curious look before she closes the kitchen door behind her.

Nicoletta puts her bag over her arm. 'I was just heading out,' she says. 'Work stuff. We can talk outside.'

Barney frowns. 'You're not rostered to work this week, Nic.'

'Is that so? I'm working on the Julia Bridges story, remember?' She waits while he follows her, and she closes the door behind them. 'Well, I have some things to do on that.' She begins to descend the grotty stairwell, but he catches her by the elbow.

'Marie's gone,' he says, matter-of-factly. 'This time she's taken Liam.'

He waits for a response, but she doesn't know what to say. 'I'll fight for custody but we're getting a divorce. That's it.'

'That's terrible about Liam.' She's halfway down the stairs when he calls her name. By the time she reluctantly looks back, she sees that he's on both knees. She can't help but burst out laughing. 'That carpet's filthy. You'll ruin your trousers.'

He shrugs. 'I don't give a shite about the trousers.'

She comes back up the stairs, slowly, and as she does so, he takes a maroon velvet box from his pocket. He opens it. A small diamond solitaire flashes in the weak light. 'You're the one I want to be with,' he says. 'Nicoletta Sarto, will you marry me?'

She feels a sob rise in her throat and she swallows it down.

'I . . . I'll think about it,' she says. 'But now I have to go.'

He doesn't call after her this time.

She walks as far as O'Connell Street, catching a bus at the Gresham. A heavy rain shower starts abruptly as the doors close and the bus pulls away from the kerb. The address she'd scribbled down leads her to a large Victorian square in Rathmines. Miss M. Swan lives at number 4E. It's a tall, red-brick house which has been chaotically divided into flats. 4E is on the top floor. The rain has slowed to a light drizzle when a young man wheeling a bicycle lets her in the main entrance and she smiles her thanks. She winces as she edges up a steep flight of stairs before she reaches the flat and gives a brisk knock. There's no answer. She puts her ear to the lock: silence. She tries again and waits for a minute or two, before going back down. The young man who let her in is chaining his bicycle to a banister.

'Excuse me, do you happen to know if Marian Swan lives upstairs?'

The man squints up at her through a longish fringe. 'Miss Swan? Yeah. Can I help you?'

Nicoletta can feel her palms dampen. 'I was hoping to speak to her today, but she doesn't seem to be at home. Any idea when she might be back?'

The man blows his hair out of his eyes before standing

up. 'She's at work. Grosvenor's Nursing Home up the road. You could try her later this evening, I guess. Or I could pass on a message, Miss ...' He stands up a little straighter and holds out his hand.

'It's Mrs, actually,' Nicoletta says, shaking it. 'Mrs King.'

'Oh,' the man – boy, really – says, visibly disappointed. 'Well, I hope you find her, Mrs King. And Happy New Year.'

'Many happy returns,' Nicoletta says, clipping away at a brusque pace, realising how much she likes the way 'Mrs King' sounds when said aloud.

Grosvenor's Nursing Home is halfway between Rathmines and Rathgar. Nicoletta hears a baby screaming before she's even rung the bell. A middle-aged blonde woman in a starched nurse's uniform answers the door after a minute's pause and stares through huge insect-like eyelashes.

'Could I speak to Marian Swan?'

The nurse's eyelashes don't budge as she holds the door open. It would seem that a young woman calling to this establishment doesn't raise many questions after all.

'I'll see if she's available.'

'Thank you.' Nicoletta almost knocks over an over-grown potted spider plant as she passes through.

'Who will I say wishes to see her?'

'Nicoletta Sarto.'

The nurse blinks, her eyelashes beating like wings. Nicoletta reaches into her bag for a piece of paper. 'Here, I'll write it down for you,' she says, plonking herself on a fold-up vinyl chair.

The nurse goes off through a connecting door. After

twenty minutes, Nicoletta starts getting restless. She can hear whispering, a kettle whirring from the adjacent room and another far-off baby crying. She wonders if it's a different baby from before. She's considering getting up and knocking to remind the nurse that she's still there, when the door opens and a dark-haired woman with a dignified walk comes towards her with her hand outstretched.

'Miss Sarto,' she says. 'Come in.'

Nicoletta stands up, disarmed by this welcome. She'd been expecting Miss Swan to perhaps refuse to see her, or at least to be slightly hostile.

She follows Miss Swan into a bright, hopelessly untidy office strewn with files and papers. A gaudy plastic Christmas tree stands in the corner, dwarfed by a tall metal filing cabinet. Miss Swan lifts a heap of papers off a chair and gestures for Nicoletta to sit, before sitting down opposite her on an upturned box.

'I apologise for the mess,' she says. 'We're updating our filing system before the new year.'

Nicoletta shrugs and takes an inward breath. 'Miss Swan, my name is Nicoletta Sarto and I'm—'

Miss Swan raises her hand. 'I know who you are.'

Nicoletta is momentarily lost for words. 'You do?'

'Yes. I read the papers. Julia Bridges was found on Christmas Eve. And the other body, the baby. Gosh. What do you want to talk to me for? I told the Guards everything at the time.'

'Did you?' Nicoletta looks her dead in the eye. Miss Swan's eyes are a soft blue; she looks away, laying her hands flat in her lap.

Nicoletta takes a deep, shuddery breath. 'Miss Swan, what if I told you that I'm here because I have reason to believe that there was an adoption racket going on at St Bridget's ...'

Miss Swan's face gives nothing away. Nicoletta decides to continue. 'I think I'm the natural child of Gloria Fitzpatrick. I know you worked at St Bridget's at that time, and I believe you witnessed my birth, and the subsequent switching of another baby, a boy, who was stillborn, so that I was wrongfully registered as the legal child of Daniela and Ettore Sarto. I wonder if you could confirm or deny that.'

Miss Swan shakes her head. 'It was nothing to do with me, Miss Sarto.'

Nicoletta's chest constricts as though someone has just stepped on it. 'I'm not here just as a reporter. I'm here as a human being. I've a right to know.'

Miss Swan stands up and walks over to a small electric kettle plugged into the wall. She flicks a switch and waits as it comes to the boil. She spoons instant coffee into two mugs and fills them with hot water before giving them a brisk stir. 'Do you take milk?' Nicoletta gives a shaky nod and Miss Swan gives the mug a generous splash. She sits back down opposite Nicoletta. 'Look, nothing I can say can change the past. Mrs Higgins is dead now. I suppose you know that she was fined in the district court for forging the national birth register a couple of years ago?'

Nicoletta nods.

'A tap on the wrist, that's all she got. She knew the right people. It was simple, really. A single girl would come to St Bridget's – usually someone Mrs Higgins had taken pity on, someone who would work for her keep up until the birth. And someone else, usually someone who desperately wanted a child, would arrive pretending they were pregnant. Sometimes American couples who wanted an Irish baby. Mrs Higgins would register the single girl's baby as the married woman's. She had a priest who was willing to do the baptisms, no questions asked.'

'And what about Gloria?'

'With Gloria it was simple. She was having a baby. She'd had to sell her business, her house. She didn't have a midwifery licence anymore. The father of her baby was married.'

'Did she say who he was?' Nicoletta takes a hot swallow of her coffee, preparing herself for information she mightn't want to hear.

'Yes, she did, as a matter of fact. Charles Creighton, she said his name was. I wondered if it was the same as the jewellers.'

Nicoletta lets the information sit for a moment before anger bubbles up her throat. 'My whole life has been a lie.'

Miss Swan leans forward. 'Many lies were told, I agree. It wasn't right.'

Nicoletta can feel a sour taste rushing into her mouth. She takes another gulp of the coffee, and it burns her tongue. 'It was just wrong.'

She looks Miss Swan in the eye. 'You brought me into the world. Placed me in my mother's arms.' Her voice cracks slightly on the word *mother*. 'Did you take me away from her?'

Miss Swan's mug lands on the table with a thud. 'I'll always remember it. It was Valentine's Day of 1942, because I was meant to go out for a meal with my fiancé and Mrs Higgins wouldn't let me take the time off. I was fuming.' She laces her fingers under her bust. 'Mrs Higgins assured me it was all for the best. Especially for you. And that was the most important thing at the end of the day.'

Nicoletta takes another gulp of bitter coffee. She quickly puts it down again. 'What happened when you voiced your concerns?'

Miss Swan scrunches her nose. Nicoletta can't help noticing that it's lightly sprinkled with freckles. This was the first face she ever saw when she took her first breath. She realises she's been staring for a few seconds too long and looks down at her hands.

Miss Swan picks up her mug again. 'After Julia Bridges went missing, I gave a broad enough statement to the police. But to myself, I said enough was enough. I went and spoke to Mrs Higgins and said I wouldn't tolerate all the goings-on. Between herself and Gloria, it's a wonder we weren't all thrown in prison, I said.' She gives a rueful smile. 'She sacked me the next day. I had to grovel so that she'd give me a decent reference. And that was that. But they're both dead now, so I don't mind telling you. Especially as it all relates directly to you. I hope you don't feel too badly about it. But as you've said, you do have a right to know.'

Marian Swan stands up, setting the coffee down on a stack of salmon-pink cardboard-covered files. 'Anyway, it's all over the papers now. About Julia Bridges, and the baby found in Charles Creighton's garden.'

Nicoletta's head swims. She struggles to keep her thoughts above water. 'Yes. My father's house.' She gives a brittle laugh that goes on for a moment too long. She drains the rest of her coffee and stands up. Her legs feel like rubber bands. 'Thank you, Miss Swan,' she says, almost choking on the words. 'It's a relief to hear the truth at last.'

Nicoletta opens the door. The nurse from before with the spidery eyelashes is standing outside, and Nicoletta has the feeling she's been listening in to every word.

'Just coming back to take your mugs.'

'Thank you, Eilish,' says Miss Swan weakly. Eilish doesn't leave, instead she leans against the desk, clutching the mugs against her chest.

'I read your report about Julia Bridges being found,' she says to Nicoletta at last, in a slightly husky voice. 'I'm glad she was laid to rest.'

'Did you know Mrs Bridges?' Nicoletta doesn't know where this is going, but Eilish seems keen to talk.

'No.' Eilish shakes her head emphatically. 'I worked for Mrs Higgins at St Bridget's as a maid before I qualified as a midwife.'

Miss Swan comes over and pats Eilish's arm. 'Eilish is very bright. I helped her get settled here.'

She smiles down at Eilish, before addressing Nicoletta, her tone apologetic, but firm. 'I'm afraid Gloria took advantage of Eilish. It's what she was like.'

Eilish nods. 'I didn't know about anything that went

on.' She steals a sideways look at Miss Swan, who stead-
fastly looks down at her hands. 'All I know is she got her
comeuppance.'

Chapter Twenty-Eight

The sky is dark and leaden as Nicoletta wanders list-lessly back in the direction of town. The windows of the grand Victorian squares and neat Edwardian terraces of Rathmines and Ranelagh are swaddled at this hour, though it's only mid-afternoon. A premature dusk has already descended, hanging limply over the rust-coloured brick chimneys like residual smoke after a conjurer's final act. The ache in her chest spikes to her throat as she tries to make sense of what she's just heard. She'd needed to speak to Marian Swan, the sole witness to her birth and the sub-sequent switching of the babies; to hear it from the horse's mouth. The definitive and final proof. And now she knows.

She sits down heavily on one of the low perimeters ringing a frost-ravaged patch of garden. The cold from the weather-beaten brick, bare and exposed to the elements through all seasons, seeps through her clothes. She feels helpless as a newborn. She closes her eyes for a moment, that blonde midwife Eilish's words sending a shiver through her bones, starting at the base of her skull. *She got her comeuppance.*

She glances behind and sees a curtain twitch, so she gets unsteadily to her feet. She needs now to speak to someone else who knew Gloria, but this time someone who actually loved her. Could she find one more person who'd be willing to speak to her about Gloria Fitzpatrick? Someone who'd seen the best in her. No one is all bad, surely. Nor all good, for that matter. She thinks of the nurse at Clyde Hall who lost her job because of Gloria. *Gloria was Bernie's pet,* according to what the husband, Cyril, had said. She could do without seeing him again, another drunken monologue that may or may not mean much at all.

Her teeth are chattering in a way that feels false, like ill-fitting dentures, and she realises she has to get in out of the cold. Her steps quicken with purpose when she sees a taxi whizz towards her. She sticks out an arm, but it doesn't stop. She keeps walking, back towards the triangle in Ranelagh village where she finds a cab, the driver reading the *Sentinel* propped against the steering wheel. The sight gives her a static jolt of reality. Is she going to speak to Nurse Brennan as a reporter, or as Gloria's daughter? She examines her motives as she clambers into the back of the cab and slams the door shut behind her, grateful to the driver for turning the heater up to high. It's ten to four and already getting dark. The minute hand is ticking by, spinning in perpetuity, and it will soon be the second of January, when Duffy will announce his decision on her fate. She can't lose the women's page editor job to Anne. But right now, all she knows is that she's desperate to speak to Bernadette Brennan, off the record if needs be, for both their sakes.

When the taxi passes the asylum, Nicoletta asks the driver to stop. She hands him a few crumpled notes and exits the car, leaning sideways against the high, austere stone wall to catch her breath, while the driver seems to take an eternity reversing and turning, before giving her a curious look and eventually driving off. Nicoletta touches the stone with her bare fingertips. It's as cold as a grave. She crosses the road and knocks on Bernadette Brennan's unassuming front door. Bernadette opens it almost immediately.

'Yes?' she says, with a nervous tilt to her neck.

'Nurse Brennan. It's Nicoletta Sarto. We met a few days ago ... I'm a reporter from the *Sentinel*.'

Bernadette blinks. 'I'm not a nurse anymore. Haven't been for ten years. Since my daughter was born.'

'Is that true?' Nicoletta says before she can stop herself. 'Or is it because you lost your job after helping Gloria Fitzpatrick commit suicide?' The words gather over her head like clouds.

The door begins closing and Nicoletta inserts her foot into the gap.

'Look, I'm sorry. Please, Bernadette. I need to speak to you. Not as a reporter.'

'Why are you here?' Bernadette's voice is quiet, but rigid with anger. She doesn't make any move to open the door any wider.

Nicoletta's face is pressed to the gap. She must look all mouth to the person behind the door.

'Because I'm Gloria's daughter.' There's a moment's silence, then the door opens a few inches, allowing Nicoletta inside.

The hallway is cool, but the kitchen is warm and cosy. Nicoletta stands awkwardly beside the Formica table, hunched into her coat, and Bernadette doesn't offer her a seat.

'Why are you really here?' Bernadette doesn't sit down either, instead leaning over the table on her knuckles opposite Nicoletta. 'Haven't you done enough?' There's a quiet fury in her tone. 'How dare you ambush my family on St Stephen's Day?'

Nicoletta shakes her head. 'I want to find out the truth about my mother.'

Bernadette gives her a grim smile. 'The truth? Do you think I'm an idiot? How do I know you're not just pretending to be Gloria's long-lost daughter, to get me to say something and incriminate myself?'

Nicoletta clasps her bag tightly. 'Did Gloria ever mention a daughter?'

Bernadette sighs noisily. 'If she did, why should I tell you?'

'I'm sorry for interrupting your family lunch the other day.' Nicoletta begins to perspire from the heat of the kitchen, but she doesn't make a move to take off her coat. She clasps her hands together in supplication. 'Truly, I am. But I've just found out that Gloria gave birth to me in secret in February 1942 and I was then illegally adopted. I've just found out that my birth mother was a convicted murderer and my whole life has been a lie.'

Bernadette looks her defiantly in the eyes. 'Why should I believe you?'

Nicoletta meets her gaze. 'Why would I make it up?'

Bernadette sits down at the table and gestures for Nicoletta to sit opposite her. She puts her bag on the floor beside her, not daring to take out her notebook. When they're seated, Bernadette speaks. Her voice is softer than it was before. 'I'm curious,' she says. 'What could you possibly want to know about Gloria that you think you'll find out from me?'

Nicoletta goes to speak but the words crumble to dust in her throat. 'I'm desperate to speak to someone who knew Gloria. Who knew what she was *really* like. And not just knew her, but maybe even loved her.'

'What makes you think I loved her?' Bernadette stands up and puts on the kettle with a brisk flick of her wrist.

'You lost your job over Gloria's death. Surely that means you stuck your neck out for her.'

Bernadette brings over tea things on a tray and Nicoletta takes off her coat and exhales slowly, before taking a shuddery sip of black tea. She's too focused on what will come next to break her train of thought in order to stop and add milk.

Bernadette laughs, a slow unexpected gurgle of mirth. 'I suppose, when you put it like that.'

'What was she like?' Nicoletta wraps her fingers around the warm cup despite the heat of the room. She is hungry for details. She feels like a baby bird, helpless, with its beak open, waiting for tasty morsels of information.

Bernadette shrugs. 'She was a pain in the neck, was Gloria. Could be a liar, depending on her mood. She definitely enjoyed her notoriety among the other patients. Lived in her own little world if you like. But she could be very kind.'

'In what way?'

'There was a woman who slept in the bed beside Gloria on the ward. She was a troubled soul, serving a life sentence for poisoning her whole family. Every morning when she woke up, the first thing she used to do on the way to chapel, she used to tell Gloria she was having a baby. Every morning.'

'And was she?' Nicoletta takes a tiny sip of tea. It's bitter without milk or sugar.

'God, no. This woman was at least sixty-five if she were a day. She'd been there for most of her life. Anyway, Gloria always acted like she believed her. One day I asked her why, and she said, "It's all any of us want."'

Nicoletta puts her hands in her lap. She can feel them trembling. 'I've heard such terrible things about her, it's a relief to hear she wasn't a total monster.'

Bernadette's brow creases. 'Oh God no, not at all. She was marvellous fun, was Gloria. She used to sit with me every evening at the nurses' station and I'd give her bottles of stout while she did her knitting.' Bernadette shakes her head. 'That got me in terrible trouble in the end. Along with everything else.'

'Everything else?'

Bernadette keeps talking, as though she hasn't heard. 'What else can I tell you about Gloria?' Her mouth curves into a rueful smile. 'She was a breath of fresh air . . . I must have loved her to do what I did.'

'Which was?' Nicoletta can barely speak.

Bernadette shrugs. She hasn't touched her own tea. 'I knew Gloria was ill, and unhappy. She'd started hearing voices again. I knew she wasn't taking her medication. She didn't say what she had planned in so many words. But I knew. And I turned a blind eye. Because I guess I wanted her to be free.'

Neither of them speak until Bernadette stands up and carries the tray over to the sink, dumping everything into it though the tea is unfinished. 'I've regretted it every day since,' she says with her back to Nicoletta. 'It cost me my job. But do I still think it was the right thing to do? Yes.'

Nicoletta takes her cue to stand up and put on her coat, thanking Bernadette for the tea. But Bernadette won't look at her. She walks her to the door. Just as Nicoletta thinks she's going to leave without the other woman saying anything at all, Bernadette grabs her hand. Her palms are cold, her breath hot in Nicoletta's face.

'Go and find Gloria's solicitor, Leslie White. Gloria left a letter among her effects.'

'Why are you telling me this?' Nicoletta stands poised on the threshold, halfway in and halfway out.

Bernadette takes her hand from Nicoletta's to wipe her face before she answers. 'Because I think you should be the one to read it.'

Chapter Twenty-Nine

The journey back into town takes an age. There are no taxis to be had and, in sheer frustration, Nicoletta walks from Windy Arbour to Ranelagh, adrenaline keeping her warm with every impatient stride. The bus she eventually boards wheezes to a stop every few minutes, spluttering with protest when it's time to move off again. She alights at Merrion Row, the pavement already beginning to frost over. The stars twinkle overhead, the night stretching out like a shroud, clear and cold. From here, at the junction with St Stephen's Green, she can see a liveried doorman at the Shelbourne Hotel holding an umbrella for a smart couple, the woman swathed in furs, with jewels gleaming at wrists and throat, the doors spinning like a gold-handled top in their wake. Nicoletta forces herself to look in the other direction. She can see the tall spindly rooftops of nearby Ely Place, where Gloria Fitzpatrick lived in disgrace, after losing her business and her midwifery licence, until she was subsequently charged, tried and convicted of a woman's murder. Did she also walk these dark streets, watchful as a small animal? Gloria Fitzpatrick. *Nurse*

Fitzpatrick. *My mother.* A woman everybody knew, yet nobody had a clue what she was up to. A creature of the night, a scavenger, like a fox or an alley cat, never to be treated with grand deference like the couple going into the hotel.

Nicoletta shrinks against the edges of the buildings, willing herself to escape notice. She hasn't prayed in a long time, but she inwardly pleads with some higher power for her not to bump into anyone she knows. Not now. Dublin is a small place; there's always the possibility. She imagines she knows how Gloria must have felt, in those lost final years. Affinity stretches between them, an outstretched hand bridging the decades, until Nicoletta almost feels like Gloria is two steps behind, shadowing her through the unlit maze of streets between Merrion Row and Merrion Square. The thought brings her a brittle sort of comfort and emboldens her to stalk the perimeter of the square until she finds the brass plaque with the right name. White and Son, Solicitors. There's a light on upstairs, and she hammers on the door until it opens a crack. A bloodshot eye observes Nicoletta through the gap.

'Miss Sarto,' the voice says with a slight slur. 'To what do I owe this pleasure?'

'I want the letter,' Nicoletta says, both hands on the brass door handle, pulling it with all her might.

'Which letter?'

'Gloria Fitzpatrick's letter, the one she left with her personal effects. I know you have it. And it belongs to me.'

The door opens a bit wider. 'My dear. I'm loath to have this conversation on the street.'

Nicoletta stands in the lobby looking around. The front reception desk and every available floor space is covered with files and papers.

'I thought your office was closed for Christmas.'

Leslie White blinks. He's wearing a red woollen pullover that's far too big for him and his collarbones jut up under it like coat hangers. 'It is. I'm doing a final clear out before I have to go into hospital for treatment in the new year. My wife wants me to have the treatment. But I don't expect to survive it.'

Nicoletta gestures at all the files. 'But what about your son? Can't he take over?'

White grimaces. 'I am the son. I'm all that's left.' He blows his nose into a large hanky which he shoves back into his sleeve. 'Now, what's all this about a letter?'

Nicoletta leans against the reception desk, a vast wooden vessel, solid as a ship, and tries to breathe evenly. 'Bernadette Brennan was a nurse at Clyde Hall Asylum in Gloria Fitzpatrick's final days. She says that when they cleared out Gloria's personal effects as no family members came to claim them, they found a letter. Nurse Brennan was dismissed after the circumstances surrounding Gloria's death came to light, but she said you took the letter, as Gloria's solicitor.' She exhales and waits for White to speak.

'Yes, I took the letter. Even though she sacked me after the trial, I kept it all these years. Haven't opened it. But I thought I should keep it safe. I was actually about to destroy it, along with some other documents,' White says with a slight slur. He smiles at her, his teeth too large for his head, his eyes not quite in focus, breath sharp with alcohol.

'Please don't. Give it to me.' Nicoletta's voice is low and urgent.

'And why should I do that?'

Nicoletta leans against the desk. She feels weary. 'Because I'm Gloria's daughter.'

White looks at her for a few seconds longer than is comfortable, then swipes a large greying envelope from the middle of a large pile on the floor. He presses it into her hands. 'Here you are, my dear.'

'Don't you want to hear proof?'

'Proof of what?'

'That I'm telling the truth about being Gloria's daughter.' She smiles, despite herself.

White looks at her, as though searching for something in her face. He smiles, the bones in his face painfully visible under the papery skin. 'The proof is standing in front of me. You're the image of Gloria when you smile. Has no one ever told you that?'

Nicoletta shakes her head, slotting the letter carefully into her bag, where it jostles side by side with the picture of Julia Bridges on stage with Daniela Stagg. Both Gloria and Daniela had given her life, in their own ways.

'Thank you,' she says, but White has already turned back to a towering stack of files. She closes the door with a bang and dashes onto Merrion Square. Exhaustion envelops her like a cloud of fumes as a bus judders to a stop. It's heading in the opposite direction to where she wants to go. She doesn't care, she just wants to sit down. She pays her fare and takes a seat behind the driver, shakily taking the letter out and tearing open the slightly damp envelope. She begins to read as the bus rounds a corner and picks up speed.

Chapter Thirty

GLORIA

When you're young, you don't think about time. You assume there's an ocean of it ahead, enough to drown in. The hours and minutes tick themselves into oblivion, second by second, as you wait for life – your *real* life – to begin. I suppose I was like that once. Impatient, but not in too much of a hurry to dive in either. Now I'm suspended somewhere in between. Poised to jump, but liable to change my mind at the last second. Charles used to charge straight ahead of me at the Forty Foot, the sky between us velvet as the inside of a jewellery box. He was – *is* – a strong swimmer. Graceful, instinctive. Too much thinking just spoils it.

There's a mural of da Vinci's *Last Supper* on the passageway wall leading into the refectory. Twelve men, flanking Jesus, like a jury. *One of you will betray me.* Betrayal the most bitter pill of all. Da Vinci's masterpiece, a commission from a patron. *I like to think of myself as a patron of the arts*. I'd said that to Charles one night at the Athena, as the cast of *The Importance of Being Earnest* filed onto the stage for an encore. He'd laughed out of the corner of his mouth.

'Of course you do.' He turned back as Lady Bracknell tossed her fan in a cascade of grey feathers into the orchestra pit. I'd had the ostrich feather fan specially made, along with all the other costumes. Everyone coming back to that fine, tall house of mine on Mount Pleasant Square when the pubs closed. The Downings. The Persian rug by the fireplace, the brocade curtains, the baby grand. The actors draped across my settee like permanent soft furnishings. Night after night, Charles' hair slick as a wing against my cheek, his eyes scanning the room. His first wife being nursed at home; I imagined the air in her bedroom thick and sweet. An unmentionable disease. Or rather, Charles didn't like to mention it.

Another night: the chorus girls at the Athena summer revue, shimmying around a large papier-mâché seashell. The supine Venus within, her body stocking glittering under the spotlight as she turned, her hands parting her long, artificial hair. The mermaid. The part that would later be played by Julia Bridges. I paid a seamstress to sew countless sequins onto those costumes. Going to Jammet's after, taking the whole cast. Charles ordered champagne, hang the expense. Before it arrived, he was summoned from the table to the telephone. His eyes glazed when he came back, forehead beaded with sweat.

'What's wrong, darling?'

We went back to The Downings then, just the two of

us. Eilish brought us drinks in the drawing room. We stretched out on the floor, where Charles spilled his over the blue Persian rug. He barely noticed. I mopped it up with one of my monogrammed towels, before giving him a fresh one, which he drank in two swallows. We settled back, me cradling his head in my lap. It was only then I was able to say it. 'Is she gone, darling?'

He nodded, his teeth chattering despite the warmth of the room. His lips on mine, movements slow and tender as a knife gliding through butter, laying me back against the damp Persian rug, hungry for me, all of a sudden, hitting out like a drowning man. Afterwards, he trailed a finger down my cheek. 'Just give me time,' he said. Hope soared in my chest.

Tempus fugit, as my former solicitor might say. Poor old Leslie. The sale of my worldly goods contributed to his wealth, but in the end, he didn't have the stomach for it. Or for me: for what I did. He just wanted me to stay quiet.

'Though if you ask me, they're at nothing without the presence of Mrs Bridges' body.' That's what he'd said. Over and over. Her body. I thought of Charles' face as I peered at the stage. *She's very beautiful. Those legs!*

The day I was sentenced to hang began like the rest, with me standing at my stunted attic window on Ely Place, looking down at the inky pavement below. A tall, narrow house divided into tiny flats, mine was on the top floor, an eyrie from which I could watch and listen. A milk cart clopped past, a boy leaping out from the cab at the front to clink deliveries onto doorsteps and fire the empties back. The sheer ordinariness of it all made me want to weep because I knew it was all about to tilt sideways. I was about to go and put fresh sixpences in the metre and fetch some water from the hopper downstairs, before having a wash, flicking on the wireless and making tea, in an elaborate sequence of mundane tasks. Anything to convince myself it was mustering up to be a day like any other.

It was then I heard the door bang. Alan Doyle from downstairs hurried prissily down the steps, turning up the collar of his overcoat so it grazed his jaw, his mass of sandy hair styled into a rigid swirl. He didn't look up, but I knew he knew I was there, looking out, the way I always did. And I knew where he was going. Down to the Four Courts, for my sentencing, to get a seat in the public gallery. Alan Doyle, the prosecution's first witness. He worked nights as a porter in a hotel on Drury Street. He'd sworn that he'd been shaving at midnight on 2nd April 1956, when he'd run out of water. He'd stepped into the service staircase at the back of the building, where it was crowded with broken perambulators, rusty bicycles, old flashlights. It was a short cut to get to the hopper on the ground floor, the only source of the building's water. He said he'd seen me, going downstairs in the same direction, with a bundle in my arms. It looked like towels. He said they'd been covered in blood. But it had been dark, and he admitted he hadn't been able to get a close enough look then, as I'd stuffed them into a cardboard box which had been nestled among the debris on the landing when I saw him. He'd asked what I was doing, and I said I was doing a clear-out. Spring cleaning, if you like. But the box wasn't big enough for the bundle I'd been carrying, and there had been a corner of fabric clearly sticking out, streaked with blood. He saw it as plain as day, he said.

I'd happened to meet Mr Doyle's eye from the public gallery and he'd smirked, then looked away. Not brave enough to face me properly. The cowardly rat must've felt my eyes following his path. He stuck his hands in his pockets, and I knew I had to get ready for whatever awaited me.

I dressed for my audience. A simple wool tunic in deepest indigo, a fresh pair of nylons. High-heeled navy court shoes which rounded me to nearly six foot. They wouldn't see those. What they'd notice were my mink coat and cap – a bit moth-eaten by then, but still biddable – and a string of green stones around my neck. Costume jewellery. Little more than glass and paste. *Must be the last bit of finery she owns*, they'd say. Serried ranks of little bottles and jars lined my kitchen table, and I dipped in and out of each one, painting on the face I wanted the world to see. My eyebrows, curved as question marks and quite blonde, appeared in due course, as I painted them with as much finesse as Michelangelo. A well made-up face never apologised for itself. But they'd focus on the bright swathe of lipstick and wonder why I still bothered. I stood in my coat and watched the sun bob above the rooftops. I'd done all I could, and I felt calm, in that moment.

I left Ely Place behind at a brisk pace. The weak winter sun warmed my face, infusing it with something like hope. A sharp wind tied in with the type of day promised on the horizon. Fresh and bright. Alive. A day for flying a kite. I was early, but I needed this time, before it got gobbled up by other people. I hailed a taxi at St Stephen's Green. The driver seemed to recognise me; he looked poised to ask me something, but I didn't utter a word from the time I stated my destination until he dropped me off at Merchant's Quay. I entered the dark, musty vestibule of the Church of the Immaculate Conception and rested my head against the coffin-like wood panelling for a minute or two, letting the solitude envelop me, until I couldn't bear it any longer. I pushed the heavy doors open and took a seat in the back pew. There wasn't another soul about. I waited for the words to come, but my mind was blank. I didn't know what I expected to find. I heard the door whoosh open and shut behind me.

'Gloria,' said a low voice. It had an expensive note to it, as well it might. My solicitor, Leslie White. I sat back and waited for him to join me.

'What are you doing here?'

'Same as you, I expect. Hoping for divine intervention.'

'A stained towel does not make a woman a murderer,' I said, but he just patted my arm.

'Let me buy you breakfast,' he said.

By the time yet another taxi deposited us at Inns Quay, photographers and reporters were huddled in an awkward-looking scrum against one of the Four Courts' granite pillars. They were all male, all young, dressed for the season in full-length overcoats, gloves and wide-brimmed hats, so I couldn't see their faces. Once they got a glimpse of Leslie hopping out of the taxi, slightly worse for wear, they moved as one. It charged my veins with a giddy purpose. Leslie opened my door.

I beamed, the wind from the river scolding the smile off my face. The alcohol had warmed my bones, oiled my joints. I glanced in the car's wing mirror. My cheeks were flushed, my eyes bright. I tried to bring it back a notch or two, setting my shoulders back, my head held high. Nothing to be ashamed of. Nothing to hide, not today. The flashbulbs started to pop and a fat young pup of a reporter leaned forward, keen as mustard. 'Gloria, Tim Duffy from the *Sentinel*.' *Gloria*. Not Miss Fitzpatrick.

'Yes?' I gave him what I hoped was a hard, icy stare, but I was all too aware that the papers would use the most unflattering photo they could, so I relaxed my face into a smile, as another flash went off and startled me.

'Are you hopeful about today's outcome?'

I laughed, in spite of everything. 'Yes,' I said. 'I'm very hopeful I'll be celebrating my birthday tomorrow with my freedom.'

This Duffy fellow laboriously wrote something down, leaning into the crook of his arm. 'It's your birthday on Christmas Day?' He looked up.

'Yes,' I said. He had a scribble of a moustache on his upper lip, which he kept touching, as though checking it was still there.

'Is it true you were born in America?'

'Yes,' I said. Before he could ask me anything else, I leaned forward. 'To tell you the truth, I regard myself as an American citizen. This is not my country. I do not recognise the Irish state.' I could sense a collective intake of breath, a whisper of excitement, as the pressmen caught a glimmer of something like good copy, before proceedings had even begun.

'What will you do if you're found guilty?'

I was about to say there was no way, but Leslie steered me by the elbow into the recesses of the buildings. 'That's enough,' he said, waving at someone he knew. I realised then how ordinary this was for him, how run-of-the-mill. It was just his job. Whereas my life was on the line. A thin film of something like hate settled into my bloodstream, cooling the roar of alcohol, making my ears buzz.

'What do you think will happen to me, Leslie? Honestly?'

I stopped in the middle of the marble floor and sank down heavily on my haunches. My voice must have risen in volume, because several men in wigs and gowns averted their eyes, as though they'd just witnessed something unsavoury.

Leslie swallowed, making his face look more sunken than ever. 'Most of the evidence is circumstantial,' he said, taking me under the oxter and almost lifting me one-handed onto a wooden bench nearby.

'That's what I've been saying.' I wrenched away and wrapped my arms around myself. I didn't care who saw.

'You haven't always been co-operative, Gloria. There's a lot stacked against you. But the jury has been out for two days now. And juries are flawed. Honestly, I think it could go either way.'

He leaned in, so that his mouth was close to my ear, and I got a whiff of brandy fumes. 'If it's bad news, we'll appeal on the grounds of insanity. All right, Gloria?'

I took a moment to let that sink in. My fate was in the hands of a dozen know-nothing men. I sat for what felt like a long time. Leslie gave me a mint and I accepted it, but I didn't take it out of its wrapper. I just held it in my hot little hand, until it dropped to the floor, warm and sticky. Leslie picked it up and pulled me back to a standing position.

'It's time,' he said in my ear. 'Just try and stay quiet, for the love of God. That's all I ask.'

There was a serious look in his eye, and I knew it meant something was about to happen. I followed him meekly into the court.

'All rise . . .'

I stood as the judge hunched forward, asking the foreman, a shiny fat man, if the jury had reached its decision.

'We have,' he said with a swagger of self-importance. Sweat patches had already begun to form under his arms. I felt nothing.

'How do you find the accused, Gloria Fitzpatrick, for the murder of Elizabeth Rourke, guilty or not guilty?'

The word 'guilty' brought everything to a standstill, like a storm. I felt submerged under the sea, desperately trying to break the surface. Leslie was speaking, but I couldn't quite make out the words. His face was too close, the uneasy proximity of someone trying to save a drowning woman. I pushed against him, my teeth chattering. I looked out at a wave of faces, pitying me, gloating, observing me like a zoo animal. A man in the public gallery stood up, and for a second, something about his movement, his mound of sandy hair, reminded me of my brother Gerard.

I couldn't see his face as he was half turned towards the door. I was flooded with relief. Gerard had made the trip to Dublin without that wife of his. I thought of the last time we'd been to Dublin together, when I was twelve and Gerard thirteen. Daddy had brought us to the zoo. We'd been standing outside the snow leopards' enclosure; it was nothing but a mesh wire fence and a few shrubs. It felt terribly cruel to have them locked away like that. There had been a mother, sleek and elegant, and her cub, the size of a teddy bear. *Don't get too close to the fence*, Gerard had said. *The mother could rip your arm off through the wire if she thinks you'll take her cub.* My lips started to move, but the man turned, and I realised it was that prick Alan Doyle, my downstairs neighbour at Ely Place, the prosecution's star witness. He looked right at me then, for the last time. That smirk. His testimony had sealed my fate. *We all knew what she was up to . . . all hours of the day and night . . . a very peculiar woman . . .* Why wasn't I nicer to him? And those soiled, bloody towels, black with Elizabeth Rourke's blood, it all could've been explained away so easily if he'd actually liked me in the first place.

Chapter Thirty-One

GLORIA

Morris never liked me either. All the questions about my car. It was a wonder Lilian Higgins allowed me to keep it when I went to work for her.

'You're fond of that car, aren't you? How much did it set you back? A car like that must've cost a fair bit.'

'I paid for it in instalments,' I'd said with what I hoped was a flat finality. 'So, it didn't seem like much, not when it was set out over a few years.'

'Really?' Morris had shuffled his chair closer to the table. 'I'm surprised you were allowed to do that. Most places would have to order a car like that specially from England or further afield. You don't see many MGs on the roads here. Still, it's something we can easily confirm with the garage.'

I thought back to Mr Harris at Harris Autos. The way he'd addressed Charles the whole time as he'd opened the driver's door.

'Sir, she's the kind of car that demands to be driven. Your wife will love it.'

Charles had looked amused. He'd looked from me to the car. 'My wife can't drive,' was what he said, but I was too excited to mind. My blood fizzed, giddy with the prospect of driving up and down the coast road, flooring it to over eighty miles per hour. The sun came out after a blustery rain shower, the road shining with promise.

When we got back to the garage, I handed Mr Harris £500 cash in a wrinkled brown envelope.

'I'll take it,' I said, kicking up each heel behind me like the dancers at the Athena, so that Charles laughed. Mr Harris eyed the cash.

'Certainly, madam,' he said.

I wondered if Mr Harris had ever driven past my fine, tall house on Mount Pleasant Square. Wondered what was inside. The tiled mosaic in the hall, depicting a bird of paradise. He wouldn't have guessed there was a half-empty suitcase of money under my bed. If he'd knocked, Eilish would've shown him into the drawing room, where he and Charles might've sat by the fire, Mr Harris unsure of what to do or say, probably lost in the beautiful surroundings. The powder-blue Persian rug by the grate, since saturated with Julia Bridges' blood. Startling in its brightness, the way the sight of blood always is.

If only I'd raced up the stairs, the day I'd bought the car, and grabbed the suitcase, emptied it out on the counterpane and deposited the dwindling contents in a bank.

Instead, I'd driven Charles back to Seaview House and parked on the street. Let them all see. I wanted to show the world, peel off my skin, reveal myself layer by layer.

Charles looked at his watch.

'Come in,' he said. 'There's no one home. I have a bottle of champagne somewhere.'

I didn't ask who 'no one' was. He could save his answers for someone else.

But he smiled at me then, and that smile felt like it was the truest thing I'd seen all day. He plucked a key from a tiny recess in the wall and unlocked a side gate. We ambled through the garden hand in hand, then sat in the Creightons' jumbled sitting room, drinking our champagne.

When the empty bottle was dangling in the ice bucket, I sat back, happiness settling like a fine dust. The Creightons' sitting room was too warm for a summer's day.

'Let's dance,' Charles said, grabbing my hand.

'Not here,' I said, indicating the mass of chairs and tables stuck together in a mishmash of styles.

'No, of course not here,' he said, with that smile again. 'Out there.' He put Lee Wiley on the gramophone and began twirling me around. He danced me down the steps, out to the yew trees at the front, through a rose garden, where we swayed in time to the far-off music as dusk began to fall. There we were, the two of us. I knew how much I wanted him, more than ever. We made love on the grass, moving against each other as though we were still dancing, the scent of the roses heady above us, the dry earth under our skin. The last time. We were catching our breath, straightening our clothes, when I saw someone, a woman, close the sitting room window with a bang.

'Mother's here,' Charles muttered. 'We'd better go.' I didn't ask him where Sally was. I didn't ask him anything at all as I charged back out, into the world.

We went swimming at the Forty Foot. It was deserted, the silence eerie. A seagull cawed mournfully overhead; the waves lapped against the wall, urgently tilting against it, wearing it away. The stone steps were greased with foam from the constant swell of the water, which was cold and thick.

When we got out, we put dry clothes on over our wet bodies and sat on the back seat, huddled together, teeth chattering.

Charles rubbed the window with his sleeve, eyes glittering in the moonlight.

'Shall we go home?' I said, keeping my tone light.

'Best get back, yes. I'm sure you understand.'

I didn't question it. Let someone else have his excuses. I simply sped off in my new car. I thought it meant my freedom. But it was to prove my downfall.

Chapter Thirty-Two

GLORIA

I underestimated Eilish, I'll admit. At first, I thought she wanted Charles to pay. The way he'd looked at her, called her 'pet', when she'd worked for me at The Downings, though she wasn't much to look at, no. A long thin face, a block of a figure, no way about her. But she wanted someone to pay. And that someone was me.

Mrs Higgins didn't take to Eilish straight away.

'She looks like she's sucked on a piss-soaked nettle,' she said, after Eilish came in to meet her. 'Dour-looking. We need someone strong and cheerful. A pleasant girl from the country with few airs and graces.'

I inwardly grimaced. *Good luck with finding someone who'll stick you.*

Mrs Higgins flicked through her ledger. 'I'm not sure we can afford another pair of hands here at the moment. It's just more expense.'

'Think of all those fireplaces that need cleaning every

morning,' I said. 'The breakfasts brought to the rooms. Sadie can't do them all.'

'Fireplaces? It's the middle of summer,' Mrs Higgins had replied, writing something down. She always homed in on whatever trivial bit of argument she could unravel and pluck out, thread by thread.

'There's lots she can help with.' I'd sat down on one of Mrs Higgins' fake antique chairs, fidgeting with my hands in my lap. They'd only just started to pain me then.

Mrs Higgins looked up. 'Hands at you again?' She shook her head. 'I told you to go back to the hospital.'

I smiled through gritted teeth, rubbing my right hand with my left thumb. 'I'm fine. I don't need a doctor to tell me to stop working so hard.'

She guffawed at that.

I exhaled loudly. 'We need someone else to help out. We're full up here until the end of the summer. Think of all the fetching, carrying, cooking and cleaning. Sadie can't do everything.'

'Why do you care so much about Sadie's workload and whether or not I hire this Eilish, anyhow?' Mrs Higgins looked up from her accounts. 'Is there something I should be aware of?'

I gave a tiny shrug. 'I want this place to be as efficiently run as we can make it. That's all.'

Mrs Higgins arched a pencilled-on eyebrow. 'Is that so? Not good enough for you, the way I do things, is it?'

I lowered my eyes. 'Of course, you know best, Mrs Higgins.'

She laughed at that. 'You're damn right I do. Tell me, what's so special about this girl?'

I pretended to think. 'I just think Eilish would be an asset to us. And she comes with an excellent reference from her former employer.'

'Who's that?'

I laughed. 'Me.'

She clucked her tongue and shut the accounts book. 'Oh, what the hell, tell her she can take the box room beside yours. But if anything goes wrong, it's on you.'

'Of course,' I murmured, delighted to finally get my way. Out in the hallway, Eilish had crouched on a tiny stool beside the telephone table, with a suitcase at her feet. I wondered how much she'd overheard.

'When can you start?'

Eilish just nodded, all serious, as though she were still considering her options.

'Now?'

Mrs Higgins went out shortly after our conversation and Eilish took her case to the box room. I brought her a cup of cocoa when she'd finished unpacking. It was still bright, though nearly ten o'clock. She was sitting on the narrow divan, fully dressed, kicking her feet against the dull oak floor. She took the cup and muttered something. I was about to leave her to her own devices, when she said, out of nowhere:

'Those pills you gave me.'

'Yes, dear?' Unease settled on my tongue like a bad taste before I swallowed it down.

'They worked. Thank you.' She drank down the cocoa in one gulp, though it must've been quite hot, before handing me the empty cup. I took it, not quite sure of how to respond.

'Try and get some rest,' I said finally, pausing at the door. 'And best not to mention it to anyone.'

She didn't answer. Dusty streams of light filtered through the window. She flopped back against the sagging pillow, still fully dressed, her long eyes narrowed against the evening glare. I had the strongest feeling she might be even more trouble, but I dismissed it out of hand. Surely, the worst had passed.

The evening it all happened, Mrs Higgins called me into her study.

'Eilish is working out well,' she said, her hair in curling papers, her head bent over a page onto which she squiggled numbers. Her fountain pen moved rapidly, swirling out neat figures in navy ink. She barely paused to look up. 'Seems a bit brighter, now, somehow. I think she likes it here. Either that, or there's a man.' She gave me a meaningful look. My cheeks burned.

'Indeed,' I said, not trusting myself to say any more.

'Gloria, I'm leaving you in charge,' she said, capping her pen. I noticed her nails were painted the pearliest, most delicate shade of pink. The colour of a seashell's insides, or the eyelids of a newborn babe.

'Terrific, Mrs Higgins. I won't let you down.'

She leaned forward to grab a blotter at the end of the desk, the deep V of her décolletage papery in the harsh summer light. I caught a rustle of silk, a flash of lace, before she looked down and straightened her bodice.

She blotted the page and closed the ledger with a thump. 'Don't make me regret it,' she said, standing up and closing the window. 'Now, scram, I've to finish packing and call a car to bring me to the boat in the morning.'

I was outside the door when I heard her whispering into the phone, sighing after a long pause, slamming the receiver into its cradle. I didn't believe for a moment she was going on holiday, either alone, or to the Isle of Man. But with her, it was best to sing from the same hymn sheet. I always had.

I was in my room later that night, about to listen to my radiogram, the air treacle-thick, when I heard her hammering at the door. Black Coat. She'd come back, as agreed. I took a few minutes changing out of my slippers and straightening my blouse. I powdered my face and applied a bright swathe of lipstick. I smiled in the mirror, the effect grotesque in its obvious artifice. I wiped off the lipstick and sidled back onto the landing. I could hear raised voices below in the hall. Eilish and another: lower, slower, a bit gravelly, but definitely female. When I got to the foot of the stairs, I saw a figure swaddled in black mink, sunk into Mrs Higgins' telephone stool. Missing her sequinned tail, her face hidden, but I knew it was her: Julia Bridges, the mermaid. Her head was almost horizontal on the little table where the telephone was kept alongside a Wedgwood bowl with large wax oranges. From here, she looked like a large furry animal, with smooth, bare legs splayed under her. Her little teeth bit down into one of the oranges, before she realised her mistake and threw it back into the bowl with a shriek.

'Eilish!' I called, stalling for time. 'What's going on here?'

Eilish reappeared from the kitchen with a glass of

water. She held it under Julia's nose, then thought better of it and placed it beside her on the little table. 'She's drunk,' she whispered.

'Well, I can see that,' I said. 'But what's she doing here? Get her out at once.'

'I can't,' Eilish said, with a pout. 'It's her. Black Coat. You said you'd see her.'

'Black Coat?' I feigned ignorance, prodding her furry elbow with one of my swollen fingers.

A muffled grunt was all I got in reply.

'It's Julia Bridges,' Eilish said in my ear. 'That actress from the Athena. The mermaid.'

'Help me move her,' I said. 'She'll be trouble. She can't stay here a minute longer.'

Eilish took her by the shoulders, and I held her under one arm. We got her standing and then somehow lying down on the bed in my room. I'd forgotten that I'd put on the radiogram before I went out but I hadn't tuned it in, so that all we heard was a load of static.

'Now then,' I said to Eilish. 'Go back to your duties.' I leaned in close to her face, the eyes half closed as they always were. 'And not a word of this to anyone.' When I heard the door click behind her, and the pad of Eilish's feet on the stairs, I put Billie Holiday on the turntable. It took a few goes because my hands were trembling, but then the room quickly filled with her sad, sweet voice. I turned to the prone figure on the bed. She was long and slender, her skin smooth, almost see-through. She opened her eyes. They were large and wide apart, aquamarine. Appropriate, for a mermaid. I could see the appeal, though I was reluctant to admit it. But I started to relax. She was young. That was all. And who was to say her visit to me had anything to do with Charles? I heaved a little sigh. I'd get Mrs Bridges sobered up, tell her I couldn't help her and call her a taxi. I'd even pay for it myself; call it a good deed.

I sat by her on the bed. She opened her mouth as though to speak, but a rush of liquid spurted out and she was sick on the floor.

'Please leave now. I'll call you a car.' I wasn't getting through to her, I didn't think. Her eyes weren't even in focus. 'I can't help you.'

She shook her head, pulling a pile of crumpled £10 notes from her brassiere and handing them over. I let them fall. They lay between us on the bed, scattered between the folds of the comforter.

'Who sent you?'

Her alabaster face was growing blotchy in the golden evening light. Her shoulders slumped miserably.

'Who is responsible for you?'

She exhaled a little sigh.

'He said you might help me.'

'Who?'

She didn't answer. There was no need. I closed my eyes for a moment, the edges blurring black. Charles. I took a series of shallow breaths, the rage pummelling my chest. I went into the hall and shut the door with a soft click, even though there was no one else around at this end of the house.

I looked out the window, my gaze steadfast, as two

jackdaws shuffled together on the railing, taut as dancers, neat in a row. They reminded me of the chorus girls at the Athena Theatre, turning one by one, elongated limbs outstretched, teeth glinting like shards of scattered glass. Ballet slippers gliding over the parquet floor, shifting like tidal sands. Charles' breath at my shoulder. And there she was. Julia Bridges, the first time I saw her. Emerging from a giant papier-mâché seashell, platinum hair draped around her body, limp as dyed seaweed. Her youth cleaving to her, glistening on her skin like seawater.

'It's not her real hair.'

Charles spoke out of the corner of his mouth, lips enunciating every syllable. 'I can see that. But she's very beautiful. Those legs!'

I'd crossed my own legs, rigid in my seat, as she swayed in time to the music.

Charles had laughed. 'It's all smoke and mirrors.'

I was rapt, watching the mermaid writhe, until all the chorus girls shimmied around her. She disappeared back into the seashell and the curtain went down. '*The Birth of Venus*,' Charles said. A nod to a painting by Botticelli. A poor imitation.

When I looked into his face, all I could see was my own reflection. He'd looked around, over my head, not visibly gauging my reaction. Oblivious to the low thrum of my rage. Underestimating it.

It rose like bile in my throat as I went further into the corridor and listened, almost tasting the air, the way a small, burrowing creature might. We don't have moles in Ireland. Charles had told me that once, long ago, on one of our drives. The thought made my chest constrict, but I tried to stay calm, clinical. I could hear the clang and clatter of tea things being collected, the cry of a newborn infant, Eilish saying something in a low voice, followed by Sadie's raucous laughter. Then silence. I came back in and sat on the bed. Julia had her eyes closed. She looked very ordinary; she could have been anybody. Charles had always been careless – with money, things, people. With us. Typical that he wanted me to tidy up his mess. I should've sent her away. But I eyed the pile of bank notes fluttering prettily in the slight breeze from the open window. *He owes me.*

I fetched two buckets of water from the bathroom and brought them back to my bedroom, closing the door behind me. Julia's fur-clad arm was flung back, almost obscuring her face. When she heard me, she stirred.

'Is this going to take long?'

'Oh, I shouldn't think so,' I said. I set the buckets down on the floor, where water sloshed over the side onto the powder-blue Persian rug. 'One moment, please.' My tone was brisk, professional, and I could almost fool myself that the mask fit. I fetched some equipment from an examination room: forceps, tubing, a speculum, and returned. No one saw me.

Julia sat up when I came back into the room.

'Please get on with it,' she said. 'I need this to be over.' I felt a flare of indignation burn in my throat, but I stayed silent.

'It'll take as long as it takes,' I said.

After I had everything set up, the solution of Jeyes Fluid

and water mixed and ready, I inserted the rubber tubing, pumping the water in. I was just about to drain it with a flick of my thumb when I felt pain searing my hand. I frowned, and she frowned back at me, still conscious.

'What's wrong?' She tried to sit up, but I wouldn't let her.

'Nothing,' I said.

But by then it was only a matter of time. I didn't have the luxury of panic. The world stood still for a few seconds, with me bent over Julia Bridges' pale, prone body. The pains were still shooting through my hand, fizzing like sherbet. I shook it out, massaging it with the other, but it felt giddy, with a mind of its own.

She tried to say something, but her speech was thick and liquified and all wrong. Her head lolled to the side and her eyes closed. The blood started then, treacle-thick, leaching from the counterpane onto the Persian rug. I dabbed at it with a hanky, realising how stupid I must seem, to anyone else, but especially to myself. I sank to my knees and muttered something. There wasn't a god I wanted to beg, or to bargain with, but I thought of my mother. Anne Fitzpatrick, née Chance. We'd left her behind, when we came back to Ireland, all by herself in a Philadelphia graveyard, and I was thankful she hadn't lived to see my disgrace. I heard voices fading outside, footsteps, a knock at the door.

'Who is it?' I said, as calmly as possible. I hadn't allowed the tide of panic to rise and drown me. Not yet.

'It's Eilish,' came a familiar voice. 'Would you like a cup of tea?'

It took a split second of pacing before I decided what

to do. God knows, the girl owed me. What choice did she have?

'Yes, Eilish, I would like a cup of tea. Come in here a moment, would you, dear?'

When she was inside the room, I banged the door shut behind her. She took fright when she saw Julia on the bed.

'She's dead! You need to call the police!'

I put my hand over Eilish's mouth to shush her. 'You silly girl! We need to stay calm.'

She looked at me then, eyes huge in her head. 'We?'

'Yes, that's right,' I said. 'And first things first, we need to get her out of here.'

Eilish crossed her stringy arms against her chest and leaned against the door, cool as a breeze. I started to realise my folly in trusting her. 'Why should I help you? Everyone knows what you do. It's only a matter of time before you're caught. Nothing to do with me.'

'You ungrateful wretch!' I kept my voice low; I couldn't keep my eyes off the dead woman on the bed, her blood seeping out of her, life ebbed away. I needed Eilish's co-operation, and fast. 'It's thanks to me you got away from Charles Creighton. Thanks to me you got a cushy number here. Thanks to me Mrs Higgins hasn't turned you out on your ear.'

'Is that what you think?' She cocked her pointy chin at me then, a smirk on her face. 'You think you did me some sort of favour? It was me did you the favour. Everyone at the Athena feels sorry for you. You still moon after Charles Creighton, though he only goes there for the mermaid.'

She whispered the last bit so furiously that a speck of saliva landed on my cheek. I wiped it away with a handkerchief before I replied. She thought I might strike her, because she cowered away from me, and I was afraid she might open the door and bolt, summoning people to the room. Fortunately, it seemed as though everyone was occupied with one of the labouring mothers, her roars rising to a crescendo. I took a moment to speak, and when I did, it was slowly and calmly, the way you might reason with a child.

'If you don't help me move this woman to my car, right this second, I will tell Mrs Higgins – and anyone else who cares to find out – that you are here because you feared you were pregnant by Charles Creighton, a married man almost three times your age, and you sought a termination from me, but I did not give you one. You'll be out of here so quick there'll be sparks flying off your heels. Who's Mrs Higgins going to believe, you or me?'

She opened her mouth to say something, but bit her lip instead, and lowered her gaze to her shoes. She knew she'd been cornered. At least, that's what I thought.

We wrapped Julia in the blue Persian rug, shrouded in her own blood. Eilish fetched a clean double comforter from the airing cupboard – one of Mrs Higgins' – and we wrapped her over in it several times so that her face and feet were completely covered. Eilish began to weep, noisy, self-indulgent sobs.

'Oh, save it for the stage,' I snapped. 'You didn't know her.'

'That doesn't mean I wanted her to die,' she wailed. 'What are we going to do if we meet someone?'

'You leave that to me,' I hissed at her back. 'I'm going to say I'm dropping some things to the nuns' laundry in Donnybrook.'

'At this hour?' Eilish bit her nails.

'Babies are born here at all hours of the day and night,' I replied evenly. 'We often need things laundered at irregular times. Besides, we might not meet anyone.'

I could still hear the labouring mother screaming the house down, Marian Swan running in and out of her room dancing attendance. The others were hiding out in their rooms. Who could blame them, with that racket going on? I hoped the coast might be clear for a little while. I grasped the bundle at the feet end, while Eilish took it gingerly under the shoulders. I saw her wince, but the expression was fleeting. I knew she wanted this to be over as much as I did. We tiptoed down the stairs and out the back door. My car was parked to the side of the premises, obscured from the road due to Mrs Higgins' thick ring of laurel bushes. It occurred to me – too late – that the car was perfectly visible to any of the occupants of the bedrooms should anyone happen to look out. As it was, all the curtains were closed. We placed the body across the back seat, buffered by the rug and all the bedclothes. It was still soft and yielding. The legs stuck up slightly at the end. I'd forgotten how tall Julia was. Those long dancer's legs. The thought made me grimace. Her shiny dark hair, divested of its gaudy stage wig, now dulled. Eilish wordlessly went back into the house. I half followed her to the door at the rear.

'Not a word to anyone, mind,' I said in her ear. 'Or it'll

be the end for both of us.' I was foolish to think that when it came down to my word against hers, mine would carry the most weight.

The engine took a few twists of the key to start, my hands were shaking so much, and the pain jangled into every last nerve ending. It let out a deathly roar. The drive I'd taken so many times before then took on a surreal, ghoulish tinge as I sped along the coast road, a dead body jostling against my back seat. The air felt heavy with an unshed storm, and yet when I looked out at the sea it was flat and glassy as the surface of a lake. The seagulls of the night shot ahead of our cortege, heralding its arrival with howls of indignation, but the air remained perfectly balmy and still. A summer's evening for a stroll, or a moonlit swim. A night for lovers.

I wanted to park on the seafront and leave her on the beach, for the waves to gently lap against and eventually tow out to sea, but I was afraid. I stopped the car near the James Joyce tower and cut the engine. The moon was high and bright. I took a deep breath and got out. I was reaching for the back door when my hand seized up again and I felt paralysed with the spasms. I howled then, great rips of anguish, into the clear night sky. If anyone heard, they didn't give me the slightest indication. After a moment, I got back into the driver's seat and rooted around in the glove box for the pills the doctor at the hospital had given me for my arthritis. I was only meant to take one, but I took three, swallowed dry. I waited for the sobs to wither in my throat, down to a feeble hiccup. The pain started to subside. I could think clearly. Charles. Why had I ever loved him? He was a jackdaw in peacock's feathers, as my mother might've said. I thought of Sally Creighton's ghastly peacocks at Seaview House and grimaced. Poor Sally. Those squawking birds her only joy. She didn't know how to handle Charles. I clamped down the howls and tried to think straight. There was a reason I'd driven all the way out to Sandycove. Let Charles deal with Julia how he saw fit. He didn't give enough of a damn about her to look after her in life. Let him do so in death. I fired up the engine and slammed into reverse. I skidded onto the road, riding up on the pavement on the opposite side, before straightening out. I continued very slowly, as though a lack of speed might slow down my racing thoughts.

I knew the front gates to Seaview House would be locked. They always were. But I wasn't going to be deterred. I took the key to the side gate from inside the tiny cavity crumbling away from the wall, as I'd seen Charles do. A laugh drifted towards me, carried on the breeze, and I heard a splash from the water, a female voice shout, then fade. Moonlit swimming. I unlocked the gate and relocked it from the other side, putting the key back in the wall. Then I marched up to the front door and pounded on it. Sally's peacocks must've sensed the rage bulging my veins like boiling oil because they stayed away.

The door opened after a minute or two. Just a crack. An inch so that a small eye could cast a look out.

'What do you want?' A small voice. It matched the eye. I caught the gleam of a white frilly nightdress. Poor child. 'There's no one here, just me. And I'll call the Guards if you don't go away.'

I jammed my toes into the gap at the bottom of the door. 'I'm not going anywhere, Delia,' I said. 'Call the Guards if you like. I'd be happy to tell them a few things.'

I managed to wedge my whole foot into the gap and the strength of my rage was no match for this child. I put out my hands in a coaxing gesture and tried to appear calm.

'I'd like to speak to Charles, please,' I said. 'Then I'll be on my way.'

'Charles isn't here,' said another voice from behind Delia. Then a face appeared in the doorway. 'Hello, Gloria.'

I blushed. I knew I must look a sight, spots of blood on my clothes, my hair wild and frizzed, eyes dancing in my head.

'You've let yourself go.'

'Thank you, Mrs Creighton,' I said, through bared teeth.

She opened the door fully and took a step towards me.

'How did you get in here?' She turned to the girl, who was trembling.

'I knew where to find the key,' I said.

She shuffled further forwards, her slippers scratching against the tiles. 'Get out,' she said. 'Or I really will call the Guards.'

I lowered my eyes. 'You have a situation.'

'What are you talking about, woman?' She turned to the child again, putting a hand on her shoulder. 'Delia, you go back to bed. I'll deal with this.'

She took me into the drawing room and poured me something dark and strong-looking from a crystal decanter. It took three goes to get the glass to my lips. My hands wouldn't stop shaking.

'It's Julia Bridges,' I said, loudly. Too loud for this quiet room. 'She's dead.'

Her eyes widened. 'Who's that? And what's she got to do with my Charles?'

I cleared my throat. 'She was his mistress. And now she's dead.'

Those eyebrows, zealously over-pruned like the roses in her garden, shot up. I leaned in towards them, until they ran together as one.

'And I'm not leaving until you help me. Otherwise, I'll go straight upstairs and tell that child what kind of man her father is. I'll tell everyone.'

She sighed. 'Where is this person?'

'In my car,' I said.

'All right,' she said. 'Then we know what we must do. Wait here, please.'

She came back a moment later wearing a waxed jacket and wellington boots.

'Thank you, Mrs Creighton,' I said.

'I think we're beyond "Mrs Creighton", Gloria. It's Ruth,' she replied.

Chapter Thirty-Three

GLORIA

The minutes of my life fizz away, drop by drop, precious as spilt champagne. I realise I am gripping a stout bottle in my throbbing fist, still cold and full. I feel light as a balloon. As though I have dragged each memory out into the light. The wisp of a song that won't go away.

Fai la ninna,
fai la nanna,
ninna oh, ninna oh,
Lo darmemo alla Befana ...

I drain the bottle in one long swallow and let the thick stout bubble down my throat before I try to get my thoughts in a straight line. But they won't go straight.

The girl next door wouldn't stop singing. The same four lines, over and over. 'It's an Italian lullaby,' Mrs Higgins said briskly, checking my blood pressure with a snap of rubber tubing around my arm. Each contraction building inside me, tightening around my abdomen like the blood pressure gauge, but I wouldn't give her the pleasure of seeing me wince.

'I don't like the look of this. I'll have to call Dr O'Neill. It's probably to do with your age.' She curled her mouth in distaste.

I was overtaken by a dragging in my insides. I turned my head. After a minute or two, I sat back. 'Why's she singing when the baby's quiet?'

Mrs Higgins' voice was sharp. 'Stillbirth,' she said. 'Poor Daniela's out of her mind.'

She swept out of the room. A crushing pain shot through me, but I didn't want to make a noise in case *poor Daniela* heard me. I remembered her from *Julius Caesar.* A competent actress, though lacking Julia Bridges' natural flair. I'd heard she remarried quickly after her husband was killed in the bombings. Bad luck.

Fai la ninna ... I reached for the bell by my bed as I was hit by another contraction. It felt as though I were pinned by an enormous wave, and I couldn't for the life of me get up.

I struggle, wrenching free, my knees hitting the table, my hands flinging themselves wide, so I knock the stout bottle with a stray elbow. It smashes into smithereens on the tiled floor, the glass smooth as sea pebbles. The tiles now thick with scattered sand, dark and damp from the salt spray. The girl was only eighteen months old. She toddled up and down the shore, gathering bits of shell polished by the incoming tide, shrieking with delight as the wind whipped her hair around her face. Daniela stood over her, protective, as though I could have been about to grab her and run. I took the kite out of its brown paper wrapping and held it up, letting it taste the wind. It fluttered and writhed, charmed by the breeze, looping itself around our heads and off, up into the sky. Dancing from side to side, the girl matched the kite beat for beat, her little hands tracing its ascent, her laugh carried out to sea as the kite crashed to shore, collapsing like a spent animal. Born on the feast of St Valentine, a Roman martyr. I never stopped looking at her, trying to memorise every angle of her face. But when I try to picture it now, it's gone. A voice whispers through the darkness instead.

Let the child sleep. I opened my eyes to see Mrs Higgins folding towels. There were voices all around me, but those were the first clear words I could make out.

'I'm not a child,' I said, my tongue thick and furred. 'I'm forty-one years of age, for pity's sake.'

Mrs Higgins tittered. 'Alleluia. Sleeping Beauty is awake.'

I swallowed several times before I trusted myself to speak again.

'What did I have?' I felt as though I'd been sawn in half. I didn't dare look down.

'A little girl.' Mrs Higgins said something to Marian, the midwife, who slammed the door behind her. Mrs Higgins lowered her voice. 'Dr O'Neill has just left. You almost died.'

I closed my eyes for a moment. The room looked brighter when I opened them again. 'I feel fine. Better than fine, actually. I'd like to see her now.'

'Not a good idea.' Mrs Higgins ticked something off on a chart at the end of my bed.

'What do you mean?'

She poured water into a stubby glass. It felt like a doorstop in my hand. After I'd taken a gulp, I tried to sit up. I fell back, the pain twisting around me. Mrs Higgins patted my hand. 'You've decided to give up your child. Why not give her to Mrs Sarto?'

The words oozed out of me. 'I've changed my mind. I'm keeping her.'

Mrs Higgins gave a toneless laugh. 'Well now. I've heard it all.' She poured herself some water and took a dainty sip. 'You need to rest. Mrs Sarto, and, of course, Mr Sarto, will give this child everything you can't.'

I tried to sit up again but couldn't. Mrs Higgins' hand on my shoulder, her voice like plum syrup. 'Believe me, I know how difficult this is.' I looked down, not wanting her to see that I didn't believe her, though I think I wanted to. 'You're in no position to support a child on your own, dear. It's been arranged now. You should be thanking me.'

'I'm not on my own,' I said, unconvincing even to my own ears. 'We'd have each other.'

Mrs Higgins snorted. 'You're on your own, with a criminal record. No situation for a baby.' She rearranged the blankets across my feet. 'Try and get some sleep.' I thought of Charles, what he'd say if he knew what was happening, but I couldn't even picture his face, or imagine where he was at that moment, or what he was doing. His fortress of a life seemed so impenetrable to me, even then. I sank back into the pillow and tears pricked my eyes in defeat.

'Can I see her, at least?' My voice was small, but hopeful.

Mrs Higgins sighed. 'Go on, then,' she said, ringing the bell for Marian. 'Only for a minute, mind.'

Marian entered the room quietly, carrying a white bundle. After conferring with Mrs Higgins, she placed the bundle in my arms. The pain was forgotten. 'This is Nicoletta.' Marian hovered, fussing over the cocoon of blankets around the child's face. Mrs Higgins frowned, as though Marian shouldn't have said it, but I repeated the word in my head over and over until I knew it would never leave. An Italian name, of course. I frowned over the baby's head at Mrs Higgins. She didn't catch my eye, instead jerking a thumb at Marian. I knew I didn't have long.

I breathed in the soft newness of her. Nicoletta. The gentle in and out of her cheeks. Her seashell eyelids began to flutter. 'She's awake,' I whispered. Marian looked to Mrs Higgins and took a step forward, but I held on tight.

Her eyes locked on mine for a long second or two, deep blue, the colour of forget-me-nots, before Mrs Higgins was beside us, whisking her out of my arms and ushering Marian out of the way. 'Let the child sleep,' Mrs Higgins said, almost to herself, as the door closed. I heard the door open and shut in the other room, and the singing started up again.

Ninna oh, ninna oh,

Lo darmemo alla Befana . . .

I closed my eyes, breathing as deeply as the wound would allow. Mrs Higgins was right. I had nothing to offer a baby. I kept breathing, the breath constant and comforting, until I floated somewhere between waking and sleeping. The in and out of her breath, pulse quickening under the skin as she woke up, the delighted little gurgling laugh as she splayed her tiny hands heavenward, as the kite chased itself to ground. Watching rapt, as it soared, anchored to my wrist, the wind breathing it to life. A beating heart in the sky, a flash in the dark bright as a smile. *My, what a beautiful smile.* That's what he said, the first time he saw me. Like pearls.

It was an elaborately plastered old building at the top of Grafton Street, looking onto St Stephen's Green. The name of the shop was spelled out in blocky gilt letters above the door. Charles Creighton and Son. The windows were full of an array of colourful gemstones in rings, watches, necklaces and earrings.

I pushed open the door and a bell chimed. The noise made me jump. A man looked up from a glass-topped desk, where he was examining some tiny jewel under a microscope. Something long and thick smouldered deliciously in an ashtray. He nodded at me, not exactly friendly, but not unfriendly either.

'Can I be of assistance?' he'd asked in a clipped voice.

'I'm just taking a look around.'

'American, are you?' He'd eyed my brand-new kidskin handbag, the tissue paper barely yanked from the lining. 'Here on vacation, is it? Welcome to Dublin.'

I'd smiled, going to a glass case and peering inside. It was filled with rings. He followed me. 'No, I'm not on *vacation*,' I said playfully. I pointed at the rings. 'Can I try some on?'

He took a tiny key out of his pocket and opened the case. 'These are from the Art Deco period. Beautiful, aren't they?'

I looked around, dazzled by all the gleaming surfaces, shining like racehorses' coats. 'Here we have sapphires and diamonds in a white-gold setting; diamonds and rubies in a platinum setting; onyx and diamonds and pearls . . .' He took out the sapphire and diamond ring and slipped it on my finger, winding strung pearls around my neck. My image bounced off the mirror opposite, refracted into a million tiny shards of light. The effect was dizzying.

'I'm sorry, are you all right?' The voice, softer now, had broken through my reverie.

'Yes, yes, I'm sorry, I'm all right. I . . . could I maybe have some water?'

'Yes, of course.'

He went through a back door, and I heard a tap running. He was back a second later with a mug filled with icy water. I drank it in two gulps, the sudden cold spreading an ache across the roof of my mouth and into my teeth. Pearls, he called them.

He gave me the pearls, that night, when we went dancing at the Imperial. The orchestra played a fast number with a complicated rhythm, and I was afraid I'd get lost, wouldn't keep up. But Charles was an excellent dancer; he led with ease, and slowed down with one ear on the music and one eye on what I was doing. A slow song started up, 'Someone to Watch Over Me', and the floor started to clear. I went to take my seat, but Charles clasped my hand in his and we danced cheek to cheek, me almost as tall as him, swaying together to the music. He took something from his pocket, fastening it around my neck, still perfectly in time.

'They're for you,' he said, his eyes forget-me-not blue. 'I had to give them to you. They'll always remind me of you.'

They felt cool and smooth under my touch, yet still so delicate. I smiled back at him, something rare and honest captured in that exact moment. His pearls around my neck, his eyes mine, and mine alone.

Signed, Gloria Anne Fitzpatrick, Clyde Hall Criminal Lunatic Asylum, April 1959. To be read after my death.

Chapter Thirty-Four

NICOLETTA

By the time she gets back to the newsroom, Nicoletta's head is spinning. She stuffs the pages of Gloria's letter back into the envelope and stows them in her bag, approaching her desk. Before she can sit down, the door to the stairwell opens and Barney walks in. She meets his eyes and nods her head vigorously, as though she's drunk. Before she can say anything, Dermot calls over from across the room.

'There's someone here to see you.' He strides forward, lowering his voice. 'I had to bring her up. Give her tea. She won't go away.'

He leads her into the kitchenette off the case room, where Mrs Clancy, Julia Bridges' friend, is leaning against the sink, nursing a mug.

'Miss Sarto,' she says, as soon as she sees Nicoletta. 'I may have done a terrible thing.'

Nicoletta can hear Barney pottering around the

344

newsroom, and she worries he's about to head off before she can catch him.

'What's that?' She goes to stand beside Mrs Clancy, filling a mug with water and gulping it down.

Mrs Clancy grabs her by the elbow. Her breath is stale. 'I went to see Jack Bridges. I suppose I was curious, about a few things. Whether I thought he'd still done it. If he was the bastard I remembered.'

'And was he?' Nicoletta puts down her mug impatiently, waiting for Mrs Clancy to get to the point. Mrs Clancy shrugs helplessly. 'He was crying, saying he loved Julia, and hasn't been able to live without her. I suppose I wanted to goad him a bit, see how he'd react. So, I told him that Julia had stayed with me for a bit before she went missing and that she'd told me about the married man.'

'And what did he say to that?' Nicoletta can hear footsteps, a door slam. She knows she only has a few seconds to catch Barney.

'He said he was going to make everything right.'

'Well, that's good, isn't it?' Nicoletta starts walking towards the door back into the newsroom, hoping Mrs Clancy will follow her.

Mrs Clancy catches up, wringing her hands. 'That's just it! He's started drinking again. I had a few glasses with him. Then he started ranting, saying it must be Charles Creighton who did Julia, why else would Julia have been found in his garden? I tried to stop him, but I think he's planning on going over there.'

'I'm sure he won't.' Nicoletta steps back into the

newsroom. There's no one else there, except Price, who glowers at her from the back bench.

Nicoletta places her hand on Mrs Clancy's shoulder and guides her towards the double doors. 'Try not to worry,' she says. 'I'm sure he won't do anything.'

They catch up with Barney at the bottom of the stairwell, his hat and coat on. Nicoletta gives Mrs Clancy a perfunctory wave, before turning to Barney.

'Yes,' she says simply. 'I will marry you.'

Barney lights up like a Christmas tree, the way he does when he's happy, the lines from his eyes and mouth fanning out and threatening to engulf his whole face. He lets out a whoop of laughter, before spinning her around and setting her back on her feet like a doll. She can't help but laugh as well. He takes the velvet box out of his pocket and puts the diamond solitaire on her ring finger. They walk back up the stairs hand in hand and she holds the ring up to the harsh newsroom light, watching it gleam.

Duffy appears in the doorway. He's wearing the same sports coat he always wears, with all the buttons open.

'Well now. What's all this hullabaloo?'

Barney grins. 'She said yes!'

Nicoletta looks to Barney. 'He knows about us?'

Duffy grins. 'I've always known.' He comes forward and pumps Barney's hand, before kissing Nicoletta soundly on both cheeks. 'And it's wonderful news. This calls for champagne. Right, get your coats. I'm taking you both out for dinner. We'll go to Jammet's.'

They're ensconced at the champagne bar in Jammet's before Nicoletta knows what's happening, the evening

346

sliding into night. Duffy's enthusiasm is infectious, and she can't help feeling as though the earlier part of the day didn't happen; or even if it did, it doesn't matter. Barney loves her and that's all that matters. He squeezes her thigh, as if reading her thoughts. The champagne has already gone to her head, so she excuses herself and picks up her bag, wending her way downstairs to the ladies'. She almost falls against a table, where a middle-aged couple are having a furious whispered argument. She rights herself as though she's just been slapped. It's Charles Creighton, looking relaxed in an open-necked white shirt and pinstriped trousers and jacket, with a woman with ash-blonde hair and heavily kohled eyes, whom she assumes is his wife. Sally Creighton, of the nervous turns. Miss Leonard had said she was an evacuee from London during the war, an orphan. Nicoletta had somehow pictured a wan girl with two thick plaits and a cardboard suitcase. What was it Charles had said about her on Christmas Eve? *Sally has what you might call a weak constitution.*

In the ladies' she pinches her cheeks in a bid to sober up, the happiness of earlier dulled. When she comes back to her table, it's empty. Barney and Duffy are talking to people they know. Charles Creighton is at the bar but comes over to her when he sees her approach her table on her own.

'Terrible business on Christmas Eve. Came as a shock, I can tell you.' He gives a hapless little shrug.

Nicoletta feels saliva fill her mouth. 'Can you comment on what happened to Mary Little for the *Sentinel*?' she asks, her voice slipping after the champagne.

His eyes widen in surprise. 'She drowned, I believe. Very unfortunate. Why?'

Nicoletta forces herself to look him up and down. She can barely stand it. How could *this* be her father?

'Why? Don't you wonder what happened to her? And to her baby?'

Creighton gives a stuttery laugh. 'How did you know she had a baby?'

'I'm going to expose you for what you are. You'll get what's coming to you.' Nicoletta takes a step back, her head buzzing.

Creighton puts a hand on her arm to steady her. 'I think you've had a bit too much, my dear. Are you all right?'

She pushes his hand away. Barney comes back over and beams, oblivious to what has taken place. 'We're engaged,' he says, throwing an arm around Nicoletta. Charles shakes both of their hands and admires Nicoletta's diamond ring. She snatches her hand back into a fist.

'Can I buy the happy couple a drink?' He gestures towards the bar.

Nicoletta shakes her head. Barney looks at her strangely. 'Are you all right?' His eyes flit over to Creighton, who is drifting across the room to talk to someone else. 'That was a bit rude,' he says.

Nicoletta picks up her bag. 'I have to get some air.' Outside, she drinks in the breeze like a drowning woman. Barney is at her side within minutes.

'I said our goodbyes to Duffy,' he says, slipping his hand into hers.

She takes a shuddery breath. 'I was thinking,' she says,

leading him out into the frosty night. A horse-drawn car-riage clip-clops down Nassau Street, and she shivers. It should be a magical night. Barney puts his jacket around her shoulders and holds her tight. The world starts to slot back into place.

'It's not right celebrating without my parents. I'd like us to call in to see them so they can meet you,' she says.

'Now?'

'Yes,' she says, not letting go of his hand. 'It has to be now.'

When Nicoletta knocks on her parents' door she's expecting her mother, a mass of lines gouging her fore-head, but when the door opens it's her father, standing there in his stockinged feet, his hair gleaming, even though the shop is long shut.

'Happy New Year,' she says, in the hallway, for want of anything else to say. He looks at her for a long moment, as though she's a customer that he can't quite place.

'This is Barney,' she says. 'My fiancé. This is my father, Ettore Sarto.' Her father's crumpled face splits into a smile and he claps his hands together. She holds out her arms and he pulls her close. When she breaks away, she can see tears glisten on his cheeks.

There's no one else in the kitchen, and they stand there, waiting to be told what to do. Nicoletta eventually sits at the table. Barney stays standing, his back to the fridge, his hat clasped in both hands, his eyes fixed on Nicoletta.

'Your mother's in bed,' Ettore says. 'I'll go wake her up.'

'I'll make tea.' Nicoletta stands up and grabs the teapot from the table. She fills the kettle as noisily as she can, flicking the knob on the cooker and lighting a match, holding it to the small ring in the middle of the iron grid. Her hands are shaking. There's a tread on the stairs and both her parents appear.

Nicoletta puts down the tea things with a clatter. 'Mam, this is Barney King, my fiancé.'

Barney holds out his hand. Daniela shakes it stiffly, then Ettore claps him on the shoulder.

'Congratulations,' Daniela says quietly. Nicoletta feels wretched.

Ettore takes Barney under the arm. 'Come have a drink with me in the shop. I'd like to get to know my future son-in-law. We'll leave the women here.'

Daniela hunches her shoulders and lets them fall. 'Such a shock. We didn't even know you were going out with someone. How did you meet him?'

'At work.' Nicoletta shrugs. 'We work together.'

'And when were you planning on telling us?'

Nicoletta can feel her good humour ebb away. 'Now seems as good a time as any. When were you planning on telling me that you were married before to someone called Tommy Stagg? Or that Gloria Fitzpatrick is my natural mother?'

Daniela's face looks bleached under the harsh kitchen light. She tightens her dressing gown and looks down at the belt strung between her fingers like a cat's cradle.

'So, you found out,' she says quietly. 'I knew when you came here on Christmas Eve no good could come of this story.'

'How could you not tell me?' Nicoletta whispers.

Daniela gives a wry smile. 'I take it you haven't told your man?'

Nicoletta shakes her head and grips her mug between both hands. 'Is it true?'

Daniela bows her head. 'My first husband died during the war, when the Germans bombed Dublin. I found out shortly after he died that I was pregnant. Ettore had always loved me, and he married me. But my baby boy was stillborn. Mrs Higgins said we'd switch the babies. It was so simple.'

'Does Dad know?'

Daniela shakes her head. 'No. As far as he's concerned, you're Tommy's child. He always knew you weren't his, but he loved me. And he loves you. He thought you and he were very alike in some ways.'

'I see,' Nicoletta says, hoping her mother will keep talking, now she's started.

'Once I'd started lying, I couldn't stop. But your father loves you. That's what matters when all is said and done.'

'And you loved Enzo,' Nicoletta says, the bitterness in her voice taking her by surprise. 'Not me.'

Daniela looks up defensively. 'We gave you everything. You haven't a clue.'

'No, I obviously haven't.' Nicoletta shyly touches the back of Daniela's hand, dry as an autumn leaf. 'You were an actress at the Athena with Julia Bridges. Why did you hide that from me, too?'

Daniela sniffs. 'I didn't hide it; I just never spoke about it. I knew Gloria from the theatre.' She gives a brief smile.

'After that, I cut myself off from that world, so I'd never have to see her again.'

'Did Gloria Fitzpatrick ever fly a kite with us when I was a very small child?' Nicoletta asks in a rush.

Daniela answers slowly. 'Yes. She came back looking for you when you were little more than a baby. She brought you a kite and we went to fly it at Sandycove Beach. But years later, after she was convicted of murder, I was mortified by my lack of judgement. And above all, I wanted to protect you.' She wipes her hands on her housecoat. Nicoletta is about to reply when the two men come back in from the shop, with Ettore's arm slung around Barney's shoulders.

'A toast,' Ettore says with a smile.

Daniela stands up and fetches four sherry glasses from the dresser, and Ettore fills them with whiskey. Nicoletta's cheeks hurt from smiling as she clinks her glass, grateful for finally hearing the truth from Daniela.

They are outside Nicoletta's dark flat on Eccles Street, when Nicoletta takes Barney's hand. 'I don't feel like going home just yet.'

'There's nowhere open, Nic,' Barney says with a laugh.

She starts walking, flagging down a taxi. 'I know somewhere that'll have us.' She opens the door and beckons him to get in the back.

'Sandycove, please,' she says to the driver. She turns to face Barney, kissing his cheek.

'We were invited to John and Delia Dawkins' New Year's party, remember?' she says in a whisper, not wanting the driver to hear. He raises his eyebrows but doesn't comment.

She asks for the taxi to leave them at Seaview Terrace.

'John and Delia Dawkins are round the other side, remember?' Barney says.

'I need to speak to someone,' Nicoletta says, leading the way, halfway down the street, to number eight. Una Little answers the door after a minute or two.

'What're you doing here?' She looks behind her.

'I need to talk to you, Una. It won't take long.' Nicoletta speaks quickly, aware she doesn't have much time. 'Please tell me what happened.' Barney shrinks into the shadows.

Una goes to close the door in her face. Nicoletta aims a shot in the dark. 'Look, I know about your involvement with John Dawkins' drug racket. I'm not going to tell anyone, but you can tell me about Mary's baby.'

The door opens a fraction wider. Una steps out and closes it behind her. She takes a shaky breath. 'Two minutes. That's how long I have before they'll notice I've gone. And I have to get to work.' She beckons for Nicoletta to follow her. She reaches the concrete divide between the terrace and the seafront and rests her cheek against it with her eyes closed.

'Mary didn't say a word to anyone.' At first, Una speaks so quietly that her words are carried off by the wind. Nicoletta bends her head closer, getting a mouthful of Una's hair. It's soft and flyaway, like a baby's. Una leans her weight on one hip, the tension leaving her face in the act of telling.

'About the pregnancy?'

Una nods. 'Maybe she didn't know herself. Mary was

good at keeping secrets,' she whispers. Nicoletta gingerly puts an arm around Una's shoulders. The girl is shaking from the cold and the release.

'When did you find out?'

Una rubs at her face with the heel of her hand. 'She came home early one day, last summer, from the Creightons'. Said she wasn't feeling well and went straight to bed. She told me that evening.'

'Told you what?' Nicoletta pats her back, but Una pushes her away.

'She'd been cleaning in Sally's bedroom that morning when she felt a horrible pain. Mary lay down on the bed at first, but she had to get up and walk around. When the baby came out, she put him in the wardrobe. She went back downstairs until she collapsed in the kitchen. They sent her home.'

Nicoletta tries to speak but it comes out as a gasp. 'Who found the baby?'

'Sally. Mrs Creighton. She had one of her turns. They had to call the doctor. Ruth told Mary not to tell anyone. She said she would take care of things.'

Una's body is suddenly wracked with sobs and Nicoletta cradles her shoulders, letting her cry it out until she's left with dwindling hiccups. Eventually curiosity wins out. 'I have to ask, Una. Who was the father of Mary's baby?'

Una doesn't answer.

'Una?' A voice, husky with drink, pierces the dank evening. 'Get back here.' Nicoletta hears a clash of unsteady feet on the slick pavement.

'Da's looking for me. I'm due at work.' Una pushes

Nicoletta away with the heel of her hand, running through the concrete snicket without a backward glance, her shoes slapping against the ground, until Nicoletta hears the grumble of voices and the door of number eight slam.

Chapter Thirty-Five

Nicoletta rests her cheek against the road's clammy dividing wall and closes her eyes. She's so tired, she could sleep right here, in the unforgiving sea air. Una's stricken face flickers under her eyelids, the cheeks red and puffy from crying, the eyes round as bottle tops. It's a child's face. Nicoletta considers going home. With Barney, just the two of them. Back to the beginning, without any of this ugliness trailing in their wake. She'll wonder later what compelled her to prise herself away from the slimy wall and link Barney's arm, pulling him onwards, rounding the corner and onto the main road where the sea glitters like rough glass underneath a slanting moon. Like all split-second decisions, motivated by the curious impulses of the heart. The wind whips in off the sea as she rattles the cast-iron side gate of Seaview House with grim fury. To her surprise, it swings open. The sound of smashing glass drifts their way, followed by whoops and applause, before the soothing tones of a woman's voice and a faint tinkling as the glass is swept up and thrown away. In the middle of the sea of mud from the Garda excavation is a red-topped marquee, surrounded by wooden boards crisscrossing the murk, providing firm footpaths for the revellers gathered for the Dawkins' New Year's party. A flotsam of men and women pose for a photo at the entrance, which is decked with paper lanterns, while twinkling lights illuminate the walkways. Was that Delia's voice she heard? Delia Dawkins, her sister. The word pops in her head like a photographer's flash. She'd always wanted a sister. Someone to confide in, laugh with. Someone on her side.

'Sure you want to do this? We don't even know them.' Barney's feet are still planted firmly on the pavement outside. 'We could just go home.' He reaches out and smooths a strand of hair from across her face. His touch grounds her into decisive action.

'We're invited,' she says. 'We'll just stay for one.'

The gate clangs and Nicoletta takes a tentative step onto one of the wooden walkways, with Barney a couple of paces behind her. The peacocks, Antony and Cleopatra, jerk forward at the sound, pecking at their feet.

Barney edges away from Antony, kicking his toe into a frozen rose bush beside the wooden board. Nicoletta wonders if there are any more human remains down there, where the shallow roots meet the earthworms and soil and domestic detritus left over from the few millennia of human habitation. Antony haughtily fans his tail, strutting on to some newer arrivals behind them.

'Poor things, maybe they're hungry,' Nicoletta says half to herself. She doesn't stop to see if Barney is following her. She keeps walking, compelled to circle the marquee's entrance, dozens of tea lights spread out like twinkling daisies. Nicoletta feels like a slightly dazed moth drawn to a flame. She hovers in the doorway for a moment, contemplating the noisy fug within. A freezing gust of sea air creeping down her spine finally propels her inside, through this blank portal. She looks around. A three-piece band is setting up in one corner, with a space clear for dancing beside it. Several tables and chairs are dotted around, including the large orange L-shaped couch that Nicoletta recognises from the Dawkins' kitchen. A dozen or so people are crowded around the sofa, swilling something blue from cocktail glasses. A sulky-faced maid bursts through the entrance, grabbing a tray of blue drinks, a frilly cap jammed onto her head. It's Una Little.

'Una,' Nicoletta hisses. Una looks appalled at the sight of her. She waits for Nicoletta to speak.

'Are Delia or John here?'

Una nods tearfully and points towards the sofa. She stands for a moment, regarding Nicoletta with watchful eyes. Just then, Barney stumbles in, and Una resentfully reaches out an arm for his coat.

'Thanks, but I'll keep it,' he says. 'It's freezing in here.'

Una hands them each a drink and stands aside to let Nicoletta and Barney by. Nicoletta scans the crowd for Delia's face. She spots her laughing her head off at something a man smoking a roll-up is saying. Delia sees Nicoletta and stands up.

'Oh, hey. Didn't expect you to make it,' she says, kissing her on both cheeks. Nicoletta is momentarily lost for words. The noise from the band tuning up is vying with 'Love Me Do' blaring from a record player rigged up on a table by the far wall. A couple dance unselfconsciously in front of it, the man tall and thin, kicking up his heels and showing off. His hair curls into his collar. Nicoletta realises it's John Dawkins. Una comes back with another tray of drinks, green this time, and Nicoletta accepts another one, realising she'd drained the last glass without noticing. Delia is talking animatedly to Barney, and she wonders idly what they're talking about. They also accept a green drink from Una's tray. Barney seemingly has second thoughts about it being freezing, and hands Una his coat. He loosens his tie, like a condemned man released from a noose. A woman in dazzling mint-green silk pyjamas appears at his elbow, her smile lipsticked on in generous swathes. Everything about her reminds Nicoletta of an exotic bird. She drags Barney off to dance. He doesn't look as though it's too much of a hardship.

'Thank you for inviting us,' Nicoletta shouts in Delia's ear in order to be heard above the music. They are the same height.

Delia smiles, as though uncomfortable under Nicoletta's scrutiny, her china-doll eyes wide, before turning away.

Nicoletta drains the rest of her green drink as the track changes to 'Ask Me Why' and Barney and the woman in the green silk pyjamas decide to foxtrot by her. John Dawkins makes his way over with two fresh green drinks. 'Here,' he says, slightly sloshing one glass. 'You're all on your lonesome.'

'What are these?' Nicoletta takes a sip and blinks hard. 'They're strong, not that I'm complaining.'

'They're mint juleps.' Dawkins takes a sip of his own.

'They match your one's outfit.' He gestures to the woman in the green pyjamas being spun around the dancefloor by Barney.

'Well, very nice they are, too,' Nicoletta says, suddenly lost for words.

Dawkins gives her a sideways glance under his eyelashes. 'Why'd you come in the end? Can't stay away from us, eh?'

'Your wife is my sister,' Nicoletta says, emboldened by all the cocktails and the sight of Barney dancing with another woman; her nails, crimson to match her lipstick, digging into his chest. She hiccups. Dawkins frowns and drains his glass.

'I suppose that means we have to dance. It's only fair.' He grabs her hand, and they foxtrot past Barney and Silk Pyjamas, who's madly giggling at something Barney has just said.

The song switches to a slow set and Dawkins slides his arm around her waist. 'Are you here to report on this? On me?'

Nicoletta shakes her head. She has to wonder at the surreal nature of the situation. This marquee covers what was a crime scene only a few short days previously. This man's wife is her sister, and nobody is privy to this fact but her. And now him. She realises she is very drunk. She's about to say something when Barney snatches her hand away from Dawkins' and leads her towards the sofa.

'We're going,' he says.

She wrenches her hand out of his grip and stumbles along the edge of the sofa. He sits beside her, draping his arm around her shoulders. She tries to wriggle out of his way by moving up the seat a couple of inches, but he won't budge.

'A few more minutes,' she says, gauging his reaction. He rubs his jaw with his knuckles.

'Nic, we just got engaged and you want to spend the evening with this shower of degenerates? Give me a break.'

'A few more minutes. I don't want to go home just yet. That's all.'

Barney takes a pack of cigarettes from his pocket and takes two out. She accepts one and coughs, before he takes it back and flicks it on the ground. He smokes in silence for a while. More people have poured into the marquee since they arrived, and a swell of dancers has crowded the floor now the band is in full swing and the gramophone has been drowned out. The sofa area is a seething mass of bodies, arms and legs sticking out at right angles. Una and her tray of drinks are nowhere to be seen. A girl wearing a long diaphanous dress sits beside Nicoletta, cork platform heels crossed one over the other, and pulls a bottle of gin from her handbag. She takes a neat swig and offers it to Nicoletta, who accepts, gingerly holding the three-quarters-empty bottle to her lips.

The girl has long, wavy, orangey-red hair pulled back from her face with a bright red scarf. 'You can finish it, I've loads more,' she says with a wave, pulling a joint from an empty cigarette packet and sparking it up. The smell is powerful. Nicoletta thinks of the joss sticks burning at Henry Morton's and shuts her eyes, throwing her head back. In two gulps the rest of the gin is gone. The girl passes the joint to Nicoletta. Barney observes the exchange but doesn't say anything as Nicoletta takes it and sucks on the end. She coughs again, the world around her seeming woollier, somehow, yet also harder around the edges, in sound and colour. She passes the joint back, and the girl takes it with a wink, before kissing Nicoletta smack on the mouth as an afterthought. The girl offers Barney the joint, but he grips Nicoletta's arm and lifts her to her feet one-handed.

'Get your things,' he says. 'Right now.'

Una is still nowhere to be seen, and neither are John or Delia. The marquee has heated up due to the sheer volume of bodies, their voices barely piercing Nicoletta's mental fog.

'Fuck it, we'll leave without our coats,' Barney mutters, leading her towards the door.

Nicoletta digs her heels in, like a belligerent pony. 'I'm not going anywhere without my coat,' she shrieks, loud enough for the man coming through the entrance to glance her way. It's Charles Creighton, she realises, with a fascinated horror, unruffled-looking in the same white shirt and pinstriped trousers and jacket he'd been wearing in Jammet's earlier.

'Well, well. The happy couple. To what do we owe this honour?'

'We're looking for our coats,' Barney mutters, plunging his hands into his pockets.

Creighton nods at them both, his smile tight. 'Good.' Barney's cheeks flush, but he seems to shrug off the slight by walking away from Creighton, towards the doorway, the outside world, his and Nicoletta's new life together.

Nicoletta feels the top of her scalp prickle with a combination of fury and adrenaline.

'Who do you think you are?' She has to shout to be heard above the band, which has launched into an up-tempo cover of 'Voodoo Child'.

'I beg your pardon?' Creighton's eyes slide off her and she realises how much she's drunk.

'You heard me,' she says, the words colliding with each other. She curses herself for drinking so much. The last and only other time she's drunk near this amount was the night when Garda O'Connor rescued her at Sandycove Beach. The thought of O'Connor's kindly face sobers her up slightly. She stands up straighter, rooting herself in the moment, taking her time, careful to look Creighton in the eye, to hold his gaze. He starts to get uncomfortable and looks away. He raises a hand to where Una Little has reappeared, clearing glasses from a table in front of the melee on the sofa, but she pretends not to see him.

'You heard me,' she says, steadily, glancing around for Barney, but he's exited into the cold night. She knows she should catch up with him, try and make things right. But there are some things that have to be said. 'First, my mother. Then Eilish Smith, who worked for her. Then Mary Little. You're disgusting.'

Creighton blinks slowly, as though hoping that when he opens his eyes he'll be somewhere else. 'What on earth are you talking about?'

Nicoletta injects all her breath into making herself heard, just as 'Voodoo Child' ends abruptly. 'You're my father.'

Dozens of revellers look their way, mildly alarmed, before resuming dancing as the band starts up again with a slow number. Delia makes her way over to Charles' side and links his arm.

'Everything all right here, Dad?'

Delia's lips twitch into a question mark. Their eyes are the same forget-me-not blue, and Nicoletta can see herself in shadow. Charles kisses Delia on the cheek. 'I believe you know this young lady reporter. She may have had a bit too much gargle.' He mimes gulping from a glass. 'She was just leaving.'

He appraises Nicoletta, looking her up and down as though just now seeing her for the first time. He narrows his blue eyes. They've allowed him to get away with a lot, those eyes, but no longer, Nicoletta thinks, as she crosses her arms and faces him, shivering in the path of the breeze from the open doorway. 'There's still the small matter of her coat,' he says, addressing Delia. 'Go ask Una, my dear. She'll know where it is.'

Delia obediently strides off to ask Una, who seems to have disappeared again. Creighton takes off his jacket and drapes it across Nicoletta's shoulders. She shrugs it off and it pools at her feet on the wooden floor. 'I don't need anything from you,' she says, her gaze never leaving his. 'Just the truth.'

He picks up his jacket and slings it over the back of a chair. He smooths back his hair. Nicoletta watches him closely. She can see his hands are trembling slightly and it's an acutely gratifying detail which she embeds in her mind. A shriek of laughter rises from the crowd at the sofa and Nicoletta looks up. John Dawkins and Una are hurrying out of the marquee together, so at first she isn't sure if she heard Charles Creighton correctly.

'You must be Gloria's child. I knew there was something about you.' He touches her cheek, as though marvelling at the resemblance. She flinches, raising a hand to wipe her face where his fingers grazed the skin.

The marquee has grown warm and soupy with human breath. Creighton leans to speak into Nicoletta's ear. The gesture is intimate.

'You're remarkably like her,' he says. 'You even sound like her.'

She doesn't flinch this time. His is a nice voice, she considers, expensive, like his smell. He's half a head taller than she is.

'Yet you pretended you'd never even met her when we interviewed you on Christmas Eve.' Her own voice is now devoid of emotion, yet loud enough to draw stares from people jostling around them. 'You discarded her – and me – like a piece of rubbish. The same way you did her maid Eilish Smith and, later, your own maid Mary Little.'

Creighton draws back, a smudge of scarlet on his cheek as though he's been slapped. 'I had no idea Gloria was expecting a child, I never knew about your existence. And I never laid a hand on Eilish. I swear it. A wicked child. As for Mary Little . . .' He jerks his head as Delia approaches with Una Little bearing an empty tray, minus any sign of their coats. 'An unfortunate business. My wife and my mother only informed me of these tragic events after the baby's remains were found. My son-in-law John Dawkins is the culprit there. And now young Una seems to be in his thrall.' He clamps his lips as Delia links her arm through his. Nicoletta thinks of the intimate painting of the dark-haired young girl she'd found in John Dawkins' makeshift studio. Could it have been Mary Little, not Una, as she'd previously thought?

'I can't find your coat,' Delia tells Nicoletta, oblivious, with a frosted pink pout. 'What've you two been talking about?' She looks from Creighton to Nicoletta and back again. Nicoletta hesitates, before looking Creighton dead in the eye. 'I just want you to know that I don't believe a word of what you've just said. I think you're disgusting, and you deserve to pay. I'll see that you do.'

Creighton closes his eyes again for a long couple of seconds. It seems to be a nervous tic. 'All I can give you is my word,' he says. 'If you'd just let me prove it to you.'

'Prove what?' Delia asks her father. She turns to Nicoletta.

Nicoletta doesn't answer. Her shoulders sag in defeat. This was all a waste of time. She had hoped to feel something, she didn't know what exactly. Just not this massive sense of nothing, like a pricked balloon. She heads towards the marquee entrance and shivers. Barney is outside leaning against the statue of the armless nymph, smoking a cigarette, his teeth chattering. The cold hits her like a sledgehammer.

'I can't find our coats,' she says in a small voice. 'Thanks for waiting for me.'

He gives her one of his rare grins. 'I was always going

to wait for you.' He throws the butt into the sea of mud and shrugs. 'The women's page editor job is yours, Nic. It's in the bag. You didn't have to drag us all the way back here tonight to prove anything.'

She doesn't bother to correct him, that she only came to confront Charles Creighton. She isn't ready to tell Barney the truth. Let him believe whatever he thinks is true, for now at least.

'Let's get out of here,' she says.

Barney hesitates. 'We can't go like this; we need our coats. It's Baltic. We'll go back in and find them. They can't have gone far.'

It's almost midnight. The woman in the green pyjamas is now leading a long line of people in a conga, counting down the minutes to the New Year, snaking the perimeter, while Charles Creighton watches from the spot where Nicoletta left him, an inscrutable look on his face. Nicoletta strides by him, upending a chair piled with coats, when there's a guttural shout from behind. A vaguely familiar, drooping figure enters the marquee, at odds with the shout, bundled up into a big overcoat. It all happens in a few seconds while their backs are turned, as they look around for Una. The man in the overcoat grabs Charles Creighton and drags him in a headlock, one hand around his throat, over to the corner where the band is in full swing. The man tosses Creighton over the drum kit, as though he's little more than a shop mannequin, keeping him pinned horizontally, knuckles pressed against his windpipe. Screams erupt among the crowd. The music stops. Delia wrings her hands, calling for her husband, who is nowhere to be seen. A thick silence begins to settle as the man in the overcoat turns his head.

Nicoletta sees now that it's Jack Bridges. He's trembling with rage, his face slick with it. He's also very drunk.

'This bastard,' he says, rattling Creighton against the taut curve of the drum. 'Took everything from me. My wife, my son. I'll teach him the lesson he's had coming.'

'Wait.' Nicoletta takes a tentative step forward, her shoulders rising with a flood of delayed emotion. 'It's not what you think.'

Bridges raises the flap of his overcoat as though to circulate some air about his person. And as he does so, Nicoletta sees the glint of the gun.

'You've got the wrong man,' she says calmly.

'What do you mean?' Bridges keeps Creighton pinned to the drum with all his might, his hands shaking with the effort.

'Your so-called friend Graham Swift was Julia's married man. And the poor little baby who was found here had nothing to do with Julia at all.'

'Then why were they buried here?' Bridges' knuckles are white as he tightens his grip around Creighton's throat. 'Tell me that.' Creighton lets out a strangulated moan, his face the colour of tomato soup.

'It's all just a misunderstanding.' Nicoletta continues talking, hoping Barney will read her mind and step in. 'That's all it is.'

'Your one, Mrs Clancy. She told me some things.'

Nicoletta inwardly groans. Mrs Clancy's visit to the *Sentinel* offices pops into her mind. Hadn't Mrs Clancy warned her that Jack Bridges was drinking again and threatening Creighton? She should have done something then. But how could she have known something like *this* would happen?

Creighton is gurgling now, and Nicoletta knows she has to act fast.

'Graham Swift was the married man. Believe me.' She pushes to the front of the crowd. Nobody stops her.

'Why should I?' Bridges opens his overcoat and takes out the gun.

'Put the gun down,' Nicoletta says calmly. At the sound of the word, Delia screams, and Bridges cocks the trigger. It looks like the same weapon he'd shown Nicoletta the previous week in the props department of the Athena Theatre, which feels like a long time ago now. As he moves the gun to point it at Creighton's left temple, his grip on the man's throat falters, and Creighton is released from Bridges' grasp, free to fall to the ground, wheezing for air. It's then that Barney charges forward and attempts to wrestle the pistol out of Bridges' shaking hands. Barney and Bridges spin around in a fruitless tussle, echoing the dancing of just a few minutes ago, while Nicoletta stands frozen to the spot. Suddenly Charles Creighton springs to life and lunges forward, toppling her to the ground, just as an almighty crack echoes into the night. She bangs her head on the wooden boards and sees sparks, the world around receding for a bit.

When she comes to, she's in a sitting position with Garda O'Connor pressing a tea towel full of ice cubes to her temple, a blanket around her shoulders. She can't stop shaking. A burnt metallic smell fills her nostrils and Delia is still screaming, prostrate in front of Charles Creighton, who is spread beside the drum kit, a large red stain across his once white shirt, his staring eyes facing the striped ceiling. The wooden floor beneath him is black with blood, spreading underneath the drum kit.

'What happened?' Nicoletta's teeth won't stop chattering.

It's Barney who answers. 'Creighton stepped into the bullet's path instead of you, Nic.'

'A heroic act, indeed,' O'Connor murmurs, reapplying some pressure to Nicoletta's injury. 'We were called out here by the Creightons' neighbour, Helen Leonard. She was complaining about the noise. When I heard the gunshot from the garden, I thought it might've been a firework.'

Barney crouches beside Nicoletta. 'I'll take it from here, Garda,' he says, grabbing the tea towel before O'Connor can object.

Morris extracts Delia from Creighton and sits her down in a chair. 'If I could ask you all to step back at once,' he says to the subdued crowd, which has already thinned out considerably after the arrival of the Gardaí.

He puts his fingers to Creighton's neck. 'We'll need an ambulance as a matter of some urgency,' he says in a low voice to O'Connor. 'But I think it's obvious that it's too late.'

Chapter Thirty-Six

Wednesday, 1st January 1969
New Year's Day

The peacocks' outrage pierces the milky dawn light. The seagulls keen in sympathy, swirling wide loops overhead. The coast road is deserted. Every single New Year's reveller from the Dawkins' party has dispersed. There isn't a sinner in sight. All the windows of Seaview House are blank. Nicoletta stamps her feet in a bid to keep warm. The blue light from the single remaining Garda squad car flashes in the early morning air, ghostly as a lighthouse. Inspector Morris had already driven Jack Bridges into custody what seemed like hours before the paramedics arrived to carry the single covered stretcher out of the marquee. The body of Charles Creighton looks insignificant and slight under its woollen shroud. Nicoletta feels the lump in her throat dissolve into tears and she scrubs at her face with the back of her hand. Garda O'Connor watches as Creighton's remains are loaded into the

371

ambulance, parked beside the yew trees at the top of the driveway of the main house. Nicoletta shudders as the doors slam. It's a moment before she can speak.

'I'm sorry,' she says.

O'Connor springs back and forth on his heels. 'Not your fault.' He gets back into the squad car and Nicoletta retreats to Barney's rust heap, feeling desperately glad he's there. Flashes of gemstone pink and blue have lit up the sky by the time the grim cortege edges out onto the coast road. Barney's brow creases with concern.

'What now? Want to go home?'

Nicoletta suppresses a shudder. 'Not yet. Follow them,' she says, her voice clear as a bell.

Her hand is unsteady as she fumbles for her notebook and pen, the small solitaire on her left hand catching the racing light from the ambulance. She knows she has to go for it; it's now or never. The story she was born to tell.

Acknowledgements

I'd like to sincerely thank the following people who've helped bring this book to life: dream agents Sheila Crowley and Sabhbh Curran at Curtis Brown; all the team at Simon & Schuster UK: the fabulous Katherine Armstrong, for taking a chance on me, along with Clare Hey and Georgina Leighton; the amazing Amy Fletcher and Ben Phillips in Rights; the dream team Hannah Paget in Marketing and Jess Barratt in Publicity; Amanda Rutter for the thorough copy-edit and proofreader extraordinaire Maddy Hamey-Thomas; Pip Watkins for designing the beautiful cover; Karin Seifried for all her work in Production; and all the wonderful team in Sales: Heather Hogan, Dom Brendon, Robyn Ware, Rich Hawton, Nicola Mitchell, Naomi Burt, Andrew Wright, Rhys Thomas and Maddie Allan.

I am grateful to the Arts Council of Ireland for their support.

A big thank you goes to those from the MFA in Creative Writing at UCD from whom I learned so much: Lia Mills,

Paula McGrath, Andrea Carter, Frank McGuinness, James Ryan and Éilís Ní Dhuibhne.

My wonderful mentors: Andrea Mara – your advice about the writing life was so spot on and fun – it made me think I could do this! Thank you to Words Ireland and Kildare County Council for funding this mentorship. Tammy Cohen – you were so insightful and encouraging at an early stage of this project when I really needed it. You went above and beyond, thank you so much for your advice at various stages. And thanks to the inspiring WoMentoring Project and the equally inspiring woman behind it, Kerry Hudson. Thank you also to Vanessa Fox O'Loughlin of The Inkwell Group for the valuable critique at a pivotal stage.

Susan Stairs and Jamie O'Connell, the very best friends in writing, and in life, thank you. My parents John and Eithne Coughlan, thank you for everything. You taught me to read, and to love books, and have always encouraged me. To my late grandmother Eithne Flanagan, who also wrote. To my sisters Sarah Coughlan and Fiona Coughlan, and my brothers-in-law Rob Byrnes and John O'Donoghue, thanks for all the support, much appreciated.

My parents-in-law – Joe and Margot Cremin, thank you for being with me through the writing of this book every step of the way. You're the best. And to my sister-in-law Paula Cremin, brother-in-law Dave Cremin and sister-in-law Niki Jalali – your support means so much.

Saving the best until last: my endlessly supportive husband Chris Cremin, for always believing I could do it. Thank you for being you. To our daughter, Hannah, I've had the seed of the idea for this book in my head for years, but I wrote much of it while you were a baby. Thanks for being the best baby in the world! And to Bellamy, who purred by my side through every word.